Sold into FREEDOM

SOLD INTO FREEDOM

A PLANTING FAITH NOVEL

CAROLE TOWRISS

Book cover designed by JD&J with some stock imagery provided by Tetana Bahnenko © 123RF.com.

Edited by Natalie Hanemann.

PREVIOUSLY PUBLISHED NOVELS BY THIS AUTHOR

For those who are no longer slaves
to the power of sin
and have become slaves of God—
and those still seeking freedom.

Once when we were going to the place of prayer, we were met by a female slave who had a spirit by which she predicted the future. She earned a great deal of money for her owners by fortune-telling.

— ACTS 16:16

The crowd joined in the attack against Paul and Silas, and the magistrates ordered them to be stripped and beaten with rods. After they had been severely flogged, they were thrown into prison, and the jailer was commanded to guard them carefully.

— ACTS 16:22–23

CHARACTERS

BIBLICAL

Paulos • apostle of Yeshua
Timotheos/Timos • the youngest of Paulos's companions
Loukas • Greek companion of Paulos; a physician
Lydia • cloth dealer from Anatolia
Silas • Jewish companion of Paulos
Euodia • slave of Maximus and Cassia
Syntyche/Syn • one of Lydia's workers

HISTORICAL

Titus Flavius Vespasian •
former Roman legate (general) of the Second Augusta legion
Publius Ostorius Scapula •
Roman legate (general) of the Second Augusta legion

FICTIONAL

Elantia/Tia • a seer of a Britanni tribe in southwestern Britannia

Quintus Valerius/Quin • a Roman tribune in the Second Augusta Legion; fifth son of Julius Valerius

Attalos • Julius Valerius's Greek slave; Quin's tutor
Cassia • Maximus's wife; Gallus's cousin
Charis • Quin's female slave; Greek.
Davos • physician; Greek physician in the Second Augusta
Decimus Magius • duovir/praetor of Philippi
Dorkas • inn owner in Ostia (port of Rome)
Flavius • a Roman tribune; son of a senator
Gallus Crispus • duovir/praetor of Philippi
Gallus's slaves • Leonidas; Nicanor
Helios • Gallus's scribe; records keeper of Philippi; Greek.
Julius Valerius • Quin's father
Julia Valerius • Quin's mother
Lydia's workers • Zenobia, Demas
Mamma • Elantia's mom
Marcus • wine dealer in Philippi
Maximus • Roman; resident of Philippi; Tia's owner
Patroclus • a land broker
Philon • a young slave arrested for assault
Prison guards • Alexios, Numerius, Pandaros, Stolos
Tancorix • Elantia's younger brother
Tatos • Elantia's father; chieftain of village in Britannia
Xenia • customer of Elantia

GLOSSARY

Brittonic

bratir: brother
carami te: I love you
cariatu: sweetheart
Roumanos (pl. Roumani): Roman
tatos: dad

Latin

avia: grandmother
Britanni: inhabitants of Britannia
Camulodunum: retirement colony for soldiers in Britannia
carissima: dearest, beloved
cena: dinner
cuirass: sleeveless piece of armor covering from neck to waist
curia: meeting place for a Roman Senate
culina: kitchen
denarius (pl. denarii): silver coin of Rome worth four sesterces
domine, dominus: (*f. domina, pl. domini*) master
domus: house
dulcissima: sweetheart
duovir (pl. duoviri): magistracy of two men

duovir quinquennial: duoviri elected to conduct a census
fugitivarii: specialists in recovering runaway slaves
impluvium: sunken area in an open-air atrium
insula (pl. insulae): apartment building, usually cheaply made
lectus: backless couch
legate: leader of a legion
legio: legion
libra: ancient Roman unit of weight equal to about ¾ pound
lictors: officer, attending a ruler, who carries out sentences
mater: mother
medicus: doctor
pater: father
pugio: dagger
raeda: four-wheeled passenger carriage
scriba: scribe
sesterce (pl. sesterces): brass coin of Imperial Rome
stoa: roofed portico or colonnade
strigil: instrument used to scrape away sweat, oil, and dirt
te amo: I love you
testatio: document confirming Roman citizenship
triclinium: dining area
via: street

INTRODUCTION

In 43 A.D., Emperor Claudius sent four Roman legions to invade Britannia. After a brutal initial battle, the Legio Secunda Augusta, under the command of future emperor Vespasian, stormed west along the southern coast, fighting thirty battles, conquering two warlike tribes, and capturing more than twenty hillforts and the Isle of Wight.

One of these two tribes was located just east of what is now Cornwall and Devon, the southwest peninsula of Britain. The battles against this tribe were so fierce, Vespasian decided not to fight against their neighbors, the Dumnonii who lived on the peninsula. Instead they headed north to Wales. Vespasian returned to Rome in 47 A.D., but the legion continued battling the Britanni until 52 A.D., when they were defeated.

In 49 A.D., the apostle Paul began his second missionary journey, accompanied by Silas. In Lystra, a city in Asia Minor (present-day Turkey), Paul again connected with Timothy, whom he had met on his first visit there, and asked Timothy to join him and Silas. In a vision, God told Paul to go to Macedonia, now northern Greece, to preach the gospel. There, Luke joined them. Their first stop was Philippi.

Philippi was a Roman colony, a status of which it was justifiably proud. Though important, it was not a large city, with a population of between 10- and 15,000. Most of those would have been slaves and Greek farmers living outside the walls. Greek was the main language spoken. Philippi had a Roman form of government, and its free-born inhabitants were citizens with enormous privileges. It does not appear, however, that there were many Jews living there.

It is here that our characters meet—and change—each other.

1

> *"There are . . . things which the Lord hates, . . . that are detestable to him: . . . a heart that devises wicked schemes, [and] feet that are quick to rush into evil."*
>
> — PROVERBS 6:16,18

SOUTHWESTERN COAST OF BRITANNIA, 49 A.D.

IT WAS THE SCREAMING THAT WOKE HER UP.

Elantia rubbed the sleep from her eyes and scrambled from her straw-covered cottage in the tiny village by the sea. In the grim light of early morning, nail-studded leather pounded the ground as soldiers dragged horrified families out of their roundhouses. Blood-red cloaks whipped in the ocean breeze as the invaders set fire to anything they could burn, tearing apart what they could not.

Screeches and wails intertwined with the clang of metal against metal, the crackle of flames eating up thatch, and the soldiers' horrible, dreadful words. Thank the gods their chieftain father had insisted they learn Latin when the *Roumani* defeated their neighbors years ago, but she hated the sound of it.

Muscles tightened, ready to fight, Elantia fought through the throng of townspeople surrounding her father.

The Roumani leader, a centurion judging by his uniform, stood face-to-face with him. "Give us your best quietly or we will take them by force."

Shoulders back, *Tatos* stood his ground. "You have no right. We are at peace with Rome. After months of bloody battles with our neighbors, Commander Vespasian decided conquering us was not worth the losses to his legion. He vowed the Roumani would never attack us."

"What makes you think we answer to Vespasian?" He leaned nearer. "Now stand aside."

"I will not." Tatos pulled himself as tall as his aging body allowed. "We've done nothing to you to warrant such violence. I must protect my people."

Her heart swelled at her tatos's vow, even in the face of almost certain defeat.

The centurion shoved him aside. "Rome needs strong backs. When we're done, you'll have nothing left to protect."

In the six years since the Roumani had invaded their land, they had brought nothing but pain.

He beckoned to another, whispered to him. The younger man grabbed Tatos and *Mamma* and dragged them away.

"Mamma!" Elantia rushed to follow her parents, but a rough hand jerked her by the arm and shoved her into a sheep pen, where most of the other young adults of the tribe already waited. She ran to Tancorix.

Her brother wrapped his arms around her, held her close.

The second soldier grabbed Tancorix and pulled him from Elantia, lining them up in a loose row.

The centurion strode over. Eyeing each of them from head to toe, he hesitated when he came to their cousin. He grabbed her thin arm and turned it over once, twice.

Elantia's breath caught. The girl was weak. She'd been sick most of the winter. What would he do to her?

He yanked her out of line, thrust her toward his second in command, and then continued his inspection, nodding in satisfaction. Stopping before Elantia's brother, he fingered the thick, braided gold torque around Tancorix's neck. He yanked at it, but the opening at the neck was but a finger's breadth wide. He pulled harder, twisting.

Tancorix put his hands to his neck, wincing in pain as the stiff metal cut into his skin and cut off his air. He grasped the man's forearms, sinking to the ground, his breath coming fast.

Tia's heart pounded as she tried to pull the Roumanos's hands away. "This is the chief's son! That torque was put around his neck as a child, and he grew into it. It's not coming off!"

Tancorix struggled for air, his face turning as red as the centurion's cloak.

The Roumanos let go of the necklace to backhand her.

She stumbled but managed to stay upright. Stinging pain radiated from her cheek to her whole head. The metallic taste of blood lingered on her lip.

With a smile that sent a shiver down her back, he neared her. He ran his fingers down her face, her neck, then along the front of the sleeveless cloak she wore, the one Mamma had spent the winter months making for her. He moved behind her and wrenched it off her arms. His hot breath on her neck sent her stomach roiling. "It's a shame we are in such a hurry."

He tossed the garment to his aide, and the younger man left.

Tia's hands trembled as she reached for Tancorix. He wrapped his arm around her shoulders and kissed her temple.

The soldier returned with a long rope. Her skin burned as he wrapped it around her wrists and knotted it, far too tightly. It went from her to Tancorix to all the others in turn.

She searched for Tatos and Mamma. What had the soldiers done to them? She'd never trusted the Roumani, and today had proved her instinct right. Her father had made sure they'd been loyal, kept every provision of the truce, and then today . . .

The centurion yanked the end of the rope. Her knees hit the ground. Her face smashed against her fists. He tugged again, pulling her up, shouting some command at her. Tancorix's gentle hands steadied her as she stood.

They followed the chief soldier. At the edge of the seaside village, all that remained of her people—the old ones and the youngest—huddled together. She quickly searched for familiar clothing. Her eyes rested on the colorful tunic Mamma wore. And Tatos? He waited behind her mother, his cheek swollen, his lip cut and bleeding.

Then she saw the bodies at their feet.

Her heart sank as realization dawned. The Roumani intended to make her father watch as they slaughtered what was left of his village.

One by one the legionaries dragged a villager from the crowd, rammed a sword through, and let the body drop.

Her father still stood, battered. Bound. Silent.

Elantia's legs gave way, but Tancorix held her up. A moan escaped.

The villagers gone, the centurion neared Tatos.

Her father looked at her and mouthed the familiar command, "No tears." His moist eyes reflected the raging flames. *"Carami te."*

I love you too. Her blood pounded. Her breath came fast and shallow.

Another legionary blocked her view. His elbow shot back, and a body crumbled to the ground. The bloody sword came to rest at his side.

Elantia turned and buried her face in Tancorix's chest. She longed to grab him, wrap his arms around her, feel safe, but since they were bound, he could only whisper in her ear.

"Don't look," her brother whispered. "You don't want to remember them that way."

After a few moments, a crimson-cloaked soldier grabbed at her again, pulling her away. She glanced toward the dwindling crowd.

Tancorix shook his head. "Don't." He placed his body between her and the pile of executed villagers.

The group stumbled forward as the legionary pulled on the rope.

"Keep looking ahead," Tancorix whispered from behind.

She focused her gaze on the cloak of the man leading them. It took everything she had to put one foot in front of the other, to keep from looking back.

The best her village had to offer marched, and marched, and marched. More soldiers added young people from other villages at various points along the way, the train of captives growing longer.

Tancorix was right. She needed to cherish the memory of her mother and father in her heart, a memory of them as wonderful parents and strong leaders.

She'd need their toughness, their love to face what was to come.

Because warriors don't cry.

BATTLEFIELD, WESTERN COAST OF BRITANNIA

THE DARKNESS EVAPORATED, BUT THE agony remained.

Quintus Valerius stretched his left hand across his chest, biting back a groan as he pressed his fingers against his shoulder. He brought his hand away dipped in blood. Any attempt at movement brought excruciating pain, and he let his arm fall against the damp grass. He tried to sit up but his body screamed in protest. The iron scent of blood filled his nostrils.

Wolves hovered at the edges of the battlefield, eager to attack the decaying flesh of fallen legionaries. Slaves tended fires, keeping the animals at bay as well as bringing light to the battlefield while the Romans buried their dead.

The *Britanni* would have to wait to take care of their bodies.

How did he end up flat on his back, on this field, blood running down his arm? And where was his horse? He closed his eyes, tried to make sense of the images swirling in his mind. What was the last thing he could remember? Flashes of careening chariots and braying horses. Men shouting orders. Ground rushing toward him, slamming into him.

And pain. Overwhelming, all-encompassing anguish.

But why?

Because Flavius, that childish, arrogant tribune, had issued an order so ridiculously deadly it sent a quarter of a legion into the path of Britanni chariots. Or under them.

Rolling to his left side, he drew his left knee to his chest. Fighting through the pain, he pushed up onto his elbow. He breathed deeply, scanning the field, until the nausea subsided. So many bodies.

How many battles had he fought in his six years in Britannia as a tribune? Almost every day, during campaigning season at least. But this had to be the worst. These Britanni warriors were like none they had ever fought. Never had so many Roman lives been lost.

Noise and chatter sounded behind him. Groaning, he twisted to look over his shoulder at slaves digging out an enormous hole—yet another mass grave.

He struggled to stand, or even sit up, but his right leg refused to obey him. He tried again. His leg would bear no weight.

"Tribune." A *medicus* hurried to him. "Do you need help?"

"I-I can't stand. My leg won't move."

The young orderly, a mop of dark, curly hair falling in his eyes, glanced at Quin's leg, and his face paled.

Quin straightened his arm to push himself higher. At first, he saw no open wounds, no cuts from a blade nor punctures from a spear. Then he realized the damage, the reason he couldn't stand. His right leg was bent inward at a grotesquely unnatural angle.

Something was drastically wrong.

The youth beckoned to another, who appeared with a litter.

One knelt to slip his arm under Quin's shoulders. The other lifted his legs.

He clenched his jaw until he could no longer contain a cry. They placed him on the stretcher and rushed him to the medical tent.

The chief medicus approached him, reaching for his leg. He shook his head. "You've made quite a mess of this, Tribune."

Quin winced. "How badly am I injured, Davos?" He sucked in a breath as the Greek physician drew his fingers over Quin's skin, poking and prodding.

"Your arm or your leg?"

"Either. Both."

"I'll start with your arm." The medic held out his hand and another assistant placed a knife in it. Davos cut a slit in Quin's tunic from elbow to neck and let the fabric fall away. He gently pressed one finger after another in different places, making faces as he did so.

"Well? What?"

"Your arm seems fine. A few stitches. Now for your leg . . ." He gently touched the deformity in Quin's leg.

Quin released a loud groan.

"I'm sorry. I know that must hurt." The medic poked again closer to the knee. "And that?"

"Actually, I can't feel it."

"You can't?" Davos frowned.

"No. I can't feel anything from just above my knee down." He shrugged, but the look on Davos's face stopped him. "That's bad?"

"Yes. You've broken a bone, and that must have injured a nerve."

"And that means . . . ?" He searched the older man's weathered face for a clue as to how bad his situation really was. Davos had been the legion's physician for as long as Quin had served the Second Augusta, and Quin trusted him with his life.

"I'm not sure. I'll need to perform surgery to reset the bone. Hopefully I can see what happened then."

"Will I get the feeling back?"

He frowned and shook his gray head. "I don't know."

"Will I walk again?"

"Yes, but you may still have problems with your leg."

"Problems?"

"It may . . . end up slightly shorter than the other."

The physician's words slammed into him harder than the chariot. That couldn't be true. "Can't you do something?"

"Not when it's damaged this badly. I'm going to get you something for the pain, and one of my assistants will get you ready for surgery." Davos grasped his left shoulder. "Don't worry. I'll take good care of you. As always."

A slave—Greek by the look of him—entered with a bowl of liquid and offered it to Quin.

"What's this?"

"Opium. For the pain and for the surgery." The slave held the bowl to his lips while Quin downed the painkiller. He mumbled his thanks and lay back on the wooden bench.

The pain wasn't nearly as devastating as the physician's words. If he couldn't walk properly, he couldn't be a soldier. And if he couldn't be a soldier . . .

The poppy's juice began to cloud his thinking. As soon as he closed his eyes, images of screaming Britanni filled his head. Barefoot, half-naked, spear-wielding warriors charging across the terrain. Iron chariots rolling over Roman bodies.

He opened his eyes and shook his head, trying to dislodge the memories.

His thoughts became jumbled and his breathing slowed. His eyes drifted closed again.

As he slipped into welcome unconsciousness, he prayed to Jupiter he would wake up to a world without war.

Pushed hard by the Roumani, the captives had marched for five days. Tia's feet bled where sharp rocks sliced into her bare soles.

Her back ached from sleeping on the hard ground. Dirt and sweat stained her tunic, and rope cut into her wrists.

She looked north. Less than a half-day's walk would bring them to the fort Vespasian and his men had built on their rampage along the southern coast. It loomed large, sitting high atop a knoll, controlling everything—and everyone—in its field of vision. The burned remains of a Britanni hillfort lay nearby.

The Roumani destroyed everything they touched.

A shouted command from the centurion interrupted her thoughts, and she turned again to the sea. A colossal ship, as wide as her roundhouse and ten times longer, pulled into the natural harbor before them. Huge cloth sails drooped from towering masts. Only a few pairs of oars dangled from the rear, not the hundreds as on a Roumani warship.

A wide wooden plank was laid against the side of the ship. Shoulders and elbows jammed into her back and sides as the soldiers shoved and pushed the crowd onto the deck and then down a rickety set of wooden steps. As soon as her feet hit the floor, she was propelled toward the wall while the hold filled with the captured Britanni.

The door at the top of the stairs slammed shut. Her breath stuck in her throat. Her vision blurred. She dug her nails into her brother's arm. The closed space and utter blackness recalled memories of the time she nearly drowned as a child. She'd hated the dark ever since.

"Just breathe. Slowly." The soft, even tone of his voice calmed her fears.

They began to sit, most with their backs to the long walls.

The door above them opened again and a throng of Roumani darted down the stairs. Working in pairs, one added an iron ring to the right foot of each captive. The other untied the ropes.

Tia studied her wrists. A raw crimson ring encircled each one, too tender to touch. She tried to lift her foot, now connected to Tancorix on one side and a young girl on the other.

Just as the last manacles were connected with thick iron bolts, oars dipped and pushed against the water. The ship jerked forward in spurts until it achieved a slow but steady pace. The sailors tramped back up the stairs, and again the door crashed closed.

After a few moments, the sails could be heard snapping tight as wind surged into them. The ship lunged forward and picked up speed.

The journey had begun. Where would it end?

2

> *"The way of fools seems right to them,*
> *but the wise listen to advice."*
>
> — PROVERBS 12:15

QUINTUS LUNGED AGAIN AT THE STRAW-FILLED ENEMY SET UP IN THE camp's forum, plunging his *pugio* deep into the belly of the practice dummy.

Glancing at the sun high above him, he withdrew the dagger. He wiped the sweat from his brow with his arm as he paced. They were already well into campaigning season, and he would be no good if he couldn't fight, or at least lead his men.

Quin sheathed his dagger and reached for the sword lying nearby. Clutching the handle, he extended the blade, slowly bringing it parallel to the ground.

Out of his peripheral vision, he noticed the legion's commander approaching, the medicus at his side.

Publius Ostorius Scapula frowned as his eyes rested on the

angry scar that ran from Quin's thigh to below his knee. "How is the leg, Tribune?"

How did he answer that? The commander certainly knew the injury had left Quin's right leg a bit shorter than his left, and pain was his constant companion. Davos said the pain might lessen, but it was probable the limp would be permanent.

"It's been two weeks, Quintus. You cannot return to duty."

"I just need a little more—"

Davos shook his head, a sad smile appearing briefly. "All the time in the world will not matter. That fall ripped your hip apart, broke a bone, and damaged a nerve. Your leg will never be as it was. You have to accept that."

Quin sheathed his sword and reached down for his crutches. "So what's next?"

"I'm afraid your time in the army is over." Scapula's deep voice gave the hated words an even harsher sound.

"O-over?" It couldn't be over. The army was the only life he had ever known. How could it be taken from him when he had done nothing wrong?

"You can't march, you can't sit a horse. You cannot command," Davos explained.

Quin's breath caught in his throat. "So I'm just to be shipped back to Rome? I suppose I could do that. I never intended to leave the army, but if I must move on to the political assignments . . ." He sighed. "I have no choice."

The *legate* crossed his arms over his chest. "Actually, Rome isn't really an option for you right now."

Years of training had taught him to mask his emotions, stuff his feelings deep into an abyss where they could not interfere with action. "What? Why not?" No army. No Rome. What was left for him?

Scapula winced. "Flavius has told everyone that you defied him, insulted him. It would be very uncomfortable for you there."

Quin scoffed. "If we had followed his orders, the entire *legio* could have been destroyed. Does he tell everyone that?"

"Of course not. But the truth will come out soon. It always does. Remember, Vespasian is there. He was not here two weeks ago, but he knows Flavius, and he knows you. He'll vouch for you when the time comes. And he will speak the truth about Flavius."

"But what about now? There has to be something I can do for Rome." He spread his arms wide. "Some post somewhere in this vast Empire where I can serve Rome."

Scapula remained silent.

"My squadrons are some of the best in all of the Empire. Men fought to serve under me. I lost fewer horses and fewer men than anyone in Britannia. And if Flavius had stayed out of the cavalry's way and commanded the legionaries like he should have, we wouldn't have lost anyone two weeks ago, either."

"Nevertheless, he is the son of a senator, and you are not." Scapula shrugged. "Status is everything in Rome."

"So you just throw me away? After fourteen years. After everything I have done, and still could do." Keeping his voice calm was becoming harder with each sentence.

Davos tilted his head. "You could go to *Camulodumum*."

"Stay here? At the new retirement colony? They're all thirty years older than I am." They might as well have suggested he swim to Italia.

"Exceptions can be made."

Quin threw his hands in the air. "I don't want an exception."

"It could be a very nice life for you. A land grant, 100,000 *sesterces*—"

"For the rest of my life? Those men have spent forty years fighting for Rome. They're ready for a quiet life on a farm. I have just begun." Quin looked from Scapula to Davos and back again. "I don't want to stay here in Britannia. I can't stay in Camulodumum with old men from my own legion. How can I face them? I'll be humiliated."

"There are other wounded soldiers at Cam—"

"Not my age!" He stopped, sucked in a deep breath. Scapula was his friend, but still his superior. His voice lowered considerably. "Isn't there anywhere else?"

"Let me think." The legate paced. "Vespasian knows the governor of Macedonia. There is a colony there. I'm sure he can arrange for you to be settled there instead of here in Britannia. Augustus settled veterans of Legio XXVIII and his Praetorian guard there, but that was nearly one hundred years ago. Their grandchildren would be there now, not active soldiers. Would that be better?"

Quin blew out a long breath. "Sounds like it's the best I'll get."

"Unfortunately, yes. At least until Flavius and his lies are stopped." Scapula grasped his arm. "I am truly sorry."

After the men left him standing in the practice yard, Quin unsheathed his dagger and hurled it at the dummy.

Until the lies are stopped. How long would that take? How long until the truth was revealed, and he could go home to reassemble some sort of life?

How easily lies could be spread. How quickly they could destroy someone.

Had the truth always been so fragile?

Elantia bolted upright, unable to breathe. She clawed at her neck, desperately trying to remove whatever it was that choked the breath from her chest.

But nothing was around her neck.

Chains, however, bound her ankles.

And in the dark, it all came flooding back. The Roumani attack of their village, the strongest young men and prettiest young women marched to the shore with iron on their feet and rope on their hands. She'd walked until her feet bled, and then the man-stealers shoved them into the bottom of a dark, rickety ship.

How many days had they been on this nightmare of a journey? She turned to count the scratchings on the ship behind her, moving her fingertips. Twenty-one, plus five days of marching. Twenty-six days since she'd seen their parents, their roundhouse. Their cousins. Their friends.

"Bad dreams again?" An arm gently slid around her shoulders.

"I didn't mean to wake you. I'm sorry."

Her younger brother, now bigger than she was, kissed her cheek and pulled her back down to the wooden floor of the rocking vessel. "Go back to sleep, Tia." *How could he be so brave?*

She eventually drifted back to sleep, the gentle rocking of the ship and her *bratir's* rhythmic breathing overcoming her panic.

Her back and arms ached when she awakened. The door above them was now open, and in the faint light of the ship's hold she could see Tancorix still slept. Stretching as best she could with weighty chains on her feet, she tried to alleviate the knots the journey had tied in her muscles.

Heavy, booted footfalls sounded on the stairs. A Roumani guard carried a basket of hard bread and skins of water, tossed them on the floor, and stomped back up.

Iron rattled and scraped along the floor as the prisoners awakened. The hot air reeked of sweat, vomit, and urine. Tia silently counted the bodies—six times more than were taken from her village, all crammed in the hold of this ship the same way she stuffed glass beads in a leather pouch. They pounced at the bread as if they were wolves attacking dying prey.

A small crust of bread wasn't worth certain injury.

Beside her Tancorix leaned forward on one palm, his broad shoulders making a path. He reached with one long arm, emerging from the fray with two loaves. As he'd done every day since they'd left, he offered her the larger one. If it weren't for him, she'd have starved by now.

"Thank you."

"I keep telling you, you don't need to thank me. I have to protect you. I'm your bratir." He smiled.

Leaning back against the rough wood, she nibbled on the dry bread. Sweat ran down her back, and the small bit of food did nothing to quell the sickness bubbling in her stomach.

She ached for the green grass and blue skies of home. The warmth and light of the sun. The sweet smile of Tatos, and Mamma's warm embrace. This . . . prison . . . was hot, unbearably foul, and above all, nearly devoid of light. The sailors opened the door at the top of the stairs during the heat of the day. Surely it was not for their comfort, but because they didn't want their cargo to die, didn't want to lose their profit.

"Are you going to eat that or just squeeze the life out of it?"

"What?" She turned to see Tancorix grinning.

"The bread. You look like you're choking it."

"Only because I can't get to any of them." She gestured above board. "I hate the Roumani. We never should have trusted Vespasian or his soldiers."

"I don't think these are real soldiers," he whispered.

"What are you talking about?"

"I don't think they're really Roumani soldiers. Just dressed like them, capturing whomever they can find to sell."

"Does it make a difference? They're Roumani, soldiers or not."

He shrugged. "If you not going to eat that, give it to me."

She shoved the smushed bread in her mouth and lay back down, her back to him.

The Roumani had killed her mamma and tatos twenty-six days ago. She'd closed her eyes before their crimson lifeblood soaked into the ground, but she would never forget the look in his eyes.

And his counsel: no tears.

Like any Britanni woman, she could fight next to the men. She had the scars to prove it. She could wield a knife and a sword.

And she would do it now, if she had one.

If they hadn't been caught off guard.

That would never happen again. She would regain her freedom. She would do whatever it took to get back home to Britannia. Or die trying.

THE JOURNEY to Rome had been long and arduous, taking almost a month. His movement severely restricted by the difficulty of using crutches on deck, Quintus had spent most of his time in one of the cabins at the stern. Built for the crew, they were often rented by those who could afford it, hoping to make a sea voyage a little more comfortable. With only a straw-stuffed mattress and a few pegs in the wall, it didn't help much but it was better than sleeping on the deck and did afford him some privacy. He could avoid the awkward conversations about his crutches and his scar.

The captain, an old man with a bald head and sun-browned face, had said they would reach the port of Ostia by midday. An afternoon's carriage ride would take him into Rome.

Mater would be happy to see him.

But *Pater*?

It seemed Pater couldn't have been happier to see him go fourteen years ago. Had more or less told him to stay in the army, even after his required service was completed. Make it his career. For life. And he had. He could have been done years ago.

Would Pater change his mind now, seeing his condition? Allow him to come home? Or instead say he deserved it?

The captain steered the ship into the harbor, coming alongside a long stone dock. Emperor Claudius had upgraded the port considerably while Quin was away.

When the hustle of off-loading cargo subsided, he asked one of the crew to take his bags ashore and secure a *raeda* for him.

He tried to ignore the dread building within him as the four-wheeled carriage flew along the road to Rome. Sooner than he was ready, they pulled up to the gate of the Valerius estate, and the driver jumped off. He rounded the side and opened the door for Quin while he climbed awkwardly down.

"Shall I carry your bag up to the door?"

"No, just leave it here at the gate. I'll send someone for it later." He dropped three coins into the man's hand.

The driver dipped his head and hurried off.

Quin sucked in a breath of courage and started up the long

walk to the house. He hadn't made it halfway when a slave, blade in hand, hustled out to meet him.

Jupiter, please let him believe me. Quin stopped and raised his hands.

"You will stop, right now, or I will kill you." The husky slave had at least twenty *libra* on him and was a head taller.

"I have stopped."

"Who are you, and why have you entered the Valerius estate without invitation or permission?" His accent marked him as Egyptian.

"I am Quintus Valerius, son of Julius Valerius. I have returned after six years in Britannia, fourteen years in Rome's army."

He narrowed his eyes. "I have been here only five years. I cannot verify this."

He sighed. "Is my mater home? My pater?"

"They are at the forum."

"What about Attalos? My slave?"

The blade lowered just a bit. "Attalos? He was yours?"

"Was?" Air left his body like he'd been punched in the chest. Had Attalos died? Been sold? "Is he . . ."

The slave's eyes widened and he lowered his blade. "No, no. Do not fear. He's well. He has charge of all household slaves. I'll send for him."

The weight fell off Quin's chest. "No. I'll go to him."

"But—"

Quin raised a brow, and the slave hushed. "My bags are at the gate."

The layout of the estate hadn't changed, and he made his way to the slaves' wing west of the main house quickly enough. He raised a fist and rapped on a closed door.

"Who is it?" Attalos barked from inside.

"It's me, Attalos."

A stool scraped the floor, and quick footfalls followed. Tumblers fell as a lock unengaged and the door swung wide. Attalos's face lit up like a sunrise, his smile wide. "*Domine!* Come in.

What are you doing here, in Rome?" His eyes moved slowly over Quin's frame, head to toe, resting briefly on the ugly scar on his leg, but his smile did not dim.

"I wanted to see you."

"You should have sent for me. You know this is not proper. *Domina* Julia would be terribly upset. At me, no doubt."

"No doubt. My mater always insisted on propriety." He stepped inside and stopped short before the old man's worktable, covered with parchments and silver coin. "Attalos, did you rob a workshop this morning?" Quin laughed.

"I control all the household accounts." He led Quin to a stool and brought another to sit beside him. "I was quite wealthy before the Romans annexed my town and took my land. I'm very good at this."

"I'm certain of it. You taught me everything I know."

"You were an exceptional student, Domine."

"Please call me Quin. I am no longer your master."

"You are still a Roman, and I am still a slave. It would cause . . . hard feelings, at the very least, among the others, not to mention your mater."

"Then at least while we are in here."

"I'll try. Now what happened? Why have you returned?" Attalos poured them both a goblet of watered wine while Quin recounted the events of the last two months.

The Greek was quiet a moment. "I would hear of you now and then, while you were gone. I've always been so proud of you. You know that, don't you?"

"I do. Pater wasn't. But I always knew you would be."

He shrugged. "Your father means well. He's just blinded himself to the truth."

"If you say so." He looked toward the main part of the house. "I'm not anxious to see him."

"You must respect him as he is your pater but be proud of who you are. Not arrogant, not ashamed. And you need to concentrate on healing. That is enough of a task for now." He patted Quin's good knee. "When it comes time to deal with him, the right words will come."

His friend's serene face warmed—and calmed—Quin's heart. Attalos had never given him bad advice. Surely this time would be no different.

3

"[She] had a spirit by which she predicted the future. She earned a great deal of money for her owners by fortune-telling."

— ACTS 16.16

TIA REFUSED TO SAY THE WORDS, EVEN TO HERSELF.

She'd known what was happening ever since the soldiers had invaded their village. She'd simply refused to think about it, acknowledge it.

Until now.

The room they'd been brought to was composed of bare, white stone walls. A cold, white stone floor. Square windows, all in a row.

A spindly man, hunched over with age, entered the only door at the far end of the room carrying an enormous basket of fresh bread. Behind him trailed a string of young girls with pitchers in one hand and cloths in the other. No sooner was the food and drink placed on the table in the center of the room than it was attacked. The old man barely escaped in time.

He shuffled toward the door, amusement written all over his face.

Let him live on a piece of bread half the size of his hand each day for two months and see how he acts.

"At least the bread is fresh this time." Tancorix smiled, always finding the good in every situation.

She tried. She just couldn't. "Do you know where we are?"

He shrugged. "Near Rome. I heard them talking as we pulled into port."

After splitting the room into men and women, the young girls circulated in pairs. One had a bucket of water, the other wet cloths. Filthy tunics came off, water dumped over them, faces and bodies scrubbed down. New, gauzy tunics were provided.

Tia shoved down the implications.

The door slammed open and several older men and women barged though. They began questioning the captives, scratching on small pieces of animal skin with a reed dipped in a black liquid, leaving interesting marks behind. It reminded her of the way the men applied tattoos to skin back home.

A silver-haired man with a brisk walk and a sour face approached Tia. He began spitting out questions. Did he have to talk so fast? Her Latin wasn't that good. "How old are you? What can you do? Cook? Clean? Sew? Read and write Latin?" He grasped her face and turned her head side to side, pulled her jaw down and looked in her mouth. One finger nearly jammed down her throat. Was he counting her teeth?

Her gaze darted around the room searching for Tancorix, but the man had a firm grasp on her head, leaving her unable to move.

He lifted the hem of her tunic and felt her legs. Her breathing sped up, her heartbeat tripled as his hands crawled higher.

Brigid, my goddess, help me.

He frowned and marked numbers on the tablet, then hung the piece of skin around her neck with a string.

One woman crawled around the room with a large block of white chalk, thoroughly covering one foot of each person in white.

Some sort of sign? The soft stone scratched her already tender foot, and she started to pull it away. The woman tugged it back and continued.

When everyone had been questioned, marked, and tagged, the inspectors gathered near the door. There they chatted and stared, shaking their heads, arguing, scowling, marking again on smooth pieces of wood, and then they left.

A new guard checked the manacles around their feet, as had been done on the ship before they walked down the gangplank to the street. They filed out of the room into an open courtyard, then up a short set of stairs on the north side. The morning sun shone in her eyes.

The stone under her feet still held the cold of the night, and it crawled from her toes through her body to her head. She shivered, though her shaking was as likely due to the suggestive stares as to the temperature. What had happened to the warm, beautiful cloak Mamma had made for her, the one she was wearing when she was taken? Likely it was now on the woman of the centurion, keeping her warm instead.

An enormous square area lay before them. Columned walkways lined the other three sides. Behind those stood massive buildings. She turned to look over her shoulder. A huge, long stone structure with many doors. There were even doors far above her head. How would you even get up there to enter through them? Everywhere she looked, there was stone. No grass. No trees. No flowers. How did people live in such a cold, artless place?

"As long as we stay together we'll be safe. We can protect each other." Tancorix's voice was soothing. "They've kept us in one group so far. I can't see any reason to split us up now. We'll be fine."

It was sweet he still tried to make her think he believed that. Such a good bratir.

An ugly man with rotting teeth and thinning hair swaggered to the bottom of the steps and faced the crowd. He walked back and forth, pointing to each of them in turn and talking. She'd always hated their language. It was harsh and without music. When shouted in anger, it was even worse.

A taller, wide-shouldered man strutted behind them, a whip in his hand. A shudder ran through her body every time he flicked the end against the stone, just enough for a crack to resound and remind them he could inflict severe pain at any moment.

When the man with the teeth reached the last one in line, he returned to the beginning. The guard grasped the arm of the first girl and jerked her forward, toward the edge of the step. She was one of the youngest of the group, or at least the smallest. Her body trembled, her shoulders drooped.

Tia lifted her chin. She would not show her fear. That would only make them treat her worse.

The men called out Latin words she recognized as numbers, one after another. Finally the trader pointed to the last man who had spoken out. *"Sold."*

The word hit her like an enemy arrow. The thought she had refused to entertain for so long finally demanded to be heard.

She closed her eyes. Felt the grass beneath her feet. The wind in her hair. Heard the waves against the cliffs. Ignored what was happening.

Warriors don't cry.

The big man's hand landed on her back and she was propelled forward. She looked over her shoulder at Tancorix.

Help me.

Not so many numbers were shouted for her. The placard around her neck didn't have as many marks; she was not as skilled as some of the other girls. She had spent most of her time deep in the woods with the old ones, learning to hear the goddess instead of practicing cooking and mending. The other girls had teased her. Her grandmother had often told her to ignore them, but maybe they'd been right.

Her heart raced.

Tancorix let out a sharp whistle, beckoning the trader. He

leaned forward. Whispered something. The trader's face lit up, and he turned and announced something to the crowd.

Suddenly, men were clamoring for her. What had her brother said? She looked to him.

He smiled.

"What did you say?"

"I told him about your gift. And I told him I was the only one who could help you use it properly."

"You did *what*? Why did you do that?" she hissed.

He smirked. "I just saved your life. And I made sure we could stay together. A little gratitude would be nice."

"Sold!" the ugly man crowed, pointing to a man in the crowd. But which one?

Tancorix meant well, but at this point, was her life really worth saving? Perhaps she would be better off dead.

Then again, at least they were together.

And together they could do anything. Even escape.

QUIN RUBBED his hip as he entered the *triclinium*. "*Mmmm.* Something smells good."

"Thank you, Tribune." His parents' kitchen slave set platters of wheat bread and cheese on the table in the center of the dining couches.

"He is no longer a tribune. Do not address him as such." Julius Valerius strode into the room and reclined on a *lectus*.

"Actually, I have not yet been officially discharged, and when I am, I will retain my rank since I will be leaving due to injury."

Loaf in hand, his father sniffed, a sign the conversation was over. No need to try to explain further.

They ate in silence. When the quick meal was over, Julius sat up. "Have you decided what you will do next?" His face was impassive as always, his voice, expressionless.

Quin may as well talk to one of the statues in the hallway. "I'm not sure yet." Three days of rest, delicious food, and a soft bed had helped considerably, but his leg still wasn't as strong as it had been.

"I cannot help you. You must be aware of this." He stared at the wall beyond Quin. "You are the fifth son. My firstborn will, of course, inherit the estate. The others will inherit parts of the business." He pursed his lips. "I did not plan on five sons. This is why I told you to stay in the army even after you had completed your required service. I have nothing for you."

"I know, Pater. You never have." He wandered down the hallway and out to the garden. After six years in gloomy Britannia, the bright summer sun was mercifully warm. He'd never been as cold as he had on that perpetually damp island. One more reason to avoid Camulodunum. Macedonia—if he ended up there, and it was looking more and more certain that he would—was reportedly sunny. If he had to wait somewhere for the truth to come out, it might as well be there.

The garden fountain majestically shot water high into the air from a stone bowl almost as high as his shoulders, sending droplets far beyond the edge of the stone basin. From the sides of a wider bowl beneath that, lions' heads spat more water. The cooling spray felt good in summer's heat, and he took his time passing through it.

At the far edge of the garden, Julia Valerius rested in the shade of an enormous tree. He joined her, grunting as he dropped onto the bench next to her.

"Have you eaten?"

"I ate a little. With Pater."

She cringed. "How did that go?"

"About as well as you'd expect. I think he'd be happier if I never came home."

She cradled his hand in hers and rubbed the back of it.

"Why does he hate me?"

She closed her eyes as a tear fell.

"I'm not his, am I?"

She squeezed his hand and stared at him with wide eyes.

"That's why my hair is lighter, and my eyes are gray."

"You think so too? You think that little of me?"

Could he feel any worse? "I am so sorry. Please forgive me."

"My brothers have lighter hair and eyes, and his uncle does as well. Your looks are legitimate, and so are you. But he won't believe. He jumped to the same conclusion you did." She looked away. "At least you had his hatred of you to lead to such a lie. He had no reason at all to think such a ghastly thing of me, no reason to suspect I had been unfaithful. But he has punished me—and you—ever since."

"Even when you pointed out my uncles, and his?"

"Even so."

"No wonder he wanted me gone." All the distance and punishment his pater had inflicted on him now made sense. Painful sense, but sense nonetheless. "Was it any better once I left?"

"Slightly. As long as I never mentioned your name."

"But my sister also has light eyes."

"Yes, and he knows she cannot possibly be anyone's but his. After you were born, he made sure I was followed any time I left the house, which was almost never. But by then it didn't really matter." She brushed a tear from her cheek. "I think in his heart he knows the truth, but he just can't bear to admit he's wrong."

"I'll leave as soon as I can. As soon as the doctors give their permission."

"How is your leg?" She pushed up his tunic slightly as she drew her finger along the end of the fading red scar. "Does it hurt?"

He shook his head. "Not really. Sometimes it flares up, but mostly it doesn't bother me." That was a complete lie, but there was no need for her to know how much it bothered him. And how little sensation he had in his foot. She would worry forever.

She gently touched the other scars on his arms, his legs. "My beautiful son, so broken and beaten."

He chuckled lightly. "It's all right, Mater. They are all from years ago."

Tears filled her eyes when she looked up at him. "You don't

understand what it does to see my child like this. No mater wants her child to hurt, ever."

He slid his arm around her and pulled her into his side. *"Te amo."*

"I know." She pulled back to touch the scar that ran toward his jawline. "I love you too. And you are still beautiful to me."

"I'm glad you think so. No one else will."

Her eyes glistened. "Oh, yes. Someone will. The perfect one for you will. That's how you'll know she truly loves you."

His mater might believe that, but he knew better. The army didn't want him. His pater didn't want him.

No one would ever want him.

THE IRON RINGS rubbed fresh wounds into the tops of her already mangled feet as Tia followed their new owner, Maximus. The fading sun hovered over the rippling water in the west, but the heat remained.

"Stop dawdling." Max's belly hung over his belt, and he was barely taller than she was. Almost every Roumanos they had met so far was shorter than Tancorix. A weak people, these Roumani. Amazing they had conquered nearly all of Britannia. They were nothing without their armor and their weapons. No wonder they failed the first time they came, and only succeeded the second time through sheer force of numbers.

She bumped her bratir with her shoulder. "I didn't know it was possible for a person's stomach to get that big. He looks like he's carrying a baby."

Tancorix chuckled.

She groaned. "How can you possibly find any humor in this?"

"What's the other choice? Anger?"

"Sounds like a perfectly viable option to me."

Ahead of them, Max halted and turned to face them. "We'll stay here for a few nights."

"Isn't this where you live?" Though she deplored the idea of boarding another boat, a harbor full of them could afford many opportunities to run away from this hateful man and head toward home.

"This is Ostia. We live in Macedonia, but we'll stay here for several days before we go home." He headed toward a row of houses near the end of the dock. He didn't wait for them. Apparently, he didn't think they could go far with iron on their feet.

When they caught up, he spoke with an older woman, whose long silver hair, elegantly arranged on her head, was held in place by a blue band. A matching blue sash draped over one shoulder. By the time they arrived at the entryway, Max was dropping silver coins into her palm.

"I'm Dorkas. Follow me, then." She nodded before leading the three of them deep into the *domus*, which was much larger than it looked from the outside. "Your rooms are here." She halted before several spacious, airy rooms to her right. Beds with fluffy, wool-stuffed mattresses, trays full of fruit, and pitchers of wine awaited.

Perhaps this wouldn't be as bad as she had feared.

Max entered one room and slammed the door shut.

Tia moved toward the next one.

A man with a dagger on his hip blocked the doorway, glaring down at her.

She backed up.

The innkeeper beckoned to Tia and Tancorix and continued down the hall. "*These* are for you."

A pair of windowless rooms lay before them, each barely large enough for a sleeping mat, and smelling of sweaty feet.

Tia forced a smile and nodded. "Thank you."

"Food will be brought to you shortly." Dorkas disappeared back the way she came.

Tia glanced around. Similar rooms surrounded them. Many must already be occupied for the night, with doors pulled tight. Hulky men with sheathed blades waited at the end of the hallway, prohibiting any chance of escape, or any other unsanctioned behavior, apparently.

She entered her room and dropped to the floor. A gentle knock sounded and the door pushed open. A young boy, in a tunic that reached his feet and hung off one shoulder, waited with a plate of fresh bread, a wedge of cheese, and a large bunch of grapes. A pitcher of watered wine was also set before her.

At least she would be fed well.

A pounding on the door came too soon after a restless night. The only indication of a new day was the light shining under her door. Just as she stuffed down the bread and fruit left outside her door, the same young boy lightly rapped on her door and beckoned her to follow. She noticed her bratir's room was empty as she passed it.

She walked back along the hallway toward the front of the house until she arrived at a spacious open-air room, much like the courtyard the roundhouses shared back home. Columns surrounding the garden supported a shaded walkway.

Max reclined on his elbows on a luxurious backless couch, an overflowing platter of food on a table nearby. No wonder his belly was so large.

"Come." His mouth full of grapes, Max sat up on his lectus.

She approached, heart pounding.

"Here is what will happen today." He swallowed noisily. "I have arranged for Dorkas to bring customers here for the next few days. They will ask you questions, and you will supply the answers. If missteps are to be made, better to make them here than at home where people will remember them."

Her thoughts reeled. What had Tancorix told them? Brigid's visions had never come on command before. They simply came when they came, how they came.

Of course, she had never asked.

"Clear?" Max angrily snapped his fingers in front of her face.

"Y-yes. I'm sorry." She glanced around the room. No Tancorix. "May I . . . may I ask where my brother is?"

"He is working elsewhere. It's none of your concern. He'll return tonight." He smiled—almost, and then turned toward Dorkas. "Let's begin. Daylight is wasting."

"Wait." Dorkas's eyes skimmed her from head to toe. "I realize a slave of her talents is a new venture for you, but don't you think she might bring you more coin if she were a little more . . . presentable?"

Max stared at her, blankly. "What are you talking about?" The annoyance in his voice was evident.

Dorkas sighed. "If I wanted to talk to her, I might be inclined to pay more if she were . . . cleaner, and in a nicer tunic. She looks like her skin hasn't felt water since Britannia."

Tia shivered at the memory of the bucket of icy water dumped on her head in the cold, white room.

The innkeeper pinched her arm. "She also looks like she will drop dead at any moment. You should get some food in her."

Twenty-five days in the belly of a ship with barely enough food to keep a mouse alive had taken its toll.

Max scoffed. "We're already late. We just need to get started."

Dorkas tilted her head, grinning. "You might get more coin in the long run . . ."

Please, please, a bath would be so nice. Thoughts of washing in the river at home with soap made from fat and ash flashed through her mind.

"Fine, then, just hurry, whatever you do." Max leaned on his elbow again.

"Take care of the merchandise, and she will take care of you." Dorkas winked at Tia and took her arm. "Come on. Let's get you cleaned up and into some new clothes."

"Nothing too expensive!"

The innkeeper laughed.

"Thank you," Tia whispered.

"It's just business, dear. I take care of my customers, they keep coming back." She threw back a curtain. "Now get in here and clean up. Quickly."

Two large pitchers of water sat on a low table next to a stack of cloths. She untied the sash around her waist and pulled her tunic over her head.

Not a real bath, but better than nothing at all. At least she would be clean.

She gasped as the curtain was yanked open again, crossing her arms over her chest.

"Put this on when you're done." Dorkas tossed a garment at her.

Tia picked up the tunic that had fallen to the floor. She rubbed it against her cheek. So soft, softer than any fabric she'd ever felt. Not wool. What was it?

She finished washing as best as she could and slipped the new tunic on. At least this one would not allow the men to see right through it. She brushed through her hair and held up the polished bronze mirror.

It was as good as she could do with the amount of time and water she was given. Not to mention the lack of soap.

She sucked in a deep breath.

Now the hard part.

4

"There is a way that appears to be right,
but in the end it leads to death."

— PROVERBS 14:12

THE STONE TEMPLE OF CASTOR AND POLLUX DWARFED QUIN AS HE stood before it on the southeast side of the forum. As a child this had been his favorite building. He loved the many columns on all four sides, stretching skyward, taller than the height of four men. He used to walk along the perimeter of the temple, touching and counting each of the pillars while his father conducted business on the forum.

So many new buildings had been erected in the last sixteen years, it was a wonder he had even found the forum. To the southwest, the Temple of Jupiter sat like a sentry atop Capitoline Hill, overlooking the city, dominating the landscape. As long as that remained, he could find his way home.

He'd walked farther than he intended, and the constant ache in his thigh had worsened. It was probably best to go home, but he couldn't resist one more walk around the temple. He limped south between the Basilica Julia and the temple. Disreputable traders hovered in the shadows on this road, eager to separate the naïve from their silver.

At the temple's corner, he stepped onto a wider road. To his right, behind the basilica, a rowdy crowd gathered. A pudgy man stood atop a raised platform, in front of people wearing dirty clothes and defeated expressions.

A slave market. One of the more disreputable ones. The buyers here were not wealthy. The people offered were not the best—they were older, injured, uneducated. These were not to be used as skilled workers, merely laborers.

The trader dragged the captives one by one to the edge of the platform. Men called out prices, asked for information, and occasionally demanded the person on display be stripped for closer inspection.

He had never thought about where the many slaves in his house had come from. His pater simply made a trip to the city's center, and later that day a new slave showed up at the estate. Quin had never seen the slaves before they were cleaned up and delivered. Never watched the bidding. Never witnessed money changing hands.

He didn't want to see it now, either. He turned and headed back the way he came until he reached the *Via Sacra*, then turned east toward home.

TIA HUGGED the wall as Maximus strode toward the corner of the peristyle in Dorkas's inn. He arranged two of her couches so they faced each other.

"Sit here." His gruff voice matched the glare.

She perched on the edge of the lectus.

"Now, remember." He held up one finger. "Smile. No one will even approach you if you scowl." Another finger. "Each person gets one question. Any more than that and they must pay again." Third finger. "And above all, don't touch the coins. They should pay me before they see you, but just in case anyone should offer you any, remember they are *mine*. I'll be waiting over here."

She nodded.

He leaned over her, his hot breath washing over her face. "And you will respond to me with 'Yes, Domine.'"

"Yes, Domine."

Max stepped a few long strides away and leaned against one of the columns, glaring. Watching her every move.

Brigid, help me. I have no idea what's to happen today.

By midday, a steady stream of people had come and gone. Rarely had anyone had to wait, but Tia wasn't idle long, either.

Max tucked a customer's payment into the leather pouch he kept in his belt. "We will become less busy soon as everyone goes home for a quick meal and the baths. We'll eat then too."

"Yes, Domine." He controlled even when she ate.

An old farmer's knees creaked as he dropped onto the couch.

She plastered on a smile and searched for a familiar feature, anything that reminded her of her parents. Even Tancorix. It was the only way she could care about these strangers. This man had kind eyes. She focused on those. "Will you tell me your name?"

"Galenos." His weathered face spoke of years in the sun.

"Are you a farmer?"

He grinned. "How could you tell?"

Should she point out the dirt under his nails, his sunburnt cheeks, the mud stains on the sleeves of his tunic that probably wouldn't come clean no matter how many times his wife washed it? "I'm a seer."

His cackle rewarded her restraint.

"What's your question?"

"I don't know what to plant."

She glanced over his shoulder at Max and leaned near.

"I'm so sorry, but you can only ask a simple question. Yes or no. Either this or that. Do you have choices?" she whispered.

His wrinkled cheeks colored. "All my choices so far haven't done well. I've planted wheat, millet, vegetables . . ."

"Let me ask her." She patted his hand and closed her eyes.

Brigid, tell me how to help this sweet man. A picture slowly formed.

"I see you standing in a field of golden plants . . . and they have long hairs coming from them. But I don't know what they are called."

His face split into a wide grin. "That's barley. I haven't planted that in many years!"

"Then perhaps it's time to try this year."

"And it's a good harvest?"

"Very good."

He laughed again as he stood. "If my crop comes in as well as you say, I will come back in the spring and give you more coin, *dulcissima*."

She didn't know that word. But it must be a nice thing. He was smiling.

Max stepped in, claiming the payment. "Thank you."

"I need to go purchase seed now." Old Galenos toddled off.

"That took far too long. Why?"

"My Latin is not good enough for some of these questions yet. I didn't know the name of the crops."

"He's supposed to tell you names, then you choose one."

"He did give me names, but I didn't know what I saw."

Max drilled his stare into Elantia.

"If I find out you are giving more service than you should be, then you are stealing from me."

"I wasn't."

"Then do it faster." Max leaned nearer, his nose a hand's breadth away from hers. "I don't care if they call you *sweetheart*, or not. Your time is mine, and my time is money. I say be quicker about it."

Tia steadied her voice. "I'm going as fast as I can. The visions come when they come."

"You'd better hope they come faster then. Pray to your goddess. Sacrifice. Whatever it takes." He straightened. "Because you only have to remain pure as long as you are a seer. If you can't do that, then . . ." His eyes traveled up and down her body like a snake slithering along a tree limb. "Now let's eat." He left, expecting Tia to follow.

As if he hadn't just somehow threatened her.

At least that explained what Tancorix had told them. It was a common belief that only girls who were pure could hear from the goddess. It wasn't true. Her mamma had been a seer her entire life, as had her mamma before her. But if it would keep her safe, she could keep up the deception.

Sweet, sweet Tancorix. Still protecting her, even when he wasn't with her.

As to how long it would work, who knew? But for now, she'd take whatever she could get.

THE COOLING EVENING breeze of midsummer kissed Quin's skin as he looked over the Valerius estate from his *cubiculum* on the upper floor. Strawberries and oranges scented the air, and the *plop-plop-plop* of the bubbling fountain drifted in, soothing his frayed nerves.

Perhaps he'd build one on his new property in Philippi.

He tossed linen tunics from his cupboard into the wooden chest on the floor, along with a second pair of sandals and his studded army boots.

"What are you doing?" Mater's sharp voice behind him caused him to jump.

"Packing. I'm leaving in the morning. Pater has made it clear I can't stay here." He answered without turning around.

She came around to face him, then pulled his hands from his task, holding them between hers. "Let me talk to him. I'm sure—"

"Don't bother. He doesn't want me here." He sighed. "And what would I do if I stayed? Flavius has ruined my name in both the military and the government. Pater will never allow me into the family businesses, I won't inherit, and it would be too embarrassing to him for me to be even a paid worker, for him or anyone else. How would I live?"

Releasing him, she pointed to the pile of clothing on his sleeping couch. "You should at least let the slaves pack for you."

"I don't need them to."

Scowling, she gestured from the bed to the trunk, to him. "This is not proper."

"I don't want anyone else handling my belongings. I've been taking care of myself for the last fourteen years without slaves." After tossing the remainder of his clothes in the trunk, he knelt to fold them.

She huffed. "You have no slaves in the army?"

"Of course we do. Hundreds of slaves. But they don't pack my personal things. Every soldier takes care of himself."

She crossed the room to the window and stared at the dusky landscape for several long moments. "Where will you go?"

"Before he left Britannia, Vespasian told me I could take my retirement pay in either sesterces or land. I've chosen land. In Macedonia."

She whipped around. "Macedonia? So far away?" Her voice squeaked.

He spun on one foot to face her, the move sending pain shooting down his thigh. "It's little more than two weeks' travel. It's half as far as Britannia."

"But you had no choice then." Her eyes glistened. "Can't you at least stay in Italia?"

"There is land available in Macedonia, not Italia."

"Macedonia." She grimaced. "It's full of barbarians."

He resisted sighing. "It's a Roman colony. They don't even station a legion there because it's so civilized. Romans there are citizens, and there are more Romans than Greeks. At least in the city." He rose and then closed the distance between them.

She brightened. "Really?"

He grinned. "It's the most Roman place on earth outside Italia."

"Well, that makes me feel a little better."

"I know you don't want me to leave." His voice was soft.

"You just got home. I've seen you for two weeks in fourteen years. Germania, then Britannia, now . . ." She laid her head against his chest. "Tomorrow? Not one more day?"

"The ship to Macedonia leaves tomorrow, or not for another month." Why did he feel so awful? It wasn't as if he had a choice.

She sucked in a long breath, stepped back, and straightened her shoulders. "Then I'll see you in the morning." She smiled as she patted his chest and turned and left his room.

There was the woman Julius Valerius had molded, as he had formed his children. Accept without question. No emotion. Spine of iron.

After he finished packing, he sought out Attalos once more. As he knocked on the servant's door, he smiled at the thought that his dearest friend in the world was a slave.

A young boy opened the door, and Quin stepped inside.

Attalos stood before his parchment-covered table, wax tablet in hand, his hand rapidly moving a stylus. He looked up as Quin entered, the face Quin had come to associate with love and caring brightening the room.

"I'm leaving in the morning."

His face, always passive after years of practice, darkened for the briefest of moments. "I'm not surprised. I'm saddened, but not surprised. I know there is no future for you here."

Quin shrugged. "I don't want to go. I don't want to leave Mater. I don't want to leave you."

He set the tablet and stylus down. "My boy, I am so very grateful I was able to see you this summer. I was sure I would never see you again once you left for Britannia."

"You know if I could, I would free you."

"I am not yours. I belong to your pater."

A mirthless chuckle escaped. "And he would never in a million years free you."

"But I am free. In a way that I pray every day you will soon understand."

"How can you be free? Because you are not in chains? Because you command others?"

Attalos searched his face. "Someone may control where I live, what I do, what I eat, but no one will ever control what I think or, more importantly, what I believe."

"And what is that?"

"You are not ready to hear that now." Wrinkles appeared around his eyes, and his mouth turned down for the briefest moment. "Besides, you have much to do. You need to get a good night's sleep, for I fear you will not sleep well for a long time."

He would miss this man's wisdom. "I wish you could come with me. Pater would allow it if I asked."

"And what good would I be to you? I am old, and slow. Take someone else. Or buy another to serve you."

"I don't want someone to serve me!" He closed his eyes and took several deep breaths. "I'm sorry. I didn't mean to shout, especially at you. I don't want you as a slave. I want you as my friend, my mentor. You were a better pater to me than he ever was."

"Domine." Attalos placed his hands on Quin's cheeks. "Quin. You don't need his approval to be the great man I know you are. That you have already shown you are. Go to Macedonia. I believe great things are waiting for you there. Not that they will be easy, but they will shape you into the man you were meant to be, that all other things in your life have been leading up to."

What was that supposed to mean? Attalos had never talked in riddles. Perhaps it was his age. Maybe he *was* too old to go to Macedonia with him. Quin drew the old man into his embrace. "I'll miss you." He fought to control his voice.

After a long moment, the Greek pulled away. "Send letters when you can. And don't worry about your pater."

Quin pulled the door shut after he left.

If only he could find some way to take Attalos with him, or at least take the confidence Attalos inspired in him. Attalos was the only person in his life who had ever told him he could do anything right. Except for his mater, and she was . . . his mater. And now Attalos was saying Quin could be a great man? Was already a great man?

He was a good soldier, maybe. Perhaps even a great one. But that was over.

He was far from a great man. And until and unless the truth came out, no one would even think he was a good one.

TIA RECOILED before her furious owner.

Max grasped her arm, squeezing hard and pulling her close. "That was very foolish of you!" His hot breath smelled of garlic and leeks.

Dorkas neared them. "Let her go! Marks on her arm will not help."

Max shoved Elantia against the wall, his nostrils flaring. "You cost us profit! I will not tolerate that!"

"I don't know what you're talking about. Please explain it to me." She held back the tears. She would not appear weak before this man.

He stepped closer. No taller than she was, his protruding belly and wide shoulders nevertheless made her feel small. "You cannot give such dire predictions. No one will come if you do that."

The future was the future. How could he expect her to control that? "What am I supposed to do then? I don't know what you expect of me!"

He grabbed her forearm and twisted, hard.

She dropped to her knees to alleviate the pain.

He twisted harder.

She finally cried out.

"Get up!" Max barked at her.

She stood, gingerly touching her arm.

"That should teach you not to argue with me!" He jabbed his finger into her shoulder.

She stared at the floor and took a deep breath. "I'm very sorry, Domine." It took a huge effort to keep her voice from breaking. "I wasn't trying to argue. I was only trying to figure out what I did wrong, what you wanted."

Max groaned. "This one is too stupid. I never should have purchased her."

Dorkas's sandals entered her field of vision. "Let me try."

Heavy footsteps faded as Max stomped away. A door opened and slammed shut.

"Elantia." Dorkas's voice was softer, but far from gentle. No matter how kind she may appear, Tia knew she was only interested in keeping her customers happy.

She kept her head down.

"Elantia, look at me when I speak."

She calmed her face before she raised her head. "Yes, Domina."

"I am not your domina."

"Yes, Dorkas."

"I believe Maximus is trying to say you must give only happy prophesies. You told that man he would die soon, and then he refused to pay."

"But that is what I saw."

She tilted her head. "Can't you keep . . . listening until you find something good to say?"

"It doesn't always work that way. The goddess tells me what she tells me."

"All right, then perhaps in his case, you could say the next month looks like a good time to plant. Or harvest. Or whatever it is farmers are doing. That would be true for anyone, no? And keep the bad part to yourself."

"All right. I can try that."

"Good." Her lips turned up, but the smile was not in her eyes. "Now, wait here. I'll talk to Max."

Tia let out a long breath and collapsed against the wall.

Squeezing her eyes shut, her chest tightened, and her throat burned.

Brigid, how could you let this happen to me? This is the fate you have prepared for me? I served you well. Committed to memory everything the teachers recited for me. Practiced my gift. And this is my reward?

Dorkas reappeared, Max behind her. "Get back to your couch. But remember what we talked about."

She pushed herself up, straightened her tunic, and flicked her hair behind her shoulders. Rubbing her arm where a bruise was surely to appear by nightfall, she took her seat.

Dorkas opened her doors once again. The next person in line was an older man, wrinkled and stooped. The mud on his sandals and the dirt on his hands and the bottom of his tunic told her he, too, was a farmer.

Tia shut out the noise of those waiting and held his weathered hand in hers. Closing her eyes, she gently stroked his hand with her fingertips and waited for the images to invade her mind. *Brigid, show me his life, show me what is planned for him.* Pictures began to form, slowly coming together from the cloudy mess in her mind.

"Your wife is expecting a baby?"

The old man laughed. "Do I look like I am the age to have a baby?"

She studied him for a moment, then raised a brow. "A daughter? Sister? Someone you love very much, I think."

He grinned and bobbed his head. "Yes. My daughter."

"She will deliver a healthy boy. He will be born small, but he will grow to be a leader of men."

"Thank you." His cackle revealed several missing teeth. "Thank you, sweet girl." He stood and offered her a bronze coin.

She tilted her head in the direction of her owner, who scurried forward to accept the payment.

A girl about her own age took the seat next, and the process started again.

At the end of the day, her mind and soul drained, Elantia fell onto the mat in her tiny room. The people she'd seen paraded through her mind.

The old man, her first customer after her incident with Max . . . His daughter would have a boy, and he would be a leader of men. She just didn't tell him he would be a leader of thieves and bandits.

She didn't tell the young woman her husband wasn't cheating in his business, but on her.

She didn't tell another woman that no, she wouldn't die from the disease that took her mother, as she feared, but that she would die in a terrible accident.

Three times she had deceived today. But she had kept the prophecies happy.

Where was Tancorix? She needed his optimism, his encouragement. She'd heard his door open late last night but he was gone again before she awoke.

She turned on her mat and faced the wall. Would every day be like this?

5

> *"Fools give full vent to their rage,*
> *but the wise bring calm in the end."*
>
> — PROVERBS 29:11

QUINTUS LEANED AGAINST A BUILDING ON OSTIA'S DOCK, TRYING TO stay out the way as sailors busily carried off cargo and restocked supplies.

The captain approached, and Quin straightened.

He grinned. "You don't look like a sailor. Or like one of the dock workers."

"I'm not. Actually, I'd like to arrange passage to Macedonia."

"Of course. I still have almost all my cabins left. Do you have a preference?"

"Not really."

The captain quoted the fare and held out his hand. Quin dropped several silver coins into it. "Pick any one that is empty." He snapped his fingers at a passing sailor. "Take his belongings on deck for him."

"Yes, Captain."

Quin followed the young man up the wide plank and to the rear of the deck.

The young man halted before the doors of the cabins attached to the stern of the ship. "Which one?"

He surveyed the four rooms. All seemed to be exactly alike. "This one, on the end, I suppose." Perhaps it would be a little quieter with only one shared wall.

"Very well." He took Quin's bag and placed it just inside the door before hurrying back to the dock.

The cabin was small, just big enough for a stuffed mattress on a low platform, and a small table. An oil lamp was affixed to the wall and a small window on the back wall let in fresh sea air.

Quin opened one of his bags and withdrew one of the ripe, green pears Mater had insisted he take along. They wouldn't last the whole trip, but they would supplement the one meal a day from the crew's supplies his fare included. That food would be filling and give him energy, but wasn't likely to be tasty. Still, better than the hardtack he ate while on march.

His pear finished, he stepped out a few strides away from the cabins and tossed the core into the water. He leaned over the railing and watched as the seagulls immediately descended, fighting over it as if it were the last bite on earth.

Chuckling, he turned around and was faced with a portly man scowling at him.

"I need this cabin." He gestured toward the room Quin had claimed.

"I'm sorry?" What would it matter? They were all exactly the same.

"This one on the end. I need it. The captain said I could have it."

That was almost certainly a lie. "Let's go ask him." Quin started to step past him.

The man held up his hands. "All right. He didn't, but I do need it. I'll pay you for it."

"Why do you need it so badly? What's wrong with one of the others?"

"I need to be on the end. I need to keep an eye on my new slaves."

Quin looked over the man's shoulder. A few strides away waited a young woman with hair the color of the sun and eyes the color of sapphires. He'd only seen that in Britannia. Could it be they were Britanni war captives?

Her beauty was marred by an ugly purple bruise on her forearm. A youth who appeared to be slightly younger stood beside her. It was obvious they were newly purchased. The girl especially had the look of someone who had lost everything. When she frowned, he realized he had been staring.

She looked away and fixed her eyes on some point in the distance.

The cabin certainly wasn't worth arguing about. He shrugged. "Sure. I'll take the next one."

"Thank you. My name is Maximus."

"I am Quintus."

"Slave!" Max pointed at her. "Move his things from my cabin to one of the others."

She glared at her *dominus* and then at him.

Why choose the girl and not her much stronger companion? Was he just trying to break her? "Don't worry. I'll do it." Quin stepped inside to retrieve his bags.

"Why?" Max said when he reappeared. "She's a slave. That's what she's for. Why would you do it yourself when I have offered you a perfectly good servant?"

"She's to serve you, not me."

"She will do as I tell her." He sneered. "I paid enough for her."

Quin put his things in the cabin next to Max's. Too bad he couldn't put more distance between them. Max seemed the type to carry trouble with him wherever he went.

TIA SUCKED in a chest full of the salt air. The full moon's glow reflected in the sea's gentle waves, reminding her of pleasant nights with her family in her seacoast village. How could she be happy and sad at the same time?

Maximus had finally gone to sleep and she and Tancorix would have a few hours without his constant commands and reprisals. She stretched out on the floor beside Max's room and tucked her arm under her head. Tancorix lay down beside her, between her and the sea. It wasn't likely she'd fall off, but it was like him to do what little he could to protect her.

"Where did you go every day? You left before the day began and returned after dark. I never saw you."

"Max sent me to work in the warehouses nearby. I spent all day moving cargo from the dock to different buildings. I think they paid him for my labor." He laughed. "Maybe he was trying to earn back some of what he spent on me."

"Those coins should have been yours."

He ignored the bitterness in her voice. "What did you do?"

"He had the innkeeper bring people to me. I asked Brigid to tell me what their future would be like."

He raised up on one elbow. "See? I knew they would appreciate your gift."

"It's not as easy as it sounds. Goddesses don't speak on command. And it can't be a bad prediction, or customers become angry and won't pay. It can't sound too good, either, or they think I'm making it up." She rubbed her arm where Max had twisted it.

"Is that why there's a mark on your arm?"

She sighed but said nothing.

"If he touches you again, I'll kill him."

"I can take care of him."

"I know." His voice was soft.

She rolled onto her back and stared at the stars. Were they the same stars she saw at home? She searched for the hunter and his hound. The bears. All still proudly patrolled the bright sky.

"At least this time, we're not below deck, thank the gods."

She grinned, glad Tancorix couldn't see her. He would see it that way. Unfortunately, she didn't share his happy outlook.

Though there were a few other good things about this trip. It would be a little shorter than the first. So far the food had been better, or maybe there was just more of it. They no longer wore ankle chains.

But then there was Max. If they had to be owned by someone, couldn't it be someone who was a little kinder? Max hadn't even bothered to ask their names.

The other Roumanos, the one Max had made move, had seemed like a decent man. Had even carried his own belongings. Max didn't like him and from what she'd learned so far, that was a compliment. Why couldn't they have ended up with him?

Then again, was any Roumani better than any other?

THE SUN'S bright fingers poked their way into Quin's room through the single, small window. He rubbed his thigh as he sat up. Would the pain ever go away?

Eighteen days at sea. If he had figured correctly, they should be almost to Neapolis, the port of Macedonia. He'd be happy if he never boarded another ship. He much preferred land. He stepped outside and started his first walk of the day around the deck.

Quin felt the captain's eyes on him as he made his way around the deck. He'd tried to walk around it as often as he could each day. Davos had told him it would help strengthen his leg. All he felt it do was exhaust him.

The officer fell in step beside him. "We'll make port by nightfall."

The first good news Quin had heard in weeks.

When they returned to the stern, the captain leaned against the mast. "What legion were you in?"

"How do you know I was in the army at all?" Quin lowered

himself onto a box of ropes, trying to ignore the ache that now seemed to be his constant companion.

The captain smiled softly. "My son was a soldier. I know one when I see one. Your discipline. Strict adherence to a routine only you know. Your respect for me, and others. Your physical condition."

He scoffed. "You mean this?" He pointed to the scar that extended well below his knee.

"That, and the fact you are otherwise perfectly fit. You push yourself every day to walk on that leg, despite the pain. So, which legio?"

"Second Augusta."

"Britannia?"

Quin nodded.

"What happened?"

"Horse reared. Then a chariot."

The captain winced. "You're a tribune?"

He nodded.

"Excuse me for saying it, but aren't you a little old to be a tribune? Shouldn't you be in Rome now, with some easy job in the city?"

"Probably. Chose not to. Long story."

The captain held his gaze a moment, then pushed off the mast. "I'll check on our progress."

Quin pushed himself up and strolled again to the bow of the ship. Grasping the rail, he leaned into the wind, letting it ripple his tunic. Too bad it couldn't blow away his unease as easily.

What awaited him in Philippi? For the first time in as long as he could remember, he had no idea.

A short while later, with about an hour of sunlight left, the ship gently bounced against the dock. Sailors hustled to complete their assigned duties. The anchor was dropped. Rope ladders were thrown off the side and the ship securely tied to port. No one was idle.

Crewmen extended a walkway from the deck, carted off boxes and trunks, and stacked them at the edge of the pier.

The captain's voice startled Quin. "Ready to go ashore?"

"I suppose."

"I'll have your things taken down for you. Will someone be waiting?"

He shook his head. "No one knows I'm coming."

The captain beckoned a crewman. "Take his bags to the end of the dock and get him a raeda."

"Yes, Captain."

"Thank you."

The captain was quiet a moment. "I couldn't help my son. At least I can help you."

TIA WAITED on the wooden walkway of the dock while Max arranged transportation to his home in—what was it called again? Philippi.

Max handed some coins to the stranger he spoke with and then returned. "I hired a carriage. It's late, but I want to go home."

Within moments an iron-wheeled wagon pulled by a pair of beautiful horses the color of oak arrived at the end of the walkway.

Max pointed at Tia. "Come."

Tancorix bent to pick up Max's bag, then carried it to the raeda. He placed the bag on the rack under the seats.

Max tipped his head toward another carriage as it pulled up on the other side of the stone road. "Ah, I see your new owner is here."

"Whose new owner?" asked Tancorix.

"Yours." Max grabbed him by the upper arm and steered him toward the second vehicle.

Tia felt like one of the horses had knocked her down and stomped on her. Tancorix was the only reason she had survived this far. Without him, she would have jumped into the sea long before they reached harbor.

She hurried to catch them. "No! You can't take him! You promised we would stay together. Please!" She grabbed Tancorix's other arm.

"I made no such promise. If that is what you understood, that is not my fault. Now let go."

"Please! Let him stay with me!"

Max grabbed Tancorix's arm with one hand and her with the other. He twisted until she let go and then shoved her to the ground.

She fell on her backside, the heels of her hands landing hard against the rough stone to break her fall.

The Roumanos from the cabin next to theirs stopped on his way down the walk, standing between her and Max. "Is everything all right? Do you need help?"

He looked at her, but why would he address a slave? Surely he was speaking to Max.

"Just a disobedient slave. Sometimes you have to use a little force." A sickening grin spread across Max's face.

Her brother climbed into the carriage. "Be strong, Tia. Carami te. And remember, no tears."

I love you too.

"Get in the raeda." Max's voice sounded like the growl of the wolves back home.

She watched for a moment until Max disappeared. Then she turned back and forced her feet to carry her across the walkway to the first vehicle. He was right. She could do this. She was a fighter. Strong. Britanni. And whatever it took, she would make her father proud.

6

"A false witness will not go unpunished,
and whoever pours out lies will not go free."

— PROVERBS 19:5

TIA AWOKE TO THE NOISE OF SOMEONE OPENING THE DOOR TO HER room.

She breathed in, slowly and deeply, remembering Tancorix's words, letting them burn into her heart.

Clatter drew her to action. A young woman in a woolen slave's tunic, perhaps a year or two older than she was, added a loaf of bread to the platter of hard cheese and apple slices on the table.

"Good morning. You must awaken, eat, and prepare yourself to go to the forum. I am to help you." Her smile was sweet, her voice pleasant.

She'd been dressing herself since she was a toddler. Why would she need help?

"I'm Euodia. Change into your tunic, and I'll be right back."

Euodia handed her a fresh garment as she breezed out of the room, closing the door behind her.

At least this room had a window. Too small to be of help in an escape, but it allowed in air and light. Tia did as she was instructed, and Euodia returned just as Tia finished getting dressed.

"Much better." She grinned. "Now sit." She pointed to a stool and handed Tia the plate of food. "You eat while I'll arrange your hair."

Tia munched the crusty bread as Euodia pulled a comb through her tangled tresses.

"I love your hair. Such a beautiful color, like the gold in the mountains near here. You wouldn't believe what some of the women here will do to get their hair this color." She came around to face Tia, piling a handful of hair atop her head. "The domina wants me to arrange it like hers, but I just don't think that will work."

Was she talking to Tia, or herself?

"I have a better idea." The comb and Euodia's fingers went to work, but Tia had no idea what was happening.

Euodia checked the view from the front again. "All right, let's see if Domina approves." She led Tia to an enormous room open to the sky, much like the one in Dorkas's house. Six couches were arranged in a three-sided square in the center, Max lounging on one and busily stuffing his mouth with bread. Grass grew between walkways which crossed the room from corner to corner. Bushes and flowering plants huddled against the walls, as if trying to stay as far away from the man as possible.

He sat up and spread his hands. "This is Philippi, if you hadn't guessed by now. Though we occasionally visit other towns, this is where we live and where we spend the majority of our time. It's much larger than Neapolis but you will soon know and be known by most of the people here." He stood and wrapped his arm around a woman who had entered while he spoke. "And this is Cassia, my wife and also your domina."

The woman was shorter and mercifully thinner than Max. Her

thick, dark hair contrasted starkly with her white tunic, which was mostly hidden under another long, deep blue cloth she wore over one shoulder and under the other arm. Her gaze traveled up and down Tia and settled on her hair. She approached, then circled Tia, fingering her long locks.

She glowered at Euodia. "I thought I instructed you to arrange her hair as a Roman. Only barbarians wear it down." She patted her own elaborate hairstyle.

Euodia dipped her head. "Yes, Domina. May I explain?"

Her eyes narrowed. "Quickly."

"I did try. It looked . . . wrong. Like it didn't belong. I thought, and you are wiser than I, so I can try again, that perhaps a simple braid might convey the foreign impression you might desire without the loose nature of a barbarian. I'm assuming you do want people to know she is from Britannia, and that is why she is gifted as she is?"

Cassia raised a brow, then allowed a half smile. "There's a reason I keep you around. But she's pale." She studied Tia a moment more. "Do something with her cheeks."

"Yes, Domina."

She raised a finger. "Not with my cosmetics. There's an empty glass of wine in my room."

"Yes, Domina." Euodia steered Tia away from Cassia.

"She was worth *all* our money? You were going to buy three slaves." Cassia's shrill voice followed them down the hall.

"I retrieved some of our money when I sold the boy."

"How much?"

"Not now." Max shushed his wife.

Moments later, her cheeks stinging from the red wine remnants rubbed into them, Tia left the domus with Cassia's hand closed around her arm.

White stone houses with arched windows and balconies soared over her head on both sides of the wide street. From the outside, they all looked the same—large, imposing, without character. She studied every door, every window, every brick. Burned it into her memory. One day, maybe they wouldn't be watching her, and she could get out of this horrible place.

Familiar scents of baking bread and simmering soup calmed her nerves—somewhat. At the end of the street they turned right onto a smaller road that led into a marketplace.

A wide tiled walkway opened before her. A roof—supported by columns on one side, attached to a building on the other—offered shade for both seller and buyer. On her right, the building was divided into small rooms, about four times the length of a man lying down.

Vendors of almost every possible ware hawked their goods. Clothing, food, pottery, silver, anything imaginable. Townspeople moved from stall to stall in no particular order, stopping to chat with friends and relatives.

Max and Cassia had an apparently enviable position in the middle of the *stoa*. Everyone had to pass them in order to go anywhere.

A brightly woven cloth covered a square acacia-wood table just big enough for Tia to reach across and hold the palm of her eager customers. A modest crowd had already gathered. Perhaps word from Neapolis had arrived. She moved behind the table, pulled back the wooden stool, and took her place at the table.

Cassia remained with her while Max wandered up and down the stoa, talking to the townspeople, enticing them to visit the new seer from Britannia.

After what seemed like hours, but was surely only moments, a young woman stepped forward from those watching, a basket hanging from one arm.

Max's words—commands—from this morning rang in Tia's ears. Smile. Be pleasant. And above all, don't take the coin. The coin belongs to them.

So did she.

Tia gestured to the stool on the other side of the table and held her breath.

Brigid, help me.

The woman sat, averting her gaze. The basket rested on the floor at her feet.

Perhaps if she touched her, had some sort of connection, the woman might feel more comfortable. "May I hold your hand?"

She placed one hand on the table.

Elantia slipped her hand under the woman's.

"Will you tell me your name?"

"Xenia."

"That's a beautiful name."

She relaxed. Smiled.

Tia stroked the back of her hand. Nothing came. "Xenia, what is your question?"

Her cheeks pinked. "Will I . . . will I ever marry?"

Tia closed her eyes. Images formed. "I see a man, an older man. He is kind and gentle, and he loves you very much."

"My father?"

"Yes. And he is talking to a younger man, a man who is . . . he is shaking his head no." Tia cringed as the tears fell from Xenia's eyes—tears she had caused.

"He refused my father's offer."

"Ahhh." The images blurred and reformed. "Wait, the younger one is with your father again. He now says yes."

"I don't believe you. He already said no. He made it very clear he doesn't want me." She jerked her hand back. "You're only telling me what you believe I want to hear."

Tia gasped. "I-I'm not. I say what the visions show me."

"No. It's impossible." She stood.

Tia stood and reached for her. This was not the way to begin her time here. "Let me try to prove it."

"How?"

"Please, sit?"

Xenia scowled but perched on the edge of the stool.

"When he was saying no, your father was with him in an olive grove. The trees were full of ripe olives. When would that be?"

Cassia moved behind Xenia, blocking her exit. "Olives are ripe in the winter months."

Tia touched her arm gently. "But when he was saying yes, he was in a vineyard."

"Still proves nothing." Xenia crossed her arms over her chest. "The grape harvest is nearly over."

Cassia stepped in. "How about this? You remain quiet until the harvest is over, and you pay nothing now. If the young man does not come to you, so be it. But if her prophesy proves true, you pay double, *and* you tell everyone in town."

Xenia pondered the offer, for longer than Elantia was comfortable. "Sounds fair." She picked up her basket of fruit and wandered back into the crowd of people.

Tia released a long breath.

"Let me ask you one question." Cassia waited until she caught her gaze.

"Yes."

"Were you telling her what she wanted to hear, or was that truly what you saw?"

"It was the vision Brigid gave me. I only tell the truth. I will only ever tell the truth. You can depend on that."

Cassia stared at her a long moment. "I hope so. Or it could lead to trouble for all of us."

AFTER A NIGHT IN NEAPOLIS, Quin hired an open-topped raeda to take him to Philippi. The wide, spear-straight *Via Egnatia* stretched before him. After his years in Britannia, tramping over forest trails and slogging through rivers, Quin would be forever thankful for the precision of Roman roads. The close-set stones made traveling smooth and easy even in a bouncy iron-wheeled carriage.

Halfway from the port of Neapolis to Philippi, he reached the highest point of the half-day's journey. He looked west, drinking in the landscape. The enormous marshes southwest of the city had once been the vast battlefield where Marcus Antonius and Octavius avenged Julius Caesar, ninety-one years ago this month. Their sound defeat of Brutus and Cassius was legendary, and mandatory study for any tribune. They rewarded their loyal combatants with land. Ten years later, Octavius, after defeating Antonius and proclaiming himself Caesar Augustus, settled even more legionaries in the colony.

Quin studied the land beyond the city's walls, marked off into lots. They would now be owned by their grandchildren and great-grandchildren. Not many, if any at all, would be soldiers now.

That was fine with him. He was weary of the machinations and duplicity of the Roman army—and her men.

A modest size, Philippi nevertheless boasted loudly of the Roman status it won from Augustus, which gave them independent government, citizenship for anyone born in the city, and most importantly, freedom from taxation.

Sitting with his legs bent for so long in the carriage had taken its toll, and Quin rubbed his leg as the driver urged the horses down the gentle slope of the Via.

It was early afternoon when the carriage rolled under the arch of the Neapolis Gate. Streets lined with *insulae* branched off the Via to the south. Row after row of four- or five-story apartment buildings reached all the way to the city wall. Resplendent villas followed as he drew closer to the city's heart. To the north lay an enormous amphitheater.

The forum, though only one-quarter of the size of Rome's, was beautiful in its simplicity. The Via hugged the northern edge, a massive fountain on either end. A temple occupied the northeast corner.

At the western end, a broad walkway lined with columns faced the forum. Clearly the town's administrative buildings occupied the whole of this stoa. The northernmost building, jutting out farther than the others, must be the *curia*, the home of the senate. That left the ornate center office as the home of the *duoviri*, the pair of ruling magistrates. "Turn here, please."

The carriage stopped before a marble Fortuna seated on her throne. Perhaps the goddess of luck would be on his side for once here. The driver started to pull Quin's bag from the shelf under the seat, but Quin stopped him.

"Can you wait? I don't think I'll be long, and I'll need you to take me to my final destination."

The driver nodded and shoved the chest back in place.

He crossed the stoa and hesitated before the basilica's double doors. When was the last time he was in a civilian building? If this were a military meeting, he would know exactly what to do, what to say. There were codes, rituals, protocols to follow. But he couldn't exactly tell the *duovir* he was reporting for duty.

One door was open, so he walked in. A slave met him in the atrium to the city's main business office. "Please, come in."

"I am Quintus Valerius. I seek the duovir."

"Wait, please." He disappeared down the hallway.

Quin wandered through the spacious room. Alabaster statuary stood on pedestals. Rich tapestries hung on the walls. Black and white mosaic tiles in the center of the atrium's floor created a picture of Bacchus, the god of wine.

The slave cleared his throat, and he turned.

A man several years younger than Quin and wrapped in a purple-bordered toga strolled in. He stopped ten or twelve strides away, head held higher than necessary. His dark hair was immaculately groomed, his eyes the color of sand, his hands soft as a baby's.

"Gallus Crispus, praetor of Philippi," the slave almost shouted, although they were the only three in the room.

Quin approached, bowed, and repeated his name. He held out the scroll given to him by Vespasian.

Gallus took it silently and read the parchment. "I see Vespasian is making good use of his fame. It really is not his place to be handing out land here." He tossed the parchment to his slave.

Quin looked down on the duovir, a full head shorter. "Apparently the emperor disagrees." He quirked a brow. "Look toward the bottom."

Gallus retrieved the scroll and unrolled it again, glanced at the last line. Glared at Quin. Handed it back.

"I'll need that back." Quin held out his hand.

"It needs to be filed here in the clerk's office."

Quin flinched at the thought of his proof of ownership leaving his hands, but he had no choice. The duovir said leave it, and he must obey.

Gallus's hard stare moved from Quin's head to his toes, then he turned on his heel and left the room.

The slave stepped forward. His face was round and open, his smile bright. "I'm Leonidas. The *scriba* is not here at the moment, but if you return in the morning, he can take you to your land."

"Thank you. Your kind words are welcome at the end of a long day." Quin extended his hand, and Leonidas grasped it. "Is there somewhere I can spend the night?"

He pointed west. "Go east to the last street, *Via Augusta*, and you should find several inns where you can stay for the night."

"Leonidas. Greek?"

He nodded. "From Athens."

"My servant was from Athens."

"Did he come with you?"

Attalos's face flitted through Quin's mind. "He had to remain with my pater."

"He seems to have meant a great deal to you."

Quin nodded. The man couldn't begin to know how much.

Back in the carriage and halfway to the far end of Philippi, Quin chuckled. Gallus Crispus couldn't be yet thirty. How had he managed to be elected duovir? Either he—or his pater, or both—must have some very influential friends. Hopefully Jupiter provided an experienced magistrate for the other duovir.

No matter. Not his problem. He was retired.

Near the western edge of the city, they turned north on a smaller road where houses and inns abounded. He needed only one of them to have an empty room for the night. A sign on the door of one of the cleaner, taller buildings proclaimed a vacancy, and the carriage pulled to a halt.

Quin alighted. "How much?"

"Twenty-five *denarii.*"

He handed over the silver coins. After pulling his bag from the raeda, he rapped on the door.

A young girl answered.

"I'm looking for a room for the night."

Without a word, she disappeared.

An older man, short, bow-legged, but with bright eyes, came to the door. "Enter, please. We are honored with your presence." He bowed. "My daughter will show you to your room, where you may rest before our evening meal." He gestured to the quiet girl who had escaped earlier.

"That will be most appreciated."

"Servants will be up momentarily with hot water and towels."

She led him to an upstairs room that overlooked the forum. A large bed with a wool-stuffed mattress and a table with an oil lamp were its only furnishings, but it was clean and filled with sunlight. And Quin was tired and hungry.

The owner and his daughter were kind enough, but tomorrow he would have his own land, presumably with his own house.

Only one thought bothered him: the fact that he had left his deed in the hands of a boy who pretended to be a duovir.

But others had seen him with the scroll. What harm could the young, inexperienced magistrate of such a small colony do to him?

7

> *"Anyone who withholds kindness from a friend*
> *forsakes the fear of the Almighty."*
>
> — JOB 6:14

In the dark of night, Gallus formed a plan. One that would bring him the coin he so desperately needed and get that troublesome tribune out of his way at the same time. It was bold, risky even, but he didn't get to be magistrate at this age by being overly cautious. And if his plan failed . . . nothing much would be lost.

The position of duovir afforded him great honor, considerable power. But he wanted more. And next year was his best opportunity to grab nearly unlimited control of Philippi.

Every five years the duoviri managed the census, which allowed them to choose which new citizens would be enrolled, who remained in the senate—and who left. Only one hundred men could be members of the *ordo*, so if some had to go to allow new blood . . . well, that was a price some would have to pay so the right men—the men Gallus had in mind—would be in place.

But in the meantime his position was costing him more of his personal fortune than he had planned. Decimus had tried to warn him, but that old man blathered on and on about so many things that Gallus didn't listen most of the time. His first day in office he was required to contribute 10,0000 sesterces to the treasury. Then there were the compulsory public festivals, sponsored by him, of course . . . the list was endless. His private funds needed replenishing.

He stopped by the records office on the way to the basilica. "Helios."

Standing before a shelf piled full of rolled parchments, his scribe turned to face him, thinning gray hair sticking out in all directions. "Yes, Domine?"

"The tribune from yesterday. Where is his scroll from Vespasian? My slave delivered it earlier?"

"On this shelf."

"Bring it to me."

The lanky clerk drew his fingers along a row of parchments, stopping at one. He slid it from its space and offered it to Gallus.

Pursing his lips, he inspected the grant, reading it once, twice. "Where is the land? Show me."

Helios led him to a large map inscribed on leather attached to the wall. "May I see the grant again?"

Gallus held up the unrolled parchment, pointing to the section delineating the land.

Helios moved his long, thin fingers over the map. "That would be here." He pointed to a plot of land outside the city's walls.

"A very nice size. An excellent location. And why was it available?"

"I'd have to look." He returned to his wall and immediately retrieved the proper document. How the man could possibly know which was which from all those rolled up lengths of parchment was beyond Gallus. They all looked identical from where he stood.

Helios unrolled the scroll, his eyes scanning quickly, his lips moving silently. "This portion—a double portion—was originally assigned to Centurion Massala. His son inherited it, and his grandson recently died without an heir. It was then returned to the Empire."

"Have you taken Quintus to his land?"

"No, I had closed for the night."

Gallus paced a few moments, tapping his chin with the rolled scroll. "Here are your instructions. When he returns today, you will tell him you have no memory or record of ever receiving this document. If he has any questions, you will send him to me. Is this clear?"

Helios blinked several times. "But—"

Gallus raised his chin and stepped closer to the clerk. "In my opinion, which is, of course, the only opinion that matters in this room, this is an illegal grant. Legate Vespasian has no right to transfer land in Philippi without my consent, and I do not give my consent. So the transfer will not take place."

"But it carries the emperor's signature . . ."

Gallus leaned nearer. "Are you going to continue to question everything I say?"

"N-no, but I took an oath . . ."

"You also swore to obey me."

"Yes, Domine." The scriba fidgeted with his cloth belt.

"So, if you want to keep your highly paid and esteemed position and serve as my scriba next year when I am magistrate during the census—and there will be many, *many* documents that will need to be formalized for the new members of the *ordo*—then you will do as I say." He smiled and shrugged. "Or you can be sent to one of the lesser provinces."

Helios studied his sandals. "Yes, Domine."

"And you will not speak about any of this to anyone."

Helios nodded.

"Is there anything unclear about that?"

Shoulders slouched, he raised his head. "No, Domine."

"Good then." Gallus strode out, the scroll in his fist.

In his own more spacious office, he dropped onto a lectus and unrolled the parchment again. This land was immensely valuable. He'd need to be very careful if he wanted to turn it from farmland to coin without raising suspicion. Later today when Quintus came back to register his grant, he would be told there was no such grant. Never had been. He would, of course, tell everyone.

Let him talk. Who would people believe? Their popular duovir, or a recently arrived, dismissed soldier?

Gallus would need to wait to put enough space between Quintus's arrival and the sale, so the two couldn't be connected. He would need to find someone to act in his name, and preferably sell the land to a buyer from outside Philippi in order to gain the highest price. There were always businessmen who were less than particular about the minutia of the laws when it came to profit and who would gladly help him complete the transaction.

Only he and Helios knew which parcel belonged to the newcomer. As long as the scriba kept his mouth closed, there shouldn't be any problems. And with so many opportunities for authorizing private transactions coming to the clerk every week, at a hefty fee he was allowed to keep to himself, he had every motivation to keep his position.

No, Helios should not be a problem at all.

And if he insisted on letting his conscience get the better of him, Gallus could take care of him the same way he'd taken care of other obstacles in the past. He'd really hoped he was past such extreme measures, but nothing would stop him from following his plan, and gaining all the power he deserved.

THE SUN BEAT warm on Quin's shoulders as he took the steps down to the stoa that ran along Commercial Road. Shrill voices competed with neighing horses and rumbling oxcarts. Smells of meat and fruit and perfume collided in a somehow not unpleasant mixture, perhaps due to the strict separation and placement of various categories of goods.

Perhaps the young magistrate had some good ideas.

The merchants of household items occupied the stalls toward the west. Anything you could possibly want for your home, or your body, could be found here—pottery and cookware, gold and silver jewelry, rugs and blankets. If it wasn't there yet, from the basic and mundane to the unnecessary and opulent, someone could get it, and then sell it at a greatly inflated price.

Food was sold in the shops to the east. Fruit, vegetables, wine, and prepared foods were all available. From ground wheat to fresh bread, grapes to wine, newly slaughtered animal to roasted meat, it was all available.

Quin ambled past the shops. As in any market, the best items could be seen early in the morning. The best prices could be had late at night, but selection was worse.

"What can I get for you, Tribune?" An old man, chubby and balding, dipped his head in an exaggerated bow, his hands clasped together in front of his chest.

"Where do your rugs come from?"

"All the way from Persia. They are the finest in all the Empire."

"May I see them?"

"Of course."

Quin stepped around the man to finger the rugs piled high on a rickety table. These rugs couldn't possibly have come from Persia. Anatolia, maybe.

"How many can I sell you today?" The man bowed again.

"None today, thank you."

"Not even one? You must have at least one. At a Roman's price, of course."

"I don't even have a house yet to put it in. Perhaps another day." Perhaps never.

"I shall await your return." The man bowed again.

Quin moved on, chatting with the merchants and trying to ascertain the quality of the goods. By the time he reached the end, he noticed activity around the records office. After climbing the stairs to the forum level, he strode to the scriba's office and peeked in.

Leonidas stood near a table talking to a wiry man about his same height.

Quin rapped on the doorframe.

The man turned, and Leonidas smiled and moved to the door. "Tribune Valerius, you found us. It's good to see you. May I introduce you to Helios?"

Helios smiled weakly, shuttling rolled parchment. "Of course. I just need to adjust some records—"

A burly, hairy man barged in the door, shoving Quin as he passed. His fox skin hat and patterned load marked him as a Thracian. He pressed himself to Helios's table and leaned over it, resting on his fists.

"I just went to my stall, the one I gave good coin, lots of coin for, but someone else is there. Explain that to me!"

Helios stood straight, backed up a step. "I assure you, no one is in your stall. I would not allow it."

"Would you like to come see?" He lunged forward.

Quin stepped closer, his hand resting atop the pugio hanging from his belt.

The Thracian threw him a side-glance and moved back.

Helios unrolled a parchment with a meticulously drawn layout of Commercial Road complete with individual stalls. "Show me where you think your stall is."

He shoved a fat dirty finger at a spot on the map.

"And there is the problem. You are here."

"I am not!" He roared at the scriba.

"You most certainly are. All food vendors are here. Together, and downwind of everyone else."

"But I paid dearly for this spot." He pointed at the other spot again.

Helios pulled out another parchment. "This is your contract. Here is the spot number, and here is the price you paid. Agreed?"

He nodded warily.

"This spot"—Helios pointed at the one the man wanted—"costs triple that."

The larger man slammed his open hand on the table and growled. Quin grasped his blade, but the Thracian left without moving toward Helios again.

"That happen a lot?" Quin pointed to the door where the man had just exited.

"Once a week or so." He pointed at the stack of contracts. "I keep excellent records."

He grinned. "I'm sure you do."

"Now, how can I help you?" Helios quietly placed the contract into its proper place and rolled up the map, stowing it on a rack along the back wall.

"I arrived yesterday with a grant from Vespasian. The duovir took the grant from me and said you could show me to my land this morning."

"I have received no such grant." The scribe busied himself with arranging the scrolls on the shelf.

"But I left it with Leonidas." He looked to the Greek beside him.

"He did, and I brought it here." He shrugged.

Quin closed his eyes. His chest ached. What had happened?

"That scroll has to be here. Look again." He controlled his breathing, a skill learned from years in battle.

"I know every scroll on every shelf in this room. It. Is. Not. Here. If you have any questions, I suggest you visit the duovir." Helios walked to the door and opened it, refusing to meet Quin's eyes. "Now, please leave. I have a great deal to do."

Quin exited, as stunned as the day he had awakened bloodied on the ground in Britannia.

Leonidas came beside him. "Something's not right here."

"My land has been stolen from me. That's what's not right."

"Do you wish to see the magistrate?" Leonidas tilted his head in the direction of the basilica.

It probably wouldn't get him his land, but he might be able to gather something from what he said. Or didn't say. "Please."

They moved next door to the magistrate's office and rapped on the door. A servant let them in.

Gallus reclined on a lectus, a servant waiting nearby with a platter of sliced fruit and fresh bread. "Tribune, what brings you here?"

"You know exactly why I am here. You and I and Leonidas all know I had a grant from Vespasian yesterday that has somehow disappeared. Why?"

"This is my city. Not Vespasian's. And I want you, and Rome, and Vespasian to know it." Gallus popped a grape in his mouth.

His blood heated, but he would not show his anger. "Then you did steal my land?"

"It's not your land. Never was. Never will be. Now get out."

Rage coursed through him like one of Britannia's wild rivers. This . . . child . . . had just admitted to fraud, theft, who knew how many other crimes—and he would get away with it. Because he was the law here. The final authority.

It took all his training to keep from unsheathing his pugio and driving it deep into this man's chest. Or better, wrapping his bare hands around Gallus's scrawny neck until that smug smile disappeared with his last breath.

On the vast portico outside the office, Quin shook his head. *How could this happen?*

Fortuna mocked him, smiling down on him. He would find no luck in Philippi.

Now what? He couldn't go back to Rome. He couldn't stay here.

He had no coin, no land, and no options.

8

> *"He who diligently seeks good seeks favor, but he who seeks evil, evil will come to him."*
>
> — PROVERBS 11:27, NASB

QUINTUS LAY ON HIS SLEEPING COUCH IN HIS RENTED ROOM, STARING at the ceiling. It had been two days since Gallus had told him his land was gone.

It was the deceit that bothered him most. In the army, disorder and disobedience were deadly and dealt with at once.

But deceit . . . first Flavius, now Gallus. When you can't prove you've been wronged, what do you do?

He rose and pulled his pack from under the couch. He rummaged through it, tossing his belongings aside. He found the small leather pouch hidden at the bottom, untied it, and poured the bronze disks into his hand. Counted them out. Enough for maybe ten more days' food and nights at the inn.

He didn't have nearly enough to get back to Rome. Not that it would do him any good. His father wouldn't let him in the gate, let alone the door.

Could he hire himself out in Philippi as a laborer? He had no experience as anything other than a soldier. But he could learn. He was still strong, resourceful. He could hunt, if necessary. He'd slept in the open more than in a tent.

A tap sounded on the door.

Quickly stuffing the coins back into the purse, he shoved it into his satchel and then kicked it under the couch. He strode to the door. When he opened it, an older man with gentle eyes and a crop of gray hair stood waiting on the other side.

"Quintus Valerius?"

Quin remained silent.

"I'm Decimus Magius, the duovir. May I come in?"

Quin scoffed and started to slam it, but Decimus jammed his foot against the frame. He was remarkably robust and quick for his age.

One hand still against the door, Quin leaned his forearm against the wall. "What do you want?"

"Don't hold Gallus's actions against me. I wish only to talk."

He had a point. The man likely had no control over Gallus. "Come in." Quin widened the door and moved to the small table in his room. He poured two goblets of wine. "Anything specific you wanted to discuss?"

Decimus closed the door behind him. "I thought we could get better acquainted. You are a tribune, are you not?"

"I am." He offered the man one of the glass goblets.

"Legion?"

"Second Augusta."

"One of Caesar's best. Explains the grant from Vespasian."

"I served for six years."

"Then you just came from Britannia?"

Quin clenched his jaw. "I left earlier this year."

"Why come here? Shouldn't you have been assigned as a prefect somewhere?"

"Long story." Why was this man questioning him? Did Gallus send him? Decimus said he was the other duovir, but he wore only a simple toga, not the extravagant purple-bordered *toga praetexta* he was entitled to. He could be anyone. Military strategy had taught Quin it would be better to withhold any information Gallus didn't already possess. "I know you didn't come here just to get better acquainted. What do you want?"

Decimus glanced around the room and pulled a stool away from the corner. "I'm sorry for what Gallus did to you. If I could change it, I would. But he has almost unfettered power here, due to his position and his family name. We're supposed to work together, but it doesn't always turn out that way." He lowered himself onto the stool, adjusting the folds of his toga.

"I appreciate your concern, but it's really not necessary." He had no time for sympathy. It would not change his circumstances in the least.

"I may be able to help you."

"You can get my land back?" Hope flickered in Quin's chest . . .

"Not exactly."

And was just as quickly snuffed out. "Then what?"

"I want you to be in charge of our prison."

Quin laughed. "Impossible." He drained his goblet and set it down. "Besides, why?"

The magistrate winced. "We've had some . . . incidents. We need someone experienced, someone with leadership skills. Someone like you."

"Incidents?"

"Escapes. Brawls. Injuries to guards." He traced the rim of his cup with his thumb.

He nodded and thought a moment. "Who's in charge now?"

"A slave. It's not the most sought-after position, as you can imagine."

Quin pondered the idea. "Does it pay? I have nothing now. I chose land over money, which, in retrospect, appears to have been a bad decision. I can't afford to rent or buy anything. Even food."

Decimus set the cup on the floor and stood. "You'll be provided everything. Food, clothes, a place to live."

"What's the staff like? How many guards do you have?" He crossed his arms over his chest.

Decimus brightened, his hands moving quickly. "You'll have as many people under you as you feel necessary. We have the resources. We are a small city, but we are not poor. We simply do not have the right people. And if you can train someone well enough to take over for you, you would have more than enough saved by then to do almost anything you desire."

"Let me think about it."

"At least if you do this, you'll have a place to live and food to eat. I'll protect you from Gallus."

"He will not approve?"

"Probably not. But once I've appointed you, he cannot undo it."

"I thought you could veto one another."

"In theory. But he has the connections in Rome." He retrieved the goblet and replaced it on the table.

"I'll find you in a few days, then."

At the door, Decimus turned back. "And Quintus?"

"Yes?"

"Until then, I would not discuss this with anyone." He slipped out of the room.

Quin dropped back onto his lectus.

Prison guard. What would his pater say now?

THE MESSAGES HAD BEEN VEILED all day, and Tia was exhausted from searching for them. It was as if Brigid was hiding from her the same way the sun ducked behind the clouds. Maybe if they got out of this dingy room and outside, where she could see the sun, feel it on her face, perhaps the visions would be clearer then.

Although maybe the goddess was just tired of Elantia coming to her all day, every day, and wouldn't hear her any more, ever again.

It was worth a try . . . but she mustn't admit weakness.

She gathered all her courage. "Domina?"

Cassia frowned. "Yes."

"Do you think we might be able to go up to the forum? There might be some who rarely come down here, who only send servants to shop for them. We might find new customers."

Cassia pursed her lips. "Max is already there, talking about you."

"Perhaps if they see me . . ."

Cassia tilted her head, thought a moment. "All right. For the afternoon."

She locked the room and they ascended the stairs. Tia's golden hair brought people to her like flies to honey.

A young man in a dirty woolen tunic fought his way to be first in line. How did he come up with the money to pay her?

No matter. Not her concern. She reached for his hand. Smiled. "Can you tell me your name?"

"Philon."

"And what is your question today?"

He glanced over his shoulder, as if he were being chased. "I . . . Someone . . . I need to know if I should stand up for myself."

"Can you be any more specific?"

He shook his head, looked over his shoulder again.

"All right. Let's see what she can tell us." With so little information, and the messages blurry already, how could she know she was even asking the right question, let alone getting the right answer? A word finally came into focus.

"I believe the answer is yes, but it's hard to tell with so little to go on."

One corner of his mouth flicked up for a moment, then he bolted from the line.

Was that the answer he wanted or not? Who could know?

As the day dragged on, Tia searched the market for Xenia. The noisome celebrations throughout the night—along with the numerous empty wine bottles strewn throughout the domus and the bleary eyes of her *domini* this morning—had told her the grape harvest had ended yesterday. Had her prophesy held true? If not, Tia would be in serious danger. Perhaps life-threatening danger.

Then it wouldn't matter if Brigid answered or not. If the domini were angry at her just for saying negative things, what would they do if her visions were thought to be untrue? Surely they would beat her. Sell her.

Or even kill her.

Shivers crawled down her spine.

"Are you feeling all right, dear?" The old woman's voice startled Tia. She was hunched over, her spine so contorted the middle of her back was at the same level as her shoulders. Her hands rested on a walking stick. Yet her face revealed no pain. Instead, she seemed to be far more concerned about Tia.

"I'm sorry?"

The old woman frowned, tilting her head. "You seem a bit pale. And you're shivering. Are you ill?"

"*Avia*, you can't ask things like that." The younger Roumanos who had brought her adjusted her cloak.

"Hush, Aurelia. At my age you can." She shooed away the girl's hand. "Stop fussing. Besides, I'm truly worried about her. She doesn't look good."

"*Avia?* This is your grandmother?"

"Yes. Please forgive her. She's gotten a bit blunt in her later years."

"Oh, it's quite all right. She reminds me of my grandmother." Tia smiled at the memory. "I'm fine, really. The breeze . . . made me shudder, that's all."

"If you're sure." It was obvious the woman didn't believe her, but she didn't press further.

"I am. Now let's see if we can find out what the gods have prepared for you, shall we?" Keeping an ear open, she cradled the wrinkled hand and closed her eyes, praying for a clear message.

Brigid, show me what you have for this dear woman, whom I know not, but who has shown me care nonetheless.

The images faded in and out, more than usual. Squeezing the grandmother's hand, she waited until they stabilized.

"*Avia*, you have ten grandchildren?"

She gasped. "Why, yes."

"You will live to see four more."

She cackled as she tapped the stick on the ground. "How delightful!"

"I'm glad that makes you happy." She glanced at Aurelia, the girl's smile strained.

Still laughing, the older woman turned to leave, her feet shuffling, leaning heavily on her stick.

Aurelia leaned near Tia as she assisted her *avia*.

"Will any of them be mine?" she whispered.

Clasping her hands, Tia breathed a prayer and waited. The goddess did not give her the answer she wanted. What could she say?

"I see you with a baby in your arms." She smiled as brightly as she could.

Tears came from Aurelia's eyes as she threw her arms around Tia. "Thank you. Thank you so much."

Tia's stomach soured. She had deliberately misled this young woman.

Aurelia hurried to catch up with her avia.

Tia shook her head and caught a glimpse of Xenia hurrying toward them. Her heart rate sped up. Was she excited or angry? From this distance, it was still hard to tell.

"Domina." Tia tilted her head toward the girl.

Cassia stepped next to her. She tapped her sandaled foot on the stone floor of the forum, waiting for Xenia to arrive. "I think she's smiling."

If Cassia was trying to sound confident, she wasn't succeeding.

"Because she's in love or because she wants her money back?"

"She didn't pay us yet, remember?" Cassia grinned.

Xenia came nearer, and nearly slammed into Tia, embracing her tightly.

She stumbled back to keep from being knocked over. Tears wet her neck. "Good news, I gather?"

Xenia released her. "He agreed to my father's terms. They finally agreed on a dowry, so now we can get married!"

"So she was telling the truth?" Cassia sounded shocked.

"Yes. It seems she was." Xenia beamed. "And I am so sorry I doubted you. I hope I did not cause trouble for you."

"No, no, of course not. You did nothing wrong. You just go and enjoy your new life now."

"*After* you pay me." Cassia held out her hand, palm flat, as Xenia filled it with coin. "Double, remember? And you'll tell everyone?"

"I already have!" After one more hug, the girl flounced away.

"Looks like you're safe on this one."

"Yes. She'll have a happy life with him."

"What about the other one?"

"The other one?"

"With the old woman." She pointed toward Aurelia and her grandmother, slowly making their way across the forum.

"Aurelia?"

"You lied to her, didn't you?" Cassia narrowed her eyes. "Do I need to be worried?"

"I didn't lie. I told you I would always tell you exactly what I have seen."

Cassia tilted her head. "You weren't telling the truth. I can tell."

"I said I saw her with a baby in her arms. I did." She bit her lip. "It just wasn't hers."

"Good, then. Everyone's happy." She pulled the string on the money sack tight.

Happy? How could she say that? She and Max had coin. That made them happy.

Aurelia might be happy for now, but only because Tia had intentionally deceived her. Many others, as well. That certainly did not make her happy.

As for anyone else, Elantia really couldn't say.

SLAMMING THE DOOR BEHIND HIM, Gallus stormed into Decimus's office. "You had no authority to do that!"

Decimus slowly rose. He nodded to his scribe, who scurried from the room. "I understand you're angry with me, but you will speak to me with civility. Now, would you like to start again?"

Gallus scowled. Decimus just loved to treat him like a child. The man may be old enough to be his father, but he most certainly wasn't, and had no right to talk to him as if he were.

Still, further alienating him would not help.

Not yet, at least.

"You had no right to offer Tribune Quintus Valerius the job of prison master."

Decimus leaned forward on his palms. "I had just as much right to do *that*, as you did to steal his land from him. And what *you* did was completely illegal." His voice was calm. "It goes against every law we have and every oath you swore. And you made the scriba break his oath as well." Decimus straightened and neared Gallus, face far too calm. "Care to tell me what this is about?"

There was no way Gallus was going to admit to the old man he needed the money in order to finish his term. Not when they had been in office less than four months. Decimus would only remind him of how many times he had tried to warn him.

Gallus crossed his arms and glared. "It's none of your business."

"You think just because your family is old and wealthy and has connections in Rome, you can get away with anything. But hear me, this will catch up with you."

Stepping closer, Gallus pointed a finger. "You have no idea what you're talking about."

Decimus placed his open hand on top of Gallus's finger and pushed it down. "You cannot use this city to fill your purse."

"I can do whatever I wish!" Gallus blew out a breath. Great. He'd lost all the control he'd struggled to regain before he first came in. "If you ever do something like this behind my back again, I will ensure you are never able to transact business in this town again. I already have Helios's cooperation. I may as well use it."

Decimus raised a brow. "You would do something so foolish, so vindictive?"

"I will not let you interfere. My family has been in power in one way or another for generations here, and we will continue to do so long after you are dead, buried, and forgotten." Gallus strode to the door. With his hand on the knob, he turned back. "You are an old man with no heirs, and your name will disappear into the clouds, but the family of Crispus will live forever."

Gallus left, slamming the door again. How dare the old man defy him like that. Decimus may be the senior magistrate, but it was in name only, and he very well knew it. Gallus couldn't let Decimus upset all the plans he had laid, negate all his hard work. He only needed a little more coin, and the tribune's land would provide it.

He'd have to wait a little while to alleviate suspicion, and then the Greek he'd heard of could sell it for him.

If he could find out his name, which was proving to be harder than keeping the gods happy.

Then next year, he'd have enough to again satisfy the wealth requirement, and he would be re-elected during census year. It didn't happen often that someone as young as he served as *duovir quinquennial*, but he had the determination and distinction to be the exception. He would fill the senate with men of his choosing, men who would do whatever he wanted. The laws he wanted would be put into place, the buildings he desired would be funded, the monuments he deserved would be erected . . .

He would be the most powerful man in Philippi for a long, long, time.

9

"One of those listening was a woman from the city of Thyatira named Lydia, a dealer in purple cloth. She was a worshiper of God. The Lord opened her heart to respond to Paul's message."

— ACTS 16:14

QUIN HAD REALIZED THAT THE RUG DEALER OFTEN HAD MORE TIME ON his hands than he knew what to do with. His goods were some of the most expensive on Commercial Road, and one sale could sustain him for weeks. He'd already proved to be a good source of information. Whether that information was reliable was another matter, but his company was not unpleasant.

"Is there a fabric dealer here?" Quin ripped a chunk from the loaf of bread the innkeeper had given him.

"Of course, an excellent one. The shop is not on this road, though. You'll need to go up to the *Via Egnatia*, go east, and turn south on *Via Appia*. You'll recognize it. It's the first domus on the right."

"Thank you."

"Still not ready for a fine rug?"

"Not yet." Quin grinned and left a coin on the table. Following the man's instructions, he came to the fabric dealer's shop just as he finished his bread. The window next to the main door was full of colorfully dyed bolts of fabric, including a rich purple. At least he wouldn't have to wait for it to be imported.

He slapped his hands together to dislodge the crumbs and knocked on the doorframe. A servant appeared instantly.

"I'm looking for the cloth dealer? I need to have a new tunic made."

"One moment."

An older woman with green eyes and beautiful skin the color of walnuts appeared. "I'm Lydia. May I help you?"

"I'm looking for the owner."

"This is my shop. I can help you."

A woman who ran the shop? If her appearance didn't indicate she wasn't Roman, this fact did. He somehow managed to cover his shock. He hoped. "I need to have a new tunic made. Maybe more than one."

"Please come in." She stepped aside, and he entered a spacious atrium. "Will you remove your cloak, please . . . I'm sorry, I don't know your name."

"Quintus Valerius. Certainly." The slave accepted the garment, and gently laid it on a lectus.

Lydia fingered the top edges of his tunic. "Do you prefer linen or silk?"

His checks heated. "Wool."

"Wool?" She looked up at him through dark lashes, eyes wide.

"Linen is too fine for my new job. But I will take one linen one for other times. And two wool tunics."

"Bleached, at least?"

"If that makes you feel better." He grinned.

"It does." She smiled. "Demas can measure you, if you'll go with him." She waved an arm toward the servant who had greeted him earlier.

After his measurements were taken, he returned to the shop, but saw only Demas.

"Is Lydia still around?"

"She's in the peristyle. Come, I will take you." He retrieved the cloak and led Quin down the hall.

Quin let out a low whistle when he entered the indoor garden.

Lydia spun around. "Is something wrong, Tribune?"

"No, of course not. This is just the most beautiful place I've been in since I came to Philippi. I didn't see gardens like this in Rome."

"Thank you, very much. We've worked quite hard on it."

"These flowers are stunning. So many different kinds, different colors." He pressed his nose into a blossom and inhaled. "Smells good."

"That's a rose."

"I saw some in Rome, I think, but they looked a little different."

"Oh, there are many varieties. All these are roses." She fingered the petals of a blossom before she sat. "I love roses. Please sit."

"Impressive." He sat across from her on another couch. "How did you know I was a tribune? I'm not in uniform."

"You're patrician, judging by the stripe on your toga, and military, judging by your bearing. Simple deduction."

He chuckled. "You should be military yourself."

She slid a tray of fruit toward him. "What brings you to Macedonia? There are no campaigns here that I know of."

"No, I've retired. But there have been . . . complications, and now it looks like I will be the keeper of the prisons."

"Would you like some wine?"

Her lack of reaction stunned him. "No, I need to go back to the market. The city will give me a house, but I don't have a couch, or a blanket, or . . . many things."

"Let me go with you, then. Demas and Syntyche will join us." She rose and headed for the front of the house.

Apparently, he had no choice in the matter. Not that he minded. She was delightful and reminded him of his mater.

Lydia wrapped her arm around his bicep as they strolled back toward the market.

"Now, where do you get your meat?"

"I haven't, yet. I've been staying at the inn until this morning."

"Then I'll tell you. You get your meat from Akakios, your fruit from Maris, and your bread from Artemesia." She pointed to the vendors as she mentioned them.

"Artemesia. Another woman?"

Her laugh came easy and often. "Naturally! I always support other women when I can."

"How did you end up selling cloth?" Following her slaves, they turned south and then onto Commercial Road.

"My husband had the business, in Anatolia. His parents learned to dye in purple, and taught him. We married and moved here, bringing with us the only legitimate imported Tyrian purple cloth to the entire region. But he died shortly after we arrived. I had to fill some of his outstanding orders, and people kept coming back. I guess since I was a foreigner they didn't mind that I was a woman, and of course we had excellent product."

"A Roman woman would never be allowed to do that."

"Nor a Greek." She picked up some apples and gestured to the merchant, holding up four fingers.

"Do you have any children?"

She looked away. "We were not married very long, and I never remarried."

"I'm sorry. I didn't mean to make you sad."

"It was a long time ago. Besides, there have always been plenty of children in the house." She shrugged. "It's enough."

"What's going on over there?" He pointed to the middle of the stoa, where a crowd waited by one of the stalls.

"I'm not sure." Releasing his arm, she stepped closer. "Ahh . . . That's the new slave girl of Maximus and Cassia."

"But why so many people?"

She leaned in. "She's a seer."

He chuckled. "Really?"

He drew up next to the slave girl, and his stomach dropped.

The girl from the ship. He might have recognized her dominus's name, but *Maximus* was common.

"I heard they bought her recently at the slave market in Ostia, part of a large group taken a few months ago in Britannia."

His stomach knotted. "Where in Britannia?"

"I don't know. Why would that matter?"

"Just curious." Even here, his past followed him.

Lydia's gaze held his. "This bothers you greatly, I believe."

"Not really." He shrugged.

"You're a terrible liar. I think you've not had much practice at deception." She laughed.

"It's not really encouraged in the army, unless you're deceiving the enemy."

"It's refreshing." She laid a hand on his chest. "You must join us for *cena* tonight. I have some guests you would enjoy meeting."

He shook his head. "I really shouldn't."

"You must. You just said you have nothing in your home."

"Not tonight."

"Soon then, yes?"

"Who is your guest?"

"Just a visitor to Philippi." Her green eyes, so much like his mater's in every way except color, sparkled. She was up to something. "Someone I think you would enjoy talking to. He's quite fascinating. He has some interesting companions too. Are you sure you can't make it?"

He might as well relent. She'd just keep asking. "All right. May I bring some wine?"

"Wine you get from Marcus, no one else. And tell him you are my friend. Otherwise you'll pay twice as much because you're new in town. He has fantastic wine but he'll take advantage of anyone he can."

He wasn't really in the mood for a leisurely dinner. He had plenty to do before he reported to the prison tomorrow. But Lydia seemed to know everyone and everything about Philippi. If he intended to stay—and he appeared to have no choice for the near future—she could be a valuable resource, even an ally. And he would need all the help he could find.

Gallus reviewed the name and the directions on the tablet before him. *Patroclus.* The name had been given to him by his cousin's husband. Gallus was never quite sure what Cassia saw in him, but at least in this, Maximus had proven to be useful.

Patroclus was said to be the man to see when interested in buying or selling land. Gallus had heard of such a man but had not had the name until now. It was said he always managed to obtain a price higher than the open market allowed, but that the price came at a substantial commission. Discretion was also one of his most sought-after services.

Those who had used him were careful before recommending him to anyone else, lest they lose their own access by sending someone he disapproved of. His business was not exactly legitimate since city taxes would eat into his profit.

Gallus rubbed out the information from the wax and left his office.

Patroclus's exact location was known only to his customers. It was situated well off the forum in one of the residential blocks. As Gallus neared the area, he studied the buildings before him. He checked his memory, then the buildings again. All *insulae.* Apartments for the poorest of Philippi. This couldn't be right.

But it was the only information he had. He banged on the main door with his seal ring, three short raps.

A lanky, young Ethiopian opened the door a hand's width.

"I was sent by Marcellus Tulius."

The door slammed in Gallus's face. Not a gesture a duovir was accustomed to. He swallowed his pride and waited. If he wanted the discretion and the profit, he had no other options.

At length, the door swung open again. The dark-skinned slave stepped back and allowed Gallus to enter, then led him up several flights of stairs into the atrium of the entire uppermost floor.

Though only one floor, it was exquisitely furnished. Gallus's own domus held no finer things. Sculptures lined the walls. The hallway led to a small peristyle full of trees, shrubs, and flowers.

The slave gestured to a couch near the *impluvium* and then disappeared. The sunken area in the floor at this time of year held very little water, but that would soon change when the rains picked up. The open space above allowed fresh air and sunlight to flood the atrium, as well as allowing the domus to store water.

Voices whispered in the hallway, the slave and his master peered out several times, and finally the furtive Greek entered the room.

"How may I help you today?" His voice was sickeningly sweet.

"I wish to sell some property."

"Ah. Perhaps we should discuss this in my office." He ambled down the hall, and ducked into a side room. "Where is the property in question?" He pointed to a wall covered with maps.

It took Gallus a moment to locate the right map, but he eventually indicated the land he wanted sold.

"You have documents for the land?"

Gallus raised his fist, the scroll in it.

He seemed surprised. "That will make things much easier."

No wonder he could charge so much.

Patroclus studied the map for several moments before turning around. "My fee will be 20,000 sesterces." His posture made it clear there would be no negotiation.

Gallus nearly choked. "Twenty—are you serious? What could possibly make you think you are worth that?" The man came highly recommended, but this?

He clasped his chubby hands behind his back. "I can get you two hundred thousand."

"T-two hundred thousand? That's quite a bit more than I expected." Probably triple what he thought. Thoughts of what he could do with that much coin raced through his mind.

A sly grin crept across his face. "Hence my fee."

"Who would pay that much more?"

"I know these things. That is why you pay me."

"And you will keep my name out of it?"

"If that is your wish."

"It is. Now, is there a contract, or how do we proceed?"

"I keep nothing on parchment or even on wax. For your safety as well as mine."

"Then what protection do I have?"

"Do you trust the man who sent you here?"

He didn't, really. But what honest man would have sent him here? "I suppose."

"I see. Well then, do you think I would remain in business long if I cheated my clients? I may charge an exorbitant fee, but my customers know precisely what that fee is and exactly what my services include before our business even begins. There are no surprises, no secrets. And you owe me nothing until the transaction is final. You bring the grant, I bring the money. Minus my share, of course."

"Of course."

"Such a large parcel may take me a few weeks. I will contact you when I have a buyer."

"How?"

"You'll know." He turned to leave. "My slave will see you out." His voice floated in from the hallway.

The silent African appeared and ushered him out.

Such a strange visit. Should he feel relieved, worried, excited? Would Patroclus truly find someone willing to pay that much for a farm outside Philippi? And would he keep Gallus's name out of the sale?

All he could do was wait and see. If there was nothing in writing, he could always deny any knowledge. So far. It seemed that at this point he had nothing to lose. And 180,000 sesterces to gain.

An amphora of wine in one hand, Quin knocked on the gate of Lydia's domus. It wasn't the most expensive wine, but it was all he could afford. He'd purchased where Lydia had instructed him to, so he hoped it would be acceptable.

The same young slave who had met him before opened the door. "Tribune, welcome."

A little familiar for a slave, but maybe Lydia treated her slaves with a looser hand than had his pater.

The slave gestured toward the back of the domus. "They are in the peristyle. May I take the wine for you?"

"Thank you." Quin removed his cloak and handed it over before stepping inside. He was only half way back when Lydia met him.

"Quintus, I'm so glad you decided to join us. Come." She slipped her arm through his and led him to the garden. "I want you to meet some new friends of mine. This is Paulos and Silas. Our young friend is Timotheos. He's from Lystra, and he just joined Paulos." She left Quin to stand next to a taller man, close to her own age. "And this is one of my dearest friends, Loukas. He lives here in Philippi. I've known him for many years."

The slave from the door—what did she call him the other day? Demas?—appeared from the dining area. "Lydia, cena is waiting."

"Excellent. Shall we go?" Lydia stepped back to let the others precede her into the triclinium.

Quin waited until they were the only ones left in the garden. "Lydia?"

"Yes?"

"You let your slaves call you Lydia?"

She laughed, a soft, beautiful sound. "Oh, my dear. Quintus, they're not slaves. I've bought each of them and then freed them. I do it whenever I can. Some stay here to work for me, some leave to try to find their families." She led him into the dining area and stopped by the couch to the right.

"Come sit here, by Timos and Demas."

He sat on the couch, then leaned on his elbow.

He glanced at Paulos, Silas, and Loukas across from him, then at Lydia in the center. Beside her were Syntyche and another slave —no, not a slave any longer. Someone who worked for her.

"You remember Syntyche? And this is Zenobia." Before reclining, Lydia handed him a loaf of bread, soft and warm. It took a good deal of restraint to avoid gobbling it like a stray dog on the street.

After more bread and fresh fruit, he blew out a long breath.

Lydia pushed herself up on her arm. "Is something wrong?"

"It's just been a long time since I've eaten so well."

"But I thought you came from your father's estate."

"I did. But I ate mostly with Attalos, with my servant."

"You ate with your slave?" Syntyche giggled.

"Syn. That's none of our business." Lydia touched the young girl's arm.

Quintus shrugged. "It's a fair question. My father was not someone most people would want to share a meal with. And he wasn't particularly fond of me." He reached for a bunch of grapes. "I spent far more time with Attalos growing up than my father. He was my tutor, my friend . . ."

"You must miss him very much." Lydia's voice was soft.

"I do." He shoved several grapes in his mouth. "This is delicious, Lydia. Thank you. I've lived as a soldier so long I forgot what it felt like to have money. Which I actually don't have, anymore." He laughed. "So I shouldn't get used to this. Most of my meals will be more like what I ate this morning. Dry bread and cheese. Olives if I'm lucky."

An older man, Paulos had thinning brown hair, a full beard and a warm smile. "Quintus, Lydia said were a tribune. Your Latin tells me you are from Rome."

Quin allowed one corner of his mouth to turn up. The old man's worn woolen tunic made him appear a farmer, or a simple laborer, but his bearing and his speech indicated he was highly educated. And perceptive. "I was born and raised in Rome. I haven't lived there for many years."

"Ah. The life of a soldier. Never long in one place."

"Until now."

"You plan to stay in Philippi?"

"For now, I have no choice."

"You don't sound happy about that."

How did he explain without sounding like a child robbed of a toy? "I was injured and had to leave the army. I accepted land as my pension, but it has been . . . misappropriated."

Silas laughed, his whole body shaking. "That sounds like a polite word for a despicable action."

Quin grinned. "You could say that."

"It sounds like your life has suddenly gone in a direction you did not plan," said Paulos.

"I never expected to leave the army. I could never even have imagined this."

"You can take comfort in the knowledge that Yahweh was not caught off guard."

"Yahweh?"

Paulos smiled. "The one true God. The living God."

Quin avoided scoffing. "Oh, the Jewish god."

"He is not only the God of the Jews. And I think He may have brought you here for a very special reason."

"Why would he do that? And did he have to wound and rob me to do it?"

"You should not hold God responsible for the evils of man."

"If he is not willing or able to prevent man from such evil, perhaps he isn't all that powerful."

"Just because he is not responsible for the evil doesn't mean he can't redeem it."

Lydia should have warned Quin he would be dining with a man who talked in circles. Perhaps Paulos wasn't as smart as he first appeared.

10

> *"Many are the plans in a person's heart,*
> *but it is the* Lord*'s purpose that prevails."*
>
> — PROVERBS 19:21

WHETHER HE WANTED IT OR NOT, QUIN WAS NOW THE PRISON MASTER of Philippi. If Fortuna smiled on him, and so far she hadn't, he could save up some silver fast and get out of this sleepy outpost of a town.

He followed Decimus to the northwest corner of the forum. The terrain rose sharply northwest of the Via, and the structures, especially the prison, were built into the rocky soil.

They crossed the wide road and turned left. "The closest one is the jail, and the one next to it is your new domus. It's not large, but it is quite nice."

Decimus gestured to the jail as they passed. "There are six cells on the main floor, each of which can hold three or four if needed, though that would be an unusual case indeed, and below ground is the inner cell, which is used at night or for particularly troublesome or dangerous prisoners." The duovir halted and pulled a key from his belt, then unlocked the front door of the small house and pushed it open. "I had it cleaned in case you decided to join us here. The house comes with a cook and a house slave."

The door opened into a small atrium, complete with an impluvium. Couches were arranged on either side. A young man and woman, about the same age, waited silently.

"You can acquire your own if you prefer, but they served the previous jailers, and are well acquainted with Philippi and what you may need. Of course, either of them can also take care of your more personal needs."

The woman studied the tiled floor. The man stared over Quintus's head.

Quintus wasn't sure where to look.

"I apologize for the small size of the accommodations." Decimus moved around the pool. "This was, I believe, a bakery or some other such building. It was turned into a domus many years ago, but it's not exactly a traditional Roman house. You can use the rooms as you see fit. There are two on each side of the atrium for you to use as *cubicula*."

Decimus led Quin through the hall to the other end of the domus. He halted and turned to face him. "To your left is the *culina*, and a small dining area—not a real triclinium, of course—is here on your right. You have a garden along the back here." He stepped into the garden. "Whoever converted this into a house had this garden installed. Had the roof removed. Made the house seem even smaller, I think. The house was connected to the aqueduct for the bakery and so he also put in the fountain. Again, I do apologize, but at least you have somewhere to live until you find something more appropriate."

Quin shook his head as he circled the fountain. "This is more than enough for me. You forget I've been sleeping in a tent for most of the last six years."

"Still, it's not what you are entitled to, as a tribu—"

"It's more than enough." He approached the fountain as he

scanned the garden. Not a true peristyle, since it had no columns or portico, it was nonetheless open to the sky and abundant in flowering plants.

And it had a fountain. Not like the massive, ostentatious one his pater had in their villa in Rome. This one was quite simple. A basin about as wide as he was tall, a small column in the middle that ended in a spout that spewed water.

But that beautiful sound was the same.

Perhaps Fortuna had blessed him after all.

And after fourteen years in Rome's army, how could overseeing a jail in Macedonia be that hard?

This should be easy.

Humiliating, but easy.

THE ROUMANOS with the piercing gray eyes sat before her. Since meeting him on the ship, Tia had seen him in the forum several times. A few times she'd even caught him watching her, but he'd never come for a message. He wasn't as tall as Britanni men, and his face was as smooth as a baby's. She'd never understood why Roumani men scraped the hair from their faces each day with a blade. Grown men should have beards.

With a disarming smile, he laid his hand on the table.

She didn't need to hold his hand. Didn't need to touch him at all. But she'd set up the ruse, and now she was bound by it. She slipped her hand under his. It was warm and large, rough and strong. A gold seal ring, with a winged horse, adorned his smallest finger.

Brigid, show me. She avoided his steady gaze. "Can you tell me your name?"

"Quintus. What's yours?"

"I am called Tia. Do you have any particular question for the goddess today? Do you have travel plans? Family concerns? A decision you need help with?"

"I've made a decision, and I need to be sure I made the right one."

"Can you tell me the nature of your decision, or perhaps the choices that you had?"

"I could've said yes, or I could have declined." He grinned, accentuating the mark a blade had left on his cheek years ago.

"Very good." She studied the candle, listening, waiting for the messages. The flickering flame danced but revealed nothing.

He narrowed his eyes. "What are you doing?"

"Hush." She closed her eyes, searching her mind. "The goddess is speaking," she whispered.

"Really?" He chuckled.

She shoved his hand away. "Fine. You should go." Even if the goddess gave her an answer after such irreverence, she wouldn't pass it on. He didn't deserve it. Let him figure out the answer to his problem himself.

"I'm sorry." He reached for her hand with both of his and gently enclosed it. "I'm sorry, truly. May I have the answer?" His gaze held hers. "Please?"

She wanted to tell him no, but those eyes . . . they drew her in. He did seem truly repentant.

"One more chance. Belittle my gift—or my goddess—again—"

He shook his head vigorously. "No, I won't. Never. I apologize."

She removed his bottom hand and set it aside. "Now keep quiet."

Speak to me.

A word formed, as out of the morning mist that covered the hillsides back home.

"The right answer was yes."

He frowned briefly, blowing out a long breath. "All right."

"Was that not your plan?"

"It wasn't my preference, but I had no choice, really." He dragged his free hand though his short, dark hair. "I have another question."

"You paid for only one." She folded her hands in her lap, a hint he should go.

He didn't take it. "I'll pay for another."

She glanced behind him. No others waited. Cassia chatted with the owner of the silver shop next to theirs. Why not?

"What do you see in my future?"

She beckoned for his hand again. Closed her eyes. Crimson and black dominated a flurry of color and chaos, refusing to settle. She shuddered as the images settled into one disturbing vision. How could she say this? It was not a happy vision. Cassia and Max would punish her.

She jerked her hands free. "I see nothing. I'm sorry. You must go."

"What? What's wrong?"

"Nothing." She glanced at her owners. "Why would you ask that?"

"You frowned."

She shook her head. "No. You must go. Please." Cassia was still distracted, but how long would that last?

"Why won't you tell me?" His brow furrowed, his eyes begging her to continue.

"No. You need to go." Any moment now, Cassia would walk in.

"Are you afraid I'll be upset?" He glanced over his shoulder. "If I promise not to complain, will you tell me what you saw?"

Closing her eyes, she sighed and took his hand once more. "I see blood. Quite a bit, actually. And I feel pain, heart-rending agony." She opened her eyes.

His face paled.

He was getting angry. She should have known better.

She poured all her energy into understanding the goddess's message. "Wait—the blood is not yours. It's near you. All around you. You are immersed in trouble."

"Who? Whose blood is it?" The Roumanos's grip tightened.

Shaking her head, she opened her eyes. "I'm sorry. That's all I know. I didn't see any more. I don't often get details. Just impressions."

"Do they always come true?"

"In one way or another, yes. Maybe it's not as serious as it sounds. Once, I saw a great fall in a man's life. He was afraid he would die for months. Wouldn't go more than ten steps from his house. Then his son dropped a pottery bowl that belonged to his mother, who had recently died. Normally, he would have been furious, as it was very precious to him. But he was so relieved 'the fall' was a bowl and not him, he laughed." She smiled weakly.

Relaxing, he leaned nearer. "I have one more question."

"Don't you think you've had enough?"

One corner of his mouth turned up. "My future—will you be in it?"

She laughed dryly. "After a vision like that? I don't even have to ask the goddess that question. Not a chance."

GALLUS PACED in the peristyle of his villa. There had to be a way to undo this mess Decimus had gotten him into. Quintus Valerius as his keeper of the prison—this was never going to work. He was obviously a good little soldier—too perfect. He would follow every law perfectly, make it impossible for Gallus to use the prison as he needed to. How was he supposed to lock up his enemies if the jailer was going to require a believable charge, a sufficient number of witnesses, and knew they should only be under house arrest instead if they had sufficient means?

Gallus needed to eliminate the tribune. But how? The law allowed Decimus to appoint him, and Gallus could not undo it. He could make something up, some horrible thing Quintus was guilty of, but he'd eventually be found out. He could try to dredge up some mistake in his past, but after all his years of exemplary service, Gallus would not likely find one. After all, he came with a recommendation from Titus Flavius Vespasian himself. And

Vespasian had a great deal of influence since he'd returned from Britannia—to a *triumphalia*, no less. Vespasian was the darling of Rome at the moment, and he was not someone Gallus needed to make an enemy of.

No, the only way to get rid of the tribune was to catch him making a mistake now, here, in Philippi. To do that, Gallus would need help.

"Leonidas!" That slave was either nowhere to be found or hovering too close. "Leonidas! Come!"

His servant appeared. "Yes, Domine."

"How many days has Quintus been the prison master?"

"Five."

"Get me the names of everyone who works in the prison now that he is in charge. The scriba should have all the names."

"Yes, Domine."

Gallus returned to the peristyle and reclined on a couch. Nicanor brought him a platter of cold duck from the night before, along with fresh bread, and poured spiced wine.

His mind plotted as he swirled the wine in his golden goblet. He needed to find a few choice men who would be his allies, and he needed them on his side before Quintus could earn their loyalty. But what would be the best way to use them?

He had consumed the last bite of duck when Leonidas reappeared, wax tablet in hand.

He snapped his fingers and the slave placed the list on his lap. Wiping the grease from the duck on a cloth, he scanned the list. Recognizing a few of the names, he crossed off those he knew would be of no help to him and then placed a mark next to four of the remaining names.

"Bring me these men immediately."

Leonidas blinked. "Domine, I'm sorry. To your house?"

He glared.

Leonidas bowed. "Yes, Domine."

He waved the Greek away and drank the last of his wine as he paced. He should probably have had Leonidas flogged. Still, it wasn't a stupid question. Gallus had never conducted city business from home. But this was different. He couldn't be seen talking to these men in the basilica.

What should he say when they arrived? Should he bribe them? Simply order them? To do what exactly?

The questions came and went until Leonidas returned, four men trailing him. "The men you requested are in the atrium."

"Have them wait. I'm not ready for them yet."

After several more moments of fruitless wandering through his peristyle, he summoned them.

"Were any of you hired by Quintus Valerius, or were you there before he was appointed?"

An older man, balding and portly, scowled. "I was there. I was promised the position of keeper. I don't know why it was given to him instead."

"I assure you, that was not my decision." He studied the other three. "And the rest of you?"

"I'm new, and so is he." A young Greek, barely old enough to grow a beard but tall and strong, jerked his thumb at the man next to him.

"And where were you before?"

"We're from the mines."

Excellent. "And you?" Gallus pointed to the remaining guard.

"I've been there for over twenty years. I just want to finish my term and retire." The man sighed and hooked his thumbs in the sash of his tunic.

Gallus resisted the urge to laugh out loud. He couldn't have hand-picked a better group. "You—what's your name?"

"Alexios," the older man who wanted to be keeper answered.

"Go with Leonidas and wait in the peristyle while I finish with these three."

When Alexios disappeared, Gallus returned his attention to the others. "I have a job for you. If you do well, you"—he pointed to the oldest—"will be allowed to retire early. If you do not, I will add ten years to your time."

The old man's scowl deepened.

"And you two will be sent back to the mines. Do you understand? Quintus may be the keeper, but I am duovir. I do not wish for you to make his job easy for him in any way. Do I need to elaborate further?" He fixed his gaze on each in turn, waiting for assent. "You are dismissed."

The three exited and Leonidas ushered in Alexios.

"Bring more wine."

The slave bowed and disappeared.

"Alexios, I have a proposition for you."

"All right." The chubby man's eyes narrowed.

"I need you to watch Quintus and report to me on a regular basis."

"What do you want to know?"

"I want to know when he does something, anything, that is not lawful, or wise, or could be used against him in any way. And if it proves useful enough to remove him from his position, you will be appointed in his place."

Leonidas rapped once on the door, then entered with a tray. He set it on a nearby couch, poured two glasses, and silently left.

Alexios thought for a moment. "How do I know you will keep your promise?"

"I didn't promise, and you don't know."

He sucked in a deep breath, then shrugged. "All right."

"But the other three are watching as well, and if I hear from them what I should have heard from you, you will be sent to the mines in their place."

Alexios drained his cup. "I'll report back in three days."

"Two."

"Two, then." The older man lumbered to the door and left.

Now he only needed Quintus to do something unlawful, or at least ill-advised, and he needed Alexios to see it.

There was no doubt in his mind Alexios would report it. He wouldn't dare be stupid enough to keep it from Gallus and risk his own life in the process.

How long it would take for the supremely disciplined tribune to make a mistake was another matter entirely.

TIA WANDERED down the hall toward the peristyle.

Something was definitely different. What was it?

Smiling. The other slaves were *smiling*. Jaws weren't clenched, shoulders weren't tight, even the air seemed lighter.

Why?

The open-air room was uncharacteristically empty when she entered. The morning platter of food left by the lectus was filled with less than half the normal amount of food.

Cassia came in from the other room. "Ah. Ready to leave?"

"Where's the dominus?" She glanced around.

"He went to Amphipolis. He'll be back tonight. It's a short journey. Let's go, before the coin goes to someone else."

With Max gone, with one less set of eyes upon her, would there be a chance Tia could escape?

In the forum, a line formed quickly. She'd begun to recognize many of the questions. Some came every day, it seemed. But she waited patiently. The answers were always different. She made sure to hear the truth.

She didn't want to be struck again.

Cassia was far less watchful than Max.

And Tia knew the way out of Philippi well. From the shop, she needed to go to the end of Commercial Road, only a few steps north to the forum, then either east or west on the Via Egnatia. From here? She was already more than halfway there. Could she make it fast enough? But then where would she go? Neapolis was to the east. That was about the extent of her knowledge.

The young man who wanted to know if his wife had been unfaithful—she hadn't—left and an old woman approached.

North of town lay the mountains. Full of gold, they said. She could probably live there, for a while. Winter would come soon. But winter here was like autumn at home. She could do it.

The old woman wanted to know if it was safe to travel. It was.

Cassia neared. Why did she have to hover? Tia would never get away with her so close.

A young man asked if he should begin a new business with a friend. He should.

And so the questions, and answers, continued. When the sun reached its apex, they retired to their shop in the marketplace. Many of their regular customers came later in the day looking for bargains as the vendors lowered their prices.

As the day drew to a close, Max strolled up.

Cassia greeted him with a kiss. "Did you complete the transaction?"

"I did. Learned something else too." He grinned.

"What's that?"

"I'll tell you later." He rubbed his hands together and looked up and down the stoa. "Looks like nearly everyone has gone. We may as well close for the day."

"That's all right with me. I'm starving."

"It's warm for this time of year." Max unclasped his cloak.

Tia placed first one stool, then the other on top of the table. When she turned, she saw it.

There could be no mistaking it. It was one of a kind. It was handmade. There wasn't another like it in the world.

Max wore Tancorix's torque around his fat neck. The ends had been cut off to allow it to slip onto his oversized neck, then a clasp and chain had been added to close it.

Fury roared up within her, filling her and spilling out in an uncontrollable rush. She lunged at him. "Where did you get this?" The scream tore from her throat.

Cassia grabbed her around the waist, pulling her from Max.

Her face burned as Max slapped her. She would have fallen had Cassia still not had a death grip on her. Still she grabbed for him, though he stayed beyond reach.

"That belongs to my brother! It cannot come off unl-unless . . ."

"Max?" Cassia loosened her grip slightly.

"The man we sold the boy to said he was . . . problematic. He kept trying to run away."

"So they killed him?" Through blurry vision, she could see people crowded around their stall, gawking at the screeching, rebellious slave.

She didn't care.

"All you had to do was bring him here. He was running to me!"

"Why should I spend coin on a useless laborer?"

"You spent it on his gold fast enough." She charged at him again, only to be yanked back. Her breath forced from her chest, she coughed until she slumped to the tile floor. She laid her head on her arms. Her throat burned, her eyes stung.

Pain exploded in her stomach. Again. Again. She opened her eyes enough to see Max's sandaled foot kick her once more. She pulled her knees up to ward off the blow, but then his feet landed on her shins.

"Enough!" Cassia's voice cut through the agony. "If she can't walk tomorrow, she can't work."

Max knelt next to her, the fat of his torso spilling over his knees.

"Do you not understand what it means to be a slave? I know you had them in Britannia."

They did, but not like this. Only to work off debt.

"Your life will never be the same. You have no control over anything. Neither did your brother. You are never to speak to me like this again. You are not to question me about anything. You are not to speak unless spoken to. You go nowhere unless directed to. Are these instructions in any way unclear?"

She started to shake her head but the pain was too great. "No." Her voice was barely audible, even to herself.

"How are you to address me?"

"No, Domine."

"Excellent. Now get up." Disdain dripped from his voice.

The blood caught in the creases of her bratir's torque now achingly obvious, she shoved down the nausea.

He stood and turned from her.

She took a moment catch her breath. Slowly, agonizingly, she pushed herself to her hands and knees, pulled up one knee, then the other, and rose. Each movement sent excruciating pain to every muscle of her body.

"Now clean up the mess you made, so we can go."

What mess? She looked behind her. She must have kicked the stools and table in her rage.

Her belly screamed as she pushed the heavy table back to the center. When she placed the second stool atop it, she held onto it a moment until the pain subsided.

At least the physical pain.

The pain of losing Tancorix would never go away.

At least not until she took her revenge.

Escape now was secondary.

First, she had to kill Max.

11

"She followed Paul and the rest of us, shouting, 'These men are servants of the Most High God, who are telling you the way to be saved.' She kept this up for many days."

— ACTS 16:17–18

HIS HAND FIRMLY AROUND THE PRISONER'S UPPER ARM, QUINTUS descended the stairs. Philon, a slave, had been accused of defiling his master's daughter. With several witnesses, the trial, such as it was, had taken less than an hour. Since death sentences could come only from Macedonia's governor, the prisoner would remain here, in the inner cell, until armed guards from the provincial palace came to claim him.

Quin unlocked the massive door and stepped inside with the young man. The slave had yet to meet Quin's gaze. Could he have done such a thing?

But it was not Quin's place to question. He'd learned a man could do anything if pushed hard enough.

Philon collapsed on the cold, stone floor and stared at the opposite wall. He hadn't said a word since Quin had led him out of the basilica.

Quin lifted one of Philon's legs and placed the boy's ankle on one of the many semicircular holes carved into the side of a wooden board. Keeping them near the center, he did the same with his other ankle. Another board with matching openings closed over the first, and Quin locked them together. He reached for an iron chain lying on the floor behind Philon and dragged it closer, and then he locked it around Philon's wrist. Moving to the other side, he repeated the procedure on his other wrist, then yanked on the chain to make sure it was securely fastened to the wall.

All for a child too devastated to even think about escape.

He tramped up the stone steps. It had been a long night. Quin brushed the mud and grime from his clothes as he climbed the stairs. He'd need a cartload of new tunics from Lydia if he remained keeper.

He'd have to deal with that some other time. Right now, all he wanted to do was get some rest.

He snatched his cloak from the peg on the wall. "We only have three prisoners, so you can keep watch alone until Stolos comes."

"Yes, Tribune." Pandaros, his youngest guard, offered a half-hearted salute. "Would you mind if I left early today?"

Halfway out the door, Quin halted and turned to face the young guard. "Yes, I would mind very much. Why do you want to leave your post?"

He shrugged. "As you said, there are only three prisoners. Doesn't seem like we need two of us here."

Quin scratched the back of his neck. "Well, I'm certain I can find someone else to take your place."

Pandaros brightened. "You can?"

"Of course. There are many men aching to leave the quarries. You decide. If you still want to leave, let me know and I'll hire another guard." He turned on his heel without waiting for an answer.

On his first week as keeper, a guard asks to go home early?

Pandaros had been difficult all week. In fact, all the guards had been more difficult than he expected.

It was almost as if they were trying to make his job as hard as possible, but what purpose would that serve? None of them were qualified to be prison master, except maybe Stolos.

He climbed the four steps to his domus.

His slave opened the door before he touched it. "May I get you something to eat, Domine? You've had a long night." He reached for Quin's cloak.

Though Quin rarely saw the female slave, Epaphroditus had followed him around for three days now, whenever he was at home. If only Quin could convince him he really didn't need anything. "I'm more tired than hungry. I think I'll just go to bed."

He trudged into his *cubiculum* and then dropped onto his sleeping couch. His feet ached from standing on stone all night. Even in battle, he was usually on grass, leaves, something not quite so unforgiving. He raised one knee and reached for the laces of his boots.

Epaphras was at his feet before he could blink. "I can do that, Domine."

Quin pulled his foot back. "That's not necessary."

The young man cringed. "Are you not pleased with me, Domine? Have I not performed my duties well?"

Quin blinked. "You've done quite well. Why?"

"You will not let me care for you. This is my job."

"I'm just used to taking care of myself. You've done nothing wrong."

"I see." He frowned. "May I please wash the mud from your tunic while you sleep?"

Quin glanced at his filthy tunic. "All right."

A smile finally graced Epaphras's face. "I'll be right back to collect it." He left the room, closing the door behind him.

Quin removed his boots and tunic and set the soiled garment outside his door. No need for the slave to bother him again. He lay down on his bed.

As if he didn't have enough to worry about. Guards at the prison who hardly worked at all, and a slave at home who barely left him alone.

Maybe he should get them to trade places.

LEANING against the column of the silver shop, Quin watched the new seer. The sun reflected off her golden hair, and a red sash set off her dark blue tunic. Every move she made seemed effortless, like water flowing in a stream. She reached across the table and cupped the cheek of the woman whose future she told, smiling gently. Apparently reassured, the woman rose and left to pay the Roman woman hovering nearby.

"She's a slave, Quintus." Lydia's voice startled him.

He pushed off the column and turned to face the fabric dealer. "I didn't see you there."

"Obviously." She grinned.

"What does that mean?"

"You can't have her. She belongs to Maximus and Cassia." Lydia ambled toward the baker, a large basket on her arm.

"Who says I want her?"

"That ridiculous look on your face." She drew a circle in the air in front of him.

He huffed. "I have no look on my face at all."

"If you say so. But five young men in my house have married in the last ten years, and they all looked just like you in the months beforehand."

He waited while she paid for the bread. His molded leather *cuirass* was restrictive after not wearing it for so many months, and he wriggled his shoulders, trying to gain some comfort. At least it wasn't the even heavier, ceremonial metal one. He'd left that one in Rome.

"I served in Britannia for six years. With the Second Augusta under Vespasian."

"And?" Her brow furrowed. "Do you believe you destroyed her village?"

"I don't know. I don't know where she's from. But it doesn't matter. We were responsible for destroying thirty villages in the south. We marched in and pulled down walls, sometimes burned whatever was inside. We did whatever was necessary to ensure there would be no resistance." His stomach roiled as the sounds of screaming women and children, the sight of paths red with blood, and the smell of burning thatch ambushed his senses.

"Quintus!" Lydia pulled on his arm.

"I'm sorry."

"Where were you just now?"

He didn't answer.

Lydia halted and moved to face him. "It wasn't your choice."

He blew out a long sigh. "I suppose. I never actually met anyone my actions affected until now. Never thought about them."

"We usually don't until we're forced to." She started walking again, reaching the fruit seller's stall. "Why don't you come for cena?"

"I have to be at the prison."

"Your many guards cannot handle it without you?" She sorted through various pieces of fruit, picking up some and sniffing them.

"I have to train a new guard. Besides, it's only fair I take some night shifts as well. I never ask my men to do what I won't do."

"You're an excellent leader." Her gaze held his.

"Another night." He kissed her cheek and left, passing the seer's shop again on the way, but Elantia wasn't there. Neither were her owners. When had they slipped out? After taking the steps to the upper level, he scanned the forum as he crossed it, looking for her blue tunic. He saw her near the temple, calling out, offering her services.

Though it was the opposite way he was headed, he ambled closer to the massive building, its two lions standing guard at the bottom of the steps leading to the landing. Max hovered nearby, ready to collect payment from anyone she might convince to listen to messages from her goddess.

He stayed several strides away, not wanting to interfere.

She moved easily through the crowd, from one person to another, chatting briefly with one, smiling at another, telling the fortune of a few, promising a longer session if they came to her stall. Always flashing an easy smile. Rather than having been brought here days ago, she looked like she had grown up here and had known everyone her entire life.

Finishing a conversation with an older woman, she turned and saw him.

He looked away, but it was too late. She had to have seen him. He slowly risked a look back and found her fixing him with a glare that would melt ice. Had she noticed him following her?

Deliberately but not fast enough to draw Max's attention, she glided toward him. He aimed for the southeast exit toward the residential area, hoping to lose her among the alleys between the villas, but she followed him.

"Tribune!"

She knew his rank. Not good. How much exposure to the legions had she had?

He halted. Turned slowly to face her.

"You're a tribune?"

"I am."

"Were you one of Vespasian's marauders?"

He winced. "I was."

"And now you prance around here in your uniform, boasting about it?"

"I don't mean to boast. I came to retire. I was forced to become prison master."

She scoffed. "No one forces a Roumanos to do anything he doesn't want to do."

"More powerful Romans can."

"Maybe now you know what it feels like." She glanced over her shoulder. Seeing Max busily engaged in conversation, she apparently felt safe to continue. "You still don't know what it's like to lose everything. To watch your home burned, your parents killed in front of you. To see your friends sold and sent to cities all over the Empire. To have what you eat, what you wear, when you rise, and when you sleep decided by someone else."

He wanted to say something, anything. But what words could he offer that would take away any of her pain, erase any of his actions?

She closed the distance between them. Only moments earlier he would have relished the closeness. Her scent surrounded him. The hem of her tunic brushed his feet. He could see the flecks of green in her deep blue eyes.

But now, he wanted nothing more than to disappear.

"Stay away from me, Tribune. Never come near me again, understand?"

THE MORNING HAD BEEN LONG and exhausting. The visions would not come. No matter how hard Tia tried, nothing. Even worse than yesterday. No words, no images, no hints. Something was blocking her access to Brigid.

Something bigger, stronger.

It was as if a giant hand held back the information she knew was there, was rightfully hers. Keeping it from her.

Who? Why would someone do that to her?

Elantia turned to her owners. "I'm weak. I'm having trouble contacting the goddess. May I get something to eat?"

Cassia snarled. "Here. Go to the vendors." She handed her a coin. "Hurry back."

She wandered down the stoa, stopping at the fruit vendor. She fingered a fruit she had never seen before. Fuzzy, yellow-orange like the sun. Perhaps that would please the goddess.

"That's a Persian apple. Try it. For free." He handed her one and she bit into it. The sweet juice filled her mouth. They had nothing like this in Britannia.

She climbed up to the forum, pulling her cloak tighter around her shoulders.

Brigid, why have you left me? You are the strongest of the goddesses. I need you here, or I am in danger.

A walk might clear her thoughts, clear her way back to Brigid. Time for the afternoon snack and then the baths was nearing, and the crowd was thinning. Many of the townspeople she had come to recognize. Some had become regular customers, coming to her for advice whenever a decision or question needed to be settled. Others she had never helped, but was still familiar with. Some she knew as visitors from Amphipolis or Neapolis.

That tribune stood near the fountain with some men new to Philippi—four of them.

One was definitely in charge. An older man, he almost seemed to be teaching them, right there in the open. A thinner man, perhaps a bit younger, appeared to be a man of some wealth, or at least education, if his clothing was any indication. Another with a full white beard and a soft smile was about the same age as the teacher, and the fourth was younger than all of them.

Tia wanted to avoid the tribune, but was drawn to the leader. He spoke with authority, but he was not dressed as a scholar. His clothes were made of common wool, not tattered, but well worn. He was fairly short. Next to someone like Quintus, or the scholar with him, he was completely unassuming.

Yet the other four hung on every word he spoke.

What could he be saying that was so fascinating or important?

She drew nearer, trying to hear the conversation, yet also trying to appear as if she weren't interested at all.

Quintus interrupted the man. "But Paulos, I don't understand. What exactly do you mean?"

"Everyone has sinned; we've all fallen short of God's standard of perfection. You're a soldier, right?"

"I was."

"When a soldier commits an offense, what kind of punishments are there?"

"Anything from extra duty to execution."

"And can he remain in the army without said punishment?"

"Of course not."

"Right. Sin demands payment. God is a perfect God, and we cannot remain with Him, because we are not perfect. Our sins must be paid for. And we all commit sins every day. We all deserve execution, a death penalty. But even though we don't deserve it, Yahweh declares us blameless through Yeshua."

The closer Tia got, it seemed a force wanted to keep her away. Something, someone was calling her away. *Brigid?*

Yet her desire to hear what this man had to say grew even stronger. She wanted to hear more about this god who considered men blameless.

Stay or go? She wavered.

"How?" asked Quintus.

"Yahweh presented His own son, Yeshua, as the required sacrifice—the punishment—for our sin. When we believe that Yeshua sacrificed His life, offering His blood for us, we are made right with Yahweh. That sacrifice covers all the sins of all people—past, present, and future—and anyone who believes in Him can be saved from condemnation."

One God for all people? Only one? She had many gods. Llyr was god of the sea, Taranus was god of thunder, Brigid was goddess of healing and prophesy. There were so many more. How could only one god take care of everything?

"Yahweh, who raised Yeshua from the dead, will also raise us up, and will take us into His presence where we will live with Him, forever."

None of her gods promised she could live with them. Ever, at all. They promised she would return to another life after this one. Over and over.

She liked what Paulos's god offered.

Words filled her head, words that demanded to be set free. She struggled to hold them in. An unknown force pushed her to identify Paulos's god, but she ached to remain silent.

"These men are servants of the highest god!"

She clapped her hand over her mouth. Had she just yelled that?

Paulos stared at her, shaking his head. After a moment, he and the others moved around her.

She followed them, pulled by an unseen force as strong as if a rope held by Paulos were tied around her waist. Yearning, begging to remain silent, she failed once again. "These men are servants of the highest god, and they are telling the way to be saved!"

Could the ground just open up and let her fall into a hole? Her cheeks were on fire. She backed up, longing to escape.

Quintus stared at her like she had grown antlers.

Paulos led them past her, toward the Marsh Gate, frowning at her as he passed.

When the men were gone, people accosted her.

"How do you know about his god? Do you know all spirits?"

"Can you tell me about the spirit that attacks me?"

"You really can tell the future!"

There wasn't enough air. They were grabbing at her tunic, at her arms. She tried to get away, but they surrounded her. Her heart raced.

Max barged in and took over, pulling the customers away from her, forming them into lines like so many soldiers.

Cassia stepped between her and the crowd. Her breath slowed, her fears calmed. "Are you all right? Are you ready?"

"Yes. It's fine."

She wasn't about to admit that something was still blocking her, that she still couldn't hear Brigid.

It would probably go away, and as long as her owners didn't know, maybe they wouldn't hurt her.

Maybe.

QUINTUS WATCHED as the crowds swarmed Elantia in the forum, most holding bronze and silver coins in the air to gain her attention. Her face was pale, fists to her chest as she tried to back away. Cassia stepped in and pulled them away, but the fear in Tia's eyes didn't disappear.

His chest constricted, his heart ached. He wanted to help her, protect her. But there was nothing he could do.

She'd ordered him to stay far away.

He caught up to Paulos and the others on their way to prayer. Paulos was explaining something to his young companion Timotheos, hands gesturing animatedly as usual. Silas and Loukas strolled along behind the pair.

"What was that about?" Quin spoke as soon as Paulos took a breath.

"What?" Paulos looked at him as if nothing had happened.

"What? How can you pretend nothing happened back there?" He jogged ahead and then stopped, blocking their path. "She yelled something about a most high god. She got everyone staring, and then they all ran to her for prophecy." Then a horrible, unwanted thought entered his mind. "Was she doing that to gain business for herself?"

Paulos tilted his head. "No, I don't think so. She wasn't the one doing it, at least. It was someone else."

Someone else? "What does that mean? I heard her, saw her yelling. Who else would it be?"

One corner of Paulos's mouth turned up. "Maybe I'll explain later. Let's see what happens first."

12

"Finally Paul became so annoyed that he turned around and said to the spirit, 'In the name of Jesus Christ, I command you to come out of her!'"

— ACTS 16:18

AFTER MANY LONG HOURS IN THE PRISON, QUIN LAY ON HIS COUCH IN the dark. Had he slept at all? He sat up and swung his legs over the bed, resting his head in his hands. Dawn would be here soon. He wasn't getting any sleep; he may as well get up. He rose and slipped his tunic over his head.

How could he have thought Elantia had done that for profit? He'd seen the fear—the terror—in her eyes.

He limped into the kitchen. A half loaf of bread rested on a shelf. He dropped onto a stool and poked at the embers of the fire in the center of the culina.

Pulling off pieces of the bread, he ran through the events of the past few days.

What did she mean when she had yelled out to Paulos? *Servants of the most high god.* Which god? And what way of salvation?

She'd made it clear she didn't want to see him, but he needed to know what had happened to her yesterday. He needed some answers. If not from her, from someone else.

When the sun finally crept above the horizon, he put on his belt, his sandals, and washed his face. Grabbed his cloak and headed outside. The early morning air was chillier than he expected, and he tossed the edge of the crimson garment over his shoulder. The forum would be crawling with people soon, and she would be there to provide more prophesies.

When he stood at the entrance to Lydia's domus, fist hovering, the earliness of the hour hit him. Was anyone even up? Lydia, surely. That woman worked harder than anyone he knew. He'd need to come back at a decent hour. He turned to go, but the door swung open.

"Tribune! Come in!" Lydia's round face and cheery smile never failed to calm his spirit.

"I must apologize. I didn't realize how early it was until just now. I can return later."

"Nonsense. We were just about to eat. Join us, won't you?"

"Thank you."

Demas appeared and took his cloak.

He followed Lydia down the hall. In the triclinium, Paulos, Silas, and Timotheos were on one side. Syn and Zenobia were in the middle.

Demas entered the room and reclined on the third side.

Lydia led him to the couch next to Demas. "Come, eat." She patted the couch.

He backed away toward the hall. "I just came to talk to Paulos. Perhaps I should return later, when you're not . . . so busy."

"Quintus, please join us. I've been expecting you," Paulos said.

Quin perched on the edge of the couch next to Demas. "What happened yesterday? You said you would explain what you meant by 'someone else.'"

"I think that young girl has an evil spirit inside her."

If he hadn't been sitting down, he would have fallen down. "A what?"

Paulos sat up. "I think a spirit of divination speaks through her. How else do you think she tells the future so well? She is indeed talking to supernatural powers, and they control her mind. And they recognize the one true God that lives in us."

"Why is that bad, then? Why did you silence her?"

"Because when she calls out that we are servants of 'the most high god' it sounds like Yahweh is the highest of many gods." Paul pointed a finger. "That's why everyone ran to her. They understood her to say Yahweh is the highest, but all the others are still gods as well. His title, the Highest, actually means He is higher than anything He has created, higher than man, higher than any spirits or powers. But there are no other gods. Just created things people worship as gods."

"So what happens to her now? Will this spirit hurt her?"

Paulos shrugged. "I don't know, because I can't tell the future."

Timotheos chuckled.

Quin glared at him.

The old man grinned. "As I said, we'll have to wait and see."

ELANTIA STIFFENED as Paulos passed her.

The war that had waged within her for the last week intensified. Whenever that man came near, she felt an irresistible urge to call to him, name him. Why? As soon as she did, she wanted to hide. Forever. In the deepest, darkest cave. And Paulos and his companions apparently wanted her to go away, too, judging by the annoyance on his face.

The group came closer.

She tried to veer away. Today she *would* keep quiet. She fisted her hands, clenched her jaw. Walked in the other direction. Anything to keep those words from tumbling out.

"These men are servants of the most high god, and they are telling the way to be saved!"

Not again. The sixth day in a row. She dropped her chin to her chest. Why couldn't she control her own tongue? Especially when she didn't know—or believe—what she was saying.

She looked up to see the group approaching. Backing up, she glanced around. Where could she go? There was nowhere for her to hide.

Paulos gently held her arm. "Are you well, child?"

Nodding quickly, she searched the forum. "I-I'm well. I . . ." Where were her owners?

His eyes were gentle. Like those of her tatos. As if he really cared about her.

Behind him, the dark-haired boy shook his head in disapproval. The one with the thick, white beard smiled softly. The quiet scholar seemed to be studying her.

She avoided looking at Quintus. Though she couldn't possibly care less what that Roumanos thought of her.

"All right." Paulos smiled. "We have to go to prayer now, but I'm sure I'll see you soon." He patted her shoulder and headed toward the Marsh Gate.

Customers crowded her as soon as they left. Max and Cassia weren't far behind.

"Me first." One of her regulars shoved to the front. "Tia, I need your help." His broad shoulders and his height allowed him to shove everyone behind him. "My wife is very ill. Tell me, will she survive?" He held out his hands, one full of coins.

She cradled his hand in hers, lightly moving her fingertips over his skin. Searching the sky for the non-existent clues, she begged Brigid for the messages.

"I can only see that she will not leave you in the next day or two. That's all the goddess has shown me." She winced. "I'm sorry."

"It's enough for now." He left to pay and another came forward.

She squeezed her eyes tighter, hoping to catch a glimpse of

what the goddess had to tell this young man—this boy, really. She'd seen only a flash of pain and blood before the future left her. What was she supposed to do with that? Might be his blood or someone else's. Could be war. Could be childbirth. Those two were wildly opposed to each other, and yet both were perfectly reasonable options for a boy not remotely ready for either battle or marriage.

She hated lying.

But she had to say something. And she wouldn't be found out for years either way.

She opened her eyes and cradled his hand between hers. "I see a life of glory ahead for you."

His eyes brightened, and he stood up straighter.

"A life in which people will shout out for you, but in which pain and blood will also play a great part. Your actions alone will decide whether that glory will bring heartache or comfort to those nearest to you. Choose wisely whom you will follow."

"Whom *should* I follow?"

"I cannot tell you that. But look around you, at not only the rewards of those whom you admire, but at what they have sacrificed. What are you willing to lose, to gain the accolades you seek?"

His shoulders slumped.

"Do not be discouraged. You have many years yet to choose your path."

"Your time is up. Move on." Cassia clapped her hands once, and the boy left.

He smiled at Tia before handing over his silver.

She finished the customers that had lined up after Paulos had left. Her head felt like it was full of spider webs. She'd made up futures and faked her way through decisions for twenty or more people. It hurt to think.

They had to have made more this morning already than most days. Max had tripled the price. Maybe they would let her go early today.

She looked for Cassia. Max would definitely say no. She noted

Cassia several strides away but before she reached her, the heaviness came again. She couldn't move her feet. Was Paulos back? She looked to the Via, in the direction of the Marsh Gate.

Her heart sank.

Not again. She tried to run.

Xenia blocked her path. "Elantia!"

"No! Let me go, please."

"Tia, my dear." She looked completely confused.

Paulos came closer.

"Tia, I saved this fabric for you. I know how you love the color blue."

Closer . . .

"These men are servants of the highest god, and they are telling the way to be saved!"

Xenia backed away as Paulos strode to her, his face set.

What had she done? What was he going to do?

She cringed, shrinking before him. Her entire body shook as he looked down on her, his finger pointed at her heart. Her knees wobbled.

"I command you in the name of Yeshua to come out of her!"

Command who? Go where? Who was he talking to? She looked over her shoulder.

"I command you in the name of Yeshua of Nazareth, come out!" He repeated the same nonsense. She knew no one of this name.

Her heartbeat raced, her hot blood pounding in her ears. She felt dizzy, swaying, her vision blurring. The battle inside her rose to a fever pitch for just a moment . . . then it silenced.

And her world turned black.

WATCHING from the window of his office in the basilica, Gallus chuckled as the slave girl collapsed in a heap at the edge of the forum. Women gasped and backed away, men stood stunned.

More entertainment than he'd had in weeks.

"Leonidas!" Why was that servant never around when he nee—

The door opened. "Yes, Domine?"

He snapped his fingers, twice. "Bring me Helios. Instantly."

The Greek scurried off.

Gallus turned his attention back to the forum. Cassia knelt to examine the girl, while Max, hands balled into fists, shouted at the man who had spoken to her before she collapsed. He always was a hot-tempered one.

The visitor, completely unruffled, answered a few of the owner's questions. Max, giving up, turned away and barked at his wife. The two whispered together a moment.

Quintus, obviously shaken but ever the gallant soldier, picked her up and carried her to the home of her domini, leaving the visitors in the forum.

Gallus couldn't have scripted better theater.

Who was that man who caused the girl to faint? And what about his companions? Had he said something to scare her? Embarrass her? Hurt her?

A knock at the door signaled the scriba's arrival.

"Come."

Helios stepped inside and joined Gallus at the window.

Gallus waved his hand at the group still standing together on the south side of the forum. "See those three? Four, actually, but one is barely more than a child."

Helios nodded.

"I need you to find out who they are, where they came from, when they arrived, and what they have done since they've been here. I need to know everything, understand?"

"Yes, Domine."

"As quickly as you can."

"I shall do what I can." The clerk left.

Gallus leaned out his window. Where had they gone? He scanned the forum. There they were, strolling toward the residential district. Why would they go that way? Were they staying with someone they knew?

Even Quintus, a Roman, presumably of land and status, stayed at an inn when he first arrived. Who could these Jews know that would allow them to stay in their home? Some of the God-fearers? That would make sense. They worshipped the same god.

He watched until Paulos and the others turned south on Via Appia.

This was troublesome. He could either be buying something from one of the villa shops, which was doubtful considering his clothing, or he was staying with someone who owned one of the largest houses in Philippi.

The last thing he needed was for these men to have connections with the rich and powerful of Philippi.

Gallus stepped away from his window, fingering the purple edges of his toga. As long as it had been only women, he hadn't worried too much about the God-fearers. What could a handful of women do, after all? They could pray to any god they wanted, as far as he cared.

From what he'd been told, they only went to sit by the river and pray. These women were not even Romans. A Greek or two, but mostly slaves, and freedmen—rather, women—except for that one woman from Anatolia. And she brought a lot of business—and taxes—into his city. He needed to remain in her favor.

Earlier in the year, Emperor Claudius had kicked all the Jews out of Rome because they had been inciting riots. All that did was send the troublemakers elsewhere. Like Philippi.

And if these men had come to Philippi to stay, had come to join the God-fearers, that could signal a change in the fabric of this town.

One that wouldn't be in his best interest.

He'd come too far to let some nomadic Jews prevent him from climbing to the top of Philippi's political system and staying there.

He would need to be prepared to take whatever steps were necessary to protect what was his.

QUIN GENTLY LAY Elantia on the sleeping mat in her small room. Such a thin piece of woven reeds. It was hardly better than the bare tile floor. If only he could have taken her to his own wool-stuffed mattress.

That would hardly be appropriate. Though he would gladly vacate his house if she could stay there.

"She's fine, Tribune. You can leave now," Max barked at him from overhead.

Quin moved her hair out of her face. Her skin, always fair, was even paler than usual.

"Now, Tribune."

Quin rose, slowly. He turned to face the much shorter man; he glared down at him for a long moment. It wasn't as if *he* could have carried her. What right did he have now to order him away as if he were a servant?

Max flinched almost imperceptibly.

Quin pushed past the smaller man, bumping his shoulder with his bicep, and left the house.

But the image of her, so small, so vulnerable on that mat would not leave him.

What had happened to her? Would she recover?

He marched directly to Lydia's house, one street over. Pounded on the door until Lydia opened it, her usual smile in place.

"Come in. We've been expecting you."

Expecting him? Again? Perhaps Paulos should warn him ahead of time and avoid these heated conversations. "Where is he?" He barged past her.

She pointed down the hall.

"What was that? Explain this to me. In a way I can understand!" Quin spoke before he even entered the room.

"Quin. I'm sure you have many questions. Please sit." Paulos gestured to one of the couches.

"I'll stand." He paced in the center of the room between Paulos and Loukas.

"You really must calm down if we are to have a rational conversation." Loukas rose and crossed the room to a table. "May I pour you some wine? Are you hungry? Sometimes food can do wonders to help us think more clearly."

Was he serious? The man wanted him to eat? Now? "Wine, maybe." Just to quiet him.

Loukas poured a glass of honeyed wine and brought it to him, along with a slice of warm bread. "Eat the bread too. Trust me. You'll feel better."

Sighing, he sat and stuffed the food in his mouth, nearly swallowing it whole, then washed it down with wine. When the wine was gone, he set the cup aside and fixed his gaze on Paulos. "Now, will you please tell me what happened?" He paused, reliving the scene. "I heard you say, 'I order you to come out of her.' To whom were you speaking?"

Paulos studied his hands for several moments before he spoke. "I was speaking to the spirit that I believe was controlling her. It became clearer every day that she was losing more and more of herself to that spirit." His voice was soft. It was obvious the incident had affected him deeply. "As she cried out, I could see the battle on her face. She tried mightily, every day, to keep from saying those things. I hated seeing her devastated, humiliated each time she lost that fight. She was growing weaker." He rubbed his hand down his face. "I'm very sorry this happened to her."

"Why did she collapse?"

"That is unusual, I admit, but I have seen it before. Most of the time when a spirit leaves, the person feels free, completely liberated. But this was a different sort of spirit. The spirit was not harming her physically, so it operated in a very different manner. I really don't know."

Loukas offered Quin another piece of bread. "It may be that the constant battle she was fighting just exhausted her, and when it suddenly ended, all that energy was no longer needed. She may just need some true, deep rest."

"I'm sorry, but what do you know about this?"

"Loukas is a medicus."

Quin stared at the man sitting across from him. He'd always thought he was a scholar, a philosopher of some sort. But a physician? Then why wasn't he with her now, helping her? "Shouldn't you go tend to her then?"

Loukas chuckled. "What makes you think they would allow me in the house?"

Wouldn't he even try?

Loukas leaned forward. "Quintus, I am sure she will be all right. If she isn't, trust me, they will summon a physician. She is too valuable to them."

He returned his attention to Paulos. "You keep saying spirit, but she said she talks to her goddess. How can a goddess be in someone?"

Paulos drew in a long breath. "Let's leave the question of whether it's a goddess or spirit alone for now. You said you saw her that first day she called to me. You saw the terror on her face and you said you'd never seen her afraid before, yes?"

Quin stood to pace again. "I was in Britannia for six years. The women fight alongside the men. They *never* show fear."

"So it had to be something very powerful to frighten her."

"True."

"Or . . . control her."

"Maybe . . ."

"So whether it was *in* her, or *controlling* her, it needed to leave her alone. Agreed?"

He folded his arms across his chest. "Agreed."

"I told it to leave her alone."

"And it just obeyed you?"

"It didn't obey *me*, it obeyed God, the one true God, the only living God."

Paulos had made sense until that point. But the spirit leaving just because Paulos told it to, whether Paulos spoke on behalf of his god or not, that was too much to ask him to believe.

Gods didn't obey other gods. Gods fought other gods, argued with other gods, tricked other gods. They fell in love with each other, grew jealous of each other, hated each other.

And only one God? How could there be only one?

13

"At that moment the spirit left her."

—ACTS 16:18

GALLUS STARED AT THE NUMBER HE'D PRESSED INTO THE WAX AND tossed the stylus to the desk. The quarterly task of reviewing all fines for minor and medium offenses had his head reeling, his stomach rumbling. He could finish this tomorrow. Better yet, make someone else do it for him. The senate only wanted totals. He could just make up numbers and they'd never know the difference.

Shoving the tablet to the side he stepped to the door and called for his slaves. A rest and some food before a bath and perhaps a lecture would do him some good. Nicanor knelt and removed his sandals, then slipped Gallus's feet into his outdoor boots and tied the laces. Leonidas helped him arrange the bulky purple-bordered toga over his shoulders, around his torso, and back over his arm.

On his way out of the building, Helios stopped him, a wax tablet in hand. "Domine. I have the rest of that information you requested."

"Finally." He glared at the scriba.

Helios looked over his shoulder. "Do you want me to tell you here, out in the hallway?"

Gallus huffed. "Back in my office."

The Greek closed the heavy door behind them. "Their apparent leader is Paulos, a Jew of Tarsus. He is also known by his Hebrew name Saul. It seems that trouble follows this man and his companions. His fellow Jews rose up against him about a year ago in"—he scanned down the tablet—"Pisidian Antioch and Derbe; both the local residents and the Jews attacked him in Iconium, and the Jews then chased him to Lystra where they stoned him. He's also caused trouble on more than one occasion in Jerusalem."

"And who are the men with him?"

"The Greek is Loukas, a local physician. He travels a great deal but does own property here. That is the only reason I got the information so quickly. Otherwise I would have had to wait for it to arrive from the cities themselves. You will need to be very careful with him since he is well-respected. The youngest is . . . umm"—he again checked his notes—"Timotheos. His mater was Jewish, but his pater was Greek."

Gallus strolled to the window. "Is his family important?"

"Not that I know of. Of Lystra. He came here with Paulos."

"And the fourth?"

"A Jew named Silas of Jerusalem. Traveling with Paulos for the last year or more. From what I can tell his family is of no importance."

"Where were they before this?"

He checked the notes once more. "Lystra. Before that, Derbe, and before that, Iconium."

"Again? Where they were stoned and run out of town?"

"Apparently so. They seem to have visited without incident this time and brought the young man Timotheos with them."

"How long do they usually stay in each place?"

"A few weeks. Maybe a month or two. Not long."

"That much is encouraging, at least." Perhaps they would move on soon, without causing the commotion they had elsewhere. He waved his hand. "You may go."

This was a great deal of new information, and he would need to consider it carefully, balanced with the rest of his knowledge. He needn't move too quickly and make a mistake. Better to wait, and watch. Time was on his side, not theirs.

He crossed the forum on his way to his domus. Nearing the end of the morning, shopkeepers were eagerly trying to complete that last sale before going home for their midday meal. Calling for customers, flooding the forum with their grating voices. If he could find a way to make it illegal, he would. At least he had managed to move all the shops down onto the market and keep those with the most nauseating smells farthest away from his domus and the basilica.

Quintus huddled at the east end of the marketplace, deep in conversation with those troublesome visitors.

Normally Gallus would ask his chief lawman to keep an eye on these visitors, but Quintus seemed to be enthralled with them. Just how friendly was he with those foreigners? He'd been with them that day, when that slave girl collapsed. How involved was he in that? Was he trying to create problems for Gallus, for Philippi? Trying to get revenge for losing his land?

Surely Quintus wasn't aware of the connection between Gallus, and Cassia and Max, nor could Quintus be certain that Gallus had stolen the land, however many suspicions he may have.

Maybe Gallus needed to have a conversation with him, see exactly how involved with those Jews he was. After all, Quintus worked for him, whether Gallus liked it or not. He may as well make use of it.

Quintus could continue his friendship, spy on them for Gallus and keep the Jews in line, and Gallus could keep the peace in his little kingdom.

Everyone would get what they wanted.

After changing his clothes and trading his red army cloak for his dark woolen one, Quin sped along the western edge of the forum. Taking the steps all at once, he landed on the walkway of the market. His gaze quickly moved to the center, finding Max's shop. Only one person in line. He headed there, trying not to look like he was in too much of a hurry.

An old woman rose from the seat just as Tia came into his vision. A young girl took her place. He watched Tia take the girl's hand, smile, speak with her like she was the only other person in the world. There was genuine concern on Tia's face.

Would she talk to him like that? Talk to him at all?

Did she even know he was the one who had carried her home yesterday?

The girl left and he stepped forward.

He waited by the doorway, waited for her to acknowledge him.

She pasted on a weak smile. "Please come in."

Sitting on the stool, he gave her his hand. "It's clear you don't want me here." He kept his voice low. "Why invite me in?"

"My owners wouldn't like it very much if I turned away a paying customer." She glanced at Cassia. "You are paying, aren't you?"

He chuckled softly. "Of course."

"And what is your question for the goddess today?" She spoke loud enough for Cassia to hear.

The question seemed to take him by surprise. He hadn't bothered to formulate one. "I don't really have one. I guess I just wanted to see you. I wanted to see if you were all right. After yesterday."

She leaned near, her blue eyes flashing. "You have to at least pretend you have a question."

She closed her thumb—the only part showing from underneath his larger paw—over the back of his hand. The fingers of her other hand wandered on his skin, sending sparks of heat through his body. Her eyes closed, her head swaying gently as she waited for the messages. She was entrancing. He could sit here forever, watching her, letting her draw circles on his hand.

She frowned.

"What? What's wrong?"

Her eyes snapped open. "Nothing."

"You frowned."

"Shh!" She glanced at her owners at the entrance. "Do you try to get me in trouble, or does it just happen that way whenever you are around?"

"What are you talking about?"

For a brief moment, fear contorted her beautiful face. "I can't hear her," she whispered.

"Can't hear who?"

"My goddess, Brigid. I've been making things up. And I've been punished once already for giving a false reading."

Noticing the still discolored skin beneath her sleeve, he squeezed her hand. "Just tell me anything."

"Do you swear you won't get me punished?"

"Of course not." Why would she think that? "I would never hurt you."

She glanced over his shoulder at her owners and shook her head.

"No. Ask me something. Anything."

"Where in Britannia are you from?"

"What makes you think that's where I am from?"

"I hear things. Philippi is a small town."

"I lived on the coast."

"What people?" His voice harsher than he intended.

"What do you know about Britannia?"

"As much as any other Roman," he lied. "What people? Who was your chief?"

She shifted her weight as she glanced toward Cassia.

"Hold my hand. Pretend you are telling me more about my future."

"Why do you need to know so badly?"

"I just do. Please?"

She turned his hand over and skimmed her fingers across his palm. "We lived far to the southwest, on the sea. My father is—was—our chief."

His heart almost stopped. How was that possible? Vespasian had moved the Second Augusta north, coming to truce with the fierce warriors of that area. It didn't make sense. "How did you end up here?"

"The Roumani attacked. Before dawn. They k—" She paused and breathed deeply. "They killed my parents, and anyone else who would be of no use to Rome. They captured me and many of my friends and sold us to someone on a ship. We traveled for many weeks until we were brought to a market, where we were sold again."

"I'm sorry." A weak platitude. His heart ached for her. But would she believe him if he told her that?

"After we made peace with them, after Vespasian swore we would be safe, swore we would never be attacked, they came for us anyway. He lied. I knew we never should have trusted him."

The army regularly sold war captives of defeated peoples. But they wouldn't act the way she described. They must have been slave traders, dressed like Roman soldiers. "But they couldn't—"

Her glare could have sliced though him. "You're a Roumanos. You must have slaves. Have you never thought where they came from? That they had families? People they loved?"

She pulled her hands back, rested them in her lap. "You haven't, have you? I'll bet you never even thought of them as people."

"That is not true."

"Your time is up. Pay the other Roumanos on your way out."

"But wait—"

"Go."

He opened his mouth, but no words came forth. What could he say?

She was right. Mostly. He knew slaves were people. That they had families, loved ones.

He just never cared enough to think much about it.

TIA WAITED. No matter what she did, all that came now was stone-cold silence.

Was this because of what that man Paulos did? Said?

What was she supposed to do?

What if her owners found out? If they punished her before . . .

A young woman perched on the stool across from her, a baby in her lap. Her eyes bright, her face expectant.

"Is this your baby?"

"Yes." She lifted him so Tia could see him. The baby cooed in his mother's arms, one tiny foot escaping from the blanket he was bundled in.

Elantia's heart clenched. How could she let them down? "He's beautiful."

"Thank you. Can you tell me what the gods have planned for him?"

"May I hold him?" Maybe if she held the child, something would come to her. Maybe the goddess would be merciful to one so small.

She rose to scoop the infant from the woman's arms. The babe's weight felt good, comforting against her. How long had it been since she held a baby? Since Britannia, at least. And even there, not in some time. He grabbed for her hair. Pink cheeks. Dark curls. Chubby fingers.

Would she ever have one of her own? Not likely. Not since they believed she had to be pure. She'd never even marry.

Brigid, talk to me, I beg you.

Still nothing came. But he was an infant. Almost anything would work. He had a lifetime to make it happen.

"I see a great life for him. He will be a leader of men." *What else?* Anyone could say that. A loving aunt would say that. *You need more to make this convincing.*

She held her finger close to the baby's fist, bumping it until he wrapped his tiny fingers around hers. The gesture warmed her heart. Why couldn't she see what good things the gods had for him?

"Is that all?" The mother's voice startled her.

"Hmm?"

"Isn't there more?"

"O-of course. I was just distracted by how perfect he is." She blinked back a tear. "He, he . . ." She tried to recall how the leadership in this town worked. He couldn't really be in government unless he was born to it, if she remembered correctly. The mother might not want him in the army. So what would be left for him to lead? "He will be successful in the marketplace. And in anything else he tries. He will be a very wealthy man." Why not?

The woman's face lit up. "Successful? Wealthy?"

"Yes." She placed him back in his mother's arms.

"Thank you." Smiling gratefully at Tia, she tucked the blanket around her precious bundle. She paid Max and left.

Max stepped into the tent as soon as he had the coins in his greedy hands. "Why did that one sound so much different from your other messages?"

She lowered herself onto the stool. "I don't know what you mean." Picking at the cloth on the table, she avoided his harsh gaze.

"That sounded different from any other one I've ever heard you give."

"You don't hear very many of them, though, do you?"

"Still."

She shrugged. "He was a baby. There's not a lot for the goddess to work with."

How could he know? He couldn't. Could he? "Were you just imagining things?"

"N-no. Why would you ask that?"

"I told you. It sounded . . . off."

"I don't know what to tell you."

Max leaned on his palms, bringing his face close to hers. He waited until she raised her face. "If I find out you have been lying to our customers, it will not end well for you." His voice was rougher than usual, if that was even possible. "So for your sake, I hope you're telling the truth." He stared long enough to make her flinch, then turned and left.

Shivers ran down her back. If he could tell she was nervous, he'd be even more suspicious than he already was. If she couldn't figure out how to hear the goddess, she'd better figure out how to look like she did, and quickly.

A tall, fidgety man, who had been lurking around the edges of the forum since early morning, finally approached their stall. He sat at her table, but couldn't look her in the eye.

That would make it even more difficult.

"May I ask your name?"

"I don't want to tell you." His eyes darted around the room.

"You don't want to tell me your name?"

"No."

"Why not?"

"I just don't."

"All right, then what is your question?"

"I want to know if I should take my employer to court."

"Ah." That would explain the secrecy. "Is he mistreating you?"

His shoulders drooped. "Yes, and he is very powerful."

"So this is a risky move?"

"Very."

"Let me ask the goddess. May I have your hand?"

He slid his hand toward her, looking over his shoulder as he did.

As she had been all day, Brigid was silent. Reason was her only ally.

"She says you should avoid this perilous venture, and instead consider a new place of employment."

"Are you sure?" He looked like she'd just told him he would die. Perhaps she'd made the wrong choice.

"That is her advice. But you don't have to take it." Especially since it wasn't truly hers.

"No, no. Everyone says you're the best."

She forced a smile. "Thank you."

Oh, Brigid . . .

The day dragged on, longer than any other.

One young man asked if he would be granted citizenship. She told him yes.

Another asked if it was safe to travel. Another yes.

A young girl asked to which god she should sacrifice. The only Roman god Tia knew was Jupiter.

When the day finally came to an end, and she was safely alone in the dark, she lay on her mat staring at the ceiling. *Brigid, why have you abandoned me? Is this my fate? To be dragged to a land far away, because I can hear the goddess, to where I can no longer hear her, and then be punished for it? Killed for it?*

It's not fair.

QUIN PACED in Lydia's rose-filled peristyle.

"Why are you so quiet tonight? You hardly ate anything. Are you well?" Lydia held out a goblet of wine. "I will take one guess at what—or who—occupies your thoughts."

"How do you explain how she does what she does? How can she tell the future so accurately? She told me her goddess—Brigid, I think she called her—tells her things, shows her pictures." He winced. "But I saw her today, and she told me she can no longer hear Brigid. Do you think that's true? Do you think her goddess is angry with her?"

"I don't believe the goddess is angry with her, because I don't believe she has a goddess telling her the future. I don't believe

Brigid is a goddess." Paulos's deep but soft voice startled him as he entered the room, Silas behind him.

"You don't?"

"I believe there is only one God, the living God."

Again with that ridiculous statement. "I'm not sure I believe in the gods anymore, but I still do whatever I can to keep them from becoming angry with me. Just in case."

Paulos sat and pulled out a stack of folded parchment. He held a bone needle up to the lights and poked a length of linen thread through its eye. "Jupiter, Mars, Brigid . . . these are not gods. They are statues, idols, gods imagined in the minds of men. How can they be angry? How can they hurt you?"

The image of Elantia's face, her terror that day on the forum, the fear even today, stayed in his mind. If Paulos had seen her, he wouldn't ask such a question. "I'm worried about her. I worry what they will do to her when they find out."

Lydia set her goblet aside. "She is their property. You know that. They can do to her whatever they wish."

"I know." He dropped onto the lectus beside her.

"I would offer to buy her, but I doubt they would sell her. If she were just a house slave, perhaps . . . but with her skill, she is very valuable to them."

"And if that skill disappears?"

"You may have good cause to worry." Lydia placed her hand on his back. "These are not kind people."

Quin aimed his glare at Paulos. "You said she'd be all right."

"I said she'd be all right *physically*." He guided his needle through the parchment, on the fold. The man seemed to be perpetually busy. Did he never stop moving?

"Why don't you seem concerned?"

"Because I did what Yahweh asked me to do, and I don't believe He would ask me to do anything that would hurt her."

Silas smiled softly. "This is not over yet, Quin. You must have faith."

Quin bolted from the couch. "In what? In whom? You have no

idea how much power Gallus has in this city and what he can do to those who displease him. They are *Romans*. She is a slave, and you are a Jew, an outsider. He will be on their side. I could very well end up arresting you before this is over."

"It wouldn't be the first time." Silas chuckled.

Quin scoffed. "You are unbelievable. How can you sit there as if nothing is amiss when her life may be in danger? When your life may be in danger?"

Paulos's hands stilled for only a moment as he caught Quin's gaze. "Quin, how do you draw such drastic conclusions? I see no evidence of danger for anyone yet."

How did he not see it? "She will stop earning them money, and they will punish her severely. Then they will blame you. How else could this possibly end?"

"Are you the seer now?" Silas grinned.

"I just know how Roman society works. It's worked against me often enough."

Paulos's brow furrowed. "Is everything for you a matter of life and death?"

Quin stepped nearer to the older man. "I am a soldier. A legal, hired killer. I've caused more death in my life than you can possibly imagine. Death—on a massive scale—is what keeps the Empire alive. So, yes, everything is a matter of not life, but *death*. And when she shows up dead, you shouldn't be surprised."

"And when she doesn't, you shouldn't be."

Quin huffed and stormed out of Lydia's house.

Until now, he'd thought Paulos an intelligent man. Learned, fascinating. His theory of only one god was interesting, amusing. But this—his callous disregard for such a beautiful young woman who had done nothing to him except perhaps embarrassed him . . .

Quin knew how things worked. And he gave it a week before Paulos was in his prison, and Tia was either dead or sold as a slave to some old man who wanted a new and pretty bed partner.

His stomach roiled at the thought.

Why? It wasn't like she meant anything to him. She'd never

even had a kind word for him. Still, he had an overwhelming urge to protect her.

But he wasn't a protector. He was a killer. And even if he could save her, she'd never see him as anything else.

He shrugged off the thoughts. Time to get back to the prison.

Where he belonged.

14

"Out of the depths I cry to you, Lord."

— PSALM 130:1

As soon as Tia saw him stomping toward them, she knew there would be trouble. In the open forum, there was no place to hide. The fountains were too far away, as were the columns that fronted the basilica. She could only stand there and wait for the punishment to fall.

"Where is she?" The wiry man nearly ran into Cassia, red-faced and sweating, even in the cool autumn air.

"Who?" Cassia pulled him out of earshot of a group of Roman women admiring the new cloth one of them had purchased.

He towered over Cassia and his cloak reeked of sweat and vinegar. "Your seer! Or so she says. Her prediction did not come true. And I want my coin back." He shoved his hand out, long fingers twitching.

"Now wait, wait." Cassia gently pushed his hand down, and with her other gently patted his upper arm. "What is your name?"

"I am Drakon. I have a small farm outside the walls."

"Drakon, sometimes it takes a while for her prophecies to come about. But never once has she been wrong. What exactly did she say?"

The Macedonian blew out a breath. "I came to her a few days ago and asked her if the young women I wanted to marry would agree, if her father would accept me as a husband for his only daughter. She assured me he would."

Tia hugged her middle. Drakon was one of the first after Paulos touched her, one of the first times Brigid had withheld her voice.

"But I went to him last night, and he laughed in my face, in front of all his sons and brothers! It was the most humiliating experience of my life. Nothing can remedy this. I want my coin back, two times over, or I shall tell everyone in Philippi she is a fraud."

"Surely we can work something out. Another session, perhaps, at no charge, of course." Cassia's voice was honey-sweet—the one she used to convince Max to do what he did not wish to do.

"Why would I want to hear any more words from her? I don't trust a single thing she says."

Cassia fingered the purse on her belt. "I don't see why you should get twice your price."

"To pay me for my humiliation and suffering. Otherwise . . ." Drakon held his arms out to the side, as if to include the whole of Philippi.

She held up a finger. "But you promise, not a word to anyone else."

"Of course not."

Cassia counted out the coin into the Macedonian's hand, and then barged toward Elantia. "Explain that!" She pointed in the direction of the unsatisfied customer who was walking away.

"Well, umm . . ." She searched for words. Her stomach knotted, her face heated. "That was the day after I fainted in the forum, after that Jew talked to me. I still wasn't feeling well, and I must have misheard the goddess. It was an aberration."

Cassia pursed her lips, as if she were trying to decide whether or not to believe her.

"I promise it won't happen again." Yet another lie. How many customers had she given prophecies pulled out of thin air?

"It better not." She glanced around. A small group of three or four hovered nearby. "Get ready. You have customers."

Tia let out a long breath. She still hadn't heard from Brigid, not since that day. What would she do if it did happen again? It was bound to.

She put on a smile and beckoned to the first man waiting. She tended to everyone in the group and then she strolled through the forum, offering messages from the goddess that she wasn't really hearing.

The last one for the day was dropping a coin into Cassia's hand when Max marched across the forum.

He was not happy.

Cringing, she waited as he stormed toward her, fists clenched, sandals pounding the tile, toga slipping off his shoulder.

She felt dizzy. He had to be angry with her. He'd never embarrass Cassia in the forum like this.

Too soon, he stood face-to-face with her.

The pain was unexpected. Heat seared her cheek, her eyes watered, she stumbled. Her hip hit first, colliding with the cold tile floor, followed by her elbow and wrist. She would surely have a bruise tomorrow.

She pushed herself to a sitting position. It took a moment for the dizziness to subside.

"Max!" Cassia grabbed his arm.

"I have just had a most infuriating conversation. Several of them, actually."

"What about?"

"Our seer here doesn't seem to be seeing the future all that well lately."

"I had a similar complaint earlier."

Max raised his fist.

"No, Max, not here."

Max grabbed her arm and dragged her east out of the marketplace toward their villa.

Struggling to keep upright, she stumbled more than once. She managed to keep from falling only because he was walking so much faster than she was. They turned onto his street, speeding toward his domus.

Once inside he threw her onto the hard floor of the atrium.

Cassia rushed in after. "What do you intend to do?"

"I feel like killing her. Do you know how much coin she cost me just today? And how many more will be behind them? Word has spread that she is a fraud, and we will soon lose everything. All the money we invested in her, and now she will bring us nothing. She is utterly worthless now."

"Are you sure no one will trust her?"

"No one. I have given back coin to at least twenty people just this afternoon." Max threw his hands in the air. "How long do you think it will take before all of Philippi has heard she no longer can see the future? Before everyone knows her goddess has abandoned her?"

Cassia paced like a trapped cat. She was the only one of the pair who had even slightly cared about her, and now Elantia had lost her trust as well.

"Although, she's not quite worthless. She can serve other purposes, now." Max knelt before her and fingered a lock of her hair, causing her to shudder. "If she's not a seer, she doesn't have to remain pure. We could still sell her and regain some of our cost. Or keep her for ourselves."

Horrible, disgusting thoughts filled her mind, and her food threatened to come back up her throat. She continued to stare at the floor, but it didn't take much to imagine the lewd smile on Max's face.

He rose. "But right now I am too angry to even think about any of that. She needs to be punished."

"Fine then. Punish her. Just don't do anything that will lower the price in case we decide to sell her." Cassia's hurried footsteps faded.

Max yanked her to her feet. The first agonizing punch with his closed fist thrust her head and shoulders back so hard she slammed into the wall.

The next one knocked her to the ground. Then the kicking began, and mercifully, her mind went blank.

GALLUS RECLINED on a couch in his dining room. The day had been long and busy, and he looked forward to a simple cena and a quiet evening, as out of custom for him as that was. Even he tired of entertaining occasionally.

Leonidas entered. "Max and Cassia are here to see you."

He groaned. Not what he wanted tonight. But she was his cousin. And he'd promised his aunt he would use his power to help family, even if she did marry that *idiota*. "Give me a moment, then show them in. And bring more food." He sat up. "Wait. First bring me my toga." He'd shed it as soon as he entered the domus.

Leonidas left and sent Nicanor in with his toga.

Moments later Max and Cassia entered the dining room.

Cassia kissed his cheek. "Cousin, I apologize for coming by without an invitation."

"Nonsense. I'm so glad to see you both. I was just about to eat. You must join me." He clapped his hands. "Wine! I'm terribly sorry. My servants are so lazy. I really should purchase new ones."

"A common problem, it seems." Max moaned.

Cassia placed her hand on her husband's arm. "Max, not yet."

Gallus gestured to the couches around the low, square table. "What? Has something happened to one of your slaves?"

Cassia shrugged as she reclined next to her husband. "It's our girl from Britannia."

Leonidas entered with goblets and pitchers of honeyed wine. Nicanor placed platters of meat, fresh bread, and fruit before them.

Gallus laughed. "The seer? What could she have done? She can't refuse to prophesy, can she?"

"In a way." Max rolled his eyes.

"Explain." Gallus reached for a piece of beef.

"That newcomer. Paulos?" Cassia spoke around a fat grape in her mouth.

"Please don't tell me he's already causing problems?"

She raised a brow. "What do you mean 'already'?"

"Never mind. Go on."

Cassia frowned. "He did something to her. Now she can't tell the future."

The incident in the forum. For now, Gallus would just keep to himself that he'd seen that.

"Cassia. Let me speak." Max silenced his wife. "We invested three years' pay in her. And now she's worthless. Today I gave back almost three months' profit to people whose fortunes proved false."

"And why do you think this is the newcomer's fault?"

"Because it has happened only since he spoke to her."

"I see."

"So what remedies do we have against this Paulos?"

Just when it looked like the visitors might not cause any trouble. "Are you sure he is the one who caused your slave to not be able to tell the future?"

"I saw him talk to her. He told 'the spirit' to come out of her."

"What kind of prophecies did not come true?"

"She told a man it was safe to travel; he drowned at sea. She told another he would be granted citizenship; he was denied. She told a man his wife was faithful—he caught her in bed with his brother!"

"She told a man he should not go to court against his abusive employer. He did not. Another did and won huge damages." Cassia shrank back as Max glared at her.

"Those are all very circumstantial cases." Gallus sighed. "I'll tell you what the law says. For the second—he could still gain the citizenship later, so not necessarily false. Third case—she could have been faithful at the time the man came to see her. Fourth—doesn't mean the man in question would have won because the other man did. The only possible false case is the first. And unless he specified travel by sea, that one is in question as well."

"But she was never wrong before!" Max's voice echoed in the tiled room.

"I'm only telling you what a jurist will say." Gallus paused. "How much were you earning from her?"

"Cassia keeps the records."

"Oh, I can speak now?"

Max glared.

Thank Jupiter Gallus didn't have a wife. Wasn't worth the anguish. Slaves would suffice.

She rolled her eyes. "We haven't had her a year yet, but it would have been about 15,000 sesterces a year. We had planned to recover her purchase price in about a year and a half."

"You're going to have to let me study the laws on this and see what can be done to recover your lost income. I have a great deal of latitude on this as magistrate, but I can only stretch the law so far."

Max slammed his fist on the table. "There must be something we can do. He has ruined us!"

Jupiter, grant me patience. "Trust me, I don't want him to get away with this any more than you do. You'll have to let me research this a little more. Let me study him, study the situation."

Max smirked. "There are still other ways we can get money from her."

"You're not getting any money out of her that way any time soon," Cassia said.

Gallus looked from one to the other. "Where is she now?"

"At our house. Recovering," she said.

"Recovering? From what."

"Max punished her. She couldn't even stand up when we left."

"That makes damage nearly impossible to prove. Any harm Paulos did will be obliterated by the damage you did." Gallus took a piece of meat from the platter and bit off a piece.

Cassia smacked Max's arm. "I told you not to hit her!"

"You did not!"

"Quiet! Both of you! I will try to help you but I will not listen to you bicker. You can fight with each other, or you can fight this Jew. When you decide, let me know."

TIA PUSHED herself up on the sleeping mat, every muscle screaming in pain. Her arms were already turning blue and purple. Moving her jaw nearly caused her to cry out. She brought her fingers to her cheek—she couldn't touch it without flinching. The flesh under her eye felt swollen. When she brought her hand away, her fingertips were dipped in blood.

Max's seal ring. It must have cut her, more than once.

They obviously didn't care if her bruises were noticeable this time. It was clear she could no longer tell fortunes. Not since the incident with Paulos. They had no need to keep her presentable now, so why not hit her even on her face?

Grabbing the edges of the mat, she pushed herself to a standing position. She waited a few moments to catch her breath. Every time she pulled air into her lungs was an experience in pain. The kicks Max had delivered must have broken a few ribs. She hobbled to the table where a servant had left some bread and water. The usually good food was gone, like the normally good care she received. Another bad sign.

What would they do with her now? Turn her into a household servant? A farm slave?

Or worse? She shivered at the despicable images that rushed into her mind. Her already weak legs threatened to give way.

Grabbing a piece of crusty bread, she shuffled to the wall and leaned her back against it. Sitting on the floor again would hurt too much.

Forget killing Max. She would need to set aside revenge for Tancorix's death. She had to escape. There was no other way out. She'd never survive otherwise. If running away killed her, or her owners did when they caught her, she'd end up no worse off than she was now.

But she needed a plan. Even if she could get out of the house, she couldn't simply walk through town and out the gate. She had to think it through.

Obviously, it had to wait until after dark. There would be a full moon tonight, which would make traveling less difficult, but also finding her easier.

She had to do it alone. Surely some of the other servants would offer help, but that would only lead to retribution for them.

Should she try to take the clothes they had bought for her?

Her tunic was ripped and stained with blood. She'd need something else to wear to avoid looking like a runaway. And if she took refuge in the marsh south of town, she'd need something warmer, but on the other hand carrying anything might slow her down and draw unwanted attention.

What about food for the journey? She couldn't get any without letting someone else know what she was planning, and that was too big a risk, for her and for them.

And what about money? Was there anything small she could sell later? She scanned the room. Nothing in here. If she got out? In the main house?

Max and Cassia were at Gallus's house for cena. She'd heard them talking. With all the wine that would surely be served, they wouldn't be back until near morning.

Perhaps she could hide in the marsh awhile and head south later, toward Amphipolis. Or east of here to the port she'd been brought to after being purchased in Ephesus.

She could figure out later where to go next. Her first task was to get out of this house. Out of this room. They kept the door locked whenever they left her in here. Maybe the goddess was on her side tonight. She hobbled to the door, jiggled the handle. It was loose, but not loose enough. Her heart sank.

She jerked hard on the handle, pounded on the door a couple times. Leaning her head against it, she cried to Brigid. *Why? Why can't you help me? Have you left me completely? You obviously aren't letting me see the future anymore.*

She was going to die here, in this room. After who knew what Max would do to her.

What about Paulos's God? If he was more powerful, could he help?

But she didn't even know his name. How could she ask him?

"God of Paulos, if you are real, if you are the Most High, please help me."

The door jiggled, pushed into her.

She scurried back against the wall, bolts of pain racing through her body.

"Tia?"

Euodia. Cassia's slave—the first person to show her any kindness in this horrible place.

"Are you all right?"

Tia straightened, wincing. "I'm all right. Thank you for checking."

Euodia entered, carrying an oil lamp. She shut the door behind her. "I heard—oh my!" Her eyes were as wide as bronze coins.

"What?"

"Your face, your arms. You are one huge bruise." She covered her mouth with her hand. Her eyes blinked back tears.

"I fell. Thank you for checking. You can go now." She hobbled away.

"Are you sure? Can I bring you anything?"

"I don't think you should. You'd better go."

"I heard . . ." Euodia hesitated. "Did you call out to the God of Paulos?"

"Of course not!" she hissed. "Are you trying to get me beaten even worse than I already am?"

"No. But I believe in Yahweh, the God of Paulos. And He can help you, if that's what you want."

Her breath caught. Was this a trick? "Why would you believe in Paulos's God?"

"I heard Paulos talk by the river, and I know his God, my God, is real."

"Good for you. But no one can help me. I'm stuck here."

"I'll help you."

"You'll get caught and then we'll both be in trouble. I don't want you to end up looking like me."

"This lock has always been tricky. If it happens to fail . . . and if you happen to wander off late in the night after everyone is asleep, and go south, and then right along the wall to the Marsh Gate, who can be blamed? While the domini are getting drunk with Gallus instead of home, they have no control over what can happen."

It sounded so good, so tempting. But could she do that to this young girl? "No. No, I can't let you do that. If they beat you I would never forgive myself."

"They won't know anything."

"How do you know someone hasn't already seen you in here, and when I 'escape,' they will tell the domini, and they will think it was you, whether you help me or not."

She smiled brightly. "The domina would never let Max hurt me. I do her hair and apply her cosmetics every morning, like I did yours. She's an incredibly vain woman, so I'm too valuable to her. And you may as well let me help you. Because I believe that is why Yahweh had me in this house and let me walk by your door tonight."

15

> *"Keep me safe,* Lord, *from the hands of the wicked; protect me from the violent, who devise ways to trip my feet."*
>
> — PSALM 140:4

GALLUS YAWNED. THOSE TWO WERE GOING TO BE THE DEATH OF HIM. Between the rich food, the lack of sleep, the arguing, and the wine they'd consumed, even liberally diluted—and he'd had Leonidas dilute it even further as night dragged toward day—and Max's incessant bragging, Gallus could sleep where he stood.

But they were influential in Philippi, and Gallus needed their support, especially this early in his year of office. Not to mention she was family, and by extension, so was Max. In the morning Gallus would consult with his scriba on the law and find out exactly what could and could not be done to try to recoup some of their losses. Probably not much, but he had to at least look like he'd tried. All that could wait until his head stopped pounding and his vision cleared, though.

He let his toga and tunic fall to the floor and crawled onto his bed.

Shouting in the hallway woke him from slumber a moment later. Or what felt like only a moment.

Who would dare shout like this in his home? Not one of his slaves. They knew he wouldn't hesitate to have them flogged.

"You cannot just barge in his domus like this! I will call for the guards!"

The door to his chamber shook.

"No! I forbid it!"

Nicanor?

"Forbid it? You cannot speak to me in this manner. I'll have you beaten until you cannot stand." Had to be Max. Who else could that be at this hour?

"*He* is my dominus, not you. And if someone is to punish me for disobedience, it shall be him."

Gallus chuckled. Nicanor had more courage than he'd given him credit for. He rose and opened the door.

His slave stood in the doorway, arms spread wide, barring entrance.

"Thank you, Nicanor."

The Greek slave looked over his shoulder. His eyes held sheer terror.

"You may go. You won't be beaten. I appreciate your effort to protect me."

The man's body relaxed as if a temple had slid from his shoulders, and he scurried down the hall.

"Max. I thought we bid farewell."

"She's gone."

Gallus searched through the fog in his brain. She. Cassia? Surely not. "She?"

"The slave! The seer!" His arms flailed wildly.

"The girl from Britannia? I thought you said you beat her. Unmercifully."

"I did."

"And yet she managed to flee from your guarded domus." He tried to keep the scorn from his voice, but judging from Max's face, he hadn't.

"I didn't ask them to keep watch over her. I didn't see the need."

"Apparently you misjudged."

"Apparently." The man's dismay at his loss evidently outweighed his shame and he kept his gaze steady. "Well, are you going to help us or not?"

Gallus yawned and looked at his bare torso and legs. "May I dress first?"

At last, Max's face reddened. "Of course."

"Wait in the atrium." He shooed Max down the hall and pulled the door closed. He dropped back onto his bed. Max still wore the clothes he left in. They must have gone home, found the girl missing, and come straight back. No wonder he could barely think. He'd better come up with something before going out there.

But what?

He rose and paced. Think. How to find a runaway slave?

There were those who specialized in hunting fugitives, but he'd have to send to Amphipolis for them. It would be midmorning before the *fugitivarii* even arrived, let alone started looking for her.

He snorted. How foolish of them. They should have beaten her even more thoroughly, locked her up . . .

Wait . . .

He pulled his tunic over his head and hurried out to the atrium. "I have an idea."

"That's the last one, then." Quin walked the prisoner into the inner cell and turned the key. He climbed that stairs and returned to the small vestibule at the front of the prison. Pulling the wax tablet off the shelf, he grabbed the stylus and etched the name of the last prisoner on it as the trumpet signaled the end of second watch.

Stolos opened the main door and strolled in. "Everyone taken care of?"

He nodded and gestured toward the row of empty cells. "Numerius is sweeping up the cells. I just took the others to the inner cell for the night. When Pandaros arrives, he can go."

"Very well."

"There are three downstairs. One is only in for theft of some bread, so he'll probably be out tomorrow. Bring him up first in the morning so he'll be ready when they come for him." He released a deep sigh as he glanced toward the door. "Pandaros is late again. I'll have to let him go, I think, but I have to find someone to replace him first. I'm going home. I've been up since before dawn."

"Of course, Domine."

"Tribune Quintus Valerius!" The shout came from the street.

"Who's that?" Stolos frowned.

"I've no idea." Quin handed over the keys and exited the prison.

One of Gallus's *lictors* waited. "Quintus Valerius, Gallus Crispus commands your presence."

"Now?"

"Are you refusing?"

"Of course not. Let's go." He took two steps and turned back. "Stolos, throw me my cloak." He waited for the garment. "And Numerius had better wait here until I return. Just in case."

"Yes, Domine."

They walked southeast across the forum and turned south on one of the wide streets to the villas. The night air was cold and he threw his cloak over his shoulder.

When they passed Gallus's house, he was confused, but said nothing. They continued farther south to the villa of Max and Cassia—Tia's owners.

A chill crawled down his back. Why should he be summoned to this house at this hour? He wouldn't be called out to arrest the Jews. That left Tia—

Had his worst fear already come to pass?

The lictor opened the gate and stepped back. Quin strode to the door where a servant took over and led him into the house. "You may wait here."

The room was large and almost completely bare. A couch or two hugged the walls. There were no tapestries on the walls, no statuary on pedestals. The room was utterly devoid of any personality, much like its owners.

Gallus entered from the hall, goblet in hand. "Ahhh, Quin. We have need of your services tonight." He glanced upward through the open ceiling, at a full moon showering the sky with silver light. "And perhaps most of your men."

My men? "Whatever you need, Domine." He bowed.

"My friends' fortune-teller has run away. If she were only a house servant it would be bad enough, and I would call my lictors. But she is not a mere servant girl. She is worth a considerable sum of money to them—every day, in fact—and we need her found immediately." He handed his goblet to a server and laced his hands behind his back as he closed the distance between them. "Quin." He lowered his voice. "I want you to take personal charge of this search, and get your best watchmen searching with you. If you have any friends you can enlist, I will pay them."

"Yes, Domine." She wouldn't run away if nothing had changed. Had they hurt her? "To help me, may I ask a question?"

Gallus nodded.

"Just to determine how far she could go, had she eaten today? Is she a strong girl?"

"A moment." He disappeared and returned with Max. "Tell him what he needs to know."

Max frowned. "She was beaten. Badly."

A nearly overpowering desire to pummel the man washed over Quin, but he quenched it. "And fed?"

"She was left with bread and water but it looked untouched."

His chest ached for her, but he revealed nothing. "And when was this?"

"Last evening."

"So she couldn't have gone far, then."

Max scowled. "I would have said she couldn't cross the room, but obviously I was mistaken."

"Thank you. That will help us narrow our search." He dipped his head.

Gallus waved a hand. "If you can't find her tonight, we'll call the fugitivarii. Now go, quickly."

"At once." He bowed and marched out. When he hit the street he broke into a jog, keeping it up until he reached the prison.

What had happened? How bad had it gotten that she had fled? And what was he supposed to do? They had every legal right to beat her, even kill her, and he had no right whatsoever to stop them. Indeed, he had a duty to obey, to find her and bring her back to them.

So they could beat her again for running away. Or worse.

Stopping at the prison door, he drew in a deep breath, and froze his features into a mask before throwing open the door. He could allow no one to know his dilemma.

"Domine? Is everything all right?" Stolos asked.

"No. I need you to gather all the guards. I want everyone back here at once. Go!"

How was he going to handle this? He couldn't take her back to her domini—he couldn't let her be hurt any more than she already was. He also couldn't shirk his duty. And if he didn't find her, and the slave hunters did . . . the thought of the letters FUG carved into her forehead as a warning to other slaves made him sick.

He paced inside the jail, his stomach in knots, his mind in tangles.

Was there anyone he could trust to help him figure this out?

The men arrived in ones and twos. He needed a plan, fast.

Stolos neared him. "Quin, what's the matter?" he whispered.

"Wait until all are here. I don't want to explain twice. And keep Numerius here at the prison to keep watch."

"Our newest man?"

"We need our best men for this. There aren't any difficult prisoners. He can handle it. You'll be here."

Quin knelt at the cistern in the corner and scooped a cup of water to buy some time. After he splashed some on his face, he rose.

"We have been ordered to find an escaped slave."

"Don't the fugitivarii do that?"

"Usually. But this is an incredibly valuable slave to her owners—the girl who prophesies in the forum each day. They don't want to wait for the fugitivarii." He held his hand up level to his shoulders. "Blond hair, about this tall, blue eyes. She knows no one here that they know of, so she shouldn't have any accomplices. Look everywhere you can think of that someone might hide. Cisterns, alleys, carriages, trunks, etc. Gallus Crispus is friends with the owners, so this is a high priority. Work in pairs. Stolos will assign each pair an area so nowhere is left unsearched. Questions?"

"What do we do if we find her?"

"Bring her here. If I'm not here, wait for me. Anything else?"

Silence.

"Good. Work fast but be diligent."

The men reported to Stolos and headed off in pairs, each to a different part of the city.

"What about me?" asked Stolos.

"You wait here. If they bring her back, take her to Gallus and then come back here and wait for me."

"Yes, Domine."

But by all the gods, even the god of Paulos, he prayed no one found her before he could.

Tia kept her steps through town light, afraid any noise would attract an owner, a guard, even another slave. Euodia had said to go all the way to the end of the street and turn right, then look for the Marsh Gate. Most of the townspeople were still asleep, so there should be no one out. If she did encounter someone, hopefully she saw them before the full moon's light allowed them to see her. Maybe she could hide behind one of the shrubs adorning the walls.

When she reached the Marsh Gate, she breathed a sigh of relief and ran as long and as far as she could. Fear of being caught outweighed the pain.

Heading southwest, as best she could figure, was her smartest option. The marshes there would conceal her the rest of the night and tomorrow if she was careful. Then she could head east for Neapolis, try to slip onto a ship headed . . . anywhere.

Every step was sheer agony, every breath a torment. She kept one arm around her ribs, but it provided little comfort. Her bare feet slipped on the damp grass and she fell more than once as she ran through the night. Her feet burned, her knees stung, bruises formed on top of bruises.

She couldn't keep this up much longer. Her foot hit a wet spot and slid out from under her. Her entire body ended up in the air before it came crashing down hard on the muddy ground. The air was knocked from her chest, and she couldn't draw any more in for what felt like far too long. Just when she thought she might suffocate, she sucked in a chest full of air with a loud excruciating gasp.

Tia rolled to one side, hugging her midsection. Cuts on her feet, her arms, and her legs all demanded attention. Her back, her ribs, and her knees were sore, and she was beyond exhausted. When was the last time she slept? Or ate?

It would be easy to just give up, go to sleep. Maybe she would starve to death. Maybe some animal would get to her.

Or maybe someone even worse would find her.

It would be hard to imagine someone worse than Cassia and Max, but she'd heard horrible stories . . .

Some warrior she was. She'd already abandoned Tancorix. His death would never be avenged. Should she lie here and take whatever Max and Cassia and Philippi handed her as well? Or would she stand up and fight it like the warrior she was taught to be?

Groaning, she rolled to her hands and knees and sat up. Extending her hands, she felt the ground around her. Damp and somewhat muddy, but not soggy. Wherever there was grass, the ground was less wet, better for walking.

She pushed herself up slowly. Careful to place her feet where the grass grew, she made her way to the center of the marsh. If she could get to where the grass was the tallest and thickest, perhaps she could find a spot that wasn't too wet, where she could hide until tomorrow night.

Could she get back to Britannia? How long had it taken to get here? Weeks. She might be able to slip unnoticed onto a ship and get away from Macedonia, but she would eventually be found out and put ashore. Then what would she do? How would she support herself? She wouldn't be able to earn enough to feed herself, let alone enough to buy passage back home. Was there any reputable profession a woman—

Her head slammed against the ground again. She should have been paying closer attention instead of thinking about the future. This time she fell onto a rock. She rolled over and grimaced as she felt her left side, hissed as her fingers found yet another wound. Her ankle ached too. She must have landed on it awkwardly.

She glanced up. The grass was well over her head. Perhaps she should stay here for the night. She was well hidden. She was too tired, too hungry, and too beat up to walk any farther.

The morning wouldn't fix a single one of those problems, except for her exhaustion. She would still be hungry and sore, and it would be light out and easier for her to be found.

But for now, what else could she do? Rested, she might be able to think more clearly. She'd deal with tomorrow's problems tomorrow.

16

> *"He rescued me from my powerful enemy, from my foes, who were too strong for me."*
>
> — PSALM 18:17

SUNLIGHT POURED ONTO THE COUCH WHERE TIA SLEPT. WHY WAS HER room so bright? She tried to stretch, but unimaginable pain gripped her body. Her head pounded. Movement was impossible.

"You're awake." A beautiful woman stood beside the couch.

Who was she? She looked vaguely familiar.

"I'm going to help you sit up, and yes, it's going to hurt." She slipped a hand under Tia's right arm, placed the other one on her left to steady her, and pushed her to a sitting position.

Tia tried to help, but everything hurt. She moaned as the muscles in her stomach worked to right her, but soon enough she sat up and the pain subsided. Most of it, anyway.

"Loukas left a little medicine for you. What he gave you last night has worn off. We'll give it a little time to work, then we have to clean you up." She picked up a bottle with a small amount of liquid in it, removed the top, and handed it to her.

Tia smelled it. She held it up and stared at it. Was it poison? She didn't even know these people. Should she trust them?

Would it really matter if it was poison?

"Drink it. It will take your pain away." The woman had such a kind smile. And Quin obviously trusted her. He could have taken her to Max and Cassia, but he'd brought her here. She uncorked the tiny container and poured its contents into her mouth.

The woman replaced the bottle on the table. "Excellent. Now, I have sent all the men to the forum so we can give you a bath with no fear. Syntyche?" She called into the main house. "Can you bring the supplies?"

"Of course."

"Syntyche is going to help us. You'll like her."

"And you?" Moving her jaw nearly brought tears to her eyes.

"Oh." She laughed softly. "I never told you my name. I'm Lydia, and this is my house. Quin brought you here last night."

"I remember." She spoke keeping her teeth together.

"What else do you remember?"

"Being beaten. Escaping. Hiding in the marsh. Then Quin found me."

"How did you escape?"

"I just did." She was not going to get Euodia in trouble.

Lydia shrugged. "All right."

A young woman about her age carried a large bowl of water to the table. She had dark eyes and darker hair. A much younger girl set down a platter of soap and cloths and oil and left.

"That was Zenobia. Both Syn and Zenobia work for me." She dipped a cloth in the water and drew it over Elantia's face.

She flinched. The water was warm and felt good, but her face was so sore that any pressure at all was painful.

Lydia shook her head. "I'm sorry. I know it hurts, but we have to get all this mud off you. We have to keep your wounds clean, and make sure there aren't any we missed." She rinsed out the cloth. "Syn, hand me the knife."

A knife? What did this woman intend to do?

Lydia gently cut the tunic off Tia's body. "Quickly, Syn. Burn this one, and bring me a clean one for her."

The girl sprinted down the hall.

Her torso was bluish-purple blobs, melding into one another.

Elantia took slow, shallow breaths while Lydia washed and patted dry her abdomen, arms, back, and legs, then applied honey to the cuts. By the time she was done, Syn had returned with a fresh tunic and a pair of sandals.

"Here we are. You'll have to lift your arms once more, but we'll try to be gentle." She raised her arms over her head, sending stabbing bolts of pain through her ribs. She fisted her hands to avoid whimpering.

"Finally. We're done. Now, you must be hungry."

"I'm not sure I can eat."

"Nonsense. You have to eat. You need your strength. Even if you don't feel hungry, you must eat."

"No, I mean, I can't open my mouth."

"You can't . . . what?"

Her cheeks heated and she looked away. "It hurts too much."

"Syn, do you think you could find us some juice? We need to get something in her."

"What kind?" The girl looked at Tia as if she must eat something other than normal food.

"Anything. Whatever you like."

She nodded and left again.

The woman certainly was friendly with her slaves.

Lydia sat beside her, studied her. "Did he kick you in the face?"

Tia shrugged. "He punched me. Maybe, I don't know. I blacked out."

Lydia took her hand. "I'm so sorry. No one should be treated this way. I forget how badly slaves are treated sometimes."

Syn set two pitchers on the table next to them. "Apple and grape."

Turning to Tia, Lydia reached for a cup. "Which do you prefer?"

She shrugged. Did it matter? Would she be able to taste it?

"Grape," Lydia whispered.

The girl poured a large cup.

Elantia held the cup to her lips and winced, pulling it back. She touched her mouth with her other hand. Her lips were badly swollen. How many times had Max punched her?

She tried again, more gingerly. The grape juice was cold and sweet, and satisfied a hunger she hadn't felt until the juice hit her stomach. She drained the cup and asked for another before the pain medication started to work. "I'm feeling sleepy."

"That's the medication Loukas left for you." Lydia rose and grabbed a beautifully embroidered blanket from another couch. "Lie down."

Tia lay back as Lydia covered her with the blanket. As she drifted off, she heard Lydia and the slave girl talking.

"Were you ever beaten like that?" the girl whispered. What was her name? Elantia couldn't remember through the medicine's haze.

"Never. I was flogged, but never like that. You?"

"I was beaten many times, but not that badly."

"Come, dear. Let's let her rest." Footsteps retreated, a door closed.

She spoke so sweetly. Why couldn't Lydia have bought her instead of those horrible people? Why couldn't she just stay here now? Was that possible?

Too many questions.

One thing she was sure of—she was never going back to Max. Because she would either kill him, or herself, before she let that happen.

QUIN SPRINTED TO HIS HOUSE. His tunic was filthy, wet, and

splotched in blood. There was no way to explain all of that by saying he was only searching—unsuccessfully—for Tia. He needed to change into fresh clothes. He needed a bath, too, but that would have to wait.

Could he trust Epaphras? Or the girl? They hadn't been with him long. It was hard to tell. He slipped through the door, crept through the atrium and into his *cubiculum* before he could be seen. After tossing his cloak and leather belt to the floor, he jerked off his tunic and rolled it into a ball. Fresh water and a cloth sat by the door, as usual, and he washed the blood and dirt from his arms and neck. The memory of her cradled against him, however, remained.

The new tunics from Lydia lay on his couch. He untied the ribbon and held the first one up by the shoulders. Inspected it, shook it out. It was no wonder she had so many customers from places so far from here. The work was exquisite. He pulled it over his head and belted it.

He turned around to find his tunic had disappeared.

He padded into the kitchen. The girl—Charis?—stirred chopped apples into a huge bowl of porridge. The fire was going well, and Epaphras stood over it, the bloody tunic in hand. The Greek glanced at him briefly before tossing the garment into the fire. The cloth did not catch fire, and Quin froze for a moment. Finally, it exploded into bright orange flames. The fire consumed it quickly and left no evidence.

Without a word, Charis picked up a small bowl, ladled some porridge into it, and handed it to Quin along with a piece of bread.

"Thank you."

She glanced at him but remained silent.

"Let me wash your feet and get your sandals. Please sit," Epaphras said.

Quin shook his head. "That's not necessary."

"Domine." His eyes dropped to Quin's feet.

"What?" He spoke with a mouthful of food.

Epaphras pointed at his feet.

To appease him, Quin held his bowl to one side and looked

down. His feet and boots were caked with mud up to his shins, with splashes higher than that. How would he explain a perfectly clean tunic—obviously freshly washed—and muddy boots?

Quin sat while the young servant prepared a bowl of warm water and carefully washed his feet. Epaphras reached for a bottle of olive oil and dabbed some on each of the cuts on Quin's legs. "Are you leaving again? I think you must wear your sandals. Your boots must be cleaned."

"All right. I'm to visit the duovir and then I'm going to the prison."

"Very well." As he dabbed oil on the cuts on Quin's arms, he glanced up at Quin through his lashes. "You did not return home all night. I trust everything is all right?"

Quin sighed. "No, not really."

"May I do anything to help you, Domine?"

"Not that I can think of."

"I'll get your cloak. There was some mud at the bottom, which I brushed off, and a little blood on the inside, but I don't think anyone will see it. I'll wash it later." Epaphras returned quickly, sandals, cloak, and belt in hand. "I shall pray for you. As I do every day." He smiled and left.

Quin finished his porridge and then jogged across the forum to Gallus's villa. *Pray for me. To whom, I wonder?* And could he trust Epaphras to keep his mouth shut about the bloody tunic?

A servant unlocked the gate of Gallus's home and ushered Quin into the atrium.

Quin avoided pacing as he waited for the magistrate. He mustn't appear concerned in any way.

Gallus plodded into the room. His blotchy face and red-rimmed eyes belied his clean toga. Must have been a late, wine-soaked night. Even after the discovery of Tia's escape.

"Quin. What news do you have for us? I trust you or your men found her."

He bowed. "I must apologize. We searched all night. I just returned myself. We found not a trace of her. I had fourteen men on the detail, each assigned to a specific area so no part of the city would go unsearched. We looked in every area that could possibly hold a person. We found nothing."

"Nothing?" The ruler rubbed his palm over his stubbled cheeks. "She couldn't have left the city, do you think?"

"Where would she go, alone? She would be recognized as a runaway instantly. Her Latin is good but heavily accented."

"True. And a girl like her could never survive in the marshes or the mountains."

Quin bristled. *She's not a girl; she's a warrior. You have no idea what she's capable of.* "Perhaps she had an accomplice."

He brightened. "Then we shall post a reward. Maybe someone noticed something and will come forward. It really doesn't matter now, anyway."

"Doesn't matter?"

"Max and Cassia say she isn't worth anything to them now."

"Because she ran away?"

He laughed. "By Jupiter, no! Because she can no longer tell the future."

"She can't?"

"That's why she ran away." He accepted a goblet of wine from a servant and sipped from it.

"I don't understand."

"And it isn't necessary that you do. You may call off the search, but keep your men on the lookout for her."

"They're not just giving up such a valuable slave, are they?"

"They're not certain what to do yet. I'm meeting with them later today." He took a long draw of wine.

So much wine, so early in the morning.

"Why are you still here? I'll let you know when I need you." He waved his hand toward the gate.

As he left, Quin reviewed this new information. What did Max and Cassia have in mind? Whatever it was, it couldn't be good for Tia.

And they had Gallus's ear, so they had all the power they

needed to do whatever they wanted. To whomever they wanted. To Tia. To Paulos.

To him.

Tia may not be able to tell the future anymore, but no one needed a seer to know something bad was going to happen, and very soon.

TIA RECLINED on one of Lydia's many couches in the peristyle, her head on a few wool-stuffed silk pillows. The medicine's fog had evaporated, and her thoughts were once again clear.

This was a far cry from hiking through the marshes on her way to Neapolis to board a ship. How would she ever get out of Philippi now? Would she have to try to escape in the dead of night again? She couldn't ask Lydia and Paulos and the others to help her. She'd already put Euodia in danger—she would do that to no one else.

She'd already abandoned her plan to avenge Tancorix's murder. Should she now give up her plan to regain her freedom as well? That is not what her tatos would expect of her, not what a warrior would do.

She needed to keep thinking, keep looking for a way out.

She sat up as an older man entered the peristyle, his face brightened by his wide smile. Taller and thinner than Paulos, he seemed somehow familiar.

He stopped in front of her lectus, a leather satchel in hand. "Do you remember me?"

She searched her memory. He was one of the men who always accompanied Paulos. "Yes, I think so."

"And how is my patient today?"

"Your patient?"

"I'm a physician. I tended to your wounds when Quintus delivered you to us."

She smiled at the thought of being held close against the Roumanos's chest. "I remember."

He smirked. "You remember me, or Quin?"

Her cheeks flamed. Perhaps she should change the subject. "Thank you for helping me."

"How are your wounds today? And your head? Does it still ache?"

"Some. But much better, thanks to you."

"Yahweh has been good to us." He lowered his lanky frame to the couch, his long legs stretching toward the door. "May I check your ankle?"

"Of course." She twisted toward him.

He placed her foot in his lap and unwrapped the linen bandage. "How does it feel today?"

"Stronger. I took a step or two on it this morning."

"And?"

"I could bear my weight but it's still painful." She winced as he pressed on the ankle in various places.

"It will be for quite some time. Do you need anything for the pain?"

She shook head. "It's bearable without anything. Besides, the medicine makes me sleepy."

"Very good."

"How is she doing?" Quin strode into the room, his red cloak fluttering behind him.

"Ahh, your rescuer has come to visit." Loukas rose and grasped Quin's arm. "Did you meet with Gallus?"

"I did. Yesterday."

"And is he satisfied?"

Satisfied with what?

"For now." Quin answered the medicus but his attention was firmly fixed on her.

Loukas smiled. "I'll be in the peristyle if you need me." He gathered his instruments and left.

Quin grabbed a low stool from its place near the wall and set it before her. "I came by yesterday, but Lydia said you were resting." He lowered himself to the wooden seat, his crimson cloak puddling on the floor around him. Even seated, his frame was imposing, especially in his tribune's uniform.

"I think I slept all day and all night."

"I'm sure you were exhausted." He removed his cloak and draped it over the end of her lectus. Leaning forward, he rested muscled arms on his knees.

"Thank you, for what you did. You must have put yourself in great danger."

"Not really."

She picked at her nails, unable to meet his gaze. "Lydia said you told the magistrate you couldn't find me."

"I did."

"Is that what Loukas meant by 'satisfied'?"

"For now he believes we couldn't find you."

"What if he finds out? That you lied?"

He laughed dryly. "He's already stolen my land. I've lost my military career. I can't go back to Rome. What's left to be done? Put me in prison?"

"I'm afraid they'll find me here." Her admission shocked her. Fear was not an emotion she was familiar with. And why would she tell him that?

"They won't." He reached for her hand.

She raised her face to find his light eyes fixed on hers. "I'm even more afraid of what they'll do to all of you when they do. I know what the penalties are for runaway slaves." Apprehension washed over her like an icy north wind. "And for those who harbor them."

"Tia, I will do whatever I can to protect you. I would give my life to keep you safe."

She barely knew him. "Why?"

"Why what?"

"Why would you do that?" She'd been nothing but miserable to him ever since she'd learned he was a tribune. A leader of those who had invaded her land. And she wasn't all that nice to him to begin with. He was, after all, Roumani.

He moved to sit beside her. "I don't like what they did to you. I care about you, about what happens to you. And for some reason, I feel responsible for you."

"Because you fought in Britannia?" She studied him. A scar that began below his knee ended somewhere under his tunic. More were scattered over his arms, a couple on his face. The Britanni warriors fought when necessary, to protect their homeland, or to hunt. Bodies were damaged. But this man had been fighting almost continually for six years at least, and his body bore the evidence.

He winced. "Partly. I don't know why. I just do. Maybe I want to do something good for once."

"You already have," she whispered. "You brought me here."

He tilted his head, hovered his hand over her purple cheek. "I'm sorry they did that to you."

"I must look terrible." She turned her face away.

"No." He placed a fingertip on one of the few places without a bruise, and pulled her face back. "You're beautiful."

She knew better. She could feel the cut on her swollen lips. Knew her jaw must still be black and blue because of the pain she felt every time she opened it to speak. Felt the puffiness around her eyes. But she believed he meant what he said.

"What's wrong?"

"Nothing. Why?"

"You're frowning."

"Just thinking." Less than a year ago he was her mortal enemy. Was he now her truest ally?

She had no doubt he could protect her body. But what about her heart?

17

> *"I will save you from the hands of the wicked and deliver you from the grasp of the cruel."*
>
> — JEREMIAH 15:21

QUIN WANDERED THE DARK STREETS OF PHILIPPI. THE FACT THAT HE hadn't the slightest idea where to look only added to his apprehension. His men covered the city. There was little chance he'd find her first if she had hidden anywhere within Philippi.

That left only outside the city walls.

Would she venture that far? He would have. Any warrior would have. A good soldier would have tried to get as far away as quickly as possible. But in which direction?

Wounded, she would avoid the mountains. She couldn't travel on the roads. That left only one option.

He winced at the thought of her alone, and cold, hiding somewhere so far from home. She had no allies here that he knew of. No one would help a runaway slave; the penalties were too severe. He was risking his own life as it was.

He wasn't even sure why. She'd told him, quite clearly, to stay away from her.

Still, he couldn't abandon her. She had no one. He knew what that felt like.

She may be a woman, but she was Britanni. Gallus may not know what the Britanni were like, but he did. He'd seen them, battled them, and his body was marked with the evidence of their bravery and strength. Their women stood beside the men, spears in hand. And much like the Roman soldiers, they would rather face death than run from a battle. They didn't fear death.

He'd never seen her personally on the battlefield, but she was a warrior. Her fiery blue eyes came to mind. Her resolute face. If Tia had made up her mind to leave, she would find a way, or die trying. But even warriors needed help when wounded. He had to find her and get her tended to.

Wasn't the man traveling with Paulos a physician? Paulos was a Jew, and Jews didn't own slaves, as far as he knew. The Macedonians didn't own slaves. Macedonians were turned into slaves by Romans.

He sprinted down one street all the way to the end, around the corner, and worked his way back to Lydia's. He knocked softly on the door.

No one answered. A soft light came from under the door—someone had to be awake. He knocked harder, shifting his weight and glancing around. Footfalls from inside grew stronger.

The door opened slightly and a wide-eyed servant slammed it.

Quin's heart nearly stopped. He'd forgotten about his Roman uniform.

A moment later Lydia came to the door. She opened it wide, smiling. "Quin, I thought it might be you. You nearly scared Demas to death. He belonged to a tribune before I bought him and set him free. A tribune, I should say, who was quite cruel to him."

"Oh, I'm sorry. I didn't mean—"

"I know you didn't. Now why are you here at this hour? Are you well?" Her gaze skimmed over him.

His heart pounded. Maybe this wasn't a good idea.

"Quin?"

"I need your help."

"Of course. Whatever I can do for you, I will. What's wrong?" She led him into the atrium.

"It's Tia, the seer."

She laughed softly. "What about her? Are thoughts of her keeping you awake at night?"

"She's run away. They beat her, apparently quite badly, and she's escaped."

Her face lost its color. "Oh, Quin, you cannot get involved in this. Whatever they do to her, they will do to you as well."

"I'm already involved." He groaned. "Gallus has sent me to find her."

She let out a slow breath.

"Lydia, I have to help her."

He dropped onto the couch.

"Is this about your time in Britannia?"

He shrugged.

She took his hand. "Quin, it was your duty. And I thought once you knew where she was from, you'd figured out you hadn't destroy her village."

"Just tell me, if I find her, can I bring her back here for Loukas to treat her wounds?"

"Of course you can." The physician's voice startled both of them.

"Loukas!" Lydia stood. "It's too dangerous."

"I'm a medicus. It's my duty to help anyone who needs me. If you don't want him to bring her here, I'll meet him somewhere else."

Lydia thought for several moments. "All right. If you find her, you may bring her here. But I beg you, try not to be seen."

"What if we have Timos keep watch for them? Do you have any idea where you will look?"

"I've sent my men to look all over the city, but my best guess is she didn't stay here. She went either to the marshes or the mountains."

"Timos can wait by the gate and let you know if it's safe to come in." Loukas glanced at the stairway. "I'll ask him if you want."

She nodded, and Loukas bounded upstairs.

Lydia paced, rubbing her hands together, chewing on her bottom lip.

Loukas returned with the young man, still half asleep.

"I'll be happy to help you. I'll wait at the Marsh Gate. If I'm not there, I had to walk away for a few moments to avoid suspicion. Just wait and I'll come right back." He yawned. "Does that sound all right to you?"

"Thank you. All of you. I hope I can find her."

Loukas glanced up at the sky. "You better leave now. You don't have many hours until dawn."

"We'll be praying for you both." Lydia kissed him on the cheek.

The ache in his leg reminded him how long it had been since he slept, or even rested, and he shivered as he stepped onto the street. Was it from fear or cold? He'd faced the Britanni with less trepidation than he felt right now. He'd faced death countless times, explored new lands, spent weeks on a ship wondering if his pater would let him in the door of their home.

But he'd never been as afraid as he was right now.

TIA TOUCHED HER LIPS. Her stomach rumbled. She shivered in the bleak, pre-dawn air. When did it get so cold? Raising her head, she peeked over the grass just enough to see the barest bit of gray in the east.

God of Paulos, thank You for protecting me while I slept.

She turned onto her stomach and tucked her arms in. Even on the cold ground, the move held in some warmth.

Rustling caught her attention. Her stomach clenched. Was someone looking for her? No, it must be her imagination.

Closing her eyes, she breathed deeply. She needed to relax. If she intended to travel to Neapolis, or anywhere, she really should get a little more rest.

That noise again, the rustling. She drew her legs up, curled in a ball. Pulled the grasses down around her. No, that might leave a hole someone could notice. She let them go, watched them spring back up. Heard them rustle, and grimaced. Did anyone hear that?

The rustling grew nearer. And footfalls. Someone was coming. She clenched her fists, remained as motionless as possible. Her throat burned.

"Elantia?"

She held her breath. Who was calling her name?

"Tia?"

Was that . . . ?

The reeds above her were pulled away. Above her knelt Quin. Was he here to take her back to her owners? That was his job. If she knew anything about him, it was that he was a good soldier. And she had done nothing to make him feel anything but anger toward her.

She closed her eyes and turned away, burying her head in the mud. *Warriors don't cry.*

"Elantia." Rough fingertips softly moved her hair from her face. "I know a safe place I can take you, if you'll let me."

"Please don't take me back to them," she whispered.

"No, I won't. Of course not."

She looked up at him. "Didn't they send you to find me?"

"Yes, but I have the guards searching inside the walls. I came to look out here. This is the direction I would have gone." He smiled. "I'm so glad I found you."

"You're really not going to return me to Cassia and Max?"

"I promise."

Could she believe him? "But you're a soldier. You obey orders."

"Not this time. I'm going to take you to a doctor. But we need to hurry, before it gets too light."

The tears she'd held at bay all night threatened to fall. She nodded.

"I'm going to pick you up. I know you're bruised and sore, and I'm sorry if I hurt you. Can you roll onto your back?" As she complied, he unfastened the fibula at his shoulder, took off his cloak, and draped it over her. Slipping one arm under her knees and one under her back, he slowly stood. She wrapped an arm around his neck, and he cradled her battered body close to his. His warmth soaked into her, erasing the icy cold of the wet ground and chilled air.

She could stay here forever.

Marching quickly but smoothly, he carried her to the Marsh Gate, slowing as he neared the city walls. He bent his face next to her ear. "I've arranged for a friend to meet us here. He'll make sure no one is watching." His warm breath flowed over her skin, causing her to bury her face in his neck.

He hugged the wall, crept forward. He stopped, the gate just around the corner.

"Quin?" A voice drifted toward them.

She stiffened and pulled her arm around his neck tighter.

"It's all right. It's my friend, Timotheos."

She let out a breath, relaxing slightly.

He crept around the corner. "Are we safe?"

She peeked out over her arms. The young man who had been with Paulos waited for them. A mop of dark curly hair framed an open face as he beckoned them near. "Yes, for now. I'm Timos. Follow me. Stay back just far enough that I can signal you if someone comes out."

Quin nodded. "Go quickly."

The trio made their way through the city, quickly reaching the more lavish homes southeast of the forum. Timos opened Lydia's door and stepped aside.

Quin let out a long breath when the door latched behind them. Following the youth into the house, he carried her into the atrium, somehow managing not to jostle her.

The young man turned to him and gestured to a room off the atrium. "I'll wake Loukas."

Quin gently laid her on a couch and slipped his arms from under her.

She missed the warmth of his body next to hers, but she craved even more the way he'd made her feel safe, like nothing on earth could harm her.

Even if it wasn't true.

QUIN REMOVED his cloak from Tia and set it aside. She seemed so fragile. Her tunic was ripped and dirty, her bare feet cut and bloody. He stepped back into the atrium and located a bowl of water and fresh towels used to wash the feet of visitors. In the short time he was gone she'd fallen asleep. He sat at the end of the couch and lifted one bloody foot. Setting the bowl beside him, he soaked the cloth and drew it over her skin. Even asleep she flinched. So many cuts.

"I can do that for you." A young servant girl—Syntyche?—appeared in front of him.

"No, thank you. I'll do it."

"Something to eat for you then?"

"Sure. Thank you." He smiled at the girl and she scampered off. He dried Elantia's foot and reached for the other one.

"Quin." Loukas's voice boomed from across the room.

"Loukas. Please tell me you can help her."

"Let me see."

Quin started to rise, but the doctor put his hand on his shoulder. "Go ahead and finish. It will help me assess her wounds and I can start elsewhere."

Loukas examined her head while Quin finished washing her feet. The doctor grabbed another cloth and drew it down her arm just enough to see bruises along the length of it. After loosing her sash, he took a knife and cut a long slice in her tunic. Her torso was purple. Older, darker bruises peeked from beneath new red ones.

Quin nearly threw up. He'd seen more than his share of wounded, even dismembered soldiers. But for some reason . . . He set her feet aside and stood, began to pace. His thigh ached more than usual from the uneven ground and carrying Tia, but it had been worth it.

Lydia entered and gasped at the sight of the beaten woman. "Oh, Quin." She wrapped an arm around his waist and patted his chest. "Don't worry. Loukas can do marvelous things with God's help."

Quin scoffed. "Why did your god let this happen if he is so powerful and good?"

"I don't think you're ready to hear anything I have to say right now. Come, sit."

She led him to a couch nearby.

He sat and rested his head in his hands.

"You care very much for her, don't you?"

He didn't respond. How could he answer that? He barely knew her, yet he was inexplicably drawn to her.

He jumped up. "I have to report to Gallus."

"What will you tell him?"

"What do you think I'll tell him? That I couldn't find her. I'm going to lie."

"Do you think that's wise?"

"Would you rather I sent him here?"

"No, but I'm not sure lying is your best option, either."

"I don't know what else to do." He shrugged. "I have to go." He moved toward Loukas. "How is she?"

"A severely twisted ankle, broken and bruised ribs, lots of deep bruises and cuts. She'll be very sore for quite a while, but I think she'll recover nicely, thank Yahweh."

"If she recovers, it will be due to your expertise, not his." He snatched his cloak and stormed out, slamming the door behind him.

18

> *"The* Lord *helps them and delivers them; he delivers them from the wicked and saves them, because they take refuge in him."*
>
> — PSALM 37:40

The handball game was doing little to distract Gallus's mind from his frustrating land deal. He'd heard nothing from Patroclus for over a week, yet it shouldn't take this long for such a prime parcel to sell. At least that was what the Greek had led him to believe. Thank the gods Gallus hadn't paid him anything up front, or he would think the man had been telling him whatever he wanted to hear to get a fat fee from him for doing a lot of nothing.

Gallus smacked the ball with his open hand and sent it sailing. It bounced against the wall and flew back toward them.

Max was unable to return the serve.

"Twenty-one."

"That's enough for me. I'm ready for the baths." Max picked up the ball and took a towel from his slave.

Gallus dabbed sweat from his face and neck and tossed the

towel at Nicanor. The olive oil he'd applied before exercising snaked down his skin. Three games had tired him, and the baths would soothe his aching muscles. They left the court and stepped next door into the atrium of the baths, paying the fee at the door.

Gallus slipped his feet into the thick-soled sandals Nicanor set out for him to protect his feet from the heated floor, and then the slave removed his exercise clothing and hung it on the pegs on the wall.

Breathing deeply, Gallus stepped into the *tepidarium*. The warm, moist air calmed his muscles and his mind, and Nicanor began to scrape the sweat from his skin with the curved metal *strigil*.

Max raised his arms so his slave could reach his sides. "Cassia's been trying to find a new investment."

"Any luck yet?"

"Nothing as good as the girl. She was extraordinarily lucrative."

Gallus smacked Nicanor on the head. "Gently! Scrape the oil off, not my skin."

"New slave?"

Gallus grunted. "Just clumsy." He gestured toward the exit. "Let's move on."

The pair moved down the hallway. Their slaves followed, carrying towels, oils, and strigils.

Men crowded the heated pool, but space opened for the duovir and his friend. They stepped into the waist-high water, and Gallus took a seat around the side of the pool, allowing the heated water to further soothe his body. He closed his eyes and rested his head on the stone edge.

From the fountain of cool water in the center of the pool, Max's panicked cry disturbed his hard-won peace. "What are you doing? You can't be in here!"

Gallus sat up to see Cassia, flustered and fully clothed, kneeling beside him. Leave it to her to make it past all the bathhouse slaves, guards, and escorts. Agitated males all around the room either sniggered or frowned, sending slaves for the attendants.

Cassia tried to catch her breath. "I was on my way home from

Amphipolis, and I stopped by the marketplace. I noticed one of those visitors, the tall one."

"And?"

"And he was buying opium and bandages."

"Again, so?" Gallus beckoned her to get to the point.

"Those are all supplies a medicus would use."

Gallus groaned. "He is a physician, you know." He laid his head back on the side of the pool.

"And those are the exact supplies our seer would need should someone decide to tend to her wounds. He would need to replace them if he had used his on her."

"He could also have used them to tend to a myriad of other injuries."

"What if she was only claiming not to be able to tell the future anymore, so we would only *think* her worthless, and then sell her cheaply, so someone, like the physician, could profit from her instead?"

"That is a *huge* leap of imagination." Gallus spoke without opening his eyes. "And why would you choose him as one to try to steal her from you?"

"He travels." Beside him, Max finally spoke. "He could take her with him and see a profit everywhere he goes. Far more than he does as a medicus."

"And when did he have access to her to convince her to join him in this scheme?"

Large, well-muscled men appeared behind Cassia.

"I'm not sure about that yet," she said, glancing over her shoulder.

"This is an outrageous accusation to make." Gallus beckoned to the attendants.

The largest of the men knelt by the pool.

"She is my cousin. Handle her gently, or you answer to me, understand?"

He nodded and rose, then headed to the exit, Cassia and the others following him.

"Just one moment!" Escaping her handlers, Cassia sprinted back toward Gallus. "I still think he is treating her. He was with that Jew when he talked to her, and ever since then, she hasn't been able to see the future. Either way, those newcomers are responsible."

"*If* they have her. You still don't know if any of these claims are true. We need to verify at least one of them before we proceed."

The attendant closed his arms over his substantial chest.

"Can't we at least follow him, see where he takes the supplies?"

Gallus waved a hand. "It's your time. I can't stop you from wasting it." He glanced at the man behind her, clearly losing his patience. "You need to go, cousin." His voice was softer.

Max scrambled out of the pool to follow his wife, but Gallus remained, hoping to reclaim the relaxed state he'd had before the interruption.

Even if Cassia was right, there really wasn't much he could do. They could possibly file a claim in court, but it was doubtful the foreigners had enough silver to make good on any judgment.

Max and Cassia had enormous influence in the city. And yes, Gallus could use their support and their influence, but once elected as duovir for the census year, he wouldn't need them nearly as much.

Still, she was his cousin, and he would do whatever he could to help Cassia and that fool she married.

Because family was family.

"You have how many brothers?" Tia adjusted her new tunic—a gift from Lydia—as she shifted her position on the couch in the peristyle. The afternoon sun streamed through the open roof, warming the late fall air to a comfortable temperature.

"Four. All older than I am. And a younger sister." Quin's smile surprised her. It wasn't the grin he usually gave her in the marketplace. This was softer, almost sad. "What about you?"

"I have—had—one brother." Her throat burned at the memory

of Tancorix. Guilt set in as she realized she hadn't thought of him in several days. True, she'd been understandably distracted, but still, how could she have forgotten him?

"Tia." His voice called her back to the present. Had he called her more than once?

"What happened to your brother?"

"He was taken at the same time I was. We were both sold to Max, but Max sold him to someone else in Neapolis." She drew in a shuddering breath. "Then, one day, Maximus came back, and I knew Tancorix was dead . . ."

"I'm so sorry."

"He just laughed it off. That was the first time he hit me, because I dared to question him about it. But he was wearing—"

Noise from the front of the house drifted back to the peristyle. Someone was banging on the front door, yelling.

Zenobia raced in from the hallway, eyes wide. "You must go! They're coming!" She grabbed Quin's arm and pulled him behind her. "Lydia says take her and go!" She headed for the servant's entrance at the back of the house and opened it, looking both ways. "I will lead you to her workshop. Hurry!"

Quin grasped her hand and bolted. Thank god—any god—he didn't have his uniform on, or his red cloak would be seen all across the city.

Following the younger servant girl, they raced down the alley between the rows of houses. Pain shot through her ankle, but fear kept her going until they reached a plain building built up against the city wall. No courtyard, no gate. No decoration of any kind. Small windows were built in a neat row high in the wall. The setting sun cast eerie shadows behind them on the stone streets. Her heart pounded in her ears and her chest burned with every heavy breath.

At this time of day, most people were safely in their homes, eating with friends, halfway through their third bottle of wine. Why would Max and Cassia be coming at this hour? Something must have set them off. Did Euodia tell? No. She would never do that, unless perhaps they beat her to make her confess. Loukas wouldn't tell, and Quin was beside her, so it couldn't have been him.

One of Lydia's servants? They adored Lydia. She'd bought their freedom. They would die for her.

Then how? It was unfathomable.

Zenobia turned to face them. "I'll knock, and they'll let you in. You'll be safe inside. No one would ever look for you here. Wait until someone comes for you. Someone you know. Me, Timos, Syntyche."

"Understood." Quin nodded.

A young man opened the door but frowned when he saw a Roman and a bruised girl he apparently didn't recognize.

"It's all right. Let us in, quickly." Zenobia glanced up and down the street.

He stepped aside, and they filed in.

"Lydia wants you to hide them here."

"Not a problem." He beckoned them, and Zenobia left the way she came. "Whatever Lydia wants is fine with me."

"I doubt any respectable Roman would come near here, but just in case, you can duck behind the dye vats here." Smiling disarmingly, he gestured to several enormous vats of bubbling liquid. Purple, blue, red, and several smaller vats of other colors filled the back half of the shop. "Otherwise, you can relax. There are bowls of fruit and several loaves of bread on a table over there."

They wandered in the direction he pointed. A small area off to the side held a pair of couches, and a small table with the bowls of food, as well as two pitchers.

Tia collapsed onto a lectus.

"How's your ankle?"

"It's all right."

He quirked a brow. "May I see?" He knelt before her, his hand near her foot.

She nodded reluctantly.

He slipped his hand under her foot and put it in his lap. Ran his fingers gently over her ankle. "It's swollen again. Running like that didn't help it. You probably re-injured it a bit." He frowned.

"Did I have a choice?" What did he expect her to do? Walk?

He set her foot down gently. "I didn't mean it like that. I only meant I was concerned."

She blew out a long breath. "I know you are. I'm sorry." She leaned near and placed her hand on his cheek. "Thank you for checking it."

"You're welcome." Grinning, he rose and sat next to her.

She almost laughed, even while running for her life. How did he manage to make her feel safe? A far cry from their first encounters. She leaned back against the wall.

"You didn't finish your story. What happened to your brother? How did you know he was dead? Are you sure they didn't just send him even farther away?"

"When Max returned from Amphipolis, he was wearing my bratir's torque. It could only have been removed if—"

"I understand. I'm sorry I brought it up again."

"It's all right. You had no way of knowing." The warmth of his body next to her somehow relaxed her, and the energy of the last moments dissipated, leaving her exhausted. She stifled a yawn.

"Come here." He slipped his arm behind her, tucking her close. "Rest a while," he whispered.

She shouldn't. She should stay awake. Something might happen, and she would need to be alert.

But with his arm around her, it was easy to forget the danger.

It was nice to let someone else handle it, let someone be the protector.

Even if only for a few moments.

QUIN STRETCHED out his legs and leaned his head against the wall. When he'd moved to Philippi, his only goal had been to stay there long enough for the rumors Flavius had spread to die. To let the truth come out. To allow Vespasian to help restore his reputation so he could return to Rome.

Once there, since Pater had nothing for him, he'd have to provide for himself. With the money he'd earned from his land here, he would have enough to buy a respectable estate in the countryside. Nothing huge; just enough to settle down, raise a family.

But as much as he hated to admit it, Elantia was right. That kind of life wasn't possible without slaves. Lots of slaves. And except for Attalos, he'd never really thought about their lives.

Attalos had a wife, and Pater had bought both at the same time. They'd never had children. As educated Greeks, they were house slaves on the estate. Demetria, an excellent cook, worked in the kitchen, and Attalos was tasked with teaching the Valerius sons. The other boys were older and hadn't spent as much time with Attalos as Quin had, but spending nearly all his time with him from the time he was a child had bonded the two, especially after Demetria died. Quin's heart had nearly broken for the man as he watched him grieve.

But how many of his pater's other slaves had been separated from their families? Julius believed that a happier slave worked harder, and he generally treated them well, but that did not stop him from buying only the best, as he saw them. He fed them good food, provided decent quarters, even sent for a physician when needed, but all of that was only so in the end they would generate more for him—more profit, more comfort, more prestige.

And Quin had never even thought twice about it.

Until he met the slave asleep on his shoulder.

What kind of person did that make him?

A Roman. A Roumanos, as she called him. He could hear her saying it, the disgust evident in her voice.

Not only was he Roman, he was a soldier. A soldier who had destroyed villages much like the one she lived in as he served in the famed Legio Secundo Augusta, wiping out one village after another from Cantium to Isca.

Not her village, specifically. But what did that matter? He was part of the power that had come to dominate and destroy her world, the power that had no regard for any people, or culture—or person—that stood in its way of ruling the earth.

Including him.

So why exactly did he want so badly to return to Rome?

Rome wasn't nearly as attractive anymore as the woman in his arms.

He was falling in love with her. Right now, he would give up all he had, which admittedly wasn't much, to stay here with her. If she didn't hate him.

For now, he would enjoy what was probably the only time he would ever get to hold her.

"Quin?" A voice interrupted his thoughts. He looked up.

"Timos?"

"It's safe. They're gone."

"Max and Cassia?"

"Yes, they've left the house."

"Did Lydia convince them Tia wasn't there?"

He shrugged. "For now."

Beside him, Elantia stirred.

If he could make himself not Roman, not a soldier, he would. But he was what he was, so perhaps he could protect her, or at least try.

She would never love him, and he understood why.

So he would be the best warrior he could be.

It was the only option he had left.

19

> *"Two are better than one, because they have a good return for their labor: If either of them falls down, one can help the other up. But pity anyone who falls and has no one to help them up."*
>
> — ECCLESIASTES 4:9–10

SAFELY INSIDE LYDIA'S PERISTYLE, THE WEIGHT OF THE ROOM crashed in on Elantia. She should have known she could never escape. If only she could have kept running, all the way to her roundhouse on the coast of Britannia. In the corner farthest from the door, she huddled against one of the columns that supported the roof of the portico. Her stomach constricted. She doubled over, sobs racking her body.

They had finally won. They had broken her.

They had killed her parents, murdered her brother, sold her, beaten her, taken her goddess . . . she had nothing left. She couldn't even fight back.

A hand landed on her back, causing her to jump. "Tia?"

That familiar deep but soft voice. *Quin.* She straightened, still hugging the column.

"Are you all right?"

"They're going to take me back. They'll find me, and take me home. Even if they let me live, I'll never be free."

"No. No, they won't. Lydia and Loukas won't let them. *I* won't let them."

She turned to face him. He was serious. He believed every word he was saying. But it was impossible. She knew better. It was ridiculous to even begin to hope. "You can't stop them. You know how powerful they are in this city. Whatever they want, they end up getting." She sighed, resigning herself to the inevitable. "I might as well just walk out there and go home with them."

He pointed toward Max's villa. "*That* is not your home any longer. You will never have to go back there, I promise you. I will stop them, whatever it takes."

She drew in a shuddering breath, tears slowly tracing a trail down her cheeks. "No. You can't. There is nothing you can do."

He placed his hands on her arms. "Let me help you."

She huffed, remembering the warrior she once was—the warrior she was no longer. "If I were on the battlefield, I could take care of myself."

"I am quite sure of that."

She shot a glare at him. Was he mocking her? If she had her dagger, he'd find out how well she could defend herself.

"I fought enough of you to know that's true." He smiled weakly. "But this is not a battlefield, and you've been stripped of your weapons, and you are vastly outnumbered. Let me be on your side. Please."

It couldn't be done.

"I'm a Roman. I know how to fight Romans. At least let me try."

He had a point. Several points. She exhaled a long breath. "All right."

Though he was taller than Max, he did not intimidate her as

her dominus did. Or even as he himself had done before. Her heart raced, but not from hate, or even fear.

She laid her hand on the narrow purple stripes of his tunic. "Does this mean anything? Max doesn't have it. Gallus wears it. His is wider, though."

"It represents the kind of family I come from back in Rome. My family is somewhat wealthy and powerful, but not as powerful as Gallus's."

A tinge of fear pricked her heart. "Could you be in danger from him for helping me?"

"Only if he knows. He doesn't, and I'll make sure he never will." He placed his hand over hers, tucking his fingers under her palm.

His heart beat steadily under her hand. She brought her other hand to his chest. "You're not wearing your soldier's uniform."

"I'm not working tonight."

She smiled. "I like you better without it."

"I can still keep you safe from Max and Cassia, though, uniform or no." Keeping her hand in his, he moved it down his chest to the dagger on his hip.

"Why would you do so much for me?"

"Because you're my *carissima*."

"What does that mean?"

His brow furrowed for a moment, as if he were trying to decide how to answer. "It means you're very special to me."

She laid her head against his chest, slipping her arms around his waist. He was strong and solid, like the marble columns behind her, and whether she wanted to admit it or not, it felt good. Comfortable, safe.

His hands settled at her waist. She pulled back to study his face. A long but faded scar ran from his left ear to just under the corner of his mouth. Another slit his eyebrow. Others might see them as flaws, but to her they were proof of his skill, his willingness to suffer for her, even if they had been gained on the battlefields of her homeland. Now he'd promised to use his blade to protect her.

His eyes dropped to her mouth. He lowered his head and pressed his lips to hers.

Her lips were still tender, but his gentleness eclipsed any pain. One hand held the small of her back while the fingers of his other hand rested lightly on her cheek. And as she melted into his kiss, she tried not to think about the fact that she was falling in love with a Roumanos.

QUIN PROWLED the hall of the jail, the feel of Tia's kiss still fresh on his lips, even after a restless night.

Where was Pandaros? Late again. If that man made it until the next full moon without Quin sending him to the quarries, he'd be lucky. He'd been insolent, lazy, careless . . .

The door swung open, and the delinquent guard sauntered in. "Sorry, but I was—"

"I don't care. Just get the cells cleaned out before I return." He slammed the door behind him before Pandaros could begin his daily list of excuses.

Quin hurried to the shops on the south stoa of the forum. The sun had long passed the midpoint of the sky, and it was nearing the time when most Romans stopped working for the day and retired to the baths.

He desperately needed to purchase something from the shops before then.

When he finally reached the wine shop, Marcus was putting away his goods for the day. "Welcome, Tribune. How may I help you this afternoon?"

"I need an amphora of wine."

"Of course. Are you hosting a meal tonight? With many guests?" He skittered his fingers over the medium-sized containers of wine on his shelves. "This is a very nice size for nine or ten people."

Quin held it for a moment but shook his head. "No. One of

those." He pointed to the larger amphorae on the wall. "What about those?"

Marcus put away the smaller one and handed Quin one of those indicated.

Quin studied it a moment and returned it as well. "No. I want something even bigger. And the best you've got. Something you keep hidden, perhaps?"

The merchant smiled and pushed aside a curtain of silk. On the ground sat several amphorae, beautifully decorated, at least a cubit wide.

He leaned over and gestured to those on the very end of the row. "Ah, yes. One of those."

"You must be joking." Marcus scoffed. "That's a month's pay, even for a tribune. Who could you be entertaining that's worth this?"

Quin said nothing. Flexing his jaw, he slapped down the necessary coins on the table in the center of the shop, the last of the money he had brought from Rome.

The vendor quirked a brow and started to pick up one of the requested containers.

"May I?" Quin came alongside him. "I need to be able to carry it in one hand."

Marcus frowned, but stepped aside.

He tested several, finding the largest one that met his stipulation. "This one."

"Here you go, then." Marcus set the jar on the table. "Do you want one of my assistants to deliver it to your house?"

"That won't be necessary." Quin picked up the wine, hoisted it to his shoulder, strode down Commercial Road, and then northeast across the forum.

At the temple of Jupiter, Quin ascended the gleaming white steps and crossed the portico. One of the servants hovering in the vestibule held Quin's offering while he slipped off his sandals and washed his hands and feet. He started to go in, but the attendant touched his arm.

"Your dagger, Tribune. No weapons in the temple."

Quin unsheathed the blade and handed it over. He felt naked without it. When was the last time he'd been out of his *domus*, or tent, without a sword or dagger strapped to his body? Yet it appeared he had no choice.

His offering in his left arm, he silently entered. His bare feet glided over the cool marble floors.

An altar laden with cheese, wine, and bread spanned the width of the far wall. In the center, priests attended a smoldering heifer, black smoke winding its way to the heavens. The acrid smells of burning wood and flesh filled the room.

Quin gingerly approached the altar, surrounded by worshippers. When was the last time he'd made a sacrifice? At least one he actually believed would do any good? Maybe as a child?

He'd worshipped Jupiter when in Rome because it was required. In Britannia, in the midst of war, it was different. There were no temples on the edges of the Empire. Some of the more devout built altars, but he'd never bothered, never thought much about it.

Until now.

Now he would do anything to protect her. Even sacrifice to gods he wasn't sure were really gods at all.

He knelt and placed his offering on the floor, then lifted his right hand to the heavens. What was the prescribed prayer?

"Hail, Jupiter, first and best of all the gods, who oversees all things on earth from the heights of heaven, and rules all of creation by the flash and deafening roar of the thunderbolt. Hear me, Jupiter, to whom belongs power over us and over our foes. Graciously lend me your ears as I reverence you."

What came next? If he made a mistake, he'd have to start all over. "I pray that you will favor me, and grant me victory over my enemies. Visit my enemies, Max and Cassia, with fear and dread, for they practice evil and have harmed someone who is very dear to me. For these reasons, Jupiter, may you be pleased and honored by this gift."

Quin rose, then he lifted the amphora, holding it with one hand as he snapped the neck with the other. "To you, Jupiter, I pour out this portion of wine." He tipped the jar, and the wine splattered over the marble floor, leaving a blood-red trail as it made its way to a drain under the altar.

He set the container aside and waved one palm over the spilled wine, the other raised to the god. "Now, Jupiter, strengthened and honored by this wine that I have poured out to you, I pray that you may favor me and grant me victory over Max and Cassia, and allow me to protect the one they have wronged."

Quin backed away from the altar several steps and turned around. After retrieving his dagger and putting his sandals on, he stepped outside, then dropped onto the steps.

Did that do any good? Would his prayers reach Jupiter? Could the sky god really do anything? It was worth a chance. No one else could help Tia, protect her from those who sought to destroy her.

The only thing her domini cared about was filling their purses with coin. If that meant beating her when she didn't produce enough, that was fine with them. He couldn't let them hurt her again. He would do anything and everything he could think of to stop them.

If that meant pouring out a month's pay of wine to a probably imaginary god, that was the least he could do.

GALLUS RAPPED his gold signet ring on the door of the apartment building. Silence greeted him.

He rapped again. Still nothing. Tapped his foot. It was not wise for the ruler of the city to be seen standing here, outside a run-down *insula* in this less-than-desirable section of the city.

Then again, it couldn't be good for Patroclus, either. He banged his fist on the door, then cradled it in his other hand. The door must be much thicker than it looked.

The same slave answered the door and beckoned him inside,

glancing up and down the street before closing the door behind them.

"What took so long?" snapped Gallus.

The slave led him up the steps without answering and left him in the atrium.

Gallus fingered the sculptures along the walls of the room. They weren't nearly as nice as those in his office, now that he examined them closely. Probably replicas. Cheaper material. The tapestries were much smaller than his. Was this man really as good as he said he was?

"Magistrate!" Patroclus swept in from the other end of his residence, his gold-trimmed robe billowing behind him. "I wasn't expecting you."

Obviously. Gallus moved to meet him, folding his arms across his chest. "I haven't had any news from you in quite some time. I thought I'd come by personally to check on your progress."

Patroclus smiled, an oily smile that made the cheese and bread in Gallus's stomach begin to crawl up his throat. "As I told you, it will take a while for me to locate a buyer for a parcel of this size. As it happens, I am leaving for Amphipolis tomorrow. I have a number of contacts there who might be interested." He still stood in the entrance to the hallway, hadn't yet come fully into the atrium. Apparently, an invitation to the man's office would not be coming this time.

"And why would someone in Amphipolis want property here?"

"They wouldn't live here, of course. They would have servants work the land, and they would collect the income. Most of these men have been here long enough to have managers they trust and feel they can safely leave the property in their hands."

Gallus couldn't imagine ever trusting someone that much. But it wasn't his problem. If they wanted to rely on some manager, let them. "If you take too much longer, I may have to reduce your fee."

The smile on the Greek's face tightened. "That would be impossible. You agreed on the fee at the commencement of our business. You put no limits on the amount of time you allowed me. You may, however, cancel our deal." His voice was still pleasant, but it was clear there would be no negotiating on this point.

Gallus stepped closer. "Make no mistake. I am the duovir. Nothing is impossible for me."

"Fine, then. I shall consider our deal canceled." He turned to go.

Gallus fingered the curls on the statue of Augustus's face. "I can always have you arrested, for dealing outside the bounds of the law."

Patroclus spun back around, eyes blazing. "And I can always tell them whose land I was selling 'outside the law.'"

He picked up the bust of the emperor and turned it over, examining it. "Do you really think anyone would believe your word over mine? I can have a trial started before the week is out."

Patroclus took several hurried steps into the room. "And I can appeal to Rome." He relaxed his shoulders, smirking. "My pater was Roman."

Gallus clenched his jaw. He was a Roman citizen? A Greek like him? How had no one told him this? Then again, no one knew what he was doing. He set the sculpture down carefully. "You have your deal, and your commission. For another two weeks."

Patroclus's snaggly teeth appeared through his wide smile again. "Excellent. I shall see you in two weeks, and not before. Unless I call for you." He whipped his robe around and disappeared down the hall, leaving Gallus standing alone in the atrium.

He found the door and ambled down the stairs. The merchant hadn't even bothered to send his slave to see him out.

How dare he treat a magistrate of Rome like this? As a citizen, he should know better than to disrespect the ruler of his own city. Actions like this could come back to bite him sooner than he might realize.

Still, because he was a citizen, that limited Gallus's options dreadfully. He couldn't have him flogged or physically harmed in the slightest. He couldn't put the man in jail, even if he were able to manufacture some wildly ridiculous charge. Citizens could wait for trial in their own homes. And as Patroclus preemptively stated, he could appeal to Rome before a trial ever started.

So Gallus would just have to shut up and suffer the Greek's impertinence. The thought of 180,000 sesterces, and all that could do for him, would have to be enough to soothe his wounded pride.

20

> *"But their idols are silver and gold, made by human hands. They have mouths, but cannot speak, eyes, but cannot see."*
>
> — PSALM 115:4–5

QUIN STEPPED THROUGH THE DOOR OF LYDIA'S DOMUS AND followed Demas to the atrium.

"I'll tell Lydia you're here."

"Oh. I think I left my cloak here the other day."

"I haven't seen it, but I'll look." He nodded and left him standing by the impluvium.

Quin ambled through the room, stopping at the empty niche in the wall where the household gods normally resided. He ran his hand over the tiled shelf. Did Lydia worship no other gods besides Paulos's?

"Quin. It's good to see you."

He turned to see Paulos stroll into the room, his ever-present, worn tunic now replaced by a brand new one, certainly provided by Lydia, although still plain, brown wool.

"May I see her?"

"Of course. I'd like to talk to you first, if I may."

Quin stiffened. "About?"

"Did I see you exiting the temple earlier today?"

He'd hoped no one had seen him, obviously, but then again, he wouldn't have done it if he hadn't meant it. He exhaled a long breath. "Yes. I did."

"May I ask why?"

"I offered a sacrifice. To Jupiter."

Paulos's face was unreadable. "Again, why?"

"I didn't know what else to do."

"And that was the only option you could come up with?" The old man's voice was calm, unaccusing.

"I didn't think it would hurt."

"I see." Paulos gestured to a couch along the pool. "Sit with me for a moment, won't you?"

Quin joined him on the lectus. Was Paulos upset, disappointed? Angry?

"Tell me your reasons for making a sacrifice at this particular time. I was under the impression you hadn't visited a temple in many years."

He jumped up, throwing his hands in the air. "They came after her, Paulos!"

"I know. I was here."

"You weren't with her in Lydia's dye works. She was terrified. She feels alone, abandoned, and worst of all, guilty that she is putting all of us in danger."

"No one here is being forced to do anything against his will." He fixed his dark eyes on Quin. "Least of all you, I'm guessing."

He huffed. "Of course not. That's not the point."

"And what is the point?"

Quin reflexively fisted the handle of his dagger. "I can't protect her! I don't know how. I'm a soldier. I fight. I conquer. I *kill*. So I prayed to Jupiter for victory over my enemies."

"Who are?"

He had to ask? "Cassia and Max."

Paulos stood and paced a moment, rubbing his beard. "Hmm."

"What does that mean?"

"What?"

"That *hmm*."

"Just thinking. Why do you feel you must kill or conquer in order to protect her?"

"I don't, necessarily. I just don't know anything else. It's what I've been trained to do. It's all I've done for the past fourteen years. It's all anyone has ever wanted from me, the only thing I've ever been good at."

"And why do you believe you are the only one capable of protecting her?"

"Well, *you're* not doing a very good job of it. And neither is your god. I figured it couldn't hurt to ask mine."

"Did you ask my God?"

"To protect Tia? No. Why would I?" He wasn't sure he believed in his own gods, let alone the god of Paulos.

"Perhaps He has a plan for her life."

"Why do you say that?"

"He brought you into her life. He brought me into it."

Was he kidding? "And look at what you've done! You made her unable to hear her goddess and now they've beaten her!"

Paulos arched a brow. "You maintain she would have been better off left as she was? A slave? Barely subsisting? At the beck and call of her domini, day and night, for their amusement? You have no idea what the living God has in store for her, or for you for that matter."

"And you do?"

"No, I don't. I do only what He asks me to do. He only asked me to help free her from the bonds of the spirit that kept her bound."

Quin sighed. "And what happens now?"

"I don't know specifically. I do know this story is not over. The Father is not done with her. Or with you. You must have patience, and you must have faith."

"Faith?" Quin laughed. "Faith has never gotten me anywhere. I had faith in my pater and he disowned me. I had faith in the army, and they discarded me when I was no longer useful." He could hear his voice rising but, for once, was powerless to stop it. "I had faith in Rome and her government, and I was cheated out of my reward for my long, painful years of service. And now I have nothing!" His breath came faster, his heart pounded. He hadn't meant to yell. None of this was Paulos's fault.

"Quin. Sit with me." He sat once again on the lectus beside the pool.

Quin dragged his hand though his hair, trying to slow the pounding in his chest, a pounding he hadn't felt since he was on the fields of Britannia.

"Come." The teacher smiled.

Quin sat once again, sighing deeply. "I'm sorry."

"I understand your frustration. I, too, once felt the need to take matters into my own hands. It didn't end well. I only made things worse, much worse."

For once Quin heard a twinge of regret in the old man's voice.

"I need you to realize something, though. Yeshua loves you, and Elantia, more than you can possibly understand. As much as you want to protect her, He wants to more. As far as you will go, sacrificing to a god you no longer trust in a desperate grasp for hope, He will go further. He loves her—and you and me—with a love unquenchable, undefinable, deeper, wider, higher than you can ever dream of. And He will do whatever it takes to bring to pass what He has in store for her. He doesn't need your help."

"So I just stand and watch while they come take her away? Do nothing?"

"Ah. I never said do nothing." Paulos smiled, his eyes shining bright. "You can work with Him or against Him. Which do you think would be the more profitable way?"

"And how am I supposed to work *with* Him, exactly?"

"You can start by learning more about Him, so you can trust Him."

Quin shook his head. That all sounded very well and good, coming from someone like Paulos, but every time he trusted someone in authority, he ended up getting burned.

There was no reason to think this time would be any different.

TIA WINCED as the brush Lydia drew through her locks pulled a little. "Lydia, what am I going to do if they come back? If they find me?"

"We shall pray that they don't."

"But what if they do?" She fingered the soft petals of a rose planted nearby.

Lydia set aside the brush and moved to the other side of the couch to face her.

Tia looked up. "You know Euodia? The girl who helped me escape?"

"Yes, I know her very well. She comes to pray with us whenever she can. Whenever Max allows her."

"She says she worships Paulos's God."

Lydia nodded, her chestnut curls swaying. "She does. She was with us at the river when he told us about Yeshua."

"But she is still a slave."

"Of course."

"Then what good will it do me to worship him if I will still be a slave?"

Lydia's green eyes widened. "Why did you think that worshipping Him would make you free?"

"Because Euodia said that she believed her god led her to my door that night so she could help me escape. Why would her god want me to escape if he was just going to send me back to them?"

"That's an excellent question. Maybe He did lead her to your door. And maybe He will set you free. I don't know. It is not always possible to know the mind of God."

"But what about Euodia? Is she to remain a slave in the house of Max?"

"You know, I've been a God-fearer for most of my life, and for most of my life, I, too, was a slave."

Tia exhaled a long, slow breath. This beautiful, elegant woman, who owned this huge home, her own business, who spoke with Roumani rulers and slaves alike with the same kindness and confidence, had been a slave? How was this possible? "When? Where?"

"In Lydia. It's a city in Anatolia. A place far away from here."

"Lydia?"

"Yes. My given name is quite difficult to pronounce. When I moved here people called me "the Lydian" or "the woman from Lydia" when they couldn't remember it or say it, and eventually I just became known as Lydia."

Memories of the day Max and Cassia toyed with the idea of changing her name caused her to shudder.

"Are you all right?"

"Yes, I'm sorry. Please continue."

"I was born into slavery. There was another servant there who was a Jew. When I was only a small child, he told us about the living God. Many of us began to worship Him. We would meet late at night after our duties were complete, and he would teach us."

"Weren't you afraid of getting caught?"

"Not really. The estate was enormous, and we all lived in another building. There was little chance of the dominus finding us. But the point is, I was still a slave for many, many years after I came to know about and worship the living God. I grew up and married as a slave. I learned about dying cloth. And it was not until about ten years ago that I was given my freedom, when the dominus died and freed us all. Then my husband and I came here to Philippi, and he died shortly after we arrived."

"Oh, Lydia, I'm so sorry."

"But, Tia, think about this. If I hadn't been a slave in that household, I would not have heard about the living God, or learned to dye, or met my husband. I would not have come here to Philippi, I wouldn't have this house and I wouldn't be able to help you."

"So . . . God made you a slave so you could help me?"

Syn entered the peristyle, carrying a platter of fresh fruit and bread. She placed the food on an empty lectus and sat beside it.

"I'm not sure I would say that. I don't think He plans for evil to come into our lives. But I will say that God can enter into even the worst situations in our lives, and turn them into blessings, if we let Him."

"So, back to Euodia, then. Is she to remain a slave?"

"I can't answer that. I know that so far, she has never been beaten. God has protected her in that house. And I offered to buy her from Max, but she wanted to remain there. She believes that is where God wants her. At least for now. And it appears she was right. She helped you."

Syn closed the door of the cupboard she'd put the clothes in. "I can't believe she had an opportunity to be free and she turned it down."

"Syn—"

"Well, it's foolish!"

"Syn, not now." Lydia's voice was firm.

Tia's eyes burned. Had Euodia sacrificed her safety for Elantia? "She wanted to stay?"

Lydia nodded.

God had put her there, just for Tia. "God did that, for me, didn't He?"

"The Father loves you, more than you can possibly imagine."

"But I have done some terrible things. I have lied, I have fought in many battles . . . how can He love me?" Tears fell, chasing each other down her cheeks. "I mean, you are such a good person. I can't . . . He can't . . ."

Lydia gestured to someone over Tia's shoulder. "Paulos. Please join us."

A gentle hand landed on her shoulder. "Tia, how are you

feeling today?" He sat on the lectus across from them. "Oh, why are you crying?"

Tia wiped her cheeks and looked to Lydia.

"Tia was telling me that God couldn't love her because of the terrible things she has done."

Paulos chuckled softly.

Irritation pricked the skin of Tia's neck. Couldn't he see her pain? Why was this funny?

"Elantia, do you know what I used to do? Before I traveled the Empire telling people about Yeshua?"

She shrugged. "No."

"I was one of the Jewish leaders. And we didn't like the news of Yeshua. It angered us, because He was claiming to be God's Son. We considered it blasphemy, of the worst kind. So I spent many years chasing down His followers, dragging them out of their houses, and throwing them in jail. I even saw some of them stoned to death. And I was proud of it."

The shock she felt at Lydia's revelation paled in comparison to the impact of Paulos's. An enemy sword could not have opened her soul wider.

"That look on your face? The way you feel? That's what you expect from Yeshua, yes?"

Tia's cheeks heated. Who was she to judge this man?

Paulos came off the lectus and knelt before her. "But He won't reject you. Because He has already paid the penalty for anything you or I have done, or might do. Sin—the bad things we do—must be punished, yes, but Yeshua took that punishment for us."

"How did He do that?"

"He died. He was crucified on a cross."

"So He's dead?" What good was a dead god?

"No." Joy brightened Paulos's face like the sun after a rainstorm. "On the third day after His execution, He rose from the dead. His death was the payment for our sin, and His resurrection means He has power over death. You will be free from the power of sin over your life, free from the false spirits who take over your thoughts.

And you can live with God, now and forever. That's all He's ever wanted. To be with us, always."

Live with him, forever. That's what Paulos had said in the forum. It was almost unbelievable.

"All you have to do is acknowledge Yehsua's death as payment for your sins."

How she wanted that. Freedom. Real freedom. "I want to do that. There is still so much I need to understand about Him, but I want that."

"Good. Then we'll pray. And when we finish, you'll be a child of God."

Paulos took one hand and Lydia took the other. His deep but gentle voice filled the air. "Praise be to God, the Father of our Yeshua the Christ. You chose us before the creation of the world to be blameless in Your sight, and to be adopted as Your children. Because of Yeshua we have redemption, the forgiveness of sins. I ask that You, our glorious Father, give to Tia the spirit of wisdom and revelation, so that she may know You better. I pray also that the eyes of her heart be enlightened in order that she may know the hope You have given us. Fill her with joy and peace as she trusts in You, so that she overflows with hope."

When he said "amen," she looked up. And although nothing had changed, she knew somehow everything had.

GALLUS STARTED at the knock on the door of his office in the basilica. "Yes?"

Leonidas opened the door and poked his head in. "You asked for Helios to be brought to you?"

He'd almost forgotten. "Send him in."

Gallus rolled the parchment he'd been reading as the scribe came to the center of the room. "Helios. I need your law expertise."

"Of course, Domine." He dipped his head slightly. Not as much as he should, but Gallus would let it go. Helios knew the law better than anyone else in Macedonia. He would be swarmed by people seeking counsel if others were aware of how much Helios knew. But Gallus kept that information to himself and used Helios as his personal font of legal advice. It was illegal to charge for it, and the increase in prestige would do far more for Gallus than it ever could for a lowly freedman like Helios.

He'd make it up to him.

Some day.

"You know about the escaped slave belonging to Max?"

"I heard about her."

"Max would like to get some of his investment back. What legal options does he have?"

"Because she escaped?"

"No, fool. Because that Jew said something to her that has kept her from being able to tell the future. He has robbed Max of his income."

"Oh. In that case, let's see." Helios paced the floor, his arms crossed, the fingers of one hand drumming on the other arm. Every few seconds he mumbled. "Income . . . loss . . . damage . . . insult . . ."

Abruptly, he halted. "All right, as I see it you have three options. Shall I write them down for you?"

"No!" He hadn't meant to answer so quickly. Or firmly. But he wanted none of this in writing. He had to commit it to memory instantly and be able to let it roll off his tongue like he'd dredged it up from his own memory. "That's not necessary. Continue."

"First. Wrongful damage to property. This requires a financial loss, and also physical damage to the slave in question—"

"Which they have."

"And also a physical act on the part of Paulos."

So that option was apparently out. As far as he knew, Paulos never touched her, and they had multiple witnesses to that.

"Two. Insult. This means damage to the owner's dignity, but again usually due to physical acts."

"Do all of these require a physical act?" If so, there was nothing to be done. Max was right. They would be ruined.

"You could try for corruption of a slave."

"What does that require?"

"That you show the Jew acted maliciously and that the slave has undergone a moral degradation."

"You can find nothing else?"

"There's really no way to prove that mere words can damage property, and that another person can take away her talent. One day she could tell the future, and the next she couldn't. How can you prove who or what is responsible for that?"

"You may go."

Helios departed. If anyone could find a reason in the law to hold the Jews responsible, it would be him. If he couldn't, it wasn't there.

As he said, how do you prove someone's words are responsible?

But his words had done something. Gallus had seen it. He spoke, she dropped. And when she rose, her gift was gone.

So Gallus needed to use the man's words against him.

But he also had to stay within the law. At least in public. If he were to risk stepping outside the law, it would be for his own gain, not his cousin's.

As Julius Caesar said, "If you must break the law, do it to seize power: in all other cases observe it."

21

"When her owners realized that their hope of making money was gone, they seized Paul and Silas and dragged them into the marketplace to face the authorities."

— ACTS 16:19

QUIN STARED AT THE WAX TABLET ON HIS LAP. DID HE REALLY CARE about how many prisoners had been in the jail for the last year? He hadn't even been here. He tossed the tablet onto the low table beside him. The stylus bobbled on the edge a moment before clattering to the tile floor.

He rose from his stool and tugged on the neck of his tunic against the stale air, which felt heavier with each breath. Stalking down one side of the central aisle of the prison, he yanked on the locks of the cells, testing their strength.

He'd been on duty since midnight. He should go home and get some sleep. What he really wanted to do was visit Tia, see if she was feeling any better than the last time he saw her. If only he could somehow show her how much he would do, what he would give to keep her safe.

If only he could convince himself that anything he did would work.

He rubbed his hands down his stained tunic, wiping away sweat and grime. He'd need to change out of his jailer's uniform first. She hated seeing him in it.

"Stolos, I'll be back tomorrow."

"Yes, Tribune. Any specific orders?"

"Just keep Pandaros from destroying anything."

Stolos's chuckle followed him out the door and halfway up the stairs to his domus.

The ever-present Epaphras met him in the atrium. "Domine, how can I help you?"

"I just need to change my clothes."

"Of course."

Quin ducked into his cubiculum. He washed his face, changed his wool tunic for a fresh linen one, and headed to Lydia's, but not before Charis appeared and handed him a fresh loaf of bread.

Waiting at Lydia's front door, he reviewed the last conversation he'd had with Paulos. *Learn more about Him.* A god was a god was a god. True, Paulos's god did seem different from any other he'd heard of, but still, he had no need of any god. They'd never done him any good whatsoever.

Demas opened the door and showed him to the atrium. "Please wait. Someone will be here to greet you."

Someone? Not Lydia? In her own house? Why not?

His questions were answered when once again, Paulos joined him in the atrium. "Quin. I thought we could talk for a few moments before we joined the others."

"Have I done something wrong again?"

Paulos smiled, the familiar smile that although gentle, failed to reassure Quin. "You didn't do anything wrong the last time."

True, he had never said that. But for some reason, Quin still felt like he'd committed some grievous error.

"There is news I think you need to be aware of."

Quin's belly tightened. "Is she all right? Did they come back?"

"I assume by 'she' you mean Elantia. Yes, she is quite well. No, they haven't returned." Paulos locked his hands behind his back and fixed his gaze on Quin. "Elantia has decided to follow the Way of the living God."

Quin shrugged. "I'm not sure what that means."

"It means she has forsaken all the false gods and goddesses of her past and has chosen to worship the one and only God."

"All right . . ."

"Quin, I know you are falling in love with her."

"I don't know that that's accurate . . ." His cheeks burned. How could this old man say that? He barely knew either of them.

Paulos laughed. "I may be an old man, but I still remember what being in love looks like. And feels like."

Quin hated to admit it, but he was probably right. "What does that have to do with anything?"

"If Elantia has decided to be part of the Way, then she cannot be with you."

He huffed. "Why not? That doesn't make any sense."

"It makes perfect sense. How can you be together if you do not agree about this most essential thing? How can you build a life with someone when the most important thing in her life means absolutely nothing to you?"

Quin felt his world falling away from him. "I'll give her permission to go to your temple. Whatever she wants."

Paulos shook his head. "Quin, this is so much more than that. It is more than going to a temple on feast days and making a proscribed sacrifice. Yeshua is . . . Yeshua is everything. He is our purpose for breathing. He is the reason we can breathe. Because of Him we live and move and have a reason to exist."

Quin paced, running his hands though his hair. "Then fine, I'll worship Him too."

"It's more than just adding Yeshua to your pantheon of gods,

Quin. Yeshua must be the only God in your life, because He is the only God that exists, period. He is the only true God."

"So let's say I'm interested in this. At least in thinking about this. What do I do?"

Paulos gestured west. "Loukas has some property outside the city. What if you go spend the day with him, and learn more about Yeshua? Where it will be quiet, away from any distractions, and he can answer any questions you have, I'm sure. Loukas has been a follower of the Way for some time."

"Distractions. Like Tia."

"Actually I was thinking of the city, and your work. But yes, her too. This decision cannot be made to please her, or so you can be with her, Quin. There are those who are our enemies." Paulos grew somber, his customarily light countenance growing dark. "I have suffered mightily for following Yeshua. Understand me, this is not a decision to be taken lightly."

Why not? At least he would get answers this way. "All right." He huffed. "What do I have left to lose?"

"Your life."

That was not the response he expected. "My life?"

"Yes, but there is so much more to gain." There was that smile again, the look that held a thousand mysteries. "Loukas will explain it to you. By tomorrow it will all make sense. Whether you choose to accept it or not, that is another question entirely."

GALLUS WAS MET WITH A RED-FACED, blustering Max as he stepped into his office. Cassia stood behind him. Perhaps he should turn around and go back. It was nearing time for the baths, and if his last visit was any indication, this would not be over quickly.

"Where have you been? I want him arrested. Have you figured out a way to do that?"

"Good morning to you, too, Max. Cassia." Gallus paused at the door and allowed Leonidas to remove his outdoor shoes and replace them with his sandals. "Sit, please. Let me get you some wine." Lots and lots of wine. He snapped his fingers at the waiting slave.

Leonidas darted from the room, apparently as happy to leave as Gallus dreaded staying.

He paced before the couple, gathering his wayward thoughts. He had no good news for them.

"First, the girl."

"The foreigner drove the spirit from her. She can no longer prophesy. It's quite simple. Arrest him."

"Exorcism is not against the law."

"But he has destroyed our business!" Max prowled around the curia like a wounded lion.

"Max, you said you would control your anger." Cassia gently grasped his bicep and led him to the lectus nearest the window.

"I am controlling my anger!" The man's roar belied his rage.

"To prove damages, as far as local laws, there is a limit of 1,000 sesterces."

"I'll pay that. Happily."

Cassia patted his knee. "No, dear. I think he means that's all we can collect."

"What?" He jumped up from the lectus, fists in the air.

This was going to be so much harder than he feared. "Calm down. I am not finished." Gallus stepped to the much bigger man and placed his hand on his chest. Now sit." He glared up at Max, his patience wearing thin already. And he'd barely begun.

Max sat.

Gallus breathed a prayer of gratitude to Jupiter. "That was local law. Now, as far as Roman law is concerned, there are three options, but I'm still not sure you qualify for any of them."

Max opened his mouth, but Cassia's hand on his back kept him from speaking. Thank the gods she could control him. Most of the time.

He explained the first two options to them, the ones that

required a physical intervention by Paulos. "That leaves corruption of your slave."

"That sounds promising." Cassia bobbed her head at Max, who refused to look hopeful.

Leonidas rapped on the door.

"Come," Gallus commanded of the slave.

The Greek opened the door with one hand, an amphora of wine and three goblets on a silver platter in the other. He set the platter on Gallus's table and poured the wine.

"Lastly," Gallus sipped his drink, "although corruption is the only one that does not require a physical action on the part of Paulos, it does require that you prove he acted maliciously, and that the slave has undergone a moral degradation."

"Well, she ran away, didn't she?" Max scowled. "Isn't that *morally degraded*?" He drained his cup and thrust it toward Leonidas to be refilled.

Gallus winced. "This is more like he caused her to commit a crime."

Max rested his head in his hands. "We're ruined. That's it. We're . . . ruined."

"I do have another idea, however." Gallus snapped his fingers. "My *curule*." A shiver of pride crawled down his spine as the oversized, acacia-wood chair was placed across from the couch. No matter how many times he sat in it, the thrill never faded. "Leave us."

Leonidas shut the door behind him as he hurried out.

Gallus adjusted the voluminous folds of his toga as he sat. "We have no civil remedies, but we may have a criminal one."

Max's head popped up. "Criminal? How so? Because they're Jews?"

"No, no. It's not a crime to be Jewish. They were, however, most certainly disturbing the peace. I can at least fine them for that."

"Not that they would have much coin to pay. He's a drifter. Moving from city to city, no home . . ."

Cassia huffed. "Worse than that, he's an artisan. He works with his hands, all stooped over as if he had no dignity or mind about him at all. It's disgraceful."

Gallus leaned on one elbow, his chin on his fist. "He's staying with the fabric dealer, the Lydian woman, is he not?"

"Yes. All four of them are. Scrounging off her kindness. Parasites, all of them."

"The physician as well?"

"I believe he has land outside the walls, but he's been staying in her domus."

Another citizen he could not afford to alienate. "What did the girl say, when she followed them?"

"Something about being servants of the highest god or some such nonsense." Cassia waved her hand in the air. "I can't remember exactly."

Max leaned forward. "She said they were servants of the highest god and were showing others the way to be saved."

Gallus rose, remembering his conversation with his scriba. "We can charge them with inciting Romans to follow practices that are illegal for us. If they are encouraging Romans to join an unapproved cult, or even to become Jews, then that is a very serious charge indeed. Our beloved emperor has given them the right to practice their religion, as long as they don't try to proselytize, which is exactly what they are doing. They've strayed outside the very generous bounds Claudius drew for them."

"So you'll arrest them?"

"I'm still not sure what punishment I can inflict on them. But I'll have my lictors send for them."

"Excellent. But hear me, I want vengeance. I want someone to pay for my devastating loss. And if it isn't the foreigners—"

Gallus glared. "Are you threatening me? Do not think that because Cassia is my cousin you can say foolish things without repercussion."

Max's face relaxed, and Cassia sidled next to him. She placed her hand on her husband's chest and backed him away. "He's just expressing his frustration. We trust you'll do everything you can, Gallus. Thank you for your time." She hurried him out the door.

They had lost a great deal, that was clear. No one had seen the girl in days. But realistically, he had very few legal options, and he had to follow the law. Most of his remedies were financial, and Paulos and his friends would never be able to repay Max. He could make them Max's slaves until they could, but who wanted that? It would take a *centuria* to work off the debt, and even Max wouldn't want them around that long.

No, the only thing to do was to exile them. Get them out of Philippi and make sure they never returned.

LOUKAS'S ESTATE just beyond the walls boasted hundreds of trees—Persian apples, apricots, and olives. The aroma of sweet fruit and the rich scent of ripening olives filled the air, surrounding the men as they wandered through the carefully tended grove.

How long had they been talking? It felt like days. Still, nothing made any sense.

"So he was crucified? Why would god allow this, if he was his son?"

"Because there has to be a penalty for sin. When there is disobedience in the army, what happens?"

"There is punishment. Immediately."

"Or what happens?"

"Then the disobedience becomes rampant. Disorder abounds."

"Exactly. So the penalty had to be paid. Before, sacrifices were offered. But that was only a temporary solution. They had to be offered over and over again. Yeshua was the final, perfect sacrifice. He was the sinless lamb, without blemish, holy, so his sacrifice could pay for everyone's sin. Does that make sense?"

"I think so." Quin dug his thumb into his right hip joint as they walked. "So no more sacrifices?"

"None."

"Ever? No wine, no grain, no animals?"

"Never again."

"All right."

"Then, after that debt was paid, God raised him from the dead."

Quin halted and faced Loukas. "Oh, I can't believe that." Just when it was beginning to make sense. This was a physician, a learned man. How could he believe such nonsense?

"There are hundreds of witnesses. He walked among his disciples for weeks before he was taken back to the Father."

"It was a spirit."

"He ate and drank."

"It wasn't him, then."

"One of his disciples, Thomas, said the same thing. He put his fingers in his wounds."

Hands on his hips, Quin paced back and forth. He had run out of excuses. Why was he trying so hard not to believe? What about this frightened him so much?

"Why did he need to rise from the dead? His death already stopped the sacrifices."

"His death conquered sin, and his resurrection defeated death."

"We don't die?" This was getting as ridiculous as the stories of the Roman gods now. Pluto kidnaps Proserpine. She eats four pomegranate seeds and should have to marry the underworld god, but Mercury, the war god, makes a deal that she will return to live there four months a year. And thus we have winter, while the gods mourn her absence.

Made just as much sense as Yeshua rising from the dead after paying for everyone's sins.

Loukas glanced at the sun making its way west. He turned and began strolling toward his house. "Of course we die, but only our bodies. Our souls, our spirits, live forever with God."

"You make it sound easy." Quin lagged behind.

"It is. All you have to do is believe it. Accept the gift that Yeshua is offering you. By accepting His death and resurrection, we can become His. We are part of His family. We are forgiven, we can live victoriously in this life, and live forever with Him in the next."

"I don't know. I'm a warrior. I am trained to accept what I can see, and hear, and touch. I don't understand any of this. This is a battle that makes absolutely no sense to me. Why would a god do any of this? Why would he send his own son to die for mere mortals? This is not how gods are supposed to act."

"Because none of those gods are real, Quin. The living God, the God who created the world and everything in it, who created you and me and Elantia, loves us so much He would send His son to die. He would rather die than live without you."

"No one gives you something for nothing. There has to be a catch."

"Oh, He does want something."

"I knew it." He might as well give up now.

Loukas halted and faced him. "He wants your life. He wants you. He wants every part of you. Your every breath, your every step, your every thought. Every moment, every hour, every day. He wants it all. And in return He offers peace. Not absence-of-war-no-chariots-or-swords-peace, but a calm that digs down deep into your heart and puts it at ease. And joy, not everything-is-working-perfectly happiness, but a joy that quietly takes over your being, that no circumstance can displace."

Loukas's pointed gaze caused Quin to shift his weight. Could he even imagine feeling that way? Peace and joy—two things a soldier rarely experienced. Yet here Loukas was offering them up like fruit on a silver tray.

Could it really be that easy?

In Quin's experience, anything that easy, anything that looked like it was too good to be true, was a trap. Something to be avoided at all costs.

Even if it meant losing Tia.

22

> *"They brought them before the magistrates and . . . the magistrates ordered them to be stripped and beaten with rods."*
>
> — ACTS 16:20, 22

TIA LAUGHED AT TIMOS. "YOU CAN'T BE SERIOUS!"

"I am. My mater refused to let them leave until they ate more." Grinning, Timos pushed a lock of his dark hair, unruly even after he had just combed it, out of his face.

"Paulos and Silas?" She glanced toward the brown-robed man seated across from her. "I can't imagine anyone keeping Paulos from doing anything he wants."

Chuckling, Timos stuffed a piece of wine-soaked bread into his mouth. "She said they could not possibly survive a journey on what they had eaten. She literally stood in front of the door until they sat down and finished what she had set out."

Zenobia brought pitchers of juice from the culina and joined them in the peristyle. Syn carried another platter of fruit and cheese.

The late afternoon sun slid behind the roof of the open room, filling it with soft light. Autumn was much warmer in Macedonia than in Britannia. The sun stayed out longer. Almost everything was better here. She still missed her family, and she was hiding from Max. But now she knew Paulos, Lydia, Loukas, and Quin . . .

And Yeshua.

She selected a thick slice of Persian apple from the platter. This new fruit was so juicy and sweet.

Nodding, Paulos poked his bone needle through a stack of folded parchment covered by a piece of perfectly-sized leather. "It's true. Eunice is a very determined woman, and her mater is even more so. But that determination is the very reason Timos is here with us today. His pater worshipped the gods of Rome, but they made sure he knew the living God. I visited Lystra the first time with Barnabas, and I taught him about Yeshua. And when I returned, just weeks ago, I brought him with me." His easy smile broadened. "Convincing them to let him come was no easy task, let me assure you."

Timos laughed again. "That's an understatement. It took a lot to get her to let her only child go. Especially after what happened last—"

"Timos." Without raising his voice, Paulos stopped his much younger partner from continuing. What was he hiding? "Will you pass the grapes?"

"What happened last time?" asked Tia.

Timos concentrated on the platter of fat, purple fruit.

Paulos patted his shoulder. "He's proving to be an excellent travel companion. We're very grateful he's with us."

The young man's face softened, and he shrugged. "I haven't done much."

"You're still learn—"

"What happened last time?" she asked again.

A tremendous crash sounded in the front room, a noise like enormous animals had been let loose, sending large objects colliding with the mosaic of the tile floor. Lydia jumped up and ran toward the atrium.

Timos ran after her. "Lydia, wait!"

"Paulos and Silas!" Max's booming voice preceded heavy footfalls pounding down the hall.

Tia's chest tightened. Her blood pounded in her ears, blocking all other sound. If they found her . . . She gathered the hem of her tunic. Her gaze darted around the room filled with trees and shrubs, searching for one tall enough, bushy enough to hide her. Finding none, she bolted to the stone steps in the back corner and took them as many at a time as her legs would allow. At the top, she squatted and peered over the edge of the half wall that lined the walkway.

Max strode into the peristyle, followed by Gallus's lictors. "Paulos and Silas!"

Paulos set aside his work and stood. "You needn't shout. We are all here. We're not attempting to flee."

How could he be so calm at a moment like this?

A tall, solidly-built man stepped forward, a bundle of birch rods resting on his left shoulder. "You are being summoned by the duovir. Follow us."

Tia stifled a gasp with one hand over her mouth as Max yanked Paulos by one arm and dragged him down the hall. The shorter of the two lictors grasped Silas and followed. They quickly disappeared from sight.

Lydia and Timos followed.

Tia rested her forehead against the wall. What now? What would happen to them? If she went along, was there anything she could do to stop whatever was about to happen? Anything that would make it worth the risk of Max seeing her, taking her back? Perhaps it would be better if she waited, let the others bring back news.

She crouched in the upper hallway in the silence, going back and forth in her mind. Stay. Go. Stay. Go.

After long moments she turned her back against the wall and

slid to the floor, bringing her hand to her ribs, to the still-tender spot where Max had kicked her on the stone floor that night.

She closed her eyes. She just couldn't face another beating. And the next would be worse. Would she even survive it? And what would he do to Lydia for hiding her?

How did everything go so wrong so quickly?

Was she that much of a coward? Some warrior.

Tatos would have been so disappointed.

She pushed herself up, hugging her middle, grimacing against the pain. Running up the stairs had aggravated her broken ribs again. She hobbled down the hall, one hand on the wall.

At least she could pray. Lydia said all she had to do was talk. No special formula. No rituals.

Lydia's blue hooded cloak caught her eye as she passed the woman's cubiculum.

But what if . . .

No. It was a terrible idea.

Disastrous. Risky. To Lydia, not just herself. But she saw no other choice.

"AND THEN I need for you to—" A commotion in the forum interrupted Gallus's thoughts and he stepped to the window. A crowd of people gathered at the southwest corner, shouting over each other. What could be going on at this hour? He shouldn't even be here this time of day. He should be home eating his cena, relaxing after an afternoon at the baths. He released a low groan. "Helios, go see what's going on."

"Yes, Domine."

Gallus scanned the marketplace a moment more, but unable to discern anything, returned to the table against the wall. He dipped his reed in ink and pulled a parchment closer. The number of documents this post required was staggering. He quickly read through it and affixed his name at the bottom.

Helios burst through the door. "Max has charged the visitors with disturbing the peace and is bringing them to you for sentencing."

A sigh escaped. Had Max not listened to him at all? He tossed the reed aside, splotching a parchment with ink, and stepped outside, halting in the doorway of the basilica.

Gallus's heart skipped a beat when he scanned the forum. Nearly a quarter of the town's men followed Max. "How did he get so many people?" Gallus spoke more to himself than the scriba. Perhaps Max was more influential in this colony than he realized.

The crowd parted. Max dragged the old Jew by one arm into the marketplace. The other one—Silas? Was that his name?—followed behind, a lictor's hand around his arm.

Paulos wasn't putting up much of a fight. Maybe he thought he could talk his way out of the charges. Or maybe Max hadn't told him exactly what he was planning to do. That would be just like him. Leave all the hard work for Gallus.

Decimus joined him outside the basilica. "What's happening? Why are the visitors being dragged halfway across the forum by your friend?"

"You'll keep quiet if you know what's best for you. And for your nephews. In Rome, correct?"

Decimus blanched and stepped back.

The magistrate headed for the edge of the stoa, waiting for Max to present the Jews. He kept his gaze straight ahead, trying to gauge the opinion of the people. Were they backing Max, or just curious? He had to follow the law, but he also needed to satisfy their demand for justice. For his own sake. He still had most of his year yet to serve, and he needed the people on his side.

Max made his way to the front, Paulos's arm in one fist, Silas in the other. "These men are Jews and are causing a great deal of confusion in our city." He spoke loud enough for all of Philippi to hear. "They are inciting Romans to follow practices which our beloved Emperor, Claudius, has declared unlawful. These two are preaching we should worship only one god, when we all know we must worship the supreme emperor as god."

The crowd roared. Fists pumped the air. The town called for immediate and severe punishment. Max shoved Paulos forward, and the old Jew fell onto his hands and knees.

Gallus almost felt sorry for him.

This was not what they had agreed on. Why had Max taken things to this entirely new level? With the crowd demanding far more serious action, Gallus could no longer simply expel them from town.

"These men are not Romans!"

"They do not value our ways!"

"They must be punished!"

One upon another, the cries filled the air. It was clear what he needed to do.

It wouldn't get Max his money. But it would make the town happy, which made Gallus happy.

He nodded to the brawny men behind Max. Servius grabbed the visitors and the other shoved everyone else aside, including Max.

"Have them stripped, and flog them." If only Max had listened, Gallus wouldn't have been pushed to do this.

The lictors set their rods aside. Each snatched one of the foreigners, grabbed his tunic, and yanked the fabric, ripping it from neck to hem. The rent tunics were pulled off and tossed aside, followed by their loincloths, leaving the men naked and exposed.

Still without protest.

They dragged Paulos and his friend to the columns holding up the roof of the western stoa as the crowd backed away, leaving copious room for the coming beating. Bare arms were stretched around the columns as far as they could go, then their hands were tied with rope, pulling their bodies tight against the marble.

Servius loosened the red leather strap on his bundle of elm rods. He selected one rod and then tossed the bundle to the ground. His cloak landed on top of it.

Gallus glanced at the crowd, at the lictors, at Paulos. He'd seen too many of these displays.

The accused man's head was against the column, his arms shoulder-high, only reaching halfway around the column.

Just before Gallus turned away, the man opened his eyes. Gallus froze. He couldn't look elsewhere, no matter how hard he tried.

But there was no condemnation in Paulos's eyes. No guilt. No shame.

Only sadness.

For whom? Not self-pity. Sorrow . . . For Gallus? Why should Paulos feel sorry for Gallus?

The audacity! Gallus walked away.

The lictors took their time, flexed their muscles. How they loved making a show of this. And the crowd loved watching it.

Servius drew his long right arm back and brought it down on bare skin.

The other lictor followed suit, his rod attacking Silas's back.

The thwack was sickening. Gallus had never liked it.

He closed his eyes and pretended to be somewhere else.

Anywhere but here.

"Can we talk more tomorrow?" Quin threw his woolen cloak over his shoulder as he and Loukas approached the Krenides Gate on the west end of the Via. The afternoon sun threw long, misshapen shadows ahead of them, and settled an orange glow on the limestone buildings. "I have to report to the jail as soon as we arrive, but I have many more questions."

Loukas chuckled. "If you have many more like our last few, we may need to consult Paulos."

"Can't you answer them?" Quin would be just as happy to avoid Paulos after their last conversation.

"I'll try. You ask the hard ones. Why?" The medicus cast a sideways glance at him. "You don't want to talk to him?"

Did he want to go into this with him? How much did Paulos's companion know already? Actually, he probably knew all of it. Paulos must have spoken to him before he sent Quin off to be schooled in the mysteries of the Way.

They ambled along the Via Egnatia in silence. Loukas seemed not to be bothered, but Quin felt as if he were under scrutiny.

As they neared the forum, sounds drifted toward them. Not the usual marketplace sounds, which on a good day could be best described as organized chaos. Vendors often shouted over one another to attract attention to their wares. Besides, it was much too late in the day for such noise.

This was altogether different. This was . . . ominous.

"What's that?" Loukas frowned.

"I don't know, but it doesn't sound good." Quin broke into a sprint. As he reached the northwest corner of the forum, he bounded down the steps and forced his way through the crowd.

The scene before him made his blood run cold. In front of the basilica, Paulos and Silas stood with their arms wrapped around pillars, stripped bare. Gallus's officers struck them over and over again with the rods of their office.

The taller of the two lictors slammed a stick of elm against Paulos's bare skin, and the crowd cheered its approval.

His partner did the same, applying his rod to Silas's back.

The first man—Quin searched his memory for a name, Servius?—struck Paulos again. Silent, Paulos struggled to arch his back against the pillar, trying in vain to evade the blows that came with sickening regularity.

Gallus stood in the doorway, arms crossed, overseeing the whole out-of-control situation. What he hoped to accomplish with this was anyone's guess. The support of Max? Other loyal Romans? It appeared to have worked. As far as Quin could tell, Gallus had found favor in the eyes of nearly every Roman with any status in Philippi.

How had this escalated to such a state? What charge could possibly warrant such punishment? Quin skirted the crowd, angling for a view of the faces of Paulos and Silas. He stepped onto the stoa and turned to look on the disgusting scene.

The rod snapped, and Servius tossed it aside. He bent to pick up another from his red leather-strapped bundle, and continued the beating.

Pain wracked Paulos's face. He bared his teeth, squeezed his eyes shut, and alternately arched his back or hunched his shoulders.

When the third rod broke, pieces flying the air, Gallus spoke to the scriba beside him etching marks on a tablet.

Helios answered quickly.

"Enough!" called Helios.

The lictors stepped back, brows raised. Servius scoffed, tossing his fourth rod to his feet. He evidently didn't appreciate having his work interrupted.

Paulos crumbled to the ground, at least as far as his bound arms allowed. Silas merely rested his head against the pillar, chest heaving.

Timos appeared at Quin's side.

Eyes still on Paulos, Quin held his hands up in surrender. "I promise you I had no idea Gallus had anything like this in mind."

"I know. Trust me. As long as Paulos is still on his feet, he's been through worse."

Quin turned to the young man to see if he was joking. He wasn't.

"How? When?"

"In Lystra. That's where I met him. Where I learned of Yeshua. The Jews from Iconium followed him to Lystra and stoned him. They thought he was dead. He nearly was."

How could a man his age survive this? Twice?

"What happened?"

"I took him to my home and my mater tended to his bruises."

Quin looked from Paulos to Timos and back. "You carried him? Forgive me, but he's much bigger than you are."

"Oh, he walked to my home, under his own power."

"You can't be serious."

Timos shrugged. "I am. I don't know how he did it, except for Yahweh's healing power."

This was unbelievable. Along with everything he'd learned yesterday—

"Quintus Valerius!"

Servius's voice broke into his reverie.

He glanced to where the senior lictor beckoned him. "The magistrate wants you."

"I better go." He rolled his eyes at Timos.

Quin approached Gallus.

"I want you to put these two in the jail overnight. Make sure they are kept safe. I don't want them escaping, and I don't want them hurt."

Quin's gaze swept their bloody backs.

As if Gallus read his thoughts, he added, "By the crowds. Or by Max, for that matter. He may have gotten some revenge, but he's still out a great deal of coin."

"I understand." He turned to go.

"And Tribune?"

He looked over his shoulder.

"You know the penalty if he escapes."

"I do."

A thousand iron Britanni chariots couldn't have crushed Quin's soul any more than Gallus's order. His message was clear. He was to take Paulos down to the inner prison. Quin may have doubts about the old man's god, but Paulos had become a friend, a mentor.

And Quin wasn't at all sure Paulos would survive.

23

> *"When he received these orders, he put them in the inner cell and fastened their feet in the stocks."*
>
> —ACTS 16:24

PEEKING OUT FROM BEHIND LYDIA, TIA PULLED THE HOOD OF THE indigo cloak around her face with one hand as she gripped Lydia's arm with the other. Perhaps she had made a grave error after all, leaving the safety of the domus.

The implacable faces of the lictors were burned into her memory. The rippling muscles of their arms and backs each time they drew back to apply the rod. The slight sneer of their lips. They almost seemed to enjoy their perverse chore.

Poor Paulos—how could they do this to him and Silas? This was unspeakable.

And Quin . . . She'd seen his face when the duovir ordered him to take them away. He may have been a soldier, but this was different. Paulos was his friend, not an enemy in battle. What would this do to him?

The crowd began to disperse, and sweaty bodies jolted hers. She dared not be discovered.

Max's laughter boomed from the western stoa.

She slipped her hand from Lydia's and raced back to the domus. The hood of her cloak slipped off as she turned south on Via Appia and her heart nearly stopped. Her loose, blond hair would give her away in a heartbeat. She reached for the hood with both hands and held it in place until she reached the front gate, her feet never slowing until she had regained the safety of her room.

She unfastened the fibula at the neck of the cloak, letting it fall to the floor in a puddle at her feet. Why would Paulos's God—her God now—let this happen? Things seemed to be going from bad to worse. Paulos and Silas were in jail, and Quin had to keep them there. She'd escaped Max's brutality, but would she spend the rest of her life running from him? If Lydia were to be found out, she could be charged with theft, and pay dearly.

Quin's fallen face drifted through her mind as she climbed the steps to her room and dropped onto the bed. He had offered to be her protector, but now she couldn't have him in her life. Not unless he too decided to accept Yeshua as his savior.

Paulos said Quin didn't really believe in any gods. After this, would he ever accept Yeshua? If not, he would be lost to Yeshua, and to her, forever.

She reached under her bed and retrieved his red cloak. She shouldn't have kept it, but now she was glad she had. The sobs burst from deep within her, and she held the garment to her chest.

When they subsided, a gentle tap sounded on the door. "May I come in?"

Swiping the tears from her cheeks, she opened the door. Lydia waited in the hall. "Of course. I could use some company."

Lydia joined her on the lectus. "That was quite a scene in the forum."

"Have you heard anything from Paulos? Or Silas?"

"Loukas went to the prison, but all they would say is that the prisoners were taken to the inner cell."

"I don't know what that means."

"The inner cell is deeper inside the jail. That usually means they consider them dangerous."

How could Paulos and Silas be dangerous? They were quiet, old men.

"Aren't you going to ask about Quin?"

She drew in a shuddering breath. "I'm afraid to, I think."

"What are you afraid of?"

How could she admit it? Would Lydia be disappointed in her?

"I know you love him, Tia." She fingered the cloak in her lap.

Tia dropped her head. "I'm sorry, I know I'm not supposed to."

Lydia laughed. "Who told you that?"

"Paulos did."

"You can't control your heart. We love who we love. What he meant was, it is unwise to build a life with someone who does not follow Yeshua. You cannot be at peace with someone who is at war with God."

"Then what do I do?"

"Pray for him. Pray for him to accept God's love, as you have. The warrior in him is having a difficult time with this. You must know how that feels." She dried Tia's face with her hands.

Why was she crying again? Warriors didn't cry. She'd cried more in the last week than she had in her entire life. "Lydia?"

"Yes?" She moved Tia's hair back from her face.

"Aren't you worried? You look so . . . peaceful."

"I'm not worried."

Tia gasped, pulling away. "How can you not be? Aren't you upset? Don't you care about them at all?" She shouldn't have said that. Obviously Lydia cared, but why wouldn't she show it?

"Tia, I am upset. I'm very concerned for them. I know they are cold, and hungry, and in pain. But I am not worried."

"I don't understand. Is it my Latin? I don't see a difference."

"No. I'm upset that they are hurting and there is not much I can do about it. But I'm not worried, because I know our Heavenly

Father is with them. And worrying will accomplish nothing but keep us from thinking clearly."

Lydia may be able to trust it all to Him, but Tia couldn't. Not yet, anyway.

Lydia slipped an arm around her shoulders. "We were just about to pray for them all. Would you like to join us?"

She shrugged. "I don't even know what to pray for."

"Just tell God what you're thinking."

"I'm not sure He wants to hear what I have to say."

"Why don't you try?"

Tia remained seated.

"Come on. You can just listen." Lydia took her hand and gently pulled her into the peristyle, where Syn, Zenobia, and Demas waited with Loukas and Timos.

Loukas rose and embraced her. "How are you, Tia?"

She shrugged again. What could she say?

Loukas prayed first. "Father, we ask for Your wisdom. Our friends are in trouble. We ask that You grant them peace, Your peace, that is beyond the understanding of the world. Fill their hearts and minds with Your joy even in the midst of this trial. Let everything about this situation bring glory to You. We pray that we may be delivered from wicked and evil men, and that You will return our brothers to us soon."

"And Father, I pray for Quin." Lydia drew Tia close to her as she prayed. "I ask that he will be able to understand all that he and Loukas discussed yesterday, that You will open his mind to the mysteries of Yeshua. I ask that he will be able to grasp how wide and long and high and deep is Your love for him, that he will know Your peace that surpasses our comprehending. Amen."

There were far too many words in her heart for Tia to say them aloud, or even make sense of. Instead, she kept them bottled up inside, like one of Lydia's expensive perfumes in exquisite alabaster jars. If God was as powerful and all-knowing as Paulos said, He'd be able to untangle her words and string them together for her, and then, hopefully, do something wonderful.

QUIN LED THEM SILENTLY NORTH, Paulos and Silas behind him, Servius bringing up the rear. At the end, he turned east, and after several paces, he halted at the prison.

He blocked Servius' entrance. "We'll take it from here."

The lictor raised a brow. "I'm sure the duovir would like to know I have guaranteed the prisoners were seen secured in the inner prisons as he desired."

One of the few who could match the lictors in size, Quin stepped closer to the man. "That's my job. Are you questioning my integrity?"

Servius stared him down a moment longer, then left without a word.

Quin snapped his fingers, and a guard tossed him a heavy ring of keys. He trudged through the main vestibule, its wide stone floor echoing every step, four cells on either side.

Guards stood to the right and left. It appeared every guard in the city had shown up in the forum, and then raced to the prison to be on hand for this spectacle.

They didn't all need to be here. They'd seen the sensational part, the show Gallus felt he had to put on. There was nothing left to do but lock Paulos and Silas away. But for how long?

"Stolos, did you put the others downstairs for the night?"

"Yes, there are four down there now."

"Four? When I left there was only one."

"The lictors brought three young men in for theft."

The inner cell would be full tonight.

Quin stopped at the far end of the room, then turned on his heel. "You are all dismissed except Numerius. You will stand first and second watch with me. Stolos and Pandaros, third watch. Fourth with Stolos and Alexios. One man inside, one on the door."

They descended to the lower floor. A broad, wooden door waited, with one small barred window. A heavy iron lock reflected the dim light from the torches hung on the walls.

He unlocked the door and leaned his shoulders against it, shoving it into the dank inner chamber. He stumbled briefly, but righted himself and spread an arm, allowing the others to enter.

In the center of the roughhewn floor lay eight sets of stocks, wooden frames bolted to the floor. The air was thick and foul, and the floor was covered in dried filth. Philon huddled against the side wall. The three thieves stayed against the back.

Quin swallowed. "I am so sorry. You know I don't want to do this, but I have no choice." He could barely breathe. His chest felt as if an iron band kept it from expanding.

Paulos placed a hand on his shoulder. "I have been under authority. There is no need to place yourself in danger. Do what you must."

Quin kicked away some of the dried excrement, then grabbed two handfuls of straw from along the edges of the cell and scattered it in a small pile.

Paulos and Silas sat and stretched out their legs.

Quin reached for more straw and turned to see their bare backs, thick blood caking along the mangled stripes. Thankful they couldn't see his face, he knelt before them. "Gallus said I had to *secure* you in this cell, but he didn't say *how* secure." He lifted the top wooden bar of the leg piece. "Your feet, please."

Paulos gestured to the ten half-holes cut into the bar. "Which ones?"

"The middle ones."

"Are you sure?"

He placed one foot into a hole. "There's no need to torture you further by spreading your legs so far your body will split in two." He set the other ankle down and brought the top of the board down, then closed the lock.

"What if the duovir finds out?" Paulos said.

"Do you really think he would come in here? He wouldn't dare come close enough to breathe the air." He fastened Silas into the stocks in the same way as Paulos, then stood.

"Not our hands, our heads?" asked Paulos.

"Your feet are bolted to the floor, you've lost a good deal of blood, and you are behind a locked door with no light once the sun goes down. Even if you could somehow get to the other side of that door, you would have to climb the stairs, get past another locked door, and get beyond more cells and armed guards. Do you think it necessary I secure your hands and head?"

"I'm only trying to keep you from getting into trouble."

Quin threw his hands in the air. "Why? Why do you care?" He hadn't meant to yell. "I apologize."

"Why don't you care, I think is the question."

He leaned against the wall. "No, why should I? That is a better question. I've spent my life following orders. To the letter. Except one time, when following it would have cost countless lives. And that one time, that one and only time, is why I end up here. And now I have nothing. I have disappointed my pater. I can't return to Rome. I have no land, no coin, no career, and I've probably ruined this one as well. And the only bright spot in my life has been snuffed out, as I now cannot have any kind of life with Elantia. So what have I got left?"

"You have a great deal left. You are alive. And you are free and a Roman citizen. Those two things alone make your life better than over three-quarters of the world."

That was true. So why did he feel so hopeless? He slid down the wall, sitting on the cold, stone floor. "And why are you not in despair? You have been slandered, beaten for no reason, thrown into prison, and who knows when he will release you?"

"This is a bit of a setback, I must admit."

"A bit of a setback?" He huffed. "You are truly insane. You could still be executed in the morning."

"No, we couldn't."

Quin rubbed his hand down his face. "Only if you know something I don't." Which was entirely possible. Paulos always seemed to know something no one else did. "Even if you manage to escape death, who would listen to you now? Max has made a fool of you."

"Ah, but God has chosen things the world considers foolish in order to shame those who think they are wise. And he chooses things that are powerless to shame those who are powerful."

Was he smiling? It was too dark to tell.

"Am I supposed to be one of those powerful things that will be shamed? Because I have no power left. And I've already been shamed. I'm sitting here with you in human waste."

"No, Quin, that was not meant for you." Silas's voice was soft.

"What is meant for you, my friend, is the love of Christ." Paulos always sounded so sure. Even here, in a Roman prison. "A love so ferocious and pure it will pick you up, set you on your feet, and never let you go."

He leaned his head against the wall. If only that could be true.

But not for him. It was too late for him. No one could want him. No one could love him. Not even the god of Paulos.

GALLUS DIPPED his fingers into the bowl of water presented to him by one of Max's slaves, then dried them on his napkin. Max and Cassia had insisted on preparing a celebratory cena. He'd rather have put the whole thing out of his mind, but it had proven to be a wise decision to join them. Cassia was an excellent hostess.

The first course was unimpressive—eggs, mushrooms, clams in a sweet wine sauce. But the next one—she must have some connections in Neapolis. And Max must have spent most of whatever silver he had left. Roast pheasant with onion sauce. Ham rubbed with honey and baked in a pastry.

If only he were a bigger man, he could eat more. But the Romans had a way around that. "Excuse me. I'll be back in a moment." Both Cassia and Max had already left the table once to empty their stomachs. Max twice, in fact.

After he did what was necessary, he swished his mouth with diluted wine and spit into the bucket Cassia had thoughtfully provided.

"Better?" She giggled.

"Much." He reached for a chunk of the ham. "You must give me the name of your cook. Or did your slaves do all this?" He waved his hand over the generous amount of meat spread on the table in the center of the couches.

"Of course not!" She cackled heartily. "I knew you would rule properly, so I hired a cook from Amphipolis. I went there this morning, found the cook—we've used him before for our bigger dinners—and told him what we had in mind. He bought the supplies. He knows all the right people, where to get the best food at the best prices."

"Of course sometimes"—Max leaned in and lowered his voice, though no one else was anywhere near—"you have to pay a premium for some of this."

Some of this was against the law. How did they know he wouldn't fine them? Or worse? Did they think he was that much under their control?

But the food was extraordinary.

Worth turning a blind eye to.

Gallus took the last piece of peacock, cooked in a spiced wine. By Jupiter, it was delicious. It was too bad it was gone. He would have loved to take some home.

"Are you ready for some more wine? We can clear this away for a bit and enjoy a special treat before the sweets are brought out."

"Whatever you want. It's your home. I am only a guest." He wasn't usually so agreeable. How much wine had he consumed so far? Since they drank it quite watered, it took a lot to get him drunk. And when he was drunk, he made questionable decisions, so he rarely drank too much.

"Euodia! Bring the wine!"

A half-full amphora sat on the floor beside Max. Why was he calling for more wine?

A slender girl with dark hair, Greek by the look of her, brought a small amphora to the triclinium.

Max took it and dismissed the slave. "This"—he held the clay container high—"is Falernian wine."

"Where did you get that? It's so difficult to find out here in—" He stopped himself before disparaging the man's precious city.

Max snapped the neck of the amphora and poured Gallus a goblet.

"You know the story of this wine, don't you?"

"No. I just know it's the best. It cost me six times as much as the next best wine. But you, my friend, my magistrate, are worth it." He lifted his glass. "To the health of Tiberius Claudius Caesar Augustus Germanicus."

Gallus barely lifted his goblet in response. It may be a law, but he didn't have to mean it. "Now the tale of the wine."

Of course someone like Max wouldn't be familiar with it. It was all about appearances with him. He was a phony. He knew nothing about this wine or any other. He drank it only because he knew it was the best. Had no idea why, and overpaid dearly because of it. It shouldn't have cost more than four times more. Although Gallus was impressed Max saved it for this point in the meal instead at the beginning, as most hosts did, then followed with the lesser vintages as the guests became more intoxicated.

"The story, the myth, is that a simple farmer, Falernus, was in his field scratching out a living when Bacchus came to him in disguise. The man made for him a simple meal, so in return the god of wine filled the cups at the table. While the hungover Falernus slept, in gratitude Bacchus cultivated the whole mountainside with vines, and ordained that the region forever after be known for his wine. It truly is the drink of the gods."

Max roared. "What a wonderful story! No wonder we can't get it here! They keep it all to themselves in Rome!" He took a long draw from the cup. "It is exceptional, though. Excellent. Would you like more?"

"Not yet." He cradled his still half-full silver goblet. He wasn't going to gulp his down like this barbarian. He intended to savor it.

The slaves paraded out again, with trays full of sliced fruit and honey cakes. Max turned his attention from the wine to a honey cake.

With all that sat before him there might be some left over. Perhaps he was too critical of his friends, such as they were. Perhaps he worried too much.

Paulos and Silas were safely tucked away in his prison. Tomorrow he would banish them, and soon he would have his silver from Patroclus. He drained his wine and shoved it at the nearest slave. "One more."

Max's laughter nearly shook the domus. "*There* is the guest I have all night waited for! Now we celebrate. Bring out the dancers! Bring out the girls!"

Why not? He was the magistrate.

He was invincible.

24

"About midnight Paul and Silas were praying and singing hymns to God, and the other prisoners were listening to them."

— ACTS 16:25

QUIN TOOK ANOTHER LONG DRINK OF WINE FROM HIS GOBLET AS HE paced the prison floor. Romans said only barbarians drank wine straight, without water, spice, or honey, but who cared? He felt like a barbarian. He had nothing left. No family, no career, no land. No Elantia. And after this, even if they weren't executed, Paulos and his friends would surely be banished from Philippi.

Yes, he was feeling sorry for himself. What would Attalos say? What was it he had said, just before Quin left Rome? *"Great things are waiting for you there. They will not be easy, but they will shape you into the man you were meant to be, that all other things in your life have been leading up to."*

Quin chuckled. "Not easy" was an understatement. The last two months of his life had been harder than any six months of campaigning in Britannia.

Britannia. Tia. She was his carissima. But he was no longer hers. Maybe never had been.

He poured the last of the wine into his goblet and hurled the amphora against the wall. The jar shattered, littering the floor with shards of clay.

Alexios peered out from the cell he was sweeping. "Domine? Something wrong?" He studied the broken pottery, then returned his gaze to Quin.

"Nothing's wrong. Thank you for being so alert."

Alexios frowned but returned to his duty.

Quin regarded the pieces of the amphora against the wall. Too bad he didn't have another. Then again, if he did, he'd probably fall asleep, and sleeping on duty was an offense punishable by death. At least in the army. If he were discovered, and that wasn't likely to happen here. By the time anyone unlocked the doors, he'd be awake. Still, he couldn't.

He ambled to the corner he used as his working space and dropped onto the stool. How did he end up this way? Two days ago, his life was perfect. Well, not perfect, but . . .

Then Tia decided to follow the Way, and he'd lost her. Because of the man called Christ.

He rested his head in his hands. Paulos said he, too, could follow the Way.

That was illegal for a Roman citizen. Not so much the following the Way part, but refusing to worship the emperor.

But what more could he lose?

Moaning drifted up from the inner cell. Was Paulos or Silas hurt? More than before? Dying? It was not unheard of for men to die after a Roman beating.

He bolted from his seat. Almost to the stairs, he skidded to a halt. This wasn't moaning.

He slowed his breathing, tried to still the thumping of his heart. Concentrated on the noises, now settling into a comforting rhythm. Took each step on his toes, irresistibly drawn to the sounds woven into a beautiful dance.

This was . . . singing? How could they possibly be singing? They had been slandered. Tortured. Humiliated. Paulos could barely breathe. How could his chest expand enough to sing without excruciating agony tearing through his body?

And yet, the song continued.

He is the image of the invisible God, the firstborn of all creation.
For in Him all things in heaven and on earth were created,
things visible and invisible,
whether thrones or dominions or rulers or powers.
All things have been created through Him and for Him.

A more glorious sound had never existed. Paulos's deeper melody was accented by Silas's higher harmony, and the song filled the prison. It surrounded and engulfed Quin more palpably than the air he breathed.

When the last note faded, he moved to the door. "Paulos?" He spoke through the bars on the tiny window.

"Yes, Quin." Paulos's familiar voice was like a balm to his wounded soul.

"Are you sure your god could love someone like me?"

"Of course. If He can love me, the chief of sinners, He can certainly love you."

He laid his head against the rough wood. "I have lost everything and everyone I love."

"You will never lose His love."

How he needed to believe that. "How can you be sure?"

"I know, as sure as I am sitting here, that nothing can separate us from His love."

"Nothing?"

"Nothing. Not life, not death, not angels or spirits or magistrates. Nothing in the present or the future. Nothing. You can never lose His love."

"I wish I could let you out of here."

"May I pray for you?"

What an odd question. Paulos was the one who should need comfort. "Pray for me? I suppose so."

"Our Father in heaven, I ask that you give our dear friend Quin a hunger to know You better. I pray also that the eyes of his heart may be enlightened so that he may know the hope to which You have called him."

"And we ask that you fill him with all joy and peace as he trusts in You," added Silas.

"Thank you," Quin whispered.

Hope. Joy. Peace. Those concepts were foreign to him. He plodded back up the stairs and to his corner.

"Sing some more!" Philon's voice drifted up from the cell.

God also highly exalted Him and gave Him the name
that is above every name
so that at the name of Yeshua every knee should bend
in heaven and on earth and under the earth,
and every tongue should confess that
Yeshua Christ is Lord to the glory of God the Father.

Quin lay his head back against the wall. "*Every* knee should bend." What was stopping him? Fear? Of what, exactly?

Maybe he could talk to Paulos more tomorrow, when his head was clearer and not so full of wine. He'd come down just before dawn. The magistrate would never rise before the sun, so even if Gallus was planning something wicked, Quin should have time to talk to Paulos.

He couldn't be more miserable. So why not give Yeshua a chance?

THE WOOL-STUFFED MATTRESS was softer than the mat she slept on in Max's house, even softer than the straw-filled mattress back at home. The deep blue cover was luxurious and kept her warm, warmer than the animal skins she'd grown up sleeping under. The pillow was perfect and still Tia was as restless as a rabbit caught in one of her bratir's cages.

She curled up into a ball, facing the wall, as if making herself as small as possible could somehow hide her from the onslaught of emotions that attacked her.

This was not the enemy she had been trained to fight.

Quin's agonized face refused to leave her memory. She longed to comfort, to hold him. But what could she say? Or do? He was under orders. He had no choice.

His last words echoed. *Because you're my carissima.*

Except now she wasn't. And she understood Paulos's explanation. All his reasons made perfect sense. If they were together—she following the Way, he still worshipping his Roumani gods, even if half-heartedly—it would end in disaster. There would be an irrevocable clash. She would be forced, at some point, to choose between her husband and Yeshua. And what about children? She'd spoken with Timos about growing up with a Greek pater and a Jewish mater. It wasn't good for any of them.

But none of those reasons soothed the ache in her heart.

Father, I know Quin is in pain. Not like Paulos and Silas are, but I know what he is doing now must be one of the most difficult things he has ever done. I know he'll think this makes him a terrible person. Please, somehow, can You help him see that's not true? He's all alone in that horrible place. Can you help him remember everything Loukas told him? If I can understand it, and You can forgive me, surely You can forgive him too.

She pulled his crimson cloak close to her face. The smell of leather and oil had faded, but it still brought her some comfort. His feelings couldn't fade as fast as his scent, could they? She had to believe he would still protect her, still fight for her, if Max came for her.

If he were able.

If not, she could defend herself. She was still a Britanni warrior. She could wield a sword, though she had none. She'd find something. Max would not defeat her.

It felt like she had barely fallen asleep when she was awakened. With one hand Tia held tight to the side of the iron bed. The other hand clutched a handful of mattress. Why was the room shaking?

The glass cup on the bedside table rattled and bobbled until it fell onto the tile floor, shattering. The legs of the table bounced, sounding very much like one of the spotted woodpeckers back home.

The shaking slowed, stopped. Tia did not release her grip. Would it start again? She wasn't risking it. She held fast, staring at a spot on the wall. The shaking slowed, then stopped.

"Tia?"

A voice hovered on the edges of her mind.

"Tia?" Lydia spoke louder, then peeked in her room. "Are you all right?"

No. The world is breaking apart.

Lydia opened the door wide and stepped inside. How did this woman always look so elegant? In the middle of the night, fresh from sleep, when the world was shaking? "It was just an earthquake."

Tia searched her memory. Even translated into her native tongue, she couldn't think of anything like it. "I don't know that word."

"Earthquake? It's when the ground moves. Does that not ever happen in Britannia?" Avoiding the shattered cup, Lydia tip-toed near. Sitting on the bed, she brushed the hair from Tia's face.

"Not that I remember. Or that anyone else remembers and speaks of."

"They happen in Macedonia and Achaia all the time. Usually you can barely feel them. That was a moderately strong one."

If that was a moderately strong one, she'd hate to see a really strong one.

Lydia gently pried Tia's hands from the mattress as she spoke. "Oh, yes. Earthquakes can go from where they barely tickle your feet, to rumbling the floor, to knocking the dishes off the shelves, to destroying whole cities."

"Destroying cities?" She shuddered. "I wouldn't want to feel one like that."

"I know. It's a horrible thing."

Tia gasped. "You've been in one?"

Lydia picked at her fingernails, exhibiting discomfort for the first time. "When I was a little girl. In Lydia. They say it was the worst earthquake in history. It destroyed *twelve* cities. It was so bad, Tiberius—the emperor at the time—not only sent ten million sesterces to help in rebuilding, he declared we wouldn't have to pay taxes for five years." She smiled weakly. "It takes a lot for Rome to give up taxes."

"How bad was it?" She sat up, tucking her legs under her.

"It was bad enough that houses fell down, temples collapsed. But the shaking wasn't the worst part."

"What could be worse than buildings falling?"

"In such a violent quake as that one, the earth not only goes up and down, it breaks apart. Roads, even buildings, end up with huge gaps in them. There were landslides, floods. Fire broke out everywhere because it happened at night, and the small fires people had to keep warm were thrown around, tossed onto broken parts of houses and stray bits of wood. Long after the shaking stopped the whole city was ablaze. It seemed like the flames went on forever."

"Is that when you left?"

"No, not then. Not till later." She glanced at the door and stood. "I think everyone is awake. Syn was gathering something for us to eat. As always."

How that girl wasn't tremendously fat was a mystery.

Pushing her covers off, Tia got out of bed and followed Lydia down the hall. "Do you think they felt the quake at the jail too?"

"They must have." Lydia descended the stairs to the peristyle, Elantia behind.

"Do you think they're all right?"

"I don't see why not. There shouldn't be any more damage there than here."

Syn entered the peristyle with a tray of sliced fruit. "A few of the bowls broke when they fell, but it's not too bad." Smiling, she offered Tia a Persian apple.

Tia shook her head. "No, thank you. I'm not hungry." Her

stomach was queasy enough as it was, just waiting for morning to come so she could find out what would happen to Paulos and Silas.

Not to mention Quintus.

"Do you think—"

Her words were interrupted by a loud banging at the front door.

Lydia rose. "Who could be coming in the middle of the night?"

A shiver ran down Tia's spine. The moment always in the back of her mind had finally come. Someone had recognized her last night.

The pounding intensified.

She wrapped her hands around her middle, backing toward the walls. Fear huddled in her chest, refusing to leave.

There was only one person who would come at this hour, be this insistent.

Max.

THE SOUND of shattered pottery awakened Gallus from a deep sleep. He bolted upright in his bed, eyes wide. With no windows, it was impossible to discern what had made such a noise. He certainly was not climbing out of his bed until he knew. What if he stepped on broken terra cotta?

He felt for the handbell hanging from his headboard. He yanked it free and rang it.

Nicanor appeared almost instantly.

"Light the lamp. Something broke." His voice was rough. Too much wine last night. He rarely drank that much.

"Yes, Domine."

Nicanor left, stopping only to roll up the sleeping mat outside Gallus's room and tuck it under his arm. He returned with a broom and a lit oil lamp. Holding the lamp low, he gingerly stepped into the room, scanning the floor around his feet.

"Ah, the amphora you brought from your friends' house has fallen."

"Good thing it was empty then." Gallus cackled and fell back on his pillow. The sound of the pottery scratching against the tile floor drilled into his head. "Are you done yet?"

"Yes, Domine. The floor is safe."

"I need to relieve myself." He sat up, his feet on the steps beside the bed, but the room spun. He stretched his hands out to steady himself.

"Do you need help, Domine?"

"Perhaps." He hated admitting that to a slave.

Nicanor put out his arm for Gallus to hold onto as he descended the three steps and stumbled to the door. He kept one hand on the wall as he made his way down the hall to the toilet.

On the way back, he brought his hand to his forehead to shade his eyes. The moonlight shining through the open ceiling of the atrium bounced off the water in the impluvium. Far too bright. But what was that just at the end of the hall? A toppled sculpture? That couldn't have been there last night. He surely would have tripped over it. What else was amiss? He would have to wait until morning to check.

"Nicanor, is that a sculpture on the floor?"

"Yes, Domine. I noticed it, too, but it's too heavy for me to pick up alone. I'll have to wait until morning when one of the other slaves can help me."

"Why is it on the floor?"

Nicanor frowned. "For the same reason the amphora is?"

Was Nicanor being impertinent? This was not like him.

The Greek tilted his head. "Did you not feel the trembling?"

"Trembling?"

"There was an earthquake."

"I must have slept through it. Was it a bad one?"

"A small one. No damage to the house that I know of. A few objects toppled."

"Good, then." He padded to the bed.

Nicanor offered his arm, but Gallus smacked it away. "I don't need your help."

He turned and plopped on the mattress, rubbing his temple with his thumb and forefinger.

"Does your head ache, Domine?"

"It does. I just need to sleep."

"Yes, Domine. But if it still aches in the morning, I have two owl's eggs."

"When did you get those?"

"I bought them as soon as I heard Max and Cassia were preparing such an extravagant dinner, and that you were attending."

Gallus waved his hand at the slave beside his bed. "That will be all."

Nicanor left, taking the lamp with him and closing the door. The room was shrouded in darkness once again.

Gallus lay back, pulling his linen covers to his chin.

So, this lowly slave already had the cure for his alcohol-induced headache prepared. Should he be insulted Nicanor assumed he would get this drunk, or pleased he had thought ahead?

His eyes felt like they had sand in them. He tried keep them open, but it felt so much better when they were closed.

He'd just have to figure this out later. Max's situation was taken care of. The culprits were in prison. Everything should be calmer tomorrow.

25

"The jailer woke up, and when he saw the prison doors open, he drew his sword . . ."

— ACTS 16:27

A KNOCK SOUNDED ON THE PRISON DOOR. QUIN APPROACHED. "WHO'S there?"

"Pandaros. It's almost the third watch."

He slid the heavy bolt to one side and opened the door, allowing his subordinate to enter. "It's past time. You're late. Stolos is already here, on the door."

"Any instructions before you go?" Pandaros obviously noticed the pottery shards in the corner, but wisely refrained from comment.

"Switch places with Stolos at the midpoint. Everything's been pretty quiet. Except the prisoners in the inner cell have been singing off and on."

"Singing?"

"When they haven't been praying."

"You mean like wailing and calling on their god to rescue them?"

"No, I mean like offering praises."

Pandaros shuddered. "That's just odd."

"I know. But it sounds nice. A lot better than wailing, so I wouldn't complain if I were you."

"Men do strange things when faced with death."

Quin winced. "You don't know they'll be executed."

"They should be."

"Why?" His question came out harsher than he intended.

Pandaros stepped back, his hands up in surrender. "I apologize. I know they're friends of yours. Didn't mean anything."

Quin drained the last drops of wine from his goblet and slammed it on the small table by the door. "I'm going to sleep. Lock the door behind me." He stomped out and up the stairs to his domus.

His servant met him in the atrium with a glass of honeyed wine and a loaf of bread.

Charis peeked out of her room for a brief moment, then shut the door quickly.

"Epaphras. What are you doing up at this hour?"

"I thought you might need one or the other." He grinned.

"Since I've already had too much wine, I'll take the bread." He reached for the food. "Thank you. You shouldn't have waited."

"I know you've had a hard day. Let me help you out of your boots."

Quin allowed the young Greek to remove his shoes. His servant was right, but Quin didn't want to talk about it.

"How are the prisoners, if I may ask?"

"The Jews?"

"Yes, Domine, the teacher and his friend. May I ask how they are doing after what happened in the forum?"

Why would Epaphras ask about Paulos and Silas? "Do you know them?"

His face flushed. "Some."

Quin stared at the young man a moment. "Are you a follower of the Way?"

Epaphras cringed.

"You're not in trouble."

"I do believe in the living God."

"So every time you say you'll pray for me, you pray to Paulos's God?"

He nodded.

"I talked all day to Loukas about Yeshua. And all night to Paulos." He yawned. "Now I'm going to sleep."

"Good night, Domine. I'll see you tomorrow."

Quin waved acknowledgement as he fell onto his bed without changing out of his tunic. Sleep had barely overtaken him when he was jerked awake. What was that noise? His gaze shot to the door of his room. It rattled. Was someone entering?

His bed moved, bumping against the wall. He got out of bed and took a step. He fell, banging his knees on the cold tile floor.

He'd had quite a bit of wine earlier, but he couldn't be that drunk. Rising to his full height, he stretched his hands out to his sides. He was not unsteady. He didn't *feel* drunk. He mumbled the names of his brothers, his uncles, all four emperors. He was thinking clearly, not slurring his words.

He definitely wasn't drunk.

Taking a step, he remained upright. Again. Again. He quickened his pace and opened the door.

Rumbling filled the atrium. The floor trembled. Walls cracked. A small piece of the ceiling fell. He backed out of the way just in time, slamming his shoulder into the wall.

Epaphras and Charis ran from the back of the domus. Tears streamed down her pale face. "What's happening?"

She had never before spoken to him. Barely looked at him.

"I don't know. But get out of the house. It's not safe. The whole house could collapse."

Maybe he *was* drunk. Or out of his mind, and this was all his imagination. A nightmare. But his knees and his shoulder still stung, and nightmares weren't usually painful.

Gods of Rome. God of Paulos. Does anyone hear me?

A horrifying thought struck. His prisoners! He reached around the doorway behind him and grabbed the belt holding his short sword from the peg on the wall. Wrapping it around his waist, he bolted out of the door and down the steps, glancing east. He could see the front door to the jail standing wide open. Not a good sign. Panic gripped his heart.

He raced inside the prison, skidding to a stop in the center of the outer room. The torches burned bright on the walls, shining a bright light on this unending nightmare.

Each door on either side stood open. Every cell empty. Thank the gods the prisoners had all been locked in the inner cell for the night.

Every muscle in his body taut, he forced himself toward the stairs. The light dimmed with each step along the circular staircase until everything was a cloudy gray.

The torches had burnt out. There was just enough light from the stairwell for him to see the enormous door was split in two, the pieces lying on the stone floor as if a giant animal had head-butt it from the inside.

His vision narrowed to that empty cell. His blood pounded in his ears, his chest heaved. They would execute him. There was no way around it. If he let six prisoners escape, especially Paulos and Silas, he would be beheaded. After whatever other punishment they decided to inflict on him.

His knees hit the cold stone, his head fell into his hands. It was over.

At least he could die like a Roman soldier. Proud, before they humiliated him.

God, help me.

He sat up on his knees and felt for his short sword. Wrapping his fist around the hilt, he slid it from its sheath. He carefully placed the point just behind his collarbone, aimed toward his heart. Eyes closed, Elantia's face flashed though his mind.

Carissima, forgive me.

"Quin, stop!"

He jumped. *Paulos?* What a cruel trick for his mind to play on him. He gripped the blade more tightly.

"Quin!"

He opened his eyes.

"Paulos?"

"Don't do this. We're all here. No one has escaped."

He let out a breath, squinting, trying to see something, anything, through the darkness. "Why not?" he croaked.

Silas chucked. "They wanted to hear about the freedom Yeshua can offer."

Quin struggled to stand. "They're *all* in there?"

"Every one of them," said Paulos. "And your guards. There's no need for you to die."

TIA PRAYED as the hammering on the door echoed the pounding of her heart. Should she hide? Run?

No. She wouldn't spend her life in fear. *Father, give me strength.*

"Come in and calm down." Lydia led a young man and woman, slaves by their dress, into the room. "Now sit down and start again."

Father, thank You. Tia breathed out all the tension. He had protected her yet again.

Lydia steered them to a lectus, and Syn immediately appeared with goblets of watered wine.

The two of them talked at once, words tumbling out on top of one another. Tia doubted she would understand even if her Latin was perfect.

Lydia held up a hand. "Epaphras, you first. Slowly."

He sucked in a deep breath. "You felt the earthquake?"

"Of course."

"The dominus was quite upset—"

"At the shaking?" Tia couldn't help interrupting. Who wouldn't be upset if their house began to shake?

"Well, no. We've all felt that before. Although this one was quite powerful."

Lydia shrugged. "I don't know about that . . . A few bowls fell, but—"

"There's a huge crack in the atrium wall. And in the ceiling of our room," the young man said.

Lydia's arm swept the peristyle. "Not here. Look around you. It frightened Tia. They apparently don't have earthquakes in Britannia. But other than some tremors, no damage. Still, I can't imagine even that upsetting your dominus. He must have been through far worse."

Twin lines appeared between his brows. "That wasn't it. It was what might be happening next door. He ran out. And . . ."

The girl grasped his hand, whether to calm him or herself was unclear.

"What? Epaphras, you must tell us." Loukas entered the peristyle from the staircase, Timos close on his heels.

"He took his weapon."

"Doesn't he always wear his pugio?" Timos asked.

"Not his dagger. His *sword*." Epaphras paused a long moment. "The doors of the prison were wide open."

Lydia sat as her hand went to her throat. "Oh, my."

Everyone seemed to be in on some enormous secret except for her. Tia grasped Lydia's arm. "What? What's happening? Is this man going to hurt someone?" she whispered harshly.

Lydia clasped her hand in both of hers. "Oh, Tia. You don't know who these people are, do you? Who their dominus is?" She pointed to the pair. "They are Epaphroditus and Charis. They serve Quintus."

"Oh, she's the one—"

"Shh!" Lydia hissed at Epaphras.

Tia rose slowly, holding to the end of the lectus to remain steady. She took two steps and halted. Quin wouldn't harm anyone. So why would he take his sword? She slowly turned back to the group, her thumb and fingers to her forehead. "But . . ."

"What might be happening below . . ." Suddenly Epaphras's words made sense. She felt the blood drain from her face. If she didn't ask, maybe they wouldn't tell her. But she knew. She'd seen his face. Felt his pain. Knew what such a failure, a lack of honor, would do to him. There was only one way for a warrior to end this. "I have to see him." If it wasn't already too late.

Lydia pulled her close. "No, you mustn't. What if you are seen? You've already risked it once. The guards will all be there by now, and they know your description. If you're seen, you will be returned immediately to Max."

A thousand horrible scenarios spun through her mind. What if she never saw him again? Or worse, what if she could have stopped him and didn't even try? "I have to see him. Please, Lydia. I beg you."

Charis stood. "She doesn't look so different from me. Put her in my clothes. No one would think twice." She gestured to the slave beside her. "We're always together."

Epaphras's eyes widened for a moment.

"If we're caught, you'll be punished for helping me, Charis. Are you sure?"

"We're sure." Epaphras rose. "We all love him. Go."

No one had escaped? Not a single one? Quin could see Paulos and Silas staying, but the other four?

Granted, the three youngest above were only in here because they were being taught a lesson. They would have been released as soon as their parents came for them. Still, perhaps at least one of them . . .

He rose. "No one left? You're sure?"

"We're all here. You're safe." Silas beckoned. His feet free, the man had backed away from the stocks. Silas stood, but Paulos, still obviously weakened from the beating, remained on the floor.

Clutching his blade, Quin stumbled toward the cell. "Stolos, get some torches down here." They didn't really need them. But Quin needed time to compose his thoughts. He'd also rather Stolos not be around for a few moments. Or anyone else, but there wasn't much he could do about Philon and the boys.

Quin sheathed his sword, the weight of a thousand battles fallen from his shoulders. Had the God of Paulos and Silas done this? Saved his life? Saved . . . everything?

Such a God deserved worship. Far more than the gods of Rome ever did. This God . . . was real.

And Quin wanted to know Him. His composure shattered, he fell at the feet of Paulos and Silas. His eyes burned with hot tears. He wept silently, his body nearly convulsing. He hadn't cried like that since . . . the night he had first killed a man.

Paulos seemed to instinctively know when the storm was nearing its end, and placed a gentle hand on his shoulder.

Quin sat back. He scrubbed his hands over his face, smearing his tears. Head still down, out of the corners of his eyes he could see Philon sitting silently, staring. The trio of troublemakers huddled against the far wall. He dared not look at them.

He raised his gaze to only the two old men before him. "Domini, what must I do to be saved?"

"We are not domini. Please don't call us that again." Silas frowned.

Quin scrambled to his feet, casting a glance at the bemused prisoners surrounding them. "Let's get you out of here. Come on. Up." Quin slipped an arm under Paulos's bicep and pulled him up.

In the outer room, he looked from one to the other. "Now, tell me."

"You must believe in Yeshua the Christ, and you will be saved," Paulos said.

"Believe what?"

"Believe that Christ died for your sins, as was foretold in the Scriptures, that He was buried, and that He was raised up from the dead on the third day as was also foretold."

It was the rising from the dead part that still had him bothered. He pinned Paulos down with a stare. "Did *you* see Him after He rose?"

"I did. Years later. As I'm sure Loukas told you, I persecuted Him mightily. I am the least of the apostles, the chief of sinners, but He came to me, and asked me why I was doing such a thing. And He told me I was chosen to take the news of His death and resurrection to all those outside of Israel. To people like . . . *you*."

"Me?"

"Yes, think about that. He sent me here, perhaps into this very prison, just for you."

Stolos returned, a flaming stave in his hand.

Could God really have sent Paulos to prison just for him? Quin's throat burned again. He needed to get out of there, where he could think. Where he could talk to Paulos and Silas, alone. "Stolos, take the others to a cell upstairs and secure them somehow. Wait . . . where's Pandaros?"

Stolos scoffed. "He ran out of here at the first rumble, like a scared rabbit."

"All right, I'll deal with him later. For now, take care of these four. You two, come up to my domus. Let me tend to your wounds. Get some food in you before you collapse."

One corner of Silas's mouth turned up. "Paulos, let's go. You really do look even worse than you did in Lystra."

"Thank you, my friend. I can always count on you to encourage me." He chuckled weakly.

With Paulos leaning heavily on him, Quin made his way up the stairs and across the stone floor of the jail. Aside from the wooden doors, the stone building was relatively undamaged.

Remarkable, after the violent shaking they had experienced. Before they could exit, Alexios, a torch in hand, blocked the doorway.

“Alexios, what are you doing here? You’re supposed to be off for the rest of the night.”

“I should ask you the same question.”

“I’m taking them upstairs for a while. I need to tend to his wounds. You don’t want them dying, do you?”

“I really don’t care whether they live or die, as long as they stay here.”

“I’ll bring them back. But he’s about to collapse. Let me through.” Quin took a step forward.

“I’m afraid I can’t let you do that. They are prisoners of the Roman Empire. They must remain here until the magistrate says they are released.”

“Look, Alexios. If they had wanted to leave they would have done so already. They not only didn’t escape, they persuaded everyone else to stay.”

“That’s not the way I remember it.” The smirk on his face sent a chill down Quin’s spine.

“Remember it? You weren’t even here.”

“I do remember the wine, though.”

A sickening realization flooded him. “You want my position.”

“Yes. And Gallus wants me to have it. I’ve been watching you since you started.” He laughed. “So again, you can’t leave.”

“But we can.” Paulos’s voice was raspy, weak.

“Who are you to question me, old man? A Jew, no less?” Alexios spat. “Get back into your cell.”

“I may be a Jew, but I am also a Roman citizen.”

Alexios’s eyes grew wide. “A-a cit—”

“So am I.” Silas spoke more forcefully than Quin had ever heard him.

Quin suppressed the surprise—and frustration—that built within him. Citizens? Why hadn’t they said so? They could have avoided all the suffering and pain they had endured. With just five little words. “Out of the way, Alexios. We’ll be upstairs. In fact, why don’t you go back home now? Your watch is over.”

The guard huffed but marched across the Via toward the forum.

They climbed the stone steps to his house. The door hung open. Quin lowered Paulos onto a couch by the pool and went to the culina.

Searching through the supplies that had all been knocked off the shelves, he found a large bowl still intact, several cloths, and some honey to take to the men.

"The kitchen is quite a mess. Everything is on the floor. I did manage to find some honey, though." Quin scooped up some water from the pool and began to wash their backs. "Now, tell me more about Yeshua."

26

> *"At that hour of the nightthe jailer took them and washed their wounds . . ."*
>
> — ACTS 16:33

Elantia scurried across the forum, the hood of Charis's cloak pulled low over her head. The chill of the stone soaked into her bare feet and moved all the way through her body.

Epaphras grabbed her hand. "Hurry!" He kept them close to the east edge, then turned west.

She would have preferred to run straight across, but there was no need to expose herself any more than necessary. In moments they arrived at the jail.

"Wait here. Let me see if I can tell what's going on." He tucked her beside the stone wall that rose far above her head. "Don't move." He glared at her for good measure.

The moments stretched out. Where had he gone? She crept to the edge of the wall and peered around it—and nearly jumped out of her skin.

Epaphras moved around her and pulled her farther back along the wall. "What are you doing? I told you not to move!"

Who was he to order her? "You were gone too long."

"From what I overheard, Quin took them to his house." He yanked on the hem of her hood and grabbed her hand. "I'll watch to see when the guard isn't looking, and you run past the door."

They crept around the corner. His hand on her shoulder, Epaphras peered into the space between the door hanging ajar and the jamb.

Tia's heart pounded against her chest. If the guard saw them . . . She pushed the terrifying thoughts away.

"Go!" Epaphras's hard whisper sliced though the silence.

She bolted toward the domus. She nearly slammed into the wall, stopping herself with outstretched palms, then dropped to a crouch. She looked behind her.

Where was Epaphras?

Once again, time seemed to go on forever. Finally, she caught a glimpse of his brown wool tunic as he darted in front of the light spilling out of the prison.

Epaphras joined her a moment later. He looked back at the prison, and when no one followed, he stood. "Come on." Grabbing her hand again, he walked around to the front of the domus and climbed the steps, Tia following.

Hesitating, she stood in the doorway. Quin knelt before Paulos, washing his striped back. Her heart broke. So much dried blood for someone not a warrior.

Epaphras gestured to her.

Quin turned at the movement. Setting the bowl aside, he hurried to her and pulled her close.

She'd forgotten what it felt like to have his arms around her. For the briefest moment, she was back in Lydia's peristyle, before the earthquake, before the beatings, before life had become so abysmally complicated.

"What are you doing here?" he whispered.

She pulled back to meet his gaze. "I had to know you were safe."

"I am. For now."

For now? What did that mean?

"Paulos has been telling me about the Way."

"About Yeshua?"

"Yes. I want to know all about Him. Come, sit." He pulled her inside, then again tended to Paulos.

She moved to the other side of the impluvium. Dipping a cloth into a second bowl, she began to cleanse Silas's back. "Is he serious? About the Way?"

"I believe so."

"This . . . this isn't because of me, is it?" She rinsed out the cloth.

"I don't think so. He hasn't stopped asking questions since he arrived at the jail, and not one of them has been about you. And notice, you're here, and he's not with you."

"I noticed." She tried to keep the disappointment out of her voice.

Silas chuckled.

"I'm thrilled, of course I am. I've just been so worried about him." She blotted the angry stripes, trying not to open them again.

"I know. You know, though, even if he decides to follow Yeshua, this is not over."

Her hand stilled. "What do you mean?"

"We have no idea what will happen tomorrow, or later today, actually. How the magistrate will react."

"But no one escaped. Everyone is still here." She dunked the cloth in the crimson water.

"Exactly. We are *here*, not in a cell where he ordered we stay."

Too many scenarios ran through her mind as she drew circles in the scarlet liquid with her finger. "What will happen to Quin—?"

Noise at the door drowned out the rest of her question.

Loukas entered the room, medicine box in hand and a grin on his face. "I thought you might have need of a physician." He stepped nearer to Paulos, and his nimble fingers skimmed over the older man's back.

Timos followed him in, carrying a large bundle. “We were concerned about you. All of you. And Lydia sent new clothes.”

Quin set aside his bowl and cloth. “No need to worry. All is well. In fact, I want to be baptized.”

“Me too.” Epaphras spoke up.

“You do?” Paulos asked.

“I’ve been talking to Timos. And I believe.”

“And me.” Charis slipped her arm though the young Greek’s.

“Charis? You weren’t even here.” Tia stared at her.

“I heard Paulos at the river. And at the house, Lydia and Loukas were praying and . . . I believe Yeshua died for me too.”

Loukas clapped his hands together in front of his chest. “Marvelous. We can do it as soon as—”

“No, now.” Quin stood.

“Now?” Loukas’s mouth hung open.

“In the middle of the night?” Silas asked.

“Right now.”

She’d seen that look before. They should stop debating with him. They would lose.

“He wants to do it now. And we can, so we should,” said Paulos.

Tia’s stomach flip-flopped. Going to the river was much too risky. If even one person saw them . . . Why couldn’t he wait? Did it really make that much difference?

Paulos looked up at Loukas, wincing. “Can you do it?”

“I’d be delighted.”

“But where? Is this deep enough?” Timos pointed to the impluvium. “Or do we have to go to the river? I hate to do that at this time of night. That might draw a lot of unwanted attention.”

“What about my fountain?” Quin said.

“Your fountain?” asked Timos.

He pointed to his garden in the back of the house. “The previous owner put a fountain in. I think the building was the bakery before it was made to move to the market with the other workshops, so they needed the water. The aqueduct isn’t far from here.”

Loukas smiled widely. "That's perfect. We have three, then."

"I—"

Everyone turned to stare at Tia.

Loukas neared her. "Are you all right?"

She fought to speak past the lump in her throat. "I haven't been baptized yet. I hadn't been able to leave the house."

Loukas's broad smile returned. "Then I guess we have four."

Quin was risking his life. She could too.

QUIN FIDGETED. Had he acted too rashly? If just one person—the wrong person—found out, they could all be put in prison, or executed.

Too late now. God would have to protect them.

Paulos and Silas sat on a couch to the side, silent but smiling. Timos stood near the fountain, ready to assist Loukas if needed.

Charis stood in the water, soaking wet.

A beaming Epaphras, in a damp tunic, hair wet, held up a towel for her.

Charis twisted her hair until it stopped dripping. She shook the water from her hands and moved to the edge.

Epaphras reached for her and helped her out.

Quin smiled. They were perfect for one another.

"Tia?" Loukas held out a hand. The basin was big enough for only one person to immerse themselves, so Loukas had remained outside the fountain.

She stepped into the basin and faced him.

Quin shifted his position slightly so he could see her face.

Tia caught his stare and smiled for a moment before returning her attention to the man in front of her. How could any one person be so beautiful?

"Tia, I know you've already said all this before, but I'm going to ask you again. Do you believe in Yeshua, that He died for your sins, that He rose again, and that by this belief you are forgiven and will live forever with Him in heaven?"

"Yes, I do."

"Do you participate in this baptism as a sign of your death to this world, your repentance of sin, and your resurrection in Christ?"

"I do."

She dropped to her knees before he continued. "Then I baptize you in the name of God the Father, God the Son, and the Holy Spirit." Loukas knelt beside her. Leaning over the low wall of the basin, he placed one hand behind her head, and one on her waist. She lay back, Loukas supporting her as she sank under the water for just a moment.

When she came up, she was radiant. Her blue eyes sparkled in the moonlight. She laughed, softly, as Loukas helped her to stand.

Charis met her at the edge of the fountain. She wrapped a towel around Tia's shoulders as she stepped over the wall.

He was now the only one left.

"Quin?"

He dragged his gaze from Tia to Loukas.

"Second thoughts?"

"No, no."

Loukas smiled. Or maybe smirked. It was hard to tell. "All right then. Quietly."

Quin climbed into the water.

The physician's smile disappeared. "I'm going to ask you the same questions everyone else has answered. I want you to think very carefully before you answer."

"Why do only I get this warning?"

"Because only for you is this illegal."

Of course. The charges against Paulos and Silas. Only approved gods were allowed to be worshiped by Romans. "Go ahead."

"Are you sure? Along with what else you've done tonight, the penalty could be death."

Quin chuckled dryly. "I've faced death many times. Almost every day in battle. And for nothing more than the glory of Rome. I may not even live to see another sunrise." He couldn't bring himself to look at Tia. "I'd rather die with Yeshua than without. No Roman god has offered me peace, forgiveness, love . . . I'm more certain of this than I've ever been of anything in my life."

Loukas smiled. "Very well."

Tia remained. He could feel the chill on his own wet hands. Soaked to the bone, she must be freezing. And yet she waited for him.

After the questions, Quin knelt. Loukas tipped him back. The water rushed in over his head, washing away his past, washing away his sin. As if he'd been buried and would emerge an entirely new creature. Was that even possible?

Suddenly all the things Paulos had been saying made perfect sense. He'd been buried with Yeshua through baptism into death, and now he'd be raised from the dead to live a new life.

His old self had been crucified and he had been set free from sin.

Just when he felt his chest would be crushed from lack of air, Loukas pulled him up. He sucked in a great breath of air and blinked the water from his eyes.

He felt like a new man. Yeshua had recreated him. He had the same body, he faced the same circumstances, but he had a new spirit.

And a new family.

He understood the look on Tia's face from moments ago. Doubtless he had the same look.

He stood, rubbing the water from his face and hair.

Loukas grinned. "All right?"

"Never better."

"I love baptizing people." He smiled as he picked up a towel and gave it to Quin, then headed inside.

Quin clambered out.

Elantia neared him.

Still dripping wet, he grabbed her, enveloping her in a fierce embrace. He buried his face in her neck. He had no words to describe the onslaught of emotions he was battling. None were necessary.

THE AROMA of roasting root vegetables and flatbread filled the domus. Tia breathed deeply. When had she last enjoyed eating? Britannia?

Charis and Epaphras had changed into dry clothes and were filling trays with flatbread, carrots, turnips, and onions.

"May I help?" asked Tia.

"No." Charis flashed a bright smile as she handed Epaphras the tray of vegetables. "You can come get a dry tunic with me."

Tia followed her back to the front of the domus. The doors to the rooms on the left of the atrium hung askew. A large crack punctuated the wall.

No wonder Charis had been so panicked when she arrived at Lydia's. The quake had indeed been far more powerful here.

"Wait here. There's a huge crack in the ceiling. Let me just grab one."

"What is she doing?" Quin's harsh voice startled both of them.

Tia pulled at her soaked clothing. "She's getting me a dry tunic."

Quin moved toward the room. "Charis, come out! What if the roof collapses on you?"

Charis emerged, tunic in hand, face pale. "I'm sorry, Domine." She bowed her head and took two steps back.

Quin closed his eyes and rubbed his hand down his face. "Charis, I'm the one who is sorry. I didn't mean to shout. I just . . . don't want you to get hurt."

She raised her head. "I did nothing wrong?"

He smiled. Or tried to. "Of course not. Just stay in the back of the house, all right? Preferably the garden."

She nodded, just a hint of a smile on her lips. Handing the garment to Tia, she hurried down the hall.

"What was that?"

He sighed. "Apparently I frighten her."

She narrowed her eyes. "What did you do to her?"

He brought his hand to his chest. "I did nothing to her! Her former owner did something awful, but I don't know who. Or what. But I guess I somehow remind her of him. That's only the second time she's spoken to me since we've met."

"Maybe she'll trust you more now."

"I hope." He gestured across the atrium. "You can change in my room. It appears to be undamaged."

After changing into dry clothes, she joined the others in the garden. All the couches had been dragged into the area.

"I'm sorry this is so small." Quin hunched his shoulders and looked around sheepishly.

"After the room we were in, this is luxurious." Silas, in a fresh tunic and sandals, laughed.

"You really didn't need to go to such trouble." Paulos gestured to the food now on a low table in the center of the group.

Quin scoffed. "When was the last time you ate?"

Paulos thought a moment. "Yesterday morning."

"That's what I thought."

"I was very happy to make this for you," Charis said. "I wish we had more."

"This is more than enough. We've gone with much less. Sometimes nothing at all. May I thank God for this food, and this night?" asked Paulos.

"Please."

"Our gracious Father, we thank You for these new lives in You. We thank You that You have delivered them from the domain of darkness and transferred them to the kingdom of Your beloved Son, in order to accomplish the good work that You have prepared for them. We ask that You would help them walk in a manner worthy of You, bearing fruit in every good work and increasing in the knowledge of You. Strengthen them with Your power, according to Your glorious might, and keep them safe until that work is finished. We thank You for this food that You have provided for us. In the name of Yeshua. Amen."

The bowls emptied quickly with five hungry men. Tia helped Charis refill them with anything they could find in the disordered culina that normally held only enough to feed three.

Tia ached to talk to Quin, but he peppered Paulos with more questions. She tried to content herself with the knowledge that he was safe, and a follower of the Way, but was he avoiding her? Or just trying to satisfy his insatiable curiosity while he had Paulos's attention?

She dropped onto a lectus next to Silas.

"He's not really trying to ignore you, you know."

She snapped her head around toward the gentle old man. "I'm sorry?"

"My guess? He's worried about growing even closer to you than he already is, not knowing what might happen later today."

Her breathing sped up. Did his safety depend on Paulos and Silas remaining in chains? This was not fair. He had just decided to follow the Way. "What will they do to him?"

Silas shrugged. "It depends. On what they would have done to us."

Her heart sank. In her fear for Quin, she had forgotten all about them. "I'm so sorry. I wasn't thinking about . . ." She grasped his hand. "What will they do to you?"

"I wouldn't worry too much about that." He grinned. "They can't do much to us"—his smile faded—"but I don't know about Quin. He let prisoners escape. At least that's the way they could see it. We shall simply have to pray for him."

Her heart felt as if it had been ripped into tiny pieces. And stomped on. How could everything go from so wonderful, to so achingly horrible, in only moments?

"How many times has God answered your prayers already in the last few days? There is no reason to think He cannot do so again."

Easy for Silas to say. But this trusting God part was new for her. And getting harder.

27

> *"When it was daylight, the magistrates sent their officers to the jailer . . ."*
>
> — ACTS 16:35

THE MOON HAD LONG SINCE RETREATED, AND THE RISING SUN WAS winning its battle with the darkness. Soft pink and orange dared peek over the eastern horizon, growing bolder by the moment.

In his doorway, Quin peered over Elantia's shoulder at the rest of the group, waiting at the bottom of the stairs. Loukas looked up protectively every few moments. "The sun will be fully risen soon. Gallus and his lictors may be here any time. You need to go."

She lay her head against his chest. "I know. I don't want to, though." She shivered.

"Cold?"

"A little."

He fingered the edge of Charis's cloak around her shoulders. "I have no idea what will happen today."

"Silas told me some of what might happen. I'll be praying for you."

His heart warmed at the thought. Yesterday that would have meant nothing, but this morning . . . "You have no idea how wonderful that sounds."

"I've been praying for you ever since Paulos told me—" Her voice broke. Unshed tears made her eyes sparkle like sapphires.

He tucked a loose strand of golden hair into her hood. "Carissima," he whispered. He longed to kiss her again, but as uncertain as things were . . . he was playing with fire already.

"Good-bye, *cariatu*." She hurried down the stairs.

He watched until she was safely in the care of Loukas and then ducked back inside.

"All right. Let's get you both back down to the jail. Loukas and Epaphras carried a lectus down for you before they left so you won't have to sit on the floor while we wait to see what Gallus does." Quin helped Paulos down the steps, and Epaphras escorted Silas.

Once the pair settled, Quin checked on the others. In the main hall, Stolos had each of the prisoners back in the cells, which still had intact chains, while Pandaros swept up rubble in the cells farthest from the door. At least he had returned. That spoke well of him. Perhaps he was learning.

"The men seem to be secure, even though the doors are destroyed. Fourth watch is nearly over, so Pandaros, as soon as you are relieved, please find the blacksmith and the carpenter."

"Yes, Domine."

He fisted his hands on his hips and scanned the jail. "We're going to need a great deal of wood. Make sure you give them a general idea of what happened before they come. I don't want a lot of time wasted going back and forth. Have them bring as much material with them as they can the first time. I'm sure Gallus will make this a priority. It doesn't need to be pretty, just secure."

"Domine?"

Quin spun around. "Yes, Pandaros?"

"Is there nothing else you want to say to me?"

He drew in a long, slow breath. "Not yet. Just get my jail repaired." He headed back to the front but halted as if he'd run into a stone wall.

Servius, *primus lictor*, stood barely four strides away. He carried himself as if he were above everyone, above the law he so forcefully represented.

"Jailer!" the lictor barked unnecessarily loudly.

Quin nodded. "Servius."

"What is this?" He wagged a finger back and forth, pointing to the fallen doors.

"The earthquake? Surely you felt it."

"A mere tremor. Nothing to cause this kind of destruction."

Quin stepped nearer. "*Here*, it was more than a tremor, as you can see. But everyone is accounted for. Would you like to see the records?"

"I would."

Of course he would. Quin nodded to Stolos, who marched toward the corner to retrieve them.

"In the meantime, Gallus Crispus Scipio has sent me to inform you that the Jewish prisoners shall be released. They are to leave the city immediately."

Paulos slowly rose from his seat, grimacing with every move. He stepped toward the lictor, Silas behind him. "You wish us to leave the city?"

"Yes. In his great mercy, the magistrate has decreed that you may go in peace."

Paulos pursed his lips and nodded. "Hmm."

Quin clenched his jaw. He knew that "hmm." It was not a good sign.

"You beat us publicly and threw us into prison."

"You were found guilty of disturbing the peace and causing Romans to worship a foreign god."

"Declared guilty? Without a trial?"

"The duovir has unfettered authority. He does not need a trial."

"To find Roman citizens guilty?"

And there was the look Quin waited for. Utter shock. Confusion. Disbelief. If the situation weren't so deadly serious, he would laugh.

"And now you wish us to disappear? Slink out of the city so no one will know the disgrace and illegality of which *you* are guilty? I think not."

Paulos was nearing the end of his strength. Servius probably couldn't tell, spending his entire life as a public official following around another official, most of the time indoors, but as a soldier, Quin knew. Paulos's breath was shallow and rapid, his cheeks were pinking—though that could also be his anger.

Paulos turned around and took his seat again. "If the duovir wants us gone, he can come and escort us from Philippi himself."

Servius looked at Quin.

Quin shrugged. "You heard him. Send Gallus."

"This is outrageous. Who are you to demand such a thing?"

Silas stepped forward. "We could always appeal directly to Rome."

Servius glared, then spun on his heel and left the hall.

Quin sprinted past the destroyed door after him. "Servius. I have a message for you to deliver to Gallus. And tell it word for word. Understand?"

IF ONLY SHE could melt into the wall. There were far too many people here in Lydia's house. Epaphras and Charis. All of Lydia's household: Demas, Syntyche, Zenobia. The men from the dyeworks. Some other women she didn't know. The grain merchant and his family—when had they believed?

Where was Euodia? Stuck at Max's house, most likely. Now that it was known what went on at the river, he'd never let her come again.

And when he finally caught Tia, as he was sure to do, she

wouldn't be allowed to come either. But she'd be strong. She'd survive. She'd weathered wars in Britannia, she'd lived through the sea voyage, she'd survived the beating . . . she could live though this. The Father would be with her.

But now, this morning, they needed all the prayer they could get, so she needed to stop thinking of her own comfort, and concentrate on Paulos, Silas, and Quin.

Timos stood. "As you know Paulos and Silas are in the prison. Years ago, Peter was in jail in Jerusalem. The believers there prayed all night, and an angel released him from his chains. I know you've been praying in your own homes, but Loukas and I thought together we could encourage each other's faith as well as lift our voices to our Father. It is likely the magistrate is even now deciding their fate, and the fate of Quin the jailer, who, if you don't know, was baptized last night, along with Epaphroditus and Charis."

Several people rose to embrace the pair.

"Tia"—Lydia drew her forward—"was also baptized, although she became a follower of the Way several days ago."

She was swarmed by hugs. Too many hugs. Eventually they left her alone and were seated again.

The time of prayer was unlike anything she'd ever experienced. Even during the festivals for the gods at home, with fire and chanting and song, with her mamma and *senomamma* beside her, she'd never felt truly connected to Brigid—or any other god. But this morning she felt the Father's unfathomable devotion and care for her, and for the men missing from her new family.

Loukas's bold, matter-of-fact way of speaking contrasted wildly with Timo's softly spoken yet surprisingly confident prayers. Lydia, arm around her, whispered nearly silent prayers the entire time. Sometimes more than one person prayed at the same time, but it wasn't like the chaos of the feasts. If the living God was all-powerful, surely He could listen to two, or three, or a world full of people at once.

Because surely Paulos and Silas and Quin were praying as well from behind their walls of stone.

When their time together came to a close, people drifted out of the peristyle. Those who were slaves scurried off immediately. She studied the people remaining in the room. Loukas and Lydia chatted near a tree. Epaphras and Charis huddled together in a far corner, awaiting news of their dominus. Lydia's freed servants went happily about their duties, chattering amongst themselves.

What was she to do now?

What was it that Paulos had told her the other day? About waiting? *"Trust in the Lord with all your heart; do not depend on your own understanding."*

That would be easy, for she had no understanding whatsoever in this situation. All she could do was trust and wait.

Father, bring him home to me. Bring them all home.

"That's impossible!" Gallus slammed his gold goblet down on his table. "I refuse to accept this!"

Servius shrugged. "That's what he said. And they're refusing to leave the jail until you go talk to them, personally."

Gallus nearly choked. "So help me all the gods, there is no way that I will go to that jail. They are not citizens. There is no possible way to prove this. Even if they are, who would believe them? I am the magistrate. I have the people on my side. This is my city." He huffed. "Now go let these men know I will not be coming and send them on their way." He picked up his goblet and shoved it at Leonidas to refill.

"Yes, Domine. Though I should let you know . . ." The lictor shifted his weight.

He spun around. "What? What, what, what?"

"The jailer is on their side."

"You cannot be serious!" Gallus roared.

"He said if you do not come and apologize, personally, he will get word to Rome that you flogged citizens without a trial. He also said to remind you that, umm . . ."—He closed his eyes as reciting from memory—"Lydia the cloth merchant and Loukas the physician are fully aware of the situation and will use all their influence to make the facts known."

Gallus slammed his freshly filled drink on his desk, splashing a good amount of it. Leaning on his palms, he thought through all his options.

He could still send his lictors back and command the outsiders to leave, or risk arrest.

Or he could send his lictors to the jail and just yank them out. Maybe beat them again. Flog them even. Keep them there forever, or banish them.

He forced out a long breath.

But would that troublesome Quin make good on his threat? And what would anyone, Vespasian perhaps, do? And how soon?

Decimus burst into the office without knocking, without announcement. "I told you this would come back to haunt you."

Gallus didn't have the energy to be outraged.

Yet another irritating old man to deal with. "Why are you here?"

Decimus stood in the middle of the office, face reddening. "How did you manage to arrest and beat *citizens*? I knew you would go too far one day, but this, this is more than even I would have imagined."

"How was I supposed to know they were citizens? They are Jews!"

"This is Philippi! Nearly everyone is a citizen! All you had to do was allow them to speak. Even for one tiny, little moment. Five words." He held up a hand, fingers spread wide. "Five. That's all they needed to say." He huffed and stomped toward the door. "You said you had this all under control. Now you very well could bring down the wrath of Rome on us."

The wrath of Rome? "You're overstating things *just* a bit, don't you think?" Did Decimus always have to be so dramatic? No wonder he was unmarried. No woman would put up with this.

"If they appeal to Rome, we could lose our positions, our homes, everything. Don't you remember Verres?"

Gallus rifled through names memorized long ago. "Governor of Sicily?"

"Besides bribing his way into power, extorting the farmers, and plundering the temples, he beat a citizen with rods."

"And?"

"And he was exiled, since because he was a citizen, that was the worst they could do to him."

"Wasn't this almost one hundred years ago?"

Decimus's face was now the color of the stripes on his tunic. "The laws haven't changed! You still can't scourge a citizen. Not only that, Philippi could lose its status as a colony. All its privileges—exemption from taxes, the right to vote—"

Now *that* was something to worry about. Something serious. More than serious. But he was not going to give Decimus the satisfaction.

He waved a hand. "I'm not even sure they are citizens. Do they have proof of their citizenship with them? Even if they do, how can we be sure it's genuine?"

"Do you really want to risk everything you own and be banished to Gaul? Or Germania?"

"If they're citizens, why didn't they bring it up beforehand? In any of the many times they talked to nearly everyone in Philippi."

"Would you have believed them any easier than you do now?"

Good question. He probably would have had them scourged longer, just for the impertinence.

"Just fix this." Decimus stormed out of the basilica.

So why bring up their citizenship now, then, after they'd suffered?

To embarrass him? He could see that.

But an apology? Could he bring himself to apologize to these foreigners? Was that really the only thing that would put a stop to this entire episode?

This was all Max's fault. He was the one who escalated this. If Max had only listened to him, they wouldn't be in this situation now.

But the time for what-ifs had passed. And if he intended to keep his position and his power, he would just have to endure the humiliation. A few moments of pain for a lifetime of power.

He drained his glass and then turned to his lictors. "Bring me Max."

If he had to suffer the indignities of an apology, then Max most certainly was going to suffer them too.

28

> *"Before a downfall the heart is haughty, but humility comes before honor."*
>
> — PROVERBS 18:12

GALLUS HALTED SEVERAL STRIDES AWAY FROM THE JAIL. HE ROLLED his neck and sucked in a deep breath. Might as well get it over with. Too bad his lictors couldn't find Max. Gallus would have to punish him later.

Stolos met them at the entrance. "The tribune and the prisoners are waiting for you."

Quintus rose as Gallus entered the prison. "Magistrate. It's good of you to come."

Another deep breath. "As if you left me a choice."

"It is you, rather, who left us no choice." The one who appeared to be the leader of the visitors stood and approached.

Gallus swallowed what pride he had left. "I'm here, as you demanded."

"We were allowed no trial. Never once did you allow us an

opportunity to speak. Even an outsider should be given a chance to address the charges against him."

Gallus kept his chin high, though he offered no retort.

"Then, even though we had no trial, no verdict, you handed down punishment."

He'd hoped just showing up would be enough. Apparently not. Was he really expected to suffer a dressing down by this . . . this Jew? "What is it, then, you require of me?"

"We are Roman citizens. What you did was massively illegal. You do realize that, don't you?" said Paulos.

Gallus closed his eyes. "I do. But it is done. What is it you want from me? Do you mean to ruin me? Destroy my career?"

"I think you've done a fairly good job yourself of that already." Quin spoke from behind him.

"Quin. We agreed I would talk." Paulos spoke gently.

Despite his nervousness, Gallus enjoyed seeing the jailer put in his place.

"What I want is for you to see us safely out of the city."

"My lictors are standing by to do just that."

"Not just yet. First, you personally will escort us to Lydia's house."

"Agreed."

"And you will allow us to remain there until we are strong enough to travel."

Gallus scoffed. "Absolutely not. I need you to leave now. Your presence here is a distraction. You're responsible for one riot already. You must leave this morning."

"That's impossible! He can barely walk across the room." Quin marched toward Gallus, the muscle in his jaw working.

He was friendly with these men, yes, but protective enough to threaten violence? When had that happened?

Before Gallus could step back, Paulos held up one finger.

The jailer stopped cold.

Astonishing. That old man could control a Roman soldier—a tribune, no less—without a word.

Quin pursed his lips and backed away. He crossed his arms over his chest, quiet, but not particularly happy about it.

Paulos returned his attention to Gallus. "You seem to be unable to grasp the fact that we are Roman citizens. We can prove it if you desire, but that of course will require we remain here while the witnesses to our *testatios* arrive from Tarsus."

By Jupiter, no. "That won't be necessary. But when you finally leave, you will never return."

"It is illegal for you to banish us."

Decimus's wiry frame blocked the doorway. "*All* of your actions so far have been illegal. You have risked not only your own future but Philippi's as well."

"You told me to handle this. If you wish me to do that, you need to stop interrupting."

"So what are they threatening?"

Silas spoke up. "We are not threatening anything."

Gallus eyed the Jews. At some point during the argument with Decimus, the old man had returned to the lectus.

"Nothing? Then what's the problem?" Decimus looked from Paulos to Gallus and back.

"They won't leave today. They want to stay at the cloth merchant's house until they are *stronger*." He mocked them on the last word. They were probably faking it anyway. They just wanted to stay here longer to embarrass him.

"Then let them! Do you have any idea what a beating can do to a man his age? Look at them." Decimus gestured to the pair.

The older man's face was sunken, his eyes were red-rimmed. His skin was pale. He looked like he was half dead already.

"Ask them to remain at Lydia's domus if you like, but let them stay."

This was ridiculous. He didn't come here to be outnumbered by all of them, including the senior duovir. He had to stand up for at least one thing. "Their presence here is dangerous! You saw what happened yesterday."

Silas stepped forward. "There was no riot yesterday. The people came to hear charges presented and see us punished. They were allowed to get out of control because you ignored proper procedure, but it was far from a riot."

"But—"

Decimus put his hand on Gallus's shoulder. "Stop talking." He looked to the visitors. "If we let you stay, you will not cause trouble for either Gallus or Philippi?"

Paulos shook his head. "We're not looking for revenge. We only want to recover and heal a bit and say good-bye before we leave."

Decimus grabbed a fistful of Gallus's tunic and pulled him away from the others. "Until now, your shortcuts have endangered only your own ambitions. Now you have put the honor of Philippi at risk. Give them whatever they want. Because if this gets back to Rome somehow . . ."

Was it possible Decimus was far more devious than Gallus had thought? "I'll destroy you if that happens. And your nephews."

"I'll take that chance. I've stood back and let you get away with too much as it is. I've watched you take advantage of nearly everyone you've come in contact with. If I lose my position by finally trying to stop you, I deserve it."

He strode from the prison.

Gallus counted the man's steps as he walked away, trying to cool his anger. Who did he think he was, coming in here, ordering him around as if he were a rebellious slave? In name Decimus was the senior duovir, but he knew very well Gallus had all the real power.

Usually.

This time, however, he seemed to have no choice but to do what the man asked.

As Decimus left, Quin cast a sideways glance at Paulos. His pain was growing worse. There was no telling what damage lay beneath the blue and purple bruises that covered his back and sides. He'd seen men die from less.

Gallus remained standing near the door, his back to them. Whatever words were exchanged between the duoviri, Gallus was not pleased. He'd never backed down before. What could have been said to make him shut up like that? And would he let them go now, or not?

Gallus turned around, glaring daggers. "I will escort you to Lydia's, I will let you stay for five days, and then you will leave." His words clipped, he was obviously still angry with his senior magistrate.

"We'll stay until we are healed." Silas spoke quietly but firmly.

He blew out a slow breath. "Will you require anything else from me?"

"Just the escort to Lydia's."

"Anything else?"

"No, thank you, Magistrate, that will be quite sufficient." Paulos struggled to stand.

"As long as *you're* happy then." Gallus marched outside, his toga fluttering behind him.

No public apology? Shouldn't they at least get that? Make sure the townspeople knew they were innocent?

Quin kept his mouth shut and moved to Paulos's side, slipping his arm under the man's bicep.

Paulos groaned as Quin helped him stand. They gingerly took the stairs down to the Via, then stepped down to the floor of the forum.

Following the duovir and his lictors, the small group dove into the sea of Romans, Greeks, and Macedonians that already crowded the forum. The primus lictor preceded his ruler, calling loudly for all to make way for the magistrate.

Quin and Silas flanked Paulos, offering some protection from the bustling townspeople.

Rather than his usual parading posture, strutting slowly and allowing time for all to notice him, Gallus fairly scurried southeast across the forum toward the residential district, head down, shoulders hunched. It was almost comical.

They had nearly reached the villa district when Max charged at their small group like a runaway carriage. Servius and his partner formed a wall in front of Gallus, but they needn't have bothered. The man ran straight for Paulos.

Moving quickly, Quin caught Max before he slammed into Paulos.

Max reached around him, grabbing for Paulos. "Why is he free? Why did you let him out?" His hands grasped at empty air.

"I had to let them go," Gallus said. "They're citizens."

"They're lying!" Max continued to try to crawl over Quin, straining to reach Paulos.

Quin struggled to hold him back. Although Quin was a head taller, Max's anger made him amazingly strong.

"He has ruined me! I've lost almost everything. I'll never be able to replace her, and now you tell me there is nothing I can do about it?" Max relaxed, nearly collapsing onto Quin. He gave up fighting and shoved Quin away from him.

The magistrate neared his friend. "Max, listen to me."

"Gallus, you can't let this happen!" he begged, his hands clasped in front of his chest. "You are the duovir. There must be something you can do."

He grasped Max's arms. "There is nothing I can do to them. But they'll be leaving Philippi soon. That's the best you can hope for." He shrugged.

"You are a traitor! And a terrible friend." Max, weeping, stumbled away, headed for his domus.

The crowds stopped talking, started whispering, gossiping. Many were pointing at their ruler, standing forlornly in the middle of the forum.

Now Quin could see why there was no need for a public apology. Everyone would know they were innocent soon enough.

When they neared Lydia's domus, Gallus didn't even slow down. He simply marched past, leaving Quin and the others to knock at the courtyard gate as he left them behind. Quin almost felt sorry for him.

Almost.

But he'd brought it all on himself.

Inside, Lydia met them with hugs, and Loukas offered pain medicine.

Syntyche brought out meat and roasted vegetables. Fruit already awaited them. "We went to the market as soon as the sun rose to purchase the best meat we could find."

"The bread hasn't had time to rise yet, but it will be ready soon. I'm so sorry it's not done." Syntyche blushed and turned back toward the culina.

"Come sit. The bread will wait. Join us in thanking our Father for the safe return of our friends." Lydia handed out goblets of honeyed wine. "I know this isn't the usual morning fare, but I also know you didn't eat most of yesterday, either. You need food for those bruises to heal."

"Then you must rest." Loukas ripped a chunk of meat from the platter. "Rest is the best medicine you can give your body."

"I thought a merry heart was good medicine," Timos said.

Paulos laughed. "Ah, Timotheos, your mater taught you well."

Quin glanced at Tia, who shrugged.

"Timos is quoting our Scriptures, Quin." Silas clasped his young friend on the shoulder. "When we found him in Lystra, he knew the Holy Writings better than anyone we had ever met. His mother and grandmother had taught him. He was the son of a Greek father in a Roman outpost, and they managed to teach him to worship the living God."

Paulos sipped his wine. "The Scriptures are true, of course. You all have made my heart lighter and I feel better already."

"Still no substitute for rest."

"Of course, dear medicus." Paulos laughed.

It was amazing how easily they could all laugh after everything that had happened. Paulos and Silas were still in pain, he could tell, even if Loukas's medicine was beginning to take its effect.

Quin had only trusted in Yeshua for a few hours. Would he ever have the faith these men had?

Because he still had no idea what his immediate future held. Did he still have a job? Did he still want it? If he didn't, where would he live? How would he live?

The questions bounced around in his head, producing no answers. He'd been thinking about all of it for too long and his mind was exhausted—most of a day with Loukas at his farm, only to return to the nightmare on the forum that had extended not only deep into the night but now past dawn.

Perhaps he should take the physician's advice before he tried to figure out anything.

But at least he was still alive, and Tia was safe. For now.

As the men finished eating, Tia and the others gathered up the dishes.

"Have you talked to him yet?" Charis bumped her with her shoulder.

"What? Who?"

She laughed. "Who else? The soldier. The one we were praying for before the sun showed its face. The one we cooked all this food for."

She frowned. "I thought we were praying for Paulos and Silas."

"Them too. But neither of them is the one who hasn't taken his eyes off you since he got here."

"That's ridiculous."

"It's true." Syntyche entered the kitchen, a stack of dishes in hand. "He's been watching every move you make."

"You're both completely mistaken." Tia tossed a cloth on the table and flounced out of the room to a flurry of giggles.

Composing herself before she entered the peristyle once again, she found the only seat available was next to Quin.

His eyes followed her as she neared him, his smile—the one she'd come to adore—bringing some light to his otherwise exhausted features.

She sat next to him and he slipped his arm around her, drawing her near.

"Are you safe now?" she whispered.

He shrugged. "I believe so. If he were going to do anything, I think he would have done it already. But who knows?"

An unseen hand reached into her chest and squeezed her heart. Could he still be executed?

"We can do this." He grinned and kissed her temple before turning his attention back to Paulos and Silas.

We?

We. He could still face death for his part in last night's debacle, and she could be reclaimed by Max at any moment.

But for now they were *we*. They had one another and they had the living God.

Tomorrow would bring its own challenges in addition to those of today yet unsolved, but for now she chose to rest in the Father.

For just this moment, it was enough.

29

> *"After Paul and Silas came out of the prison, they went to Lydia's house..."*
>
> — ACTS 16:40

QUIN AWOKE IN ONE OF LYDIA'S MANY GUEST ROOMS. YESTERDAY everyone had slept off and on, recovering from the ordeal that had felt like it would never end. At least he and Paulos and Silas had. Sleep was more than enough to bring him back to excellent physical condition, except for his hip, but the others had lost a good deal of blood and it would likely take several more days before they could travel.

He wandered downstairs and found only the two of them in the peristyle. A plate of cheese and bread sat on a low table.

"Where is everyone else?"

"It seems Lydia's household had a great deal of work to catch up on. Several are at the dyeworks, Lydia and Demas went to visit clients. They thought we might enjoy a quiet day."

Quin took a seat and reached for a piece of bread. "May I ask you something?"

"I would imagine you have a great many questions."

"I do, but I'll start with one. What are you making? You've been working very hard on that." He gestured toward the folded leather and parchment creation in Paulos's hands.

Paulos tied a knot into the thread and then bit it off. "This is a gift for you."

"For me?"

"For all of you here in Philippi. It's a codex, a copy of the Scriptures." Paulos thumbed through its pages. "The Law, the history, poetry, and the prophets. This is how you will learn more about Yahweh." He held it out for Quin.

He drew his fingers over the codex. Soft leather covered pages and pages of handwritten parchment. Each sheet, folded in half. A metal clasp to keep it closed and protected. Exquisite.

"I'll take good care of it."

"I've no doubt."

"May I ask you another question?"

"What question would that be?"

"Why did you not claim your citizenship earlier? You could have prevented all of this—the beating, the imprisonment, all of it."

Paulos nodded. "You're absolutely right. We could have prevented any pain or inconvenience. But then what happens after I leave? What happens to Lydia, or the grain merchant, or Euodia when they are accused of the same crimes? If I claim citizenship to avoid persecution, then what is to happen to those who have no citizenship to hide behind? I cannot ask those we leave behind to endure anything we have not ourselves suffered."

"I suppose I understand that." He paused. "Has this happened before? Timos said you were stoned. In Lystra, I think?"

"We were. But that was by the Jewish leaders. This is nothing new. The leaders of the synagogue have been against the Way since Yeshua began teaching about His Father. I myself was one of their most vigorous persecutors. I'm sure Loukas told you."

"Some of it."

"But what happened here is different." Silas was uncharacteristically somber. "The Roman government has never been involved before."

"We have never been treated so shamefully as we have here. To be stripped, flogged, without any chance to speak even a word . . . it is disgraceful that any man should be treated in such a manner." Paulos's voice was soft.

A lump worked its way up Quin's throat. "I'm so sorry I had any part in that. You have no idea."

"You caused none of the pain, or the shame. And if you hadn't been there, would you be here now?" Silas's grin was back.

"The persecution is only going to get worse. Trust me, this is just the beginning." Paulos focused his gaze on Quin. "There will come a day when we will be arrested and thrown in prison just for saying the name of Yeshua. And that, my son, is why I think our God has brought you to Philippi."

"What do you think *I* can do?"

"You'll be one of our leaders. That's why I made the codex for you."

Quin laughed. "I've followed Yeshua for less than two days. How can I lead anyone?"

"You'll still be ahead of most of the others that will come to know him here in this city," Silas said. "I believe God has great plans for Philippi. And he has you and Elantia, Epaphras and Charis, and Lydia and her household to lead the way."

Paulos pointed a long finger at Quin. "In your position as prison master, you may be able to help protect them. You know Gallus and Decimus, you know how the Roman world works." He drew in a long breath. "This is a whole new war, Tribune. And we need you here."

How was he supposed to protect everyone who came to know Yeshua? He couldn't countermand the magistrate's orders. He couldn't possibly know what that unpredictable man would do.

Quin might not even be here himself that long, if Gallus had his way.

As if Paulos could read his thoughts, he touched his shoulder. “Quin, no one expects you to do the impossible. But I believe our Father took you out of Britannia and placed you here, as a soldier of God, for His purposes. Just keep doing your job, the job He placed you in. Do what God asks you to do when He asks you to do it. He asked me to order the spirit to leave Elantia, and I did. He did not ask me to be responsible for everything that happened after. He asks me to tell everyone that Yeshua is the Son of God. I do. I am not responsible for what people do with that knowledge. You put us in the inner cell, but God rescued us. Just keep doing what you’re asked to do.”

“That’s all?”

“Isn’t that the way it works in the army? You should be used to this.” Silas laughed. “You simply have a different commander now.”

Quin smiled. “You’re right. I can do that.”

As long as He allows me to.

Tia had sneaked out of the house with Lydia before dawn just to have something to do, and somewhere else to do it. She picked up a piece of fabric Lydia had dyed a beautiful indigo. The dye shop was full of cloth that needed to be folded and sorted into orders for clients or stacked by color for Lydia to turn into exquisite articles of clothing. The last several days had put them behind, and until that area was cleared, she couldn’t begin dying more cloth.

Beside her, Timos picked up a stack of folded cloth and placed it into a basket to be taken to Lydia’s house. “You’re very quiet this morning.”

“I was thinking.”

“About?”

“I’m not really sure what I am.”

He smiled. “You are a child of God. A daughter of the King.”

That much was true. "That's not what I mean."

"What do you mean then?"

"Where I fit. I'm not Roman or Greek or even Macedonian. Paulos says we'll be the foundation of the church here when he leaves but . . . Quin is a tribune. People listen to him. Lydia is a successful merchant, Loukas a physician. Even Epaphras is a leader among the slaves. I'm just a fugitive. How can I be a leader of anything?"

"Oh, everyone is a slave."

She laughed. "No they're not. Look at Lydia. Look at her beautiful stola—that she made herself. And Loukas—even Gallus respects him." She thought of Quin and the way he looked in his leather cuirass molded to perfectly fit him, his gleaming sword reflecting the sun. His striking Roman figure was anything but slave-like.

She gestured to Timos. "And you—you're not a slave. How can you say something like that?"

"Because it's true. Everyone is a slave. We are either a slave to sin or to righteousness."

"I don't understand."

"What is the most important thing, as a slave?" He set the load of indigo on a table by the door.

"To obey."

"Exactly. You can either obey the evil desires of sin, which lead only to death, or you can obey the laws of God, which lead to holiness, and eternal life with Him." He began folding bleached linen to fill a new basket.

She nearly choked. "But I don't know all of the laws! I can't obey them all! What if I break one by mistake? Or still sin?" Panic set in. Would she lose everything she had just found?

"When you placed your faith in Christ, God set you free from the power of sin. This is why I say you are no longer a slave to sin, but a slave to Christ. And that faith and obedience is counted as righteousness. You don't have to know all the laws, because God is teaching them to you. He is writing them on your heart. You are growing in your faith and knowledge of Him every day."

She had spent every day since leaving Britannia trying to break free of her slavery. Could she be happy as a slave, a slave to Christ?

"Is this why Lydia could be content while she was a slave? Why Euodia refused Lydia's offer to purchase her?"

He nodded. "I'm not saying everyone should remain in bondage. Our Father has different plans for each person. Euodia believes that is where she belongs. I don't know what He has in store for you."

"What about my brother?"

"Your brother?"

"Max killed my brother. I vowed I would kill him for that."

Timos froze, his hands in mid-air. The calm smile melted from his face, and she watched a myriad of conflicting thoughts race through his mind as he tried to decide what to say. "You cannot mean to still do that." He furrowed his brow. "Do you?"

Elantia picked at her fingernails. "I know it's wrong. I don't really want to kill him anymore. But I don't know if I can forgive him. Tancorix saved my life. More than once on our trip over here." Her eyes burned, and she swiped away tears.

He took her hand. "Tia, unforgiveness will only eat a hole in *your* heart, not his. It will keep you in bondage more surely than anything in this world."

More tears flowed. "I don't know how to forgive him. How do I do that? I don't want to forget my bratir."

"You don't have to. I said forgive Max, not forget your brother."

A sob escaped her.

"May I pray for you?"

"Please?"

"Our heavenly Father, we come to You to seek Your help. Your precious child needs to forgive a tremendous wrong done to her. We all have sinned against You, and do not deserve Your forgiveness. Yet You died for us, so that we might live with You forever. Help Elantia to share that forgiveness with her dominus, so her heart can heal. Let Your love flow through her, so that perhaps he, too, can come to know Your salvation." He squeezed her hand before he let go.

There was no immediate, complete healing. She was still angry with Max. Furious. Enraged. But there was a tiny part of her that was willing to let go that wasn't there before.

And that was progress.

That was God.

QUIN PACED in Lydia's peristyle. Paulos and Silas had returned to their rooms to rest after their discussion earlier.

He hadn't spoken to Gallus since that morning, the morning they had been escorted through the forum. What would Gallus say to him if he showed up at the prison? Or the basilica?

"Quin."

He looked up at the sound of Loukas's gentle voice.

"Tell me, honestly, how are you doing? It's been two days since the earthquake. You haven't been back to the prison."

"I'm wasn't sure I would go back. I'm not sure what I'd do instead, though. I haven't had any time to save up any coin. I lose my home if I'm no longer keeper of the prison. I'm not even sure if Gallus wants me to continue. But Paulos believes I should."

"Have you prayed about this decision?"

He winced. "No, I'm afraid praying about things is not something I'm used to yet."

"It takes a while to become used to thinking that way. Making Him a part of your life is a conscious decision that has to be made over and over again, every day."

Could he do that? He didn't regret his decision, but would he disappoint God?

"Don't worry. Sometimes we have to make that decision more than once in the same day." He laughed. "God does not expect perfection."

"That's good to know."

"I'm going to find something to eat. Want anything?"

"No. I think I have something I need to do."

At the end of Lydia's street, he turned left and soon entered the forum. Nothing much seemed to have changed since the night before last, for most of Philippi. Most of the people barely felt the quake. For him, though . . .

"Quin, I've been looking for you." The senior magistrate approached him.

"Decimus."

"How are your friends? Healing, I hope?"

"They're recovering nicely, thank you."

Decimus's gaze skimmed the forum. "Can we move over here a moment?" He gestured to an open space, leading Quin away from the crowd. "I wanted to ask you about them."

"What about them?"

"I found their attitude to be . . . rather different."

Just when he thought everything was over. Was Decimus going to make trouble for them now? He'd come to think of Decimus as a friend. "What do you mean different?"

"After everything Gallus did to them, they had every reason, every right, to want to hurt him. To cause pain. At least to demand justice. Revenge, even. But they didn't. Not even a public apology. They only asked for some time to rest before traveling on. I find that odd. Commendable, but odd."

"I agree, it's definitely different. Not the way I was taught."

"So how do you explain that?"

"That's the way of their God." He paused. "My God now too."

His eyes widened. "You've decided to follow their God?"

"I have. Will that be a problem?" Had he just signed his own death warrant?

"Not with me. Not if it makes people behave like that."

"Would you like to know more about Him?"

Decimus thought for a moment, then shook his head. "No. I'm

not ready for that. I have too much to lose. And I'm too afraid. Of Gallus and of Rome."

"All right. If you change your mind, though, you know where to find me."

"In the meantime, I have some other information that might help you."

"With what?"

"If you decide you don't want to stay here as keeper of the prison, this might be of interest to you. There's no guarantee it will work, though."

After hearing Decimus's news, Quin strode toward the western stoa, resisting the urge to sprint. At the entrance to the basilica, a slave halted him.

"Quintus Valerius, for the duovir."

The slave disappeared and Leonidas met him at the door.

"Welcome, Quintus. Come in. I'll see if he has time for you."

Quin followed the Greek to the magistrate's door and waited until he was escorted in.

"Magistrate." His heart beating wildly, he bowed. What would he do?

Gallus quirked a brow. "Why the sudden display of respect?"

"I have been shown I was wrong to disrespect you. I apologize."

"Interesting." He sipped from his silver goblet. "What can I do for you today?"

"I have an arrangement I'd like to propose."

"What arrangement is that?"

"I understand you are dealing with Patroclus the broker to sell my land."

Gallus nearly choked on his wine. "Th-that is not true."

"You can deny it if you want. I know it's true."

"Why are you here exactly?"

"I'm here about Elantia."

Gallus grinned. "You want the girl."

Quin wanted her safe. He wanted her free. He wanted her at peace. But this was something Gallus's twisted mind could not grasp, so he would leave it at that. “Yes. I want Elantia. So here is my proposal. You can keep my land.”

Gallus allowed a half smile.

“But you give Max 30,000 sesterces. I figure that’s about two years’ income, at the height of her earning power. Two sesterces per customer, twenty customers a day, every day, for two years. And that’s being very generous. We all know it probably wouldn’t keep up for that long. The oracle in Delphi doesn’t cost that much.”

“And if I do this, you’ll keep quiet about what happened earlier this week?”

“About everything. I get her, free, and my job. You keep your lucrative career, my land, and your reputation.”

The shorter man thought a long moment.

Quin rubbed his hand down his face. Was Gallus really going to risk everything to keep 30,000 sesterces? Quin wouldn’t really go to Vespasian, but did Gallus know that?

He finally turned back. “Agreed.”

“Very well. Please send the letter of manumission to Lydia’s by the end of the day.”

“I don’t know if Max—”

“Oh, he will.”

Gallus sneered. “This girl better be worth it. You’re giving up a lot.”

“She is. I’m giving up nothing.”

30

"[Paul and Silas] met with the brothers and sisters and encouraged them. Then they left."

— ACTS 16:40

It had been over nine days since the quake. Quin ran his hands down the new doors in the prison—the city had done a good job of repairing both the jail and his home. If he didn't know better, he would swear they'd never been damaged at all.

Too bad the same couldn't be said for the bodies of Paulos and Silas. Their backs were covered in stripes going in all directions. The wounds were closed now, any danger of bleeding passed. But they were far from totally healed.

"Stolos, I'm leaving now."

"Yes, Domine." The man grinned. He had taken over for Alexios as second-in-command, and the prison had run much more smoothly since. Quin had convinced Gallus to allow Alexios to retire rather than be sent to the mines. After all, he had kept the magistrate well-informed of Quin's movements. And he did try to keep Quin from leaving that night.

Even Pandaros was well-behaved, though still late more than Quin liked.

After leaving Stolos in charge, Quin trudged up the steps and entered the atrium of his home. After tossing his cloak on the floor of his room, he made his way to the culina.

He poked his head in.

"Something smells good."

Charis smiled shyly. "Thank you."

"Where's Epaphras?"

"He went to get some more wood. He'll be right back." She answered quickly, waiting for Quin to respond.

"All right."

She relaxed.

Epaphras strolled in, an armful of wood.

"May I speak with you both a moment?" asked Quin.

"Of course." He nodded and dropped the load into the container in the corner.

"I'll be in the dining area."

Quin waited on one of the two couches that were placed up against the wall. A small table sat in the middle of the floor. It wasn't a triclinium where diners reclined while eating, but it was good enough.

Charis brought a plate of food—just enough for Quin—and set it on the table.

He gestured to the opposite lectus.

She sat down, and Epaphras followed a moment later.

Quin leaned forward, his arms on his knees. "Do you two like working there? In this house?"

Epaphras nodded. "Very much."

Charis nodded. "Yes." Her word was clipped.

"Charis, I don't know what happened to you before, but I have never hurt a slave." He sighed. "I can't free you. I would if I could, but you don't belong to me. You belong to Philippi, to serve whomever is keeper of the prison. Even if I saved up enough to buy you, or Lydia or Loukas did, they'd bring someone else in here and I don't want that."

"Neither do we," said Epaphras.

He sat up and raked his hand through his hair. "We're brothers and sister now, in Christ, and I can't have you as slaves. I can't have anyone as a slave. Not anymore. My family in Rome is wealthy. We had a lot of slaves, maybe a hundred. My father treated them well. My tutor was a Greek named Attalos. I loved him more than my own pater. But I rarely thought—until I came here, and met Tia—about the life he had before he was captured by the Roman war machine. I can't live in a house with slaves. Not anymore."

"So are you telling us we have to go?" Charis's voice was almost inaudible.

"No, of course not. You can *work* for me, you just can't be my slaves. I can pay you, a little"—he laughed—"and we can share everything. Just don't tell Gallus."

Her face melted into relief, and she smiled. The first real smile he had seen from her. He laughed.

"All right then. I have one more question."

"What?" Epaphras said.

"Do we have room for one more?"

TIA DRIED her hands on a towel. "Someone's here for me?"

"Yes. I think you should come quickly." Epaphras's face was as bright as the fire under the cooking pot. She touched Syntyche's arm. "I'll be right back."

Lydia was at the front door talking to a messenger when Tia entered the atrium. "I can give it to her."

The man's face was set as stone. "I was told to put it directly in her hands. Only hers."

Lydia beckoned her. "Tia, this man has something to give you."

In the center of the room, she froze. Was it an order to return to Max? No, they would just come take her. What could this be?

The messenger frowned.

She willed her feet to move. One step at a time.

He handed her the parchment and strode away.

Lydia guided her to a lectus.

Fingers shaking, she untied the ribbon. Broke the wax seal. Stared at the document in her hands.

"I can't read Latin." She handed it to Lydia.

Lydia skimmed it quickly, her face breaking into a wide smile. "It's a certificate of manumission. Max has set you free."

The word settled into her soul. *Free.* She was finally free. Legally.

She'd been free ever since she asked Yeshua to forgive her sins. That was when her life changed. Even if she'd had to return to Max and Cassia, she would have been truly free.

But now her heavenly Father had given her what she hadn't asked for. Earthly freedom.

"But how?"

"I think Quin had something to do with this. He had some land when he first came here, but Gallus stole it from him. My guess is he traded it."

"For my freedom?"

"He can't marry you if you're a slave. Now that you are both following the Way . . ."

Oh, Quin.

She raced to the peristyle and found him waiting for her, standing tall in the center of the room, in a new linen tunic. Did he already know? She hid the parchment behind her back.

Moving toward one of Lydia's rose bushes, he plucked a blossom and twirled it between his fingers. "Was something delivered to you?" He grinned.

"You gave up your land for me?"

"I told you I would give my life for you. Why not a square of dirt?"

"But what will you do now? Where will you live?"

"Paulos said I should remain the keeper of the prison. He said I could be very useful there."

She brought the parchment from behind her back, played with the seal and ribbon attached to the bottom.

"I need your help, though."

"*My* help? What help can I give you?"

"You can pray for me. Gallus and I have an . . . uneasy peace, but I'm not sure how much I trust him. He could still turn against me at any time. And I'm not sure how much Vespasian could do, even if I did go to him." He stepped nearer.

"Quin, I've been praying for you. I've never stopped."

"I need you beside me. All the time. I want to marry you."

Her heart raced, and she searched his face. "You do?"

He cupped her face. "Of course. Te amo."

"Carami te," she whispered.

"And now that you're free, it's possible, legal, very desirable . . ."

He pulled her close, lowered his head. His lips met hers in a soft kiss.

She wrapped her arms around his neck, rising up on her toes.

He deepened the kiss, and the parchment fell to the floor at their feet.

QUIN LOOKED around him at the group assembled on the riverbank. The women who had met before, the God-fearers, had come to hear Paulos one last time, as well as a few others who had decided to follow the Way since the quake.

Paulos stood before them. "Saints of Philippi. I call you saints, for that is what you are. You are the saints of God, His holy people. You are holy, because He has redeemed you. You have been bought with His blood. And because you are His, He calls you to be separate from the world around us. We still live in this world, but we follow His Way, we live according to His holy laws."

He walked back and forth before the group, his gaze meeting each person.

"We had a little incident here, didn't we?" He smiled and uneasy laughter rippled through the crowd. "It will undoubtedly happen to us again, and it may happen here again. You may think I would say ignore the rulers! Follow God! But that cannot be the way we live. Unless God's laws contradict the laws of the rulers of this world, we must still submit to the government and its officers. There will come a time, and I believe it will be soon, when we have to choose between the emperor and Yeshua. Then, of course, there is no choice. Until then, we are to be obedient whenever possible. Otherwise, what do we make Yeshua look like to the world? A troublemaker? We will have enough to answer to that is true, without bringing trouble on ourselves."

Paulos clasped his hands in front of his chest. "I'll be leaving you soon, much sooner than I had planned to." His voice began to crack. "You will always have a special place in my heart. Take care of each other. Love each other. Pray for each other. For you are the beginning of the church at Philippi, the first church in all Macedonia. And with God as your rock, you can endure anything. If I survived that"—he pointed beyond the walls to the forum—"you can endure, you can prevail over *anything* the Jewish leaders, the Roman government, or anyone else sends against you. As long as you do it together."

Quin looked at the people around him once more. Was anyone here a citizen? Other than him? Maybe the grain merchant. No wonder Paulos didn't claim his privilege loud and strong before Gallus laid a finger on him. He had to show everyone here they could survive as well.

Quin almost hadn't. He pulled Tia closer and kissed her temple. *Thank You, Yahweh, for a strong wife to walk beside me.* One who had found true freedom.

Attalos had been right. Great things had been waiting for him in Philippi. He had come to Philippi to wait for the truth. And he had found it. Not where he expected, or how.

But it was a deeper, more powerful truth than he could ever have imagined.

EPILOGUE

"I thank my God every time I remember you. In all my prayers for all of you, I always pray with joy . . ."

— PHILIPPIANS 1:3-4

Philippi was the first church established by Paul in Europe, and he maintained an unusually close relationship with them for the rest of his ministry.

When Paul was under house arrest in Rome from 59–61, the church sent a gift with Epaphroditus. Epaphras nearly died, and when he was recovered Paul sent him back with a letter in which Paul repeatedly tells the Philippians how much he loves them.

We know the jailer became a follower of the Way, but we know nothing beyond that, and nothing of what happened to the slave girl. We do know is that the care for Paul and his ministry that began with Lydia and the jailer continued until the end of his time on earth. The church remained faithful until the city was destroyed by an earthquake in 620. Today, only ruins remain.

Philippi is a testament to the power and glory of the gospel—the good news that changes men and women, rich and poor, free and slave with the love of Christ.

MY THANKS TO . . .

I must first thank Jesus Christ, the ultimate Author and Creator. Without Him, there would be no story.

My family. Thank you for allowing me the time and space to craft this novel. Your patience is unbelievable.

The Women's Bible Study at First Alliance Church, Silver Spring, Maryland. Your insights into Philippians were invaluable, as were your prayers.

Edward Hatfield, my language expert—for your help with ancient Latin and Britonnic, especially for Elantia's beautiful name. All mistakes are mine alone.

My beta readers—Rita Schuh, and Dr. Sue Pankratz, who also provided medical guidance. Your support means so much to me.

My editor—Natalie Hanemann. Thanks for your gentle, expert guidance.

And to you—Thank you for reading. May my words bring you closer to Him.

ABOUT THE AUTHOR

An unapologetic Californian, Carole Towriss now lives just north of Washington, DC. She loves her husband, her four children, the beach, and tacos, though not always in that order. In addition to writing and picking up kids' shoes, she binge-watches British crime dramas.

Visit the website for discussion questions and other resources.

For more information:

caroletowriss.com
carole@caroletowriss.com

IF YOU LIKED THIS BOOK . . .

Deep Calling Deep is the story of Paul, Timothy and Luke in Rome. You'll also meet Sextus Burrus, who was the Praetorian prefect from 51–61 A.D, and thus likely had a great deal of contact with the Apostle Paul while he was under house arrest.

CHAPTER ONE

"And when we came to Rome, the centurion delivered the prisoners to the praetorian prefect, but Paul was allowed to dwell by himself with a soldier that kept him."

— ACTS 28:16, JUB

Rome, month of September, 61 A.D.

Praetorian Prefect Sextus Afranius Burrus had imagined the scene spread out before him, but his worst nightmares weren't even close.

Lucius Secundus, the former city prefect, had been murdered by one of his slaves. Following an ancient law, the senators had called for the execution of all four hundred of the slaves who had worked for him.

The Praetorian Guards had been called out to quell the resulting riot.

The new city prefect and his *cohortes urbanae* were an astounding picture of Roman efficiency. All three cohorts, five hundred men each, gleefully took part in the bloody vengeance. Some of the urban guards pounded stakes into the ground along the Appian Way just outside the city's walls. Others guarded the remaining slaves, and still others confiscated wood from anywhere they could find it.

Sextus had seen teams of soldiers leaving the Secundus estate. Apparently, they'd razed the slaves' quarters, tearing down doorways and roof supports.

The all too familiar metallic scent of blood permeated the air. Sextus wiped sweat from his brow as he walked along the oldest of Rome's wide stone and cement roads. Crosses of all shapes lined the highway on his right and left—crossbars at the top, the middle, wherever. The victims' feet hung only a cubit or so above the ground, their anguished faces easier to see, their tormented cries easier to hear.

The Guards had started with the men. Obviously wanting to eliminate as much resistance as possible, the youngest and strongest were first to be nailed to the posts, staked at regular intervals along the *Via Appia*. Most of those had already been crucified by the time Sextus arrived.

The clanging of hammer against nail clashed with the screams of women watching husbands and sons writhe in agony. The noise grew so loud, Sextus's ears hurt. He rolled his shoulders, trying to dull the pain as he trudged south.

The condemned waited in a loose grouping on the east side of the Via surrounded by armed and angry guards.

At the end of the seemingly endless line of limp bodies, Sextus halted. With his good hand, he shaded his eyes against the brutal midsummer sun, gazing south toward the nearby Alban Hills. The *via* continued all the way to Capua, rarely veering to left or right. Even when hills, rivers, or cities stood in the proposed path, Rome's engineers barreled straight through.

Ancient pine trees lining the highway stretched toward the few wispy clouds above him, as if trying to rise above the slaughter. In the distance, family vineyards and peaceful villages dotted the landscape. If he kept walking, maybe he could reach one and forget this nightmare had ever happened.

But he had responsibilities.

He clenched his fists and spun around to trudge back toward the city's center, trying to shut out the detestable images, only to have them replaced with pictures even more gruesome.

A boy not old enough to shave trying to stop the guards from dragging his little sister away.

A mother desperately clinging to her newborn as one of Secundus's avengers ripped him from her arms.

A toddler squirming so violently, the soldier trying to pin him to the wood gave up and unsheathed his dagger. Sextus tried to avert his eyes, but the horror compelled him to watch as the soldier nailed the lifeless body to the upright.

He was already dead, so what was the point?

To incite fear. Abject dread. To remind any who dared to go against the world dominating power that was Rome, that she would always win.

Back inside the walls, Sextus ensured his men had the desperate crowd firmly under control. Held back by Praetorians, both citizens and slaves lined the street leading from the Capena Arch to the city center; he avoided meeting their accusing eyes. His stomach roiled. His heart pounded. If he stayed inside the walls, maybe the angry cries from the crowd would drown out the shrieks from beyond them.

He'd seen more death than all the senators combined. So why was he the only one who seemed to be bothered by today's slaughter? He'd served in the army since he was seventeen years old. More than forty years had passed since he'd first tasted combat. He'd been part of the deadliest battles, left entire villages bloody and burned, all in the name of the glory of Rome.

But no matter how hard he tried, today he found no glory in the death of innocents.

THE SUN SANK low in the west, as if trying to escape from a day that had been long, gory, and gruesome. Perhaps some good food and his wife's beautiful smile would improve his mood, although until Sextus could rid himself of the scent of death and the sound of screams, he likely wouldn't feel any better.

Near the top of Esquiline Hill, in one of the wealthiest sections of Rome, he opened his front door to the atrium and glanced around. He strode down the hall to the open-air peristyle at the other end of their *domus*. Empty. Where was Gaia? She'd been gone a lot lately and would only tell him she'd been visiting friends.

Their only son Afranius had been killed in Britannia the spring before last in the uprising by Boudicca, the warrior queen. The pain of that loss had almost destroyed their marriage. For over a year, other than to go to the baths, Gaia had rarely left their *domus*. She talked to no one but him. And of course, Tiberia, their only female house slave. Recently, however, things had been much improved. She almost seemed peaceful. If these "visits" of hers had made the difference, he should be happy about it.

Maybe her calm would rub off on him.

He stepped into their *cubiculum* off the atrium, where he unhooked the pin at his shoulder that held his crimson cloak in place and hung it neatly on its peg on the far wall. The leather cross-body strap that held his sword followed, along with the belt and its attached dagger sheath.

Maybe a bath would relax him. Sextus left their modest home and headed for the bathhouse reserved for the guards near the barracks. He was already sweating when he entered the large facility.

There was no admission fee here, but he paid a slave to watch his clothes. He allowed another to apply oil to his skin. It slid down his chest in rivulets, collecting into bigger blobs along the way. The room's warm air made it easy for the attendant to scrape it off along with the sweat and dirt.

Once clean, he slipped into the large heated pool and sat on the stone bench that ran along the edge. The water came to his neck, and he allowed the heat and softly rippling water to wash away the stress.

But not the horror that refused to leave his mind.

He gave up trying to relax. After drying off and dressing, he stepped outside. He had taken only a few steps toward home when the prefect of the night watch blocked his path.

Tigellinus.

The man had made it clear he wanted to rise in the ranks of Rome's protective services and would do anything to make it to the top. So far, he'd reached the level of prefect, but only of the *vigiles*, the universally hated night watchmen.

"I saw you on the *via* earlier today." Tigellinus sneered.

"And?"

"Couldn't handle Roman justice? Had to retreat within the walls?"

"It was not my job to oversee the executions." Sextus stepped around the man.

Tigellinus fell into step beside him. "I understand. You needed to supervise your men." He sneered.

"My men perform quite well without my direct supervision. That's why they are Praetorians and not merely *vigiles*." An unnecessary barb, even if true.

Tigellinus growled. "Your men are no better than any other soldiers."

Sextus chuckled as he thought about the quadruple pay, the shorter length of service, the pristine weapons they bore, and the fact that every single Guard was a citizen from Italia, not merely freedmen like the *vigiles*. He couldn't resist answering back, even though he knew it would only lead to more rancor. "If you truly believe that, you are more foolish than I thought."

Linus raised his chin. "I still say you should have been visibly supporting the retribution."

Sextus clenched his jaw. "My Guards were called out for riot control. That's their job. We took care of the people, and the City Guards were handling the executions. You were unneeded to begin with, and I most certainly will not endure a reprimand from a lower officer."

Linus glared, his face reddening. "I am the prefect of the *vigiles*. You are the prefect of the Praetorian Guard. I am not a lower officer."

Sextus halted and stared down at the much shorter man. He leaned near, using every tactic he knew to control his anger. "And yet you report to the prefect of the City Cohorts, while I answer to Nero himself." Sextus had had enough of this worm who had schemed and clawed his way to his position. "The only reason you have your position, Linus, is because the emperor shares your enjoyment of horses. Every man in Rome has seen you out at night with him, going to the houses of seduction, getting him drunk, and pouring lies into his ears."

An evil smile slid across his face. "I am closer to Nero than you will ever be. You are losing influence to me daily, and I will soon have your job, your house, and your prestige."

The modicum of relaxation he had gained in the bathhouse evaporated like steam. "Perhaps. But for now, I am your superior, and you will not address me in such a manner again." Sextus turned and left the officer standing in the street.

Linus was probably right. He would be Praetorian Prefect sooner or later. His deceit and maneuverings would pay off, and Sextus would be dismissed. But until then, he would seek justice and not acclaim, live his life with integrity, and protect the city and the emperor with honor.

Though if Rome continued in the direction it had taken today, there may not be much left worth protecting.

Sextus had been in countless battles. He'd seen bodies in worse condition. Uglier deaths, even crucifixions. The images, the smells, the sounds—these were nothing he hadn't experienced thousands of times over, but today's spectacle would not leave him, and it made him sick to his stomach. Why must this one incident bother him so fiercely?

Maybe because it was *four hundred* "incidents." Three hundred and ninety-nine innocent people slaughtered for the sins of one man.

His throat burned. He'd say it was a result of all the dust kicked up by the Urban Cohorts as they took their vengeance along the Appian Way, but it had been bothering him for a couple months now. His ears had begun to ache recently as well.

Back in his bedroom, he reached for an amphora of honeyed wine and filled a goblet. He'd been drinking too much of it lately, but the honey was one of the few things that soothed his throat. He'd lost weight from undereating, and if he wasn't careful, he would lose strength as well. The drink felt cool and smooth on the irritated flesh as it slid toward his stomach.

After unlacing his boots, he perched on the side of his bed, and whistled for Fidus. He downed one more goblet before jamming the stopper into the neck of the pottery and setting the jug on the low table next to the bed.

His enormous Molossian hound bounded in from his spot in the atrium, sitting patiently before his master.

"Good dog." Sextus scratched behind the dog's ears. The faithful animal had to worry about pleasing only one person. No scheming, no lies, no theatrics.

If only Sextus's life could be so simple.

Printed in Great Britain
by Amazon